*W*hat the critics are saying...

ဆ

"Ms. Stone has created a very vivid world where psychic beings are not all that unusual. Her descriptions of astral projection and the astral plane are particularly vivid and beautiful. The supporting characters are very well drawn and really add to the story. I especially liked the character of Stephanie. Sam and Callie's love story was very involving, as was the whole story. I read it all in one sitting. I can never get enough of the story of good triumphing over evil and this is a particularly good example of that." ~ *Coffee Time Romance*

"I liked this book as it is something completely different, and yet it has all the best elements of a good story. It is a love story. It is about good verses evil. It is new age. If you believe in the presence of the unknown, of the unity of souls and that there is something beyond our normal lives, this is the book for you." ~ *Fallen Angels Review*

"This book has something for everyone: an intriguing story about psychic terrorism, a sweet romance with some spicy sex scenes, and comedy as Callan practices her psychic skills. Astral Nights is a highly imaginative and unique story that I think everyone will enjoy." ~ *The Romance Studio*

"Astral Nights is a book that not only provides an intriguing paranormal story but also some comical passages. I enjoyed reading about Callans life and her fears in trying to protect everyone she loves. I have never read a story quite like this one where another person terrorizes one person psychically because they possess such great psychic power. It certainly was an interesting book and I liked it for the passion that shone through and how a special glow could bring the light into the darkness that had been in Callans life. Ms. Stone has definitely written a book that is worth reading by lovers of the paranormal genre." ~ *Ecataromance*

Astral
NIGHTS

Kay Stone

CERRIDWEN PRESS

A Cerridwen Press Publication

www.cerridwenpress.com

Astral Nights

ISBN 1419955012
ALL RIGHTS RESERVED.
Astral Nights Copyright© 2005 Kay Stone
Edited by Kelli Kwiatkowski
Cover art by Syneca

Electronic book Publication October 2005
Trade paperback Publication November 2006

Excerpt from *Heaven and Lace* Copyright © Linda Bleser 2006

Cerridwen Press is an imprint of Ellora's Cave Publishing, Inc.®

About the Author

ॐ

Kay Stone has created stories for as long as she can remember. For her, there's never a dull day. She just dips into her imagination and, for the moment, lives in whatever fantasy that presents itself. Her stories are liberally sprinkled with humor and the weird and wonderful.

Life has been more conventional than the stories her mind's eye creates. Although she's traveled to Mexico, Hawaii and England — and lived in Florida, Virginia and Arizona — her home is Colorado. She's raised two splendid sons, done much business writing, and obtained a Bachelor of Arts in English (creative writing and journalism emphasis).

Her elderly, eccentric Cairn terrier, Millie, keeps her company as she assaults the computer and lets the good times roll.

Kay welcomes comments from readers. You can find her website and email address on her author bio page at www.cerridwenpress.com

ASTRAL NIGHTS

ജ

Dedication

ဆ

To Hugh Phillip, the first of our new generation.

Trademarks Acknowledgement

The author acknowledges the trademarked status and trademark owners of the following wordmarks mentioned in this work of fiction:

BMW: Bayerische Motoren Werke Aktiengesellschaft

Chevy Bel Air: General Motors Corporation

Cadillac: General Motors Corporation

Disneyland: Walt Disney Company

Donald Duck: Disney Enterprises, Inc.

Jaguar: Jaguar Cars Limited Corporation

Mighty Mouse: Viacom International Inc.

Model T: Ford Motor Company

Vicks VapoRub: Procter & Gamble Company

Chapter One

ဆာ

Callan perched on the edge of the couch, twisting a soft velvet pillow and listening to the wind slam against the windows. On August afternoons, storm clouds often crested the Rocky Mountains, thundered across the hills and valleys of the city of Denver and then streamed out across the eastern prairie. The weather here was fickle. The buildup produced a burst of wind and a smattering of raindrops, hail or a full-blown storm with tornados. Whatever they got usually evaporated quickly, leaving behind a fresh, sunny day.

Change, she reflected, might make fascinating weather, but she wasn't up to the transformations necessary to fight off the creature called The Gull. All she'd ever wanted was a simple life, free of any weird paranormal nonsense. The doorbell rang and as she hurried to answer it, she hoped whoever was there wouldn't further complicate matters.

Stephanie, her neighbor and best friend, bustled through her front door. "He's here?" she asked, pushing her long auburn hair out of her face.

"Where else? Downstairs. At the rate they're banging at it, those kids will have that computer trashed by Labor Day," she complained. Lately, her son Connor and Stephanie's son Zach, both eleven years old, couldn't seem to get enough of computer games, and the distant shrieks and explosions filtering up from the basement family room all afternoon had begun to get on her nerves.

"Aren't we a little cranky this afternoon? Stop mauling that pillow or you've got a big cleanup job in your future. I won't help either," Stephanie said, steering Callan into the kitchen. "Sit!" Stephanie ordered, pulling out a chair and pushing her into it. She snatched the pillow from Callan, plopped it in the center of the kitchen table and headed for the refrigerator. "You look like you slammed a boob in the car door," Stephanie commented, rummaging around among the leftovers. "Got any beer in here?"

Callan squelched a hiccup of laughter. She'd been working on this sour depression for a night and half a day and wasn't about to give it up after just one of her friend's outrageous wisecracks. After what she'd been through, she was entitled.

"Oh, a nice little white wine. I might have known," Stephanie said as she emerged from behind the refrigerator door, bottle in hand.

That remark deserved a prickly comeback, but Callan resisted. After two years of friendship, she understood that Stephanie used sarcastic remarks to conceal that she had a marshmallow for a heart.

"So, what's got your knickers in a twist, Mighty Mouse?" Stephanie asked, after pouring the wine and settling across the table from Callan. "Did the stud-muffin doc try to feel you up on the first date?"

"Stephanie, you're incorrigible!"

"I admit I had a peek at him when he came to pick you up. I know what's the matter with you," she said slyly. "He didn't even try, did he? The rat bastard, and after you wore that incredible teal dress for him too," she dramatized in an aggrieved voice.

Sometimes Stephanie was over-the-top outrageous, but today her efforts didn't penetrate Callan's dejection. She shrugged and replied, "It's not really important." Gusty wind flung rain against the bay window. Her hanging plants in the window were outlined in a silver aura by a lightning flash.

"Not important! No wonder you looked so peeved." Thunder nearly drowned Stephanie's voice. "Boy, if my kids ever drive me loco, I wouldn't mind him realigning my head." A wide, wicked grin lit up her freckled face.

Callan sat, numbly staring down at the table, remembering the disastrous date last night. She didn't know how to explain what had happened without sounding demented. Her fingers itched to grab the velvet pillow in front of her, so she clutched the stem of her wineglass.

"Got any suggestions for an interesting neurosis I could spring on him?" Steph rattled on, ignoring the lack of response. "You can borrow it if you lighten up."

"You're welcome to him anytime," she replied with a grimace. "I've got a more complicated problem and I don't need more trouble. Besides, I misinterpreted the purpose of the so-called date," she added. "I should have known meeting an old boyfriend at the mall was a bit too lucky. Turns out, good ol' Sam Cavendar set me up. I was conned. He hunted me down on purpose."

"Why would he do that? Tell me about last night. I want to know what happened — blow by blow."

Under Stephanie's coaxing, Callan described the evening, especially the candle-lit restaurant and the fabulous food. Such a romantic setting might intensify Stephanie's outlandishness, so she edited certain feelings that she didn't want to talk about. She did mention some of Sam's more tame compliments and caresses, but she trailed off into silence when she reached their walk in the restaurant garden and the discussion they had. Her sense of betrayal was still so strong that she wanted to get up and run into the storm, as if its violence could scour away the pain.

Thunder came from the southeast. The storm was on its way out unless it unexpectedly turned back toward the mountains.

"Sooo, he sounds interested enough. What happened then?"

"There's something that you don't know about me, Steph," she answered, watching rain trickle down the window.

The paranormal was a subject she'd never discussed with Stephanie, but she had to talk to someone. Her judgment was skewed by fear and her anxiety was growing by the hour.

"It scares me," she continued, "and I'm afraid you might not like what I tell you. People usually freak out and that's the last I see of them."

"I'm a tough little bitch. I taught middle school and can handle most anything."

Callan took a deep breath and said in a rush, "Okay, you asked for it. I'm a clairvoyant--psychic. I know that sounds crazy..."

Stephanie studied her as if the revelation answered all the questions she'd never dared ask. Then she said, "Listen, Mighty Mouse. Who was it that tried to kick in my front door one night last spring? You charged upstairs when Matt opened it. My Katie was blue. We could have lost her without your warning. You gave me back my Katie. There isn't anything you can tell me that would stop me from being your friend."

She reached across the table to pat Callan's hand. "And obviously, you gave me an example of your clairvoyance that night. Your confession doesn't surprise me. I figured it was something like that. Thank god for what you can do."

Callan couldn't quite meet Stephanie's eyes. Praise on this subject embarrassed her, but some of her tension lifted. No one had ever actually thanked her for using her power.

"When the outcome is good, like what happened with Katie, I can accept this weird ability. For a while anyway."

"You know," she continued, staring out the window at the rain, "Sam said everyone at home in Apple Springs knew about me, and I can't keep the secret here any better than I did there. That time with Katie was the only precognitive vision I'd had in a long time. I thought I'd left it all back home in Wisconsin. But, according to Sam, it's followed me here."

"How so?"

"He says I've been chosen as a target for domination by a high sorceress of the supernatural. She's stalking me."

"What!"

"Last Friday, a psychic by the name of Rosemary Sabin came to see Dr. Ostherhaut, Sam's partner, claiming to have telepathically intercepted the intentions of a woman from Brazil," Callan explained. "The woman arrived in Colorado recently and is on the hunt. Rosemary insisted that I'm her target. Why a powerful psychic would be interested in me, I don't have a clue. My paranormal powers were never that extraordinary and they're definitely rusty now from lack of use. The Brazilian woman is known as The Gull and is supposed to be a dangerous criminal—some sort of psychic terrorist. Rosemary told Sam that I was in the Denver area and sent him to warn me.

"According to Sam, Dr. Ostherhaut headed a government project on the paranormal back in the Seventies. Rosemary acted as his subject, and she supposedly has astounding abilities in clairvoyance, telepathy and telekinesis. She's offered to help me fight off The Gull."

Stephanie, for once, seemed stunned into silence.

"It wasn't just imagination on Rosemary's part," Callan continued. "As a kid, a giant black bird, which I assume is this Gull person, paid me numerous visits, inflicting some damage each time, although I always managed to fight her off." Those memories from childhood now left her trembling and cold inside.

"Oh, my god," Stephanie exclaimed, her brown eyes round with astonishment.

"Rosemary also told Sam that The Gull has controlled or inhibited me in some way all my life. He had the nerve to imply that I'm her creature. Owned by her, in other words. So what does that make me? A pathetic nothing! A nonentity. In his eyes, I suppose I am."

"No, that's wrong. How dare he! You're not like that at all!" Stephanie said, half out of her chair.

Callan forced a calm, reasonable tone, careful to keep a tremor out of her voice. "Thanks for the vote of confidence. You know, I've always imagined my precognitive ability as a small, sly, twisted gnome hiding in the shadows of my mind who only occasionally whispers a beneficial tip. Usually, when needed, the little blockhead is asleep under the mental equivalent of an oak tree. It isn't surprising that that shiftless, devious imp failed me when I needed a warning about Sam and The Gull. I'm lucky this time that the imp's negligence only caused a social *faux pas* on my part, so far..."

Stephanie, eyes wide and mouth half open, and Callan, weighed down by apprehension, sat hushed as the rain gradually stopped. The sun brightened behind patchy clouds and granted them a golden, clean-washed afternoon.

Stephanie set back in her chair and slid the stem of her wineglass in a lazy arc as she considered Callan's revelation. Finally she looked up and said, "What happens to you — what you can do — is impressive. Sam's right. You need to take advantage of this Rosemary's proposal. Get some control of the situation. Otherwise, you could end up wearing feathers too. And they aren't even in style this year."

Callan snorted at the attempt to cheer her up, then took a sip of her wine. "Thanks for that thought. I'm spooked, but not enough to get cozy with the local psychic and all the hoodoo voodoo that goes with it. Can't you just see her? Some aging hippie, left over from the Sixties, in love beads and bell-bottoms with a plastic flower in her hair."

Stephanie shook her head, reached across the table and trapped Callan's hand. "Whatever. You can't let that bird woman get you, Mighty Mouse. Connor needs his mom. You've got the grit, I know it, plus an offer of help from an expert. Don't blow the chance."

"It's hopeless," Callan said, pulling her hand away. "I haven't had a reliable premonition in years except for the one about Katie. My crystal ball has a really big crack in it."

"So, stick a piece of tape on it," Stephanie snapped as she topped off their wine. "It's all so fascinating!"

"Yeah, sure. And furthermore, I don't like people looking at me like I'm something nasty stuck on the bottom of their shoe. And sometimes it's scary. I've got no control over what happens to me. You don't know what it's like."

Stephanie dismissed her complaint with a wave of her hand. "No, I don't. But guess what? Maybe Sam had two agendas last night. You wouldn't want to miss out on the good part."

Callan raised an eyebrow and asked, "How do you figure that? What good part?"

"From the way he came on to you before he delivered his message, he's obviously attracted to you. He was only doing what he had to, an unpleasant duty to warn you. Have you considered that?"

"You're suffering from blue dye poisoning from all the denim you wear," Callan countered with a grin. Stephanie, like Sam of old, always tried to put a positive face on everything. It seemed to work. In spite of Callan's protests, Stephanie's acceptance and counsel had eased the despondency and tenseness that had plagued her all day.

"You're wrong about his motive. It wasn't attraction," Callan insisted, not yet ready to alter her opinion or consider that Stephanie might be right. She clicked the stem of her wineglass against the table in emphasis. "Remember, I knew Sam from babyhood. He's a born healer. Strong on sympathy and an unusually decent person, I'll admit, but basically, even as a kid, a prying old fuddy-duddy, always wanting to get inside people's heads and fix them."

Her conscience said that her description of Sam's character wasn't entirely accurate or complete, so she added, "To be fair, back then empathy was a big part of his character. He's a genius with people with more charisma than anyone has a right to. He's got this way about him that makes you feel like you're the most important person in the world. Kids used to fight over who'd sit next to him in the lunchroom. I don't know why I forgot that. He must be extraordinarily successful as a psychiatrist."

"Tell me about him from when you were kids," Stephanie urged.

Callan remembered a time at the beginning of their lives that illustrated perfectly what kind of person Sam had been as a kid and later as a teenager. Now she wasn't sure Sam still possessed the same benevolence and sincerity. Perhaps, after he left Apple Springs at seventeen when his family moved to Chicago, he had changed greatly, so those qualities were only a veneer over a subtly altered personality. He certainly hadn't returned to Apple Springs for her as he said he would.

All last evening she had sensed that there was something different about him, something alien hidden behind his eyes that hadn't been there seventeen years ago. At first, she'd pushed the perception away as too vague and unreliable. Then, she sensed, concealed deep inside him, uneasiness, caused by her presence. She hadn't been mistaken. Her psychic sense hadn't atrophied that much. Under all his sophisticated charm, he was uncomfortable with her. His warm copper-brown eyes hid anxiety and caution. What had she done to make Sam feel those negative emotions? At the time, the disturbing shadow emotions had peppered her like pellets of hail.

Finally she said, needing to get Stephanie off her romantic roll, "I remember, when we were—oh, four—we ended up behind this dilapidated chicken coop way down behind his mom's vegetable garden. I don't remember how it started, but it was a case of 'if you'll show me yours, I'll show me mine'."

A mischievous glint brightened Stephanie's eyes and she leaned forward. "Hot damn! A nasty little kid secret. Tell all."

Callan raised an eyebrow again to let Steph know that her comment was off base. Perhaps, if she could explain Sam, as he had been long ago compared to how he was now, she would lay off her campaign to get them together. Callan propped her elbow on the table and rested her chin in her hand. She leaned forward and lowered her voice to a confidential whisper.

"There we were, standing knee-deep in weeds, with our pants down around our ankles. We each got a look, and then Sam got real stirred up. Upset, I mean," Callan clarified in response to Stephanie's snicker. "We were barely four, for crying out loud!"

"Barely, huh. Okay. Sorry."

"Okay, cornball, behave. Somehow he'd come to the conclusion that a falling toilet seat had chopped me. He got hysterical.

"'Callie, Callie,' he kept yelling, 'we got to find it, go to the doctor, get it sewed back on.'"

"Geesh, you mean, sort of a toilet seat guillotine?"

"Yeah. Can't imagine where he got the idea. But the notion really stuck in Sam's head. 'What'd you do with it, Callie? Why dinn't you get it fixed? How you going to pee straight without it?'" He went on and on, crying, almost blubbering in panic, hobbling around and getting more and more tangled up in his britches. He ended up on his naked little butt in the prickly weeds once or twice. Popped up again right away and kept yelling."

"Poor kid," Stephanie said, a sympathetic grin on her face.

"At first I was confused. Had no idea what he was talking about. Then, when I figured it out, I couldn't get through to him to reassure him that I was all in one piece, that I was fine. He wouldn't listen. Just kept hollering how 'we have to find it, get it sewed back on'. Sam the kid was way ahead of his time," she added. Stephanie hooted.

"Now I knew I was a girl and that everything was just as it should be," Callan continued. "I leaned over and checked just to be sure. No doubt at all in my mind then. Then I got mad.

Downright outraged that he believed something was wrong with me just because I didn't look like him."

"Right on, sister!" Stephanie declared with a fist punched into the air.

"I yelled that I wouldn't want one of those ugly old things anyway. His looked like 'a nasty old warty frog with its tongue hanging out,' I told him. That shut him up for a moment while he leaned over to check his out."

Stephanie sat with both elbows on the table, hands covering her mouth, a stream of titters flowing under them.

"Bravo!" she gasped out.

"Sam started yelling again but then his dad showed up. Fortunately for us, he didn't treat us like a couple of pint-sized perverts as some people might have done, but understood it was just little kid curiosity. Sam got his empathy from his dad, I think.

"Anyway, he got Sam quieted down and our britches up. I stomped off home sniveling and gave Sam the cold shoulder for two days.

"So," she concluded, "making things better, protecting, helping, that's just his nature. Obviously, he contacted me out of his need to fix things, since he believes The Gull threatens me. Nothing romantic about that, especially when he was so sneaky about the whole thing. Pretending to run into me on my way out of the gym! It makes me furious that I fell for it. And I'm supposed to be clairvoyant!"

"Wrong!" Stephanie snapped. "Don't be an ass. I'd bet money that Sam wasn't on a rescue mission or offering his medical services. He let his hands do the talking. Your description of him as a kid and your excessive distrust now are contradictory. If he's anything like the boy you described, he's not a sneaky manipulator. I don't think it'd take much to get the studly doc back on track," she said with a slap of her hand on the table. "Do you want to spend your life alone?" she asked. "That's where you're headed, you know, the way you avoid men. You've been divorced for two years. It's time to get out of your rut."

"Well, Sam's certainly not for me," Callan answered. Stephanie had hit a sore point. Her avoidance of the dating scene bothered her, but she wasn't about to admit it to Stephanie. "After the way he dumped me? I never even knew why he did it. We were really close all through our childhood and teen years. We were practically engaged. After he moved to Chicago, he changed in some way. Probably found a sophisticated city girl without a thought for me. I can't trust him."

"Being the dumpee is the pits, but play this lottery, Mighty Mouse. Don't be so hard on poor Sam. People change, especially at that age. So, maybe he did find a new girlfriend. You gotta know young guys that age walk around with a sticky dickie all the time. What else could you expect if you were apart a long time?"

Feeding Steph's earthy sense of humor with her story about Sam hadn't sidetracked her at all. Callan felt her cheeks flame up at her last comment. Gads, thirty-four years old and a mother and she sometimes still blushed like a nineteenth-century virgin. It made her feel even more like a freak.

Stephanie got up from the table and reached across to pat Callan's cheek. "It sure tickles me when you blush. I'm getting my kid and going home. Mom's orders are to arrange to meet the wizard woman. See what develops. Call Sam and give him a chance," she finished as she headed for the door.

"By the way," she said, turning back and leaning nonchalantly against the doorjamb, "if you and Sam need inspiration, Matt could build you a magnificent chicken coop in your backyard. He's real handy with that sort of thing. If you think it would help, of course."

Callan picked up the pillow from the table and pitched it at her. "See if I tell you any more secrets!"

Laughing, Stephanie caught the pillow and ducked to safety in the hallway.

* * * * *

After dinner that evening, Callan took a glass of iced tea to her front porch and settled into the cushioned swing. She set the tea on the porch railing, propped up a pillow for her head, and stretched out with a sigh. It had been a complicated and emotional weekend, and she was tired. Maybe Stephanie would come over later and keep her company for a while. That would be pleasant, although she'd probably continue to harp on Sam and The Gull.

Her son Connor, Stephanie's boy Zach and some of the other neighborhood kids were kicking a soccer ball around on the front lawn in the twilight. Their shouts seemed muffled in the soft, moist evening air. The streetlights had just come on, and soon it would be time to send the other children home.

She snuggled deeper into the swing and began to analyze Sam and the consequences of their date. Stephanie couldn't possibly realize how exhilarating, sexy, terrifying and humiliating the past day had been.

Between trying to bury the humiliation over misunderstanding Sam's intentions and the anxiety caused by the absurd news that she was the chosen puppet of a crazed psychic from Brazil, she'd spent a restless, pillow-pounding night. Memories of The Gull and Sam fluttered in her mind like sparrows in a cage, refusing to perch for more than a moment.

As an alternative, she picked over areas of her life in Apple Springs to determine what was Gull-corrupted. The possibilities were innumerable. All day she'd been trying to reconstruct the citadel of peace and security she had built during the past two years.

Creating a new home in Denver and conquering her homesickness and despair after the divorce had taken all the emotional strength she possessed. As her world broadened and the vitality of the city beside the towering mountains seeped into her spirit, she came to relish living again and now couldn't imagine returning to her small hometown in Wisconsin. Her life was further ripened through her friendships with Stephanie and a few others. Her career as a paralegal flourished. She'd done an exemplary job of banishing disturbing memories along with her psychic side. No way would she ever again become involved with the paranormal.

Abandoning her hometown for the mountains and rolling hills of Colorado was the best decision she'd ever made. Now, everything she had created was threatened by The Gull's alleged plans for her.

After she'd turned Sam down and nearly walked out on him, he tried to change her mind about accepting help from Rosemary as he drove her home. He'd certainly let his charisma loose last night. For the thousandth time, she harshly reminded herself that he wasn't interested in picking up where they'd left off seventeen years ago. He'd asked her to call him so they could get together again, no matter what her decision about Rosemary. What a crock! After his underhanded maneuvering? No way! The Sam she used to know would have been straightforward about the message from Rosemary Sabin. Why had he been so underhanded? He hadn't even tried to explain his actions.

If the compliments and hand-holding last evening were just his way of making her more amiable to his message, he had erred badly. Did he think her that much a fool? She recognized when she was being royally patronized. The idea rankled along with her other grievances.

She might have created Sam's supposed romantic interest out of his normal amiability and her own imagination. Obviously, rebuilding a relationship with him wouldn't be possible using the emotional debris left over after his long-ago abandonment. After her talk with Stephanie, she felt more relaxed and less bitter. At least her self-denigration had been whittled from turnip-headed ignoramus to credulous dimwit.

Languid in the early evening heat, she watched the playing children with half-closed eyes and yawned. Here she was, all alone, worrying and fretting over her naiveté and the fix she was in. Maybe Steph was right, and she'd been unfair to Sam. Her attitude certainly turned sour after he mentioned The Gull. The evening had grown chilly and she shivered. The least Stephanie could do was pop over to check on her morale.

Maybe it would be sensible to get some help with The Gull. From the corner of her eye, she saw a mist rise from the evergreen shrubs planted in the angle of the steps across from where she lay in the swing. Before she could turn her head to inspect it, the lawn and playing children vanished. A cold, smothering, gray blankness enveloped her in confusion and an abyss of blindness. She couldn't feel the cushions beneath her. Under the pressure of the grayness, her physical self disappeared. No arms and legs twitched in surprise. Up and down no longer existed. No inhaled or exhaled breath confirmed her reality.

Helpless, obliterated by the grayness that held her captive, there was no fighting free. No way to run. Completely vulnerable, she tried to call out but couldn't hear the sound of her own panic.

After an endless time of floating in nothingness, swaddled in terror, her inward cries dwindled into mental whimpers. The engulfing gray-place gradually opened out around her, enlarged and unfolded into separate sea and sky that extended out into a sphere. Sluggish wavelets sent her bobbing about randomly like flotsam, turning her perspective over and over. Strangely, there still was no sense of a body or of wetness lapping against it. Only vision of a sort had been restored. Sullen veils of mist drifted about, blocking what little view she had.

Hearing returned gradually, letting in the sound of the suck and slap of waves, then the screech of a bird. The scream resonated in her mind. The bird's calls gradually transformed into a voice.

Hear me, sweet sister! You permit false virtue to leech your strength! Join us, become one with us in a song of might, it challenged.

At the apex of the whirling leaden sky, Callan caught a glimpse of the bird, all stark, black angles, immense as a sun within the murky interspace. *The Gull!* She remembered it well. The creature had always filled her with a freezing horror. With no body to house or protect the incorporeal part that remained, she could only turn inward and curl the essence of her mind into a tight protective ball. As compressed as her mind was now, the feathered creature could shatter her spirit with a capricious thought.

This mental cage is my fault, she acknowledged. She could have accepted Rosemary's offer immediately and perhaps avoided this prison of the mind. With that admission, there was indulgent agreement from the great bird, leaving her feeling much like a puppy who had been praised for not piddling on the carpet.

The black bird circled then melted into the whirling ashen sky, its cawing fading. The grayness thinned, the waves calmed, and a muted halo of light materialized at the horizon. The glow broadened and brightened and the sphere world drew back like a dilating iris.

Except for a diffuse glow, it was dim in this new place. Crickets serenaded the night, wind ruffled the leaves of a tree branch hanging over a fence, but the breeze did not touch her skin. The scent of night fragrance eluded her. Apparently, no senses other than sight and hearing were to be permitted. She couldn't look right or left voluntarily or make a sound. The Gull still retained control of her body and senses. She hung somewhere, where she didn't know, like a bodiless eye.

That made her want to close down and squeeze what was left of her mind into a tighter bud. She instinctively knew if she gave up, that she would never get free. Her mind would forever remain closed off from her body. Terrified, she willed herself to stay alert and look outward into the darkness.

A sliding glass door hung before her. Then a slow, circling scan of the area began. It was a patio enclosed by a cedar fence. Potted plants lined the fence, and a table with a striped umbrella sat in a corner. Coming nearly full circle, the scan stopped at a wooden door set at right angles to the glass doors. The door glided closer and opened to reveal a storage closet fitted with rows of neatly racked tools. Small, luminous white hands appeared and began to explore among the tools. They picked up something and disappeared from view.

She realized that her worldview was from a much lower level than usual. Had her consciousness been captured and imprisoned within the body of a much smaller person? The hands she had seen weren't her own.

The perspective changed again as the glass doors again came fully into view. The door slid open with a gentle thump and they entered the house. Light filtering in from a hallway ahead dimly illuminated a dining alcove and a kitchen across a counter on the right. The rooms looked familiar, but a clear memory of where she had seen it before wouldn't surface.

Floating down a hallway, they stopped at the foot of a stairway on the right. A three-foot-high, woven wicker frog, its wide-open mouth stuffed with cattails and dried flowers, squatted on the bottom step. The silly frog arrangement triggered a memory. This house belonged to Bernie Rabney, her neighbor directly across the cul-de-sac.

They moved forward again, turned into a living room where Bernie sat slumped on the couch, his mousy gray-brown hair rumpled, a beer can in his hand. A short paunchy man in his early fifties, he was dressed in gray work pants and a blue and gray plaid shirt. Bernie started, and then quickly stood up. He took two steps forward and concern flashed across his face.

"You!" he exclaimed. He held the beer can in front of him like a shield.

Barely an arm's length now from Bernie, she could see the throbbing pulse in his temple and the frightened widening of his eyes.

"Pardon me, mistress. I didn't recognize you for a moment," he said, a tight smile stretching his mouth into a grimace.

"Good evening, Bernie dear. How have you been?" asked a childlike, accented voice.

The neck of Bernie's shirt was open, showing the edge of a white T-shirt. Callan watched in fascination as he convulsively swallowed, causing his Adam's apple to twitch and jump above it.

"Very well, thank you, mistress. Can I be of service, mistress?"

"How kind of you to offer, Bernie dear. But it's too late, our dear one, our beloved old friend. An offer of helpfulness certainly will not grant you a reprieve," the piping, saccharine voice cooed.

Bernie said nothing, simply stared vacantly back at the person before him. Within, Callan felt her mind begin to contract in upon itself again as a rage, not her own, surged around her. It seemed as though gravity had increased tenfold and was crushing her out of existence. Her peripheral vision dimmed; only directly ahead remained in view. They moved closer to Bernie.

The voice continued but the sweetness turned petulant and waspish. "You should have confined yourself to your duty of watching our dear sister and refrained from going into business for yourself. You draw the authorities' attention to our business, old friend, and we do not permit that!"

A hand, clad in a blue and red print gardening glove, jumped into view. The fingers clutched an eight-inch Phillips-head screwdriver. For a long moment, the glove and sharply pointed tool hung suspended in front of Bernie's face. He stood as if mesmerized. Then the screwdriver plunged forward and buried half its length into his left temple.

Bernie stared in wide-eyed surprise, his mouth agape and lips quivering like a child deprived of a favorite toy. The beer can hit the carpet, sounding like an explosion. He reached up and wrapped a hand around the gloved fingers. Only then did the intruder pull her hand away, breaking Bernie's grip too.

The yellow plastic handle of the screwdriver stuck out obscenely from his head like a cartoon alien's antennae. Blood oozed from around the shaft, a scarlet rivulet running down his cheekbone.

Callan's mind twisted in panic within her small, hidden place. She wanted to look away from the sight and to scream out her terror and revulsion, but she couldn't close her eyes or produce a sound.

"Oh, you are so funny-looking, Bernie darling. You should be on TV!" the voice jeered. "You're too killing for words." High-pitched titters filled the room.

The roar of a waterfall filled Callan's consciousness. Terror squeezed her mind and obscured her vision like a leaden mist.

Through the shrouding haze, she saw Bernie reach up to tentatively finger the yellow handle, exploring the object buried in his temple. His face was pallid and his lips puckered into an exaggerated kiss. He stared blankly and swayed slightly. First to the right. Then to the left. His knees buckled. In slow motion, he fell. Then the roaring enveloped her, growing in volume. The buffeting and compression drove her horrified mind to the edge of eternal oblivion.

To reclaim herself and her sanity, she clutched at her most cherished, enduring memories. Her golden-haired Connor at two, sitting in his highchair, crowing "pee-nee ba's, Mama," as he rolled bits of his peanut butter and jelly sandwich into beads that he stuck on the refrigerator door. Connor swaggering across the school yard to his first day of school, stopping at the door to turn and give her a thumbs-up. Connor's boisterous yell of joy whenever he beat her again at a computer game.

From far away, she heard his voice. "Mom, Mom!" She wanted to reassure him that everything would be all right, not to worry, but the encircling darkness held her. She couldn't form the words.

A hand touched her. Connor's hand and she heard the insistent call again. "Mom!"

How wonderful to feel a caress on her own face, hear a voice with her own ears. Dimly, she saw a figure looming over her.

A need to tell someone about Bernie nagged at her. The memory of his face as he fingered the handle of the screwdriver jutting from his temple scuttled away to hide itself in peaceful oblivion. If it buried itself, she too would cower in darkness with it. She scurried after the image, determined to corner it and drag it into the light. She caught the memory, pulled at it, back and back, and concentrated on forming words in her mind. *Bernie Rabney's dead. There's a screwdriver stuck in his head. The Gull killed him. What am I going to do?*

Chapter Two

ও

Just before noon on Monday, Callan sat by the window in the reception area of Sam's high-rise office and stared at the vista of the Rockies spread out before her.

She'd spent a sleepless night, dazed and nearly incapacitated with the migraine that developed after the nightmare vision of Bernie's murder. The headache had finally dissipated at dawn, allowing her mind to clear, but all through the morning, the foreboding never let up.

After returning to herself with Connor bending over her, she'd been confused, unable to decide how to respond to what happened. A man was dead in the house across the cul-de-sac, but she didn't dare call the police. It was the only certainty she grasped under the pain. Explaining her knowledge of the crime with the true answer, "I was shanghaied mentally and saw it in a vision," was untenable. The repercussions of the ensuing brouhaha were varied and staggering. Media coverage, jail time as a suspect or a mental facility could result in the loss of Connor. The logical equation—Callan one, police zero.

Someone apparently had taken the initiative and informed the law. Perhaps The Gull had the temerity to call them herself. The owner of the voice in the vision seemed arrogant enough to dare anything. At 10:30 Sunday night, the Rabney house was surrounded by police cars and then swarmed by cops and technicians until morning. When a policeman came by to interview her, she had played dumb.

The police hadn't revealed a suspect in Bernie's murder in the morning newspaper. It only said that the murder was possibly drug related, as a drug-manufacturing lab had been found in the basement. It was hard to imagine Bernie in the role of drug dealer. He had been self-effacing and somewhat of a fussbudget, but always friendly.

As she had read the paper, she recalled the voice of her kidnapper saying "going into business for yourself." The voice had also called Bernie "her minion." Could Bernie's murder have been a reprisal because he was engaged in drug manufacturing on his own? The voice stated that he was derelict in his duty of watching her "dear sister."

With stomach-cramping knowledge, Callan then realized that Bernie had been sent to watch her, and that the "dear sister" was herself. Sam's earlier warning hadn't moved her to face the reality of the danger hovering over her. Now, she accepted that The Gull's malicious purpose was truly aimed at her. Bernie had watched her almost the entire time that she'd lived in her new house. The idea was terrifying.

Looking back at the things she had seen The Gull do over a lifetime, she could imagine a hundred different ways the woman could hurt and torment her both physically and emotionally. When the possibility of The Gull threatening Connor hit her, panic finally pushed her toward the telephone. She had called Sam before leaving for work that morning and had set up an appointment to meet Rosemary Sabin at noon.

Other questions buzzed through her mind as she sat waiting. *Why did she call me her "dear sister"? Why would a supposedly powerful psychic need an actual watcher to keep track of someone? Just how powerful is she and in what ways? Why would she take the risk of murdering Bernie with her own hand? And why, after all these years, am I able to hear The Gull's voice telepathically?*

She sensed Sam's approach. Grateful for the interruption, she rose and crossed the waiting room to meet him at the reception desk.

Sam was still lean, but those weren't stringy adolescent muscles under the burgundy silk shirt. Thankfully, he'd retained the abundant chestnut hair with the lock that never stayed brushed back from his forehead. A square jaw and strong chin now counterbalanced the prominent nose that had once been his youthful despair. He'd grown taller since he left for Chicago so long ago. At six-three he topped her by nearly half a foot. She'd definitely have to reach up to kiss him now. He'd certainly added impressive layers of masculinity from seventeen to thirty-four.

All the longing she'd felt for him when they were teenagers rose up and blazed through her body. What would it take to get this hunk out of the elegant shirt and the finely tailored linen slacks?

Oh, lord, he still turns me on. Just like Saturday evening, not two minutes with him and I wanted to crawl all over him. What a rush! The sensual response felt fantastic and a blush warmed her cheeks.

Sam's grin broadened. He was still remarkably perceptive and probably knew exactly what she was thinking. Her face faithfully reflected her emotions and offered plenty of clues to everyone. Chagrin and awkwardness silenced her.

She looked down for a moment and then quickly back up, feeling that he would suddenly disappear if she didn't keep an eye on him. He was openly studying her. His eyes roved down her body, pausing at her legs, then back to her face. After so many years, was he disappointed in the way she looked now? No, the appreciative gleam in his eyes and the sexual interest rolling from him said otherwise. Giddy bubbles of pleasure flowed along her nerves as if she was a champagne flute and someone had poured the wine.

"Callie, I'm so glad to see you," he said, taking her hand. "I want to apologize for Saturday night. I handled it badly, pushing you the way I did. I'd like us to start over."

Sam seemed genuinely pleased to see her. However, like Saturday, he was still uncomfortable in her presence. Maybe he wasn't even conscious of his wariness, but she certainly was. Her little gnome hadn't deserted her entirely. A latent alarm, lurking far back in his mind, was definitely working on Sam. Was his problem simple guilt over a broken teenage romance?

Not likely. Even as a kid he had been wise in the ways of people and hadn't been disposed to fits of self-recrimination.

Whatever his problem was, she didn't want it to hinder the resurrection of some fragment of their former spontaneous, relaxed relationship.

He seemed sincere and an appreciative light brightened his copper-colored eyes. When she'd spoken with him early that morning, he'd sounded relieved to hear from her. His magnetism had flowed from the phone, leaving her feeling like some thirsty nomad lured to an enchanted oasis but not permitted to drink at its spring.

"No apologies needed, Sam. You were right about The Gull and the danger. Besides, it's time I explored this bizarre knack of mine."

"Thanks, Callie. Come on. We've ordered in lunch, so we can begin planning our strategy without delay."

His warmth kindled a glow in her that evaporated the icy lump that had occupied her stomach since the night before. His nearness and the warmth of his hand on her arm as he led her past the reception area and down a hall to the right sent a feeling of safety and reassurance through her. Although she needed help, nervous doubts about the wisdom of becoming involved with the psychic world again still troubled her.

As they approached the end of the hall, an older man appeared from a side door and came toward them.

"Callie, I'd like you to meet my colleague and partner, Dr. Albert Ostherhaut. Albert, this is Callan Nevins."

"I'm glad to meet you, Mrs. Nevins," he said. "I hope we can be of assistance to you."

Dr. Ostherhaut's handshake was warm and firm and she sensed in him an abundance of goodwill. He was her height and somewhat stout, with a coarse head of silvery hair and a mustache shading into white. The hazel eyes in his lined face conveyed high intelligence and a well-honed shrewdness.

"I appreciate your concern for a stranger."

"I apologize for any apprehension our rather precipitous contact may have caused you. Rosemary is waiting in here," he said, opening a door and ushering her into a large windowless conference room.

A yellow paper airplane streaked toward her, causing Callan to step back in surprise and bump into Sam. The hair on the back of her neck rose. She stepped around Sam and put her back to the wall.

The airplane zigzagged past her and headed toward Dr. Ostherhaut. It skimmed under his nose, swooped upward into a loop, then shot toward Sam. The airplane mussed Sam's hair with an audacious wiggle while dodging his groping fingers.

"Rosemary!" Dr. Ostherhaut yelled. "Cut that out!"

The paper airplane completed a few more jubilant loops and came to a halt in front of Callan's eyes. It hung suspended with its pointy tip aimed directly at her. It almost seemed to quiver in anticipation.

With a deep breath Callan cautiously reached out and plucked the hovering paper airplane from the air. It rustled and trembled for a moment like a small, trapped creature seeking its freedom. She nearly dropped it. The airplane had been folded from a sheet torn from an ordinary yellow legal pad. Amusement and delight washed away her previous apprehension. Here was a facet of the paranormal that was fun, even silly, lacking the usual ominous atmosphere that had previously surrounded her experiences.

"Hello, Callan, I'm Rosemary Sabin, your hoodoo instructor," came a mellow voice from the far corner of the room.

A figure advanced to meet her. At first, there were only the eyes. Set below wrinkled eyelids, their faded aqua was penetrating but playful. The remainder of the woman's body seemed to unfold and solidify around those eyes.

Rosemary Sabin was tall and slim but beginning to stoop with age. Her silver hair was fluffy and carefully styled, her makeup applied subtly and with precision, and her flower-print silk shirtwaist dress was tasteful and meticulously fitted.

Callan stepped forward to clasp her outstretched hand. A current flowed from Rosemary's fingers, emotionally sustaining and vital with life force. At her touch, Callan sensed that Rosemary was much like her own great Aunt Noonan, not physically or in personality, but in her psychic power and in her generous heart.

Longing poured through her. She wanted to fly a paper airplane, make it soar and tease, just as Rosemary had done, more than anything she'd craved in years. "Can you teach me that trick?" she asked.

"Perhaps, if you have the gift of telekinesis," Rosemary answered.

She still held Callan's hand firmly. Her eyes became more brilliant and all-encompassing. As their gazes remained locked, Callan sensed a mental dexterity and a peculiar power that she hadn't encountered before, even in her Aunt Noonan. Déjà vu flashed over her. Somewhere in her subconscious an awareness of a long association stirred, the memories not quite reaching the conscious level. She'd known Rosemary before, somewhere or sometime. The other woman, she knew, recognized her too.

With that knowing, the conference room, Sam, Dr. Ostherhaut and Rosemary disappeared, to be replaced by sun-dappled water and steamy heat. The odor of decaying vegetation and the scent of exotic flowers permeated the air. Calls and shrieks came from a multitude of birds and animals. Warm flowing water caressed her bare skin and splashed water drops reflected like a shattered stained glass window around her.

Hands reached toward her and lifted her up toward the sun. She looked down into a laughing, feminine, brown face with black almond eyes. She was no longer Callan, but someone young and innocent, and possessor of a bone-deep joy.

Mother?

Yes, daughter, I'm here, came the answer.

In her heart she knew what she felt and saw was authentic. There was no need to seek authentication of her vision from Rosemary. The other's thoughts radiated confirmation and joy. The experience told Callan that they had known each other in another lifetime. That philosophy didn't correlate with her conservative Midwestern upbringing. Neither did her paranormal abilities, but she'd had to accept them anyway.

In spite of the dichotomy, well-being swept through her. Under Rosemary's touch, the last of her earlier aversion to the paranormal vanished, replaced by curiosity and an eagerness to open to experiences she believed she'd rejected forever. Later, she would have to reflect on what the jungle vision meant and how it would affect her worldview. She suspected that many of her comfortable beliefs and attitudes would be challenged in the coming weeks. It wasn't a reassuring thought.

"Shall we sit down to lunch, ladies? We have a lot to accomplish this afternoon," Dr. Ostherhaut said, breaking into the emotional and psychic cocoon that surrounded the women.

"Of course, Albert," Rosemary answered, with a slanting glance at him and a delicate wrinkle of her nose. Reluctantly, they dropped hands. The abrupt cutoff of their connection left Callan feeling physically cold and emotionally bereft for a moment.

They all moved to the end of the polished conference table where a variety of sandwiches, salads and beverages waited. Sam sat beside Callan, with Rosemary across from her, and Dr. Ostherhaut as Rosemary's partner.

"Will you be able to give much time to this project, Mrs. Nevins?" Dr. Ostherhaut asked when they were seated. "It may require considerable time and effort on your part to reach a satisfactory level of psychic competence."

"I've arranged for a week's vacation from work. I hope it will be enough to make a start."

As they passed the food, a slight prickling sensation meandered across Callan's mind, not unpleasant, only mildly unsettling. Rosemary was watching her, a smile playing at the corner of her mouth. Then came a phantom thought not her own.

Don't mind Albert's formality and dictatorial ways, my dear, she suddenly heard. Rosemary's mental voice was distinct and as resonant as a temple bell. *He's been my friend for many years. He's got a good heart and is an excellent psychiatrist. You can trust him, even though at times, he can be overwhelmingly stuffy, obsessed with paperwork and numbers, and rigid with linear thinking. Do you suppose they hand out those characteristics along with the doctoral degree? You do exceptionally well in telepathic receiving, Callan. Could you reply to me?*

The voice flitted through her mind, touching lightly as butterfly wings. Open and lightly humorous, it invited a reply.

The last time she'd used telepathy was with her Aunt Noonan and she'd been a small child. She struggled to organize her thoughts and construct an answer. At first, she could only project a fuzzy mental query.

Relax, said Rosemary's mental voice again. *Be in the same mental state as when you listen to melodic music. Visualize each letter in a word, separately and distinctly, that you wish to send to me. Words formed quickly create a voice in a partner's mind. Pictures work too. Follow my mind and sense the pathway I use. Echo each word I say in your mind's eye. Experience how I do it.*

Callan followed her instructions although she felt as if she were trying to catapult her brain outside her skull.

Yes, that's right, Rosemary encouraged. *After some practice you will become accustomed to using a combination of words, pictures and emotion. You will form a telepathic voice. Okay, now, give a little push and release them from the third eye. It's situated on your forehead, just between and slightly above your physical eyes. Look at me. Can you see it?*

Rosemary's third eye looked like a miniature whirlpool, spinning out flickers of indigo light. The bizarre, hypnotic eye blazing from the middle of Rosemary's forehead made Callan catch her breath.

You…don't…care for…scientists? Callan finally got out after her astonishment quieted.

Each word departed from her mind haltingly, unlike Rosemary's smooth, efficient sending. She knew she had projected a telepathic message. She'd felt it leave her mind. She had to restrain herself from touching her own forehead in search of a third eye. Her forehead felt warm and rather peculiar, prickly as with an allergic rash. Logically, a third eye must be decorating her forehead too.

Sure I do. Their contributions are important, Rosemary answered. *They keep the plumbing flowing. Except that some older scientific types, like Albert, who have been steeped in the so-called logical mind-set for many years, can be so overbearing at times. An old poop, in other words.*

Callan fought to maintain a bland expression and edit anything more than mild amusement from the link with Rosemary. The old girl was getting to her.

Now Sam, for instance, is a treasure, Rosemary confided. *Trained in scientific methods, of course, but not a dry, stuffy bone in that superb body of his and apparently no obsession with getting a bunch of facts down on paper. There's always the possibility, however, that Albert will corrupt him eventually.*

You're right about Sam, Callan agreed. *He already has his own obsession. The inclination to be responsible for the mental health and well-being of every person to cross his path. He's always been that way.* Rosemary had opened a door in Callan's mind and let the telepathy spill out.

By the way, is it polite to be talking behind their backs, or their minds? Callan questioned as she further relaxed, the sending smoothing out with each thought she released. It was so satisfying, so relaxing, as if she had removed a too-tight hat from her brain. *I like this telepathy. It's fun. Handy, too. You can eat and talk at the same time. Try some of that pasta salad.* She formed a picture of the particular salad in her mind and included its tangy flavor along with it. *It's delicious.*

Sam broke in then, glancing suspiciously from one to the other. "What are you two up to? Something's going on here. You two keep looking at each other oddly. And what is that annoying hum I keep hearing?"

"Oh, just a little get-acquainted chat and telepathy practice for Callan," Rosemary answered, reaching across the table to pat her hand. "She has an amazing telepathic talent. A quick learner, too. Picked it up right away. Mental conversation is such a rare psychic gift. It's so good to have someone to mentally chat with again."

Callan had never voluntarily read anyone's mind, although occasionally, when she was tired, a stray phrase would get through. She'd always assumed that meaningful two-way telepathy was possible only with another psychic, such as her Aunt Noonan. The rest was just static. To preserve her sanity, she'd learned automatic blocking around others at an early age.

"You should be gratified, Sam," Rosemary added, smiling at him affectionately. "Most people aren't aware of telepathic transmissions. You must have a wee bit of ESP yourself."

Sam looked nonplused. He abruptly set down his fork as if he had found a cockroach in his salad. He looked with alarm at Dr. Ostherhaut.

"Don't be concerned, Sam. An ethical telepath won't read another mind, not word for word anyway," Dr. Ostherhaut said, as he regarded Rosemary and Callan with an ironic grin. "Since they've got it, we can expect them to flaunt it. Although not always so blatantly, I hope."

Callan got the impression that he regarded them as somewhat wayward children who had been caught in some petty mischief.

"Don't go all uptight on us, Sam," Rosemary said earnestly. "We would never poke around in your head. That would be gauche. Besides, most minds are boring or incredibly nasty. Not to say that yours is," she added hastily. "It's just that most people have such shockingly imprecise minds and poor visualizations. Mish-mash and mental yammer. So, we tune out other people's fuzzy thinking as noise."

"Fuzzy minds, hum," Sam said, regarding Rosemary with barely restrained mirth and not a little fascination. "That could become a new category of discrimination, I think."

"Not discrimination," Callan cut in. "Self-protection. I'd rather take up mud wrestling in a pig wallow than muck around in some people's minds."

"That's a rather uncharitable attitude, Callan," he answered with a mild, non-committal glance. His disapproval of her comment was kept entirely on the inside, but his altruistic nature had certainly been outraged. She knew it as surely as if he had snarled his opinion. Getting to him was kind of fun.

"Since you have your own brand of ESP, Sam," Callan added sweetly, "your amazing empathy with people, maybe you should ask Rosemary for some training and really get into the mind game." The dare showed in her voice. "Unfortunately, firsthand experience of the average psyche would likely change your opinion of people. That would be a shame."

Putting him on the spot would pay him back a fraction for his underhandedness last Saturday. It still smarted, although to be fair, Sam's intentions had likely been honest.

Sam gave that suggestion a moment's consideration, looked speculatively at Callan, grinned, and then picked up his fork to resume eating. What had just flashed through his mind? She should have peeked.

"If everyone will please finish their lunch," Dr. Ostherhaut urged firmly, "we'll proceed with the business at hand."

Subdued, they obeyed and shortly took their drinks and moved the meeting to the other end of the long conference table. They resettled in the same seating arrangement as before, with Rosemary directly across from Callan, and Dr. Ostherhaut and

Sam facing each other. They all turned expectantly to Dr. Ostherhaut as the leader.

"Callan," he said, "I want you to know that anything said in this room will be considered confidential and under the doctor-patient code of ethics by Sam and me. I have no doubt that Rosemary will also abide by this policy."

Rosemary nodded and sent her agreement to Callan.

"What we'd like to do this afternoon," he continued, "is to conduct some baseline tests of your abilities. We've brought in some psi games and measuring devices and I'd like you to try them out. I'd also like to use the electroencephalogram, an EEG that we have here to measure your brain wave activity. A biofeedback machine is available should you feel the need of it during your training sessions with Rosemary."

"What he means, dear," Rosemary whispered from across the table, "is that he wants to hook you up to his old-fashioned icky-sticky machines and try to figure out how you do what you do. Fortunately, it doesn't hurt, but it certainly wrecks your hair. Awfully tedious, too."

Dr. Ostherhaut cleared his throat and continued. "Perhaps later on you can record for me a summary of any psychic episodes you have undergone. With your permission, I would like to keep records of our findings and record our conversations. I have an ongoing interest in, and have conducted scientific research on, the various aspects of the paranormal for many years."

"What he's not telling you is that we did psi research back in the Seventies for a secret government agency that I'm not supposed to name," Rosemary informed Callan.

"Rosemary, please," Dr. Ostherhaut said. "I'd like to conduct this meeting in an orderly, business-like manner."

"Don't you forget, Albert," she shot back, "that the only reason we're here is to develop Callan's powers. That crazed psychic terrorist is bearing down on her. I don't care whether you get a pile of printouts and figures!" Rosemary punctuated each sentence with a rap of her knuckles on the table. "I want to hear, right now, all about Callan's paranormal experiences and get on with the training."

"Didn't you and Callan get her psychic history out of the way while you were talking earlier?" he asked, barely controlling his exasperation.

"No."

Rosemary slanted a pleased smirk in Callan's direction, and she caught her thought. *Dictatorial. Linear-minded. Numbers-afflicted and excruciatingly methodical. An old fart. Didn't I warn you?*

Callan, although sympathetic toward the doctor's frustration, locked down her expression and swallowed a giggle.

"Very well, Rosemary," Dr. Ostherhaut said with resignation. "Perhaps, as you say, speed is imperative under the circumstances. We'll get to the history shortly."

He snapped on a recorder sitting on the table and stated the date and time and names of the attendees. He opened a folder and removed a stack of papers.

"But first," he said, "I think we should explore the motivating force behind this project, the woman known as The Gull.

"Her name is Bianca Dias Cavalcantis. She is the head of a criminal organization headquartered in Brazil," he lectured.

"I obtained information from one of my government contacts over the weekend. Not much is known about her or the internal workings of her organization. All attempts by law enforcement agencies to infiltrate at a significant level have failed. Any undercover agent sent in either vanishes or is found dead. Rumor says that she uses her psychic powers to control her operatives, ferret out infiltrators or destroy any opposition. It's said that whole families have disappeared into her gang."

He separated a color photograph from the other papers and shoved it across to Callan.

"This is the only known photo of her. The operative who took it passed on the film only minutes before he was killed in a suspicious hit-and-run accident."

The eyes, they dwelt in Callan's nightmares. A deep sapphire blue, the eyes dominated the picture, reaching out to seize her and bring back memories of the times they had mocked and threatened her.

"We do know that her family immigrated to Brazil from Portugal just before World War II," Dr. Ostherhaut continued.

With one part of her mind, Callan absorbed what he said, but the eyes in the picture wouldn't let go of her.

"They bought an estate on the seacoast. They had a substantial fortune when they arrived, but they didn't prosper other than financially. When Bianca was four, her mother committed suicide. By the time she was fifteen, her father and three older brothers were dead in either bizarre accidents or from indeterminate illnesses. She was left as sole inheritor of the fortune and the family estate, where she still lives today. She's forty-six years old now. The original fortune has multiplied many times over.

"There are indications that she is in the process of expanding her operations in drugs, vice, illegal weapons and professional terrorism across Latin America and possibly into the United States as well."

"Callie, are you okay?" Sam asked.

She had been staring obsessively at the picture as the doctor spoke. Her left hand, white with pressure, gripped the edge of the table, and the right hand, holding the picture, trembled. Her insides quivered too.

"I know those eyes," she said in a raspy voice. Her chest felt constricted, as though a heavy object pressed against her breastbone. "The black gull, the one I have seen intermittently all my life, has those eyes. Not human eyes, but sapphire, like this woman's."

With an effort to avoid looking into the eyes again, she studied other details in the color photo. It apparently had been taken in a public area. Blurred images of people appeared in the background. The crowd didn't jostle the central figure. There was plenty of personal space around her.

The face, turned fully toward the camera, was as insipid and ageless as that of a stone cherub crowning a mausoleum. The long, blue-black curly hair accentuated the whiteness of the skin. The woman Bianca was tiny, fragile, in comparison to those around her, perhaps only four-and-a-half feet tall. The head seemed disproportionately large for the small frame. A sweet and docile sprite, except for the mesmerizing eyes. They reminded Callan of a weapon brought to bear, neutralizing the sweet childishness of the rest of the woman's appearance.

"Sam told me you spoke of a black gull when you were children," Dr. Ostherhaut said, interrupting her study. "This woman has similar eyes, you say. Can you give us examples of the circumstances under which you saw the gull with blue eyes?"

"When I was a youngster, I saw her frequently. Usually when something bad happened to me or to other people, I would see this huge gull. It had a wingspan of at least ten feet, I'd say. A light-devouring coal black with those weird, blazing, sapphire blue eyes. It would perch on a tree branch, on a fence or roof. Always glaring at me, laughing, mocking me. When it appeared, I'd usually get a headache, a pressure. An unpleasant prickle in my brain. It always scared me so." She faltered and dropped the picture onto the table.

Sam pried her left hand away from the table edge and held it on his knee. His touch drained away some of her anxiety.

"The headache, the tingling," Rosemary said, "was probably generated by Bianca trying to coerce a mental rapport with you."

"Sam told me about a few clairvoyant instances in your childhood that he knew about," Dr. Ostherhaut said. "For example, your intervention prevented a possible collision between a runaway truck and your school bus. You also located a lost fisherman. Did the black gull have anything to do with those happenings?"

Callan shook her head. "Those situations were my own clairvoyance coming out. She wasn't around." She glanced at Sam, wondering what else he had revealed to Dr. Ostherhaut. He squeezed her hand as if he knew exactly what she was thinking and gave her a reassuring smile.

"Can you tell us a particular instance when you saw The Gull and something unpleasant did happen," Dr. Ostherhaut asked.

"When I was six. The morning after my Aunt Noonan died. I saw it outside the kitchen window. My mom had just told me that Aunt Noonan had passed away in her sleep. Heart attack. The bird felt…pleased about something. The death of Aunt Noonan probably. It stayed for about ten minutes and then disappeared."

"My great Aunt Noonan," Callan explained, "was the family eccentric, full of odd quirks, spooky visions and foretelling. Undeniably, she had paranormal powers. A family mystic popped up every now and then on my dad's side. Aunt Noonan was secretive, hiding her clairvoyance from the people of Apple Springs, uselessly I suspect, although they certainly always knew about me. I become the town witch in her place."

"Was that the first time you saw The Gull? The day your Aunt died?"

"No, the first time I ever saw it, I was about four. Aunt Noonan and I were in our yard weeding the flowerbeds, talking telepathically as we worked. I remember it specifically because I had just learned how to do it. She saw the bird first. I picked up her terror and started to cry.

"The bird crouched on the old apple tree. It stared at us with those horrible blue eyes. I didn't like it at all. It was so big that the whole tree seemed to sag with its weight. The air seemed heavy, still, and it was hard to breathe. Aunt Noonan talked to the bird, but I didn't understand what they said. After a while, it wasn't there anymore. Aunt Noonan wouldn't explain it to me. Said not to talk about the bird with anyone. We went on weeding the garden."

Talking about the incident had brought out all the childish dread at that first meeting with The Gull. If Aunt Noonan hadn't died, maybe she would have provided guidance and training, and The Gull would have been banished from her life years ago. Then this ludicrous prospect of facing a showdown, unprepared and unarmed, with a Brazilian psychic would have been avoided.

"Can you give us more examples?" Dr. Ostherhaut urged.

"My eighth birthday party. Do you remember, Sam?" she asked, turning toward him.

"Your mom was upset because you wouldn't eat the birthday cake she made."

"The party was in our backyard," Callan remembered. "The Gull appeared and hunched down in the vegetable garden, wings all spread out. It stared at me. The pressure and prickly feeling came, followed by the headache. Then Mom brought out the cake. A huge gross black widow spider was crawling across the white icing between the pink rosebuds, leaving a trail of footprints. When Mom sliced the cake, she cut the spider in half and it oozed black blood.

"At first I didn't understand why she didn't see the spider. Then I realized it wasn't really there, that the bird had made me see it. It believed the shabby trick was an excellent joke. The cake had become disgusting to me, of course."

"Indeed. However, quite an extraordinary feat," Dr. Ostherhaut said. "Please go on."

"Another time, a Fourth of July picnic when we were about fourteen," Callan said, with a glance at Sam. She questioned how much of their childhood he recalled. She'd tried to forget many of those ancient episodes, and it was painful to resurrect them, along with their attendant emotions. She was glad he still held her hand.

"The bird showed up and draped itself over the sheriff's patrol car parked next to the field. It was huge. I could hear its claws scraping the car's roof. The wings slapped and fluttered against the windshield and the back window. The eyes did their whirling bit. I got the usual headache. Then it ignored me.

"The bird looked around, taking in the baseball game and the school band playing a concert. Finally, its interest turned to the tables where the picnic food was laid out. The bird had made up its mind about something. I'd gotten wise to it by that time and was scared of what it might do. I started toward the picnic tables, hoping to prevent its mischief. How, I didn't know.

"Before I could get there, a pot of baked beans exploded, peppering everyone in range. Simultaneously, bowls of potato salad and slaw erupted like volcanoes, spraying the crowd. Hamburger and hot dog buns soared like miniature flying saucers. Then the paper plates and cups went up. Bottles of mustard and ketchup exploded. The beer kegs started rumbling then spewed. People were screaming and running away, spotted with food. I got a lot of suspicious, hard looks that day. People blamed me for it."

Sam stirred and said, "That Fourth in Apple Springs became known as the day of the food fireworks. Nobody ever figured out how it happened. People didn't blame you, Callie. They knew it wasn't your style."

Sam obviously saw her psychic episodes from a more generous perspective. Of course, he hadn't felt the fear or suspicion that was directed toward her after a public paranormal incident.

"As a rule, would you say that The Gull's attention and animosity focused mainly on you rather than others?" Dr. Ostherhaut asked.

Rosemary had sat quietly, asking no questions, her face showing that she was disturbed by Callan's account.

"Yes, most of the time. However, I could go months, even years without seeing it. Sometimes I would see it, but nothing unusual would happen. The bird would just show up, watch me for a few minutes, give me a headache and then disappear. During my senior year in high school, all through college, until several years after I was married, I didn't see it at all."

"Tell us about the first time you saw it after the long hiatus," Dr. Ostherhaut requested.

"I'd always assumed The Gull only visited me for my entertainment value, to watch me squirm, under whatever circumstances randomly developed or it managed to orchestrate. Such as causing the spider illusion on my birthday cake or creating the food fireworks. The power to change someone's personality? No, that never crossed my mind then. A couple of years ago, I finally comprehended that The Gull had somehow corrupted my husband. Destroying Luke was probably easy for her. She certainly has the power. I didn't know what to do about it. How to change him back and make things right again."

The three waited patiently for her to go on. Telling them about the night when she accepted that Luke was no longer the man she married would be humiliating. She had faced her own mortality that night and knew in her heart that she was truly an adult.

"You were hurt in an attempted robbery a couple of years ago," Sam asked. "Did she have anything to do with it?"

Leave it to Sam to zero in on the exact incident. And how did he know about that? He must still have a connection in Apple Springs, she realized, and wondered who it was. She pushed the question aside, and dry-mouthed, she explained.

"Yes. Luke took Connor and me out to dinner at the pizza place at the edge of town. That was unusual. By then, Luke seldom paid attention to either of us, coming and going as he pleased. Over the years, our home became hardly more than a boarding house to him. He didn't abuse us exactly, other than being indifferent, or at the most, sarcastic." Each sentence she spoke made the next easier.

"The marriage had been over for a long time, but I just couldn't get up the gumption to end it formally. Unable to face the emptiness of my life. Not knowing how to fill it. Afraid of small town gossip, I suppose, or how Connor would feel about a divorce. Frozen with indecision, that was me.

"There was plenty of gossip about Luke circulating through Apple Springs. His fingers were in many pies, and he had become a wealthy man.

"Over the years, his reputation deteriorated under a series of questionable business deals that always came out in his favor. I heard the whispers about him and at first tried to dismiss them as jealousy over his success. But slowly I came to know the whispers and gossip were based on truth. From overheard conversations, papers left carelessly about the house, I pieced together a picture of his business practices. I didn't want to believe the evidence, but slowly I became ashamed of being his wife."

She paused, recalling the emotions and letting the details of that night pierce her once more. That June evening after the late supper, the three of them headed for the parking lot behind the pizza joint. The sun had gone down, and the parking lot lights glinted off the cars. The heat and humidity made it hard to breathe, and the hum of insects from an adjacent field rasped harshly against her ears. Connor, who had turned nine earlier that month, was delighted by the rare attention he received from Luke during dinner. He ran ahead, chattering over his shoulder about how great the pizza had been. Luke trailed behind.

As they approached their car, a figure materialized from behind a van. It was dressed in light-colored baggy shorts, T-shirt and heavy work boots. The hair was shaved on the sides of the head so that only a stiff dark ridge ran from the hairline to the back of the skull. In the shadows, the eyes were dark pits, the mouth a slash across the bottom of the face.

It held a knife, its short blade canted upward slightly, held waist-high, waving jerkily, as though uncertain which of them to threaten.

Callan grabbed Connor's arm and shoved him back behind her. The figure stood only three feet away, and she was directly in line with the waving knife.

"Okay, let's have the purse and wallet," said a boyish voice. It was hoarse and shaky with tension but definitely young.

She extended her handbag toward the boy. Hopefully, Luke would cooperate and not become belligerent and aggressive, escalating the incident. She was scared but certainly not paralyzed with fear. Give the boy money and he would leave.

Suddenly, a blow exploded against her back. The impact knocked her forward. Peering into the teenager's face from inches away, she could see his watery eyes widen in surprise. There was no pain in front, only awareness that something alien lodged within her. The knife had slipped smoothly into her stomach. The agony came from the stunning blow to her back. Confusion clouded her mind. The danger was in front, not behind. The boy stumbled back, withdrawing the knife as he went. He turned and scuttled away between the parked cars and into the darkness.

At first it seemed that the knife had only scratched her. But her fingers, pressed gingerly against her waist, instantly became sticky with blood. The coppery smell rose in the muggy air. Blood soaked her blouse and ran down to saturate her shorts. *How messy*, she thought. Connor, beside her, clutched her upper arm.

"Mom, mom, mom," he said.

Luke made no sound. No exclamation of concern. No hand reaching to support her. Nothing but coldness flowed from behind. Then she understood that the blow that propelled her onto the knife had come from Luke. He had done it deliberately. With that realization, the pain detonated, radiating from her middle, exploding in every nerve in her body.

She was on her knees, head drooping, one blood-covered hand pressed to the gritty asphalt. Dizziness sent the world tipping and spinning. Connor knelt with her, still clinging to her arm, crying now. Behind them, Luke's footsteps sounded, moving leisurely away toward the restaurant.

Inside her mind came a familiar shriek of mocking laughter. With difficulty, she raised her head. On the other side of the chain link fence that separated the parking lot from a field, The Gull's eyes glowed with sapphire glee in the darkness. Her high-pitched squawking overrode the rasp of the insects as Callan's consciousness winked out.

"I knew The Gull had orchestrated the whole thing somehow. They never caught the teenager. I didn't tell the police what Luke had done. Neither did Connor. How could he tell them what his father had done? After I got out of the hospital, I started divorce proceedings and Connor and I left for Colorado as soon as I was well enough. Luke didn't try to stop me from taking Connor away."

The others were silent. Sam looked at her with sympathy, the doctor with a restrained, almost calculating concern, and Rosemary with a poorly concealed outrage.

"Last night she further demonstrated her evil by murdering my neighbor Bernie Rabney," she stated baldly. "How do I stop her? Otherwise, I believe she'll try to take me over, make me into a carbon copy of herself."

Chapter Three

ဢ

"Murder!" Rosemary sprang from her chair and leaned toward Callan across the table. "The woman is vile!" she spat out. "I'd like to pull out all her psychic connections with red-hot pliers!"

To Callan, Rosemary's outrage felt as pungent as a spray of ammonia spreading through the room. She drew in her empathy and shut down telepathic contact with her. Rosemary was an unpredictable element. There was no telling what she could or would do psychically when aroused.

"Take it easy, Rosemary," Dr. Ostherhaut said, standing halfway up as if some decisive action might be needed.

Rosemary stood with her mouth quivering for a moment, then sat down and primly folded her hands on the table. She stared down at them as though only they restrained her from another outburst.

Dr. Ostherhaut's attention returned to Callan as Rosemary subsided. "The Gull murdered someone last night? How do you know?" he asked, and settled back into his seat. Obviously, he was no longer concerned with Rosemary.

From the corner of her eye, Callan caught a glimpse of Sam's face. His expression showed understanding for her trouble, but there was curiosity too and some well-buried awe. She didn't like seeing any of those emotions. They made her feel even more of an oddity. She slipped her hand from Sam's grasp, planted both elbows on the table, and rested her chin in her hands.

"Last night Bianca took over my mind. She killed my neighbor Bernie Rabney with her own hands and made me watch. She likes playing it down and dirty." The bald statements didn't begin to express the horror of the phenomenon.

The other three sat in silence as Callan told them of her mental kidnapping and witnessing the murder of Bernie through the mind and eyes of Bianca.

"She's never done that before, usurped my mind, woven me into the fabric of her own. The experience was so eerie, like being a fly perched on a horse's ear," she said, her voice hoarse from her long recitals. "I don't know how she did it. She's never done anything like that to me before."

She felt hollow with hopelessness, her stockpile of resiliency depleted. The others' expressions showed they were beginning to truly assimilate the magnitude of the threat.

With a sigh Sam got up, went to the other end of the table, poured four glasses of iced tea and then passed them out. Dr. Ostherhaut added two packages of artificial sweetener to his and drained the glass in two mighty gulps. Rosemary didn't seem to notice the drink. She sat slumped, her forehead resting on the back of her hand as if all verve had deserted her.

Callan's tea contained two slices of lemon. Sam had remembered that she liked extra lemon. She smiled at him, amazed that he would remember so trivial a detail after so long. He responded with the grin that had always caused a delightful trembling around her heart. It did just that again, and she wasn't sure she should allow herself to enjoy it. *Probably a bad idea. Don't be a bigger fool than you've already been*, she told herself.

Undoubtedly, he knew the effect his quirky little grin had on women. Or maybe she was just unusually susceptible to its effect. Mindful of Rosemary's likely sensitivity to any errant sexuality in the room and Dr. Ostherhaut's trained canniness, she shut down her consciousness of Sam as a desirable man, not wanting any of the others to know the impact he had on her ragged spirit. She had managed to disperse any trace of her attraction from the conference room's atmosphere.

Dampening her sensual awareness of him didn't seem to perturb Sam at all. It didn't take a clairvoyant to realize it had disappeared or at least gone underground. Unlike many men who would be annoyed at such an abrupt cut-off, he didn't seem to notice the loss of sexual undercurrent. Instead, he had remained in the background all afternoon and simply offered a neutral support, unspoiled by any resentment that she wasn't responding to his masculine appeal.

"I knew I was right when I decided forty years ago to stay out of her accursed psychic sight!" Rosemary exclaimed, exploding out of her funk. Her eyes snapped with renewed vitality. Rosemary had recaptured her feistiness without the aid of tea.

"Do you want to explain that, Rosemary?" Dr. Ostherhaut asked, in a quiet but firm voice.

"Certainly, Albert." Rosemary puffed out her lips at him, leaned back in her chair and folded her arms on the table. She looked at Callan with a confident smile. "As I said, I sensed her psychic aura long ago. She must have been a small girl at the time. At first, I only perceived her as a muddy psychic blight. As time went on, I spied her on the astral plane. She was an ominous gray-black entity by then. I put up my psychic defenses against her then and there. She doesn't even know I exist," she finished, obviously satisfied with her strategy.

"How does one do that? Wouldn't a gifted psychic notice a mental defense, even as a negative or blank spot?" Callan asked. She was curious about creating a psychic defense. After years of denial and avoidance of the subject of the paranormal, her forcible immersion in the subject had released a voracious need to know everything about it.

"That's a good question, my dear. However, you must remember I put my guard up when she was still very young. Before she had full control or use of her psi powers. Even now, as highly skilled psychically as she is, to her I'm just a mediocre spirit on the astral plane and inconsequential.

"Perhaps, for anyone with the talent to notice, like Bianca," she continued, "your pillar of light with its distinct psychic markings attracted her attention on the astral plane. Even when you were a youngster the signs would be clear. Luckily, you must possess some natural resistance to her psychic manipulations. Otherwise, you'd have been consumed spiritually by her as a child."

"Are you saying that Bianca got the drop on me simply because she was older?" Callan hadn't understood much of what Rosemary had just said, but that concept had come through.

"That's right. However, I have another theory too. This is just speculation, but I believe her physical proximity to you since she came to Colorado has given her an extra edge. Allowed her to force you into accompanying her while she murdered your neighbor. I don't know why some psychic phenomena are enhanced by physical nearness."

"How do I keep her from doing it again? How do I protect myself and keep her away?" Callan asked. Lunch was no longer sitting comfortably in her stomach. One by one, Rosemary was removing pieces of her confidence and her hope.

"I'm sorry to interrupt you, ladies," Dr. Ostherhaut said, "but it's close to 3:00 and both Sam and I have patients to see. Besides, this is Rosemary's specialty, the training of your psychic powers, Callan. However, I would appreciate it if you would come in tomorrow at 8:30. I would like the opportunity to take a few scientific readings. Rosemary, don't you arrive until 11:00. With you around, my readings undoubtedly would be skewed." He turned off the tape recorder and began gathering his papers.

Poor Albert! Callan heard Rosemary's telepathic voice say. *He hates it when I talk about the astral plane and astral spirits. His rational mind wants psi to remain strictly on the scientific level. Of course, the mystical doesn't easily yield to the scientific. I've been a burr under his intellectual collar since the day we met. My theory is that he has a secret desire to be a practicing psychic himself. The conflict makes him really uptight. Having psychic talent is as common as dandelions,* she went on with a mental sigh. *Most everyone has some. I believe that psi's easier for women to manifest because they're not so adamant about remaining in a state of strict logic all the time. It's acceptable for the female to use her intuition.*

Rosemary paused for a moment, and then added, *Albert comprehends the emotional mindset for a successful psychic event from his years of research with me. His ambition is to produce a scientific report with a manual of instructions on how to do it. He hasn't zeroed in on the particular factor that causes psi talent. For all his knowledge, I believe he feels let down, inadequate. Furthermore, he believes he has no psychic power, because he can't do my parlor tricks. I've told him and told him that it's not true, that he has psi, but he won't believe. It's his blind spot.*

I sense that Dr. Ostherhaut has his own brand of...perceptiveness, Callan replied. *I don't think he's deficient spiritually or intuitively.*

That's just my point. He's not. He's an exceptionally good man, a spiritual man. Like Sam, he's such a marvelous doctor because he cares deeply about people. He has an uncanny intuition about what makes a person tick that he uses in his work. He won't accept that his genius for helping people is a form of psychic talent. He wants fireworks. His stubborn shortsightedness makes me so mad that I can't resist rubbing it in that I've got the fancy muscles and he doesn't. I'm ashamed of my treatment of him at times, but I'm enough of a prima donna to keep tweaking his nose.

"Okay, ladies," Dr. Ostherhaut said, interrupting their subliminal conversation. "I can tell by your bland expressions that you're chattering away underneath. Roasting me, no doubt. However, may I have an answer regarding tomorrow's agenda?"

"Nonsense, Albert," Rosemary replied sweetly. "Don't be paranoid. We were just discussing some important psi theories. Your plan, of course, is acceptable to us," she said, gathering in Callan's unspoken confirmation.

"Uh-huh. I'm sure that's the case," he said, heading for the door. "Please feel free to use the conference room as long as you need it."

"Don't worry, Albert," Rosemary called after him. "I'll make sure Callan has the psychic equivalent of a ring of nuclear missiles."

"You can do that better than anyone," Dr. Ostherhaut said, giving Rosemary and then Callan a brilliant smile before disappearing into the hall.

Sam stood up to leave too. He studied Callan for a moment as if judging her state of mind after the afternoon's revelations. He touched her shoulder and let his spread fingers caress her neck just under her left ear.

"You'll call me if you need me, anytime at all, won't you, Callie?"

As usual, his slight touch coursed a tingling path through her body, which treacherously craved more. Her good sense rejected the need as dangerous to her precarious emotions. She couldn't allow unsettled feelings about him to distract her. Preoccupation with his current intentions would divert her from the dilemma she was facing. Besides, Bianca might see him as a potential hostage if they became friends again.

"Yes, Sam. Thank you." She kept her reply grave and distant.

He recognized her brush-off. She felt his dismay, but he gave a nod of acceptance and followed Dr. Ostherhaut.

Callan watched him stride away, already regretting her decision. When he disappeared through the door, she turned her attention back to Rosemary and caught a sympathetic flash in the aqua eyes.

"Sam's an enduring man, Callan. He'll be there when you want or need him."

"Perhaps. It's not a smart idea to depend on him in this situation."

"I suppose we'd best get on with the nuclear missile construction," Rosemary said, tactfully changing the subject. "First, I must ask a few background questions. Do you get clairvoyant messages of a wider nature, concerning public events, such as disasters? What about telekinesis? Have you ever moved anything deliberately or spontaneously?"

"When I was just a toddler the clairvoyance and telepathy tormented me," Callan answered after a moment. "My mother told me I had horrible nightmares and waking dreams around the time I began talking. I do vaguely remember dreams of violence and blood and being terrified. I have a strong memory of a voice that shut out the noise, crooning to me, making the nightmares go away. I suspect it was my Aunt Noonan, helping me to control. She came to live with us about that time. Without her, I don't think I'd have stayed sane.

"Later, sometime before starting school, the clairvoyance functioned only sporadically. It narrowed to only those instances where someone I was close to was in danger. After Aunt Noonan died, I never again spoke with another person telepathically. I'd never heard The Gull's voice until last night. I've never moved objects with my mind. Never wanted to."

Rosemary had listened intently to her recital. "You were lucky to have your aunt. Psychic prodigies can end up insane without a good filtering technique in place. However, you easily picked up my instructions to visualize words and send them telepathically. Clear visualization is essential for telepathy, telekinesis or to operate within the psychic realm. 'As you imagine, so shall you be,' is my family's psychic motto. How were you able to do that if your telepathy went unused after your aunt died?"

"I am, rather I used to be, an artist, so maybe visualization comes naturally to me," Callan said. "I started out as an art major in college and expected to make it my career."

"Used to be? Expected?"

"During my first year, I seemed to lose interest. The work became difficult and frustrating. I felt dissatisfied with what I produced. That time was devastating because I felt I had lost my vocation. I decided I didn't have what it took, so I changed to a business major."

"An abrupt loss of interest and skill," Rosemary mused, her lips thinning. "Bianca! If you examine that time, look deep within yourself, I suspect you will detect Bianca's meddling somewhere. She couldn't control you overtly, so she slipped in on the astral plane to attack your creative source. Subtly undercutting your confidence and blocking your creativity must have been irresistible to her."

At first Callan was astounded at Rosemary's hypothesis, but as she examined it further, the validity of the idea became believable. That first year in college had been so strange, as if all that she had been was drawn out of her and reshaped like clay. She could not speak as the possibility coalesced into certainty. The concept fit. Bianca had stolen her art. Fury and grief engulfed her.

Blindly she stood up. She wanted to run, but didn't know where to run. She needed to escape the knowledge that she had been so outrageously, frightfully manipulated. She stumbled around the table, not caring where she was headed. Abruptly, she came up against one of the consoles along the wall. Both hands were clamped over her mouth to choke off a shriek of pain and rage. Tears ran down her cheeks to dampen her fingers.

Rosemary was suddenly beside her, one fragile hand resting lightly on the back of her neck. Comfort and calmness wove their way through her mind and gradually loosened her rigidity.

She turned to Rosemary with tear-flooded eyes and choked out, "Luke and my art? What else has she taken from me? What else have I lost to her? If she could do those things, and me with no notion of what she was doing, there could be more, much more."

"Yes, there's probably more. But beware. This odyssey you have begun today will take all the courage, the integrity, you possess. To decipher the distortion of your past and create a future of your own making may require a heavy price." Rosemary's voice was stern with warning. "If you let anger rule you, Bianca will win. She thrives on hate and misery. Exploits the fears and weaknesses of others. It's her reason for being. She could own you, body and soul."

Rosemary's words sobered her, driving out the volatile emotions and replacing them with chilling fear. Rosemary urged her back to the table and produced tissues to wipe her face.

"Why don't you put your head down on the table and relax," Rosemary suggested. Exhausted, Callan pillowed her head on her crossed arms. Rosemary began massaging her shoulders.

"You have a consoling touch, Rosemary," Callan said.

"Just a little psychic healing. The laying on of hands. You can learn to do it too. Now relax. Do you remember how you felt when you painted?" she asked softly. "Or maybe during a good run or during your yoga sessions. You do all those things, don't you?" Rosemary's voice settled into a hypnotic, telepathic murmur.

When you do those things, you're relaxed, but your mind is alert. Completely focused until time almost seems to stop. That is the meditative state and the beginning of the alpha state, a smooth, regular brainwave frequency, as Albert will explain to you. Then you proceed to the theta state, where the psychic has access to her power. Be at rest and feel that way now. It's wonderful, your mind calm, clear, receptive.

As Rosemary continued the massage, Callan physically felt like melting butter, her mind opening as Rosemary continued to instruct her.

I want you to visualize a white light, a special, radiant white light, Rosemary said. *See how it glows, like liquid sunlight, like an angel's halo. Now the light is near you, it's touching your feet. Can you feel its warmth? It's slipping into you, through the soles of your feet. It flows up your legs. So warm. Warm and pure and comforting. Now it's at your hips collecting at the base of your spine. Yes...yes, you know it. It's coursing up your spine to the level of your heart.*

Enclosing your heart in its protection. Traveling up to crown your head like a tiara of diamonds. It's a lovely thing, the armor of light. Feel the tenderness that flows through it and the power. It whirls and eddies through you, reflecting outwardly through your skin, the splendor encloses you.

Each night before you sleep and when you awake, visualize the white light filling and surrounding you. You can cause the radiance to enclose and protect your home and your loved ones too. It's like lowering a crystal bell jar around them. I've put its protection around this office. Can you see it with your psychic eye? Tap into the eternal creative power, hold fast to it, and its protection is yours. Rosemary's stroking slowed and her hands rested on Callan's shoulders.

After a moment, Callan sat up. Her earlier distress had evaporated, leaving only tranquility and a hopeful outlook that her chaotic nightmare world would steady into a reliable orbit once more.

I saw the white light, she sent to Rosemary. *It was the most glorious psychic experience I've ever had. They've always been drenched in fear and darkness before. I didn't know it could be that way. Thanks, Rosemary.*

Available whenever you need it, Rosemary answered with shiny eyes. *No charge either.*

"Now go wash your face in cold water. You're all blotched," she ordered verbally. "There's a bathroom just across the hall. Take yourself home and get a good sleep. I'll see you tomorrow, and we'll go over many other odd and fascinating notions."

Callan kissed Rosemary on the cheek and retrieved her purse from under the table. "Bless you, Rosemary. See you tomorrow," she said from the doorway.

* * * * *

Later that evening a cool, rain-freshened breeze swept down from the black mountain range and whispered through the pines in her yard. As Callan stood on her backyard deck, the current lifted her hair, ruffling it against her cheek, much like Sam's touch that afternoon. The moon was in a dark phase, and only reflected city lights and the glow from windows in neighboring houses illuminated the night. The tranquility that she had achieved under Rosemary's guidance still lingered, buoying her with optimism. She would learn everything Rosemary could teach her and forever end Bianca's meddling in her life.

The evening with Connor had been blissfully uneventful after the extraordinary day in Sam's office. During dinner they had discussed Connor's expectations and plans for the new school year, which would begin later in the week. It would be his first year in middle school.

With all the excitement after meeting Sam, house cleaning had been neglected over the weekend. She always seemed to be behind with the cleaning and laundry and rushing to catch up. Her bathroom especially needed going over, so she tended to that chore while Connor straightened his room. Although it was unlikely that a speck of dust would dare deposit itself in his sanctum or one book or picture would be allowed out of alignment, he would rigorously tidy up anyway. His bathroom always looked as if it had been scrubbed with a toothbrush. No soap scum allowed in there.

Connor had become so finicky about his surroundings and belongings that sometimes she wanted to go in his room and upend a few items just to make it look lived in. Maybe rub a little dirt into his carpet. His inclination to perfectionism worried her more each day. For an eleven-year-old kid's room to look like it was part of a model home, unlike the rest of their house, wasn't normal. Mr. Connor Persnickety should take over more chores since he was probably a better housekeeper than she was. Certainly he was more dedicated. More chores. That might cure him.

Although more chores wouldn't cure his newfound vegetarianism. His adoption of the vegetarian philosophy was phony, simply a phase he was going through. Goading his mother about eating meat and making her lose her temper over it seemed to be his purpose in life lately. She'd caught him sneaking a slice of corned beef out of the refrigerator yesterday, and then he had the gall to deny his intention to eat it. That made her even madder.

As she wiped and scrubbed, she considered how expert in the paranormal arts she could become. A protective aura around the house would be reassuring. The big bad bird lady wouldn't be able to pop in on her unexpectedly. Rosemary hadn't gotten around to explaining how proficiency in telepathy, telekinesis and clairvoyance would help her fight Bianca. Maybe when she was a psychic expert she'd know when The Gull planned to attack, so she could have a stockpile of rocks handy to chuck at her using telekinesis. While swearing at her telepathically, of course.

If I got good enough at the paranormal arts, she fantasized, *maybe I could stop doing housework. Just like that funny witch on the television show* Bewitched *that I watched as a kid. Perfection at the twitch of a nose.* She looked in the bathroom mirror and tried to wiggle her nose, but the effect was ludicrous. The rest of her face wouldn't stay still.

Maybe then, she further speculated, *I could send the dust, grunge and trash of daily living into outer space with a snap of my fingers.* She tried the snap and it echoed satisfyingly off the tiled walls but nothing else happened. She grinned. *If I get telekinesis down pat, never again will I wield a vacuum cleaner or scrub a toilet.*

I could shoot the dirt and garbage out into outer space. But NASA might not appreciate greasy, dirty paper towels and dryer lint on the windshield of the space shuttle, so maybe I should rethink the idea.

With the chores finished, they'd settled down together for a *National Geographic* special on TV. Afterwards, Connor obligingly went to bed with only a couple of reminders from her. Now she was alone, eager to get on with her practice as an apprentice psychic.

In bare feet she padded down the deck stairs to the back lawn and made a circuit of the yard along the tall cedar fence. She paused in the far corner where a lilac bush and old-fashioned scented roses were planted in honor of Apple Springs. The lilacs had long since ceased to bloom, but the roses, their reds and pinks and yellows washed to a ghostly pallor in the shadowy dark, liberated their sweet fragrance on the evening breeze.

As a cricket chorus sang, she brushed a rose with the tips of her fingers, enjoying the sensuous velvety texture of the petals. Rosemary's meditative session seemed to have enhanced her sensory perceptions. From the Ellisons' house, she could hear sleepy wails from Katie. *The little cowgirl woke up.* She smiled in contentment at the homey sound.

An amorphous glow covered her hands like soft moonlight. Rosemary's gift of the protective aura, shining forth in the night, enveloped her body, encasing it in delicate splendor. She knelt beside the roses, then stretched out in the grass and looked up at the heavens. Many years had passed since she'd taken the time to truly stargaze. Awareness of the grandeur of a night sky was one practice that had fallen away over the years.

As Rosemary had instructed, she controlled her breathing as she would have done during a yoga session and sought the gateway to the theta state. Her respiration slowed into a deep, steady rhythm. The Earth radiated warmth from the heat of the day. The minutes passed, the meditative state deepened, and she became conscious only of the stars above and the Earth beneath her. Gradually, the Earth took possession of her.

Her trance deepened and, during an infinite moment in time, her mind brushed against the primal instincts of the small life that scurried over the Earth, burrowed within its sheltering soil and swam in its oceans. She became immersed and enthralled in the grandeur of the planet's abiding life cycles.

After an eternity of flowing with and absorbing the currents of earthly life, curiosity drew her upward into the atmosphere. Floating free from the Earth, her spirit diffusing upon the wind, she soared above the world. The feeling of freedom and power was intoxicating. She felt as though she'd been transformed into the tail of a comet. With the tips of ethereal, glowing fingers, she reached out and traced the world's mountain ranges.

As a flitting breeze, she danced across high, sunlit meadows, rippling the wildflowers and grasses as she went. The caressing wind became a tempest, sweeping her across an ocean to find and trace lazy designs in desert sands.

A massive dust storm buoyed her up again and whirled her into the endless circulating pattern of wind and clouds. She looked upon the man-wounded places defacing the world's surface and mourned.

A plunge into the Earth followed, there to drink at the fountain of its fiery, molten outer core. The Earth expelled her, and she drifted in the jet stream of the high stratosphere, sharing the Earth's stately rotation through the night, and its orbit around the sun.

After a long, lazy descent, she once more found herself back on mundane Earth with the crickets' song and the scent of her flowers. She arose feeling as light as a dust mote. Her aura brightened and expanded around her like silvery confetti tossed on the wind. As she lifted her arms to the night sky, the luminescent aura began to swirl around her. As the whirlwind danced faster and faster, a delicate music box melody began to chime.

She reached out and gathered an armful of the glittering, racing mass. The mist coalesced and clung to her arms, pulsing with power. She flung the double handful of aura upon the night breeze and directed it to the rooftree of her house. It clung there for a moment, than spread across the roof and down the walls like paint made of stardust. She laughed in euphoria.

The whirlwind slowly ceased its jubilant dance, the music box chimes faded, and her luminescent aura dispersed on the night breeze. The house still radiated a mellow light. She sighed with satisfaction and made her way back up the deck steps and inside.

Connor as usual slept with abandon, his pajamas twisted, his limbs flung wide and entangled in the bedclothes. She rested her hand for a moment on his hair then watched as his body was blanketed in the radiant aura.

The fairy dust is real, Connor, just like you believed when you were little.

She stumbled to her room, dropped her clothes on the floor and pulled on a nightshirt, barely making it to the bed before sleep overtook her.

Deep into the night, a shriek of enraged frustration penetrated her sleep. Startled, she jerked awake. The unearthly screech had sounded like The Gull. She had no way to be sure that she'd woven the protective shield correctly. If she hadn't, The Gull could break through.

Chapter Four

ഔ

The Gull hadn't gotten in, and after a short screeching spell had finally left. On Tuesday morning, Callan pretended to leave for work at the usual time, giving her an extra half-hour to kill before her appointment with Dr. Ostherhaut at 8:30. Only Stephanie knew about the project and where she would be spending the next few days. Explaining to Connor that she was holed up in a psychiatrist's office for a week to practice her telepathy and learn to fly a paper airplane by telekinesis was out of the question.

A few minutes after Callan arrived at the office building's underground parking garage, Sam's car pulled in. She wanted to avoid him as much as possible. She crouched down in the front seat of her car. Peeking out her window, she saw him pull into a reserved space two rows ahead near the elevator. When the car door opened and Sam got out, she ducked down again and waited. Had he noticed her car in the shadow of a pillar? Getting caught hiding in her car would be mortifying.

Sam's true feelings and motives were still questionable, as far as she was concerned, Stephanie's theories notwithstanding. Memories and hopes regarding him had broken her sleep almost as much as her worries over Bianca. She'd accept a little private chagrin at using childish tactics to avoid him. After all, darn it, Sam hadn't explicitly indicated that he was extending anything other than a helping hand during a crisis. Helping humanity and intervening in emotional emergencies were at the core of him. She certainly didn't need therapy, and she couldn't assume that she was special to him because of their past. It would be best for her poise and his safety to keep the relationship distant and businesslike. Her ego still smarted from the debacle of their date and her unwarranted assumption of a romantic interest.

Besides, it was hard to trust him again. He was the one who ended their friendship long ago. Whenever Sam was near her, their childhood and teenage years surged into memory, leaving her struggling to reconcile them with the present reality. They were different people now, so he was only leftover breadcrumbs, she reminded herself again. She couldn't afford the luxury of wanting him, even a little. Even a brief walk with him through a deserted parking garage would be uncomfortable.

A car door slammed and footsteps echoed off the concrete walls. When she judged he was safely in the elevator and on his way, she cautiously sat up, reached for her extra-large cup of cappuccino, inhaled its cinnamon bouquet, and took a deep swallow.

A fragrant bakery and specialty coffee shop two blocks from Sam's office had lured her in for a desperately needed second cup. Resistance to the aroma of the flaky pastries was just barely doable. Withstanding the coffee was not. Last night her sleep had been restless again, broken by the constant need to monitor the protective aura around the house, but Bianca hadn't shown up.

The coffee did its invigorating work. She finished it off and headed upstairs hoping that Sam had retired to the privacy of his office.

Luckily, he was nowhere in sight. The secretary at the front desk directed her to the conference room where they'd met the day before. Dr. Ostherhaut was already there, surrounded by his machines.

"Good morning, Callan. Ready to get wired up to one of my nasty machines? This is an electroencephalograph," he said with a beatific smile as he held up a handful of wires.

"Sure, wouldn't miss it."

His manner was playful and charming, and he had a dimple in his left cheek that played peek-a-boo with his mustache when he smiled fully and naturally as he did now. The doctor had been holding back yesterday.

What is it with these two psychiatrists? she wondered. *In a fatherly way, the doctor's charisma is as powerful as Sam's. They must give each other lessons in charm. Or maybe they just absorbed it from each other like vagrant bacteria in the air.*

"Okay, have a seat and I'll wire you up," he said. "I'll try not to irreparably destroy your hairdo. Long ago, Rosemary corrected my tendency to commit that misdemeanor." He added a comic twist to his mouth at the memory of Rosemary's backlash. It made Callan laugh.

After she was settled in a reclining chair, he carefully sectioned her hair and began attaching electrodes to her scalp with a sticky substance.

"The electrical activity of the brain can be measured by the use of an EEG machine," he said. "I want to measure your normal brainwave pattern first. Then your brainwave pattern in other states of consciousness.

"As Rosemary probably told you yesterday," he went on as he worked, "a psychic must achieve the alpha brainwave pattern followed by the theta pattern. That's the meditative state of a relaxed but focused mind. The biofeedback exercises will help you to enter the alpha pattern at will. From there, you go deeper into the theta state and facilitate your paranormal powers."

He placed the last of the electrodes, tilted her chair back, and fiddled with a control panel. "You don't need to do anything. Just relax and let the machine do its work."

Callan contemplated the ceiling and considered the events of the last few days. Faces appeared and reappeared over and over. Sam, Rosemary, Dr. Ostherhaut, Stephanie, Connor. Sam, Rosemary, Connor, Sam, Sam, Sam—

"You're well within the normal alpha range, alert with good focused concentration. I suspect you have a habitually calm state of mind. Do you do meditation and yoga?" Dr. Ostherhaut asked, interrupting her daydream.

"Yes, and it's good to know my hours in the lotus position have paid off," she answered, choking back any sarcasm from her voice. *And I'm certainly glad you can't read my mind!*

"How about a psi game now? It's fun." He adjusted her recliner to an upright position and moved over a console holding a box.

"This is a random number box," he announced. The box was about the same size as a small television set, with an on/off switch and lights and buttons.

"You push this button to start it," he said, pointing to a green button on the lower right side. "It generates a four-digit number electronically inside. You enter your guess on this keypad, and then push this button after each turn," he said, demonstrating the machine, "then a new number appears inside. The box automatically counts the correct and incorrect guesses. It's electronic and silent so no clicks or peeps can give away clues.

"Since no one knows the numbers being generated, it eliminates telepathy and demonstrates clairvoyance. There are one hundred numbers in a run. I've set it for three runs. A new series of numbers will start automatically when the first series is finished. Start whenever you're ready. If you have any problems, give a holler," he said as he left the room. "I'll be in my office across the hall with the door open."

Callan stared at the machine with its shiny black buttons and impudent red and green lights. She could swear the machine was leering at her, thumbing its nose and daring her to try to outsmart it. Rosemary's aversion to Dr. Ostherhaut's machines was absolutely understandable if they all looked at you as this one did.

The places where the electrodes were attached pulled slightly. She impulsively stuck her tongue out at the box and punched the start button with her thumb.

Dr. Ostherhaut returned an interminable time later. "Let's see how you did," he said cheerfully.

He pushed a button on the side of the box and a display screen on the front showed three correct, two-hundred-ninety-seven errors. He crowed with delight, much like Connor after he'd won a computer game.

Callan scowled at the box and then at the doctor.

"The test ticked you off, didn't it? An extraordinarily low score reveals your clairvoyance as much as getting every one correct! The odds of your missing that many in three runs are astronomical. You're good! Congratulations. You're clairvoyant whether you like it or not!"

She inched back slightly from the random number box and reached up to poke at a particularly annoying electrode. "Dang machine," she muttered under her breath.

Dr. Ostherhaut continued to grin at her. "Rosemary isn't due for another hour. If you can take a little more aggravation, I have another little box for you to bedevil."

He moved the random number box out of the way and rolled over what appeared to be a simple computer and monitor. When he turned it on, a green spot slowly crawled down the center of the screen. Darker green sections appeared on either side of the screen.

"This is my favorite," he said with relish. "It's used to test telekinetic ability and enhance clairvoyance. Rosemary trained on a similar apparatus to learn how to fly that paper airplane that you admired so much.

"The machine generates a random pattern of five numbers," he went on. "By clairvoyance you must first perceive the numbers and then try to telekinetically influence the computer to generate a matching sequence. If you can do it, the spot will move away from the center of the screen into the darker green zone. The EEG will produce a musical note when the dot moves. Keep the tone going for as long as you can. Are you game?" he challenged.

"Of course," she said, curious as to whether she had any telekinetic ability.

"I suggest you relax and achieve a deep theta state before you begin. I'll be back in plenty of time to free you before Rosemary arrives."

This machine was more malevolent than the random number box, although she must have matched the digits occasionally. The computer would give an anemic wail, and the spot would jiggle into a dark green zone before promptly snapping back to the center. By the time Dr. Ostherhaut returned, she was not in a relaxed, focused state. She was fuming. The doctor was sympathetic and encouraging as he removed the electrodes, telling her that it took considerable practice to command the little green dot.

When he was finished disconnecting her and his back was turned, she pointed her index finger and took a bead on the monitor screen. Jerking her thumb, she blew it away. The green spot gave a hard twitch to the right, the machine emitted a piteous yowl and its lights went out. By the time a puzzled Dr. Ostherhaut turned to inspect his equipment, she had grabbed her purse and was escaping into the hallway.

Rosemary called a "hello" as she was about to enter the rest room. When she came up and got a look at Callan's face, she grinned. "Albert's gone into his Dr. Frankenstein mode, no doubt, walking around rubbing his hands together in glee. He loves to get his paws on a talented but green subject in need of a little comeuppance. Bet you aced the random number test and bombed the telekinesis test."

"Sort of," Callan agreed, "and my hair's a mess." She could feel it sticking up in spikes. "I hope nothing in that sticky stuff will bleach the roots of my hair or make it fall out."

"It's safe. I cured him years ago of carelessness in that department. Let me say hello to him before he goes back to work. I'll be in here," she said, bustling into the conference room.

When Callan returned, Rosemary was waiting alone. *Your protective aura looks vital this morning. I assume you've also constructed one around your house?* Rosemary asked through the telepathic link they had begun to use while discussing paranormal matters in the conference room.

The experience was bliss! My house looks like it's been given a coat of paint made of moonlight.

She described her epiphany with the Earth and her dance with the luminescent whirlwind. She became subdued when she told about Bianca's efforts to break through the protective aura during the night.

Sounds as if you've made great progress. You kept her out. By the way, using the Earth's life energy field is unique. I've never heard of it being done before. To construct a protective aura substantial enough to keep Bianca out permanently will take much more power, wherever you can get it.

At Callan's worried expression, she said, *Add more protection tonight. Thick is good. Build it day by day until it's like the bell jar I described yesterday. Better still, make it as thick and intricate as your grandma's crystal cake cover. Don't be too concerned now. You're progressing nicely. It takes practice to construct a strong psychic shield. But don't ever forget she's out there waiting for you to screw up.*

"I know she is," Callan said, dropping out of telepathy. "I feel like a silly little gullible jerk for letting Bianca alter my destiny."

"I don't believe there is only one destiny issued per person," Rosemary said, looking at her sharply. "We are born into particular circumstances, but life offers choices and detours."

"I've been letting her manipulate my choices and create my detours for me! I've been Bianca's patsy and plaything. She made my childhood hell with anxiety. I was constantly watching over my shoulder for her, never knowing when she'd show up with another lousy trick. If I had developed my psychic gifts, I might have had a chance against Bianca and fought back long before now. How different my life could have been!"

"You can't blame yourself for this situation, Callan. Remember, you were hardly out of babyhood, and she was almost an adult during your first contacts. You couldn't have fought her. You didn't have the power or skills at that age. If your Aunt Noonan had lived, she undoubtedly would have stood guard over you and helped you develop. Maybe that's why she died," Rosemary finished, holding Callan's gaze. "Stopping a heart would be easy for The Gull."

Callan was stunned at her explicit statement. "Is that possible? Could Bianca have killed my aunt just because she protected me?"

"Entirely possible. Remember what Albert said about Bianca's relatives all dying off prematurely? Causing a heart attack would be easy for her."

"My Aunt Noonan. Along with Luke," she said, her eyes misting. "All because of me. Until he married me, Luke was a fine man. He deserved better than to end up as a shady small-town businessman. We could have had a good life together. We were in love at the beginning. I feel responsible for what happened to him. His potential was wasted because he married me."

Rosemary sat quietly, apparently unaffected by the negative feelings flowing from Callan.

"I docilely went where Bianca led me. Luke and I would likely have married and had a child, but the direction of our lives would have been under our control. Luke's integrity would be intact today, I'm sure. My art would never have been abandoned. How different everything would have been if I hadn't blindly submitted to her plans for me. I failed Luke and I failed myself!" At the back of her mind she acknowledged that she was wailing like a child that life wasn't fair, but she couldn't stop herself. The past few days had been too full of stress and change.

"Don't take it all on yourself, Callan," Rosemary cautioned, her face gentle, her voice calm.

"I must! I can't let her rule me anymore. I'm reclaiming my life!" she answered back, her hands clenched into fists on the table. She was filled with such rage and determination that she shook with it. She didn't know how to release the pressure.

"Bravo! I'll hold you to that vow! But first, let's get some lunch," Rosemary suggested, with a sympathetic smile on her face. "Guilt and vows are more easily handled on a full stomach, don't you think? Besides, you're going to need some fuel for this afternoon's practice."

"I'm sorry for spouting off at you like that, Rosemary." Her touch and calm suggestion seemed to have drained the negative emotions from Callan.

"Should we go find a fantastic little bistro?" Callan was starving. Her paranormal activities seemed to use a lot of calories. "Can we forget all about this psi stuff? Just be two new friends enjoying a lunch together?"

Her uncontrolled outburst was embarrassing, but she felt better, more relaxed, after the emotional venting. A lot of anger must have been bottled up.

Rosemary was silent for a moment as she studied her hands in her lap. "I don't think we should be seen together," she answered. "Bianca is probably aware that you're coming to this building since my shielding aura in itself is a giveaway. Although I've prevented her using clairvoyance to locate us inside and spy on us, that doesn't stop her from using conventional snooping methods such as following you in person. I suspect she's too arrogant to bother with that. My protection is that I'm just one more old lady in a building full of medical offices."

"I'm sorry," Callan said. "I didn't think about that. I'd forgotten you could be in danger from Bianca too. You'll be careful, won't you?" She hadn't the courage to suggest that Rosemary stop training her.

"Don't worry about me." Rosemary shrugged, dismissing her concern. "I'm one canny old clairvoyant and not easy to lay a hostile thought on. Let's see if that young lady at the front desk will help us order some lunch."

While they awaited the food's delivery, Callan asked, "You spoke yesterday of the astral plane. I've heard the term but what precisely is it? How can a corrupt person like Bianca have access to what I would expect to be a spiritual place?"

"Having psychic power doesn't require that a person be benevolent or moral here on Earth or on the astral plane. All that lives upon the Earth has a reflection on the astral plane. No matter whether the being is good or evil, whether it's human or animal, sentient or not. What resides on Earth is duplicated there. The life force radiates between the two worlds.

"I think of the astral plane as a celestial basement," she went on, "sort of a quasi underground parking garage." Rosemary's grin was saucy and the roll of her eyes suggested humor and openness about her paranormal theories. "Otherwise, just imagine all that raw, messy, disruptive life force blundering around in the pure spirits' heavenly home. All those sour, disapproving, pursed up angelic mouths! What a drag!"

"I don't understand."

"I'm not surprised," Rosemary chuckled. "I know this sounds mystical, but it's hard to describe another dimension to someone who's never been there.

"For example, a clairvoyant can sometimes perceive the past, present or the future, but how does a mind tap into those states? The astral plane is a tangible place to me, as real as this room is to you. Although it's occurred to me that it might not be an actual place at all, but only my way of dealing with the indescribable."

"How did you discover your astral plane?" Callan asked, leaning toward Rosemary in her eagerness to understand her worldview.

"My astral plane was discovered or, perhaps I should say defined, by an ancestor nearly four hundred years ago. The key to entering it has been passed down through the women of my family for generations. Legend says that the first visitor believed she had stumbled into heaven. Subsequent visits overturned that notion. I'll take you there when you're ready. Then you'll understand."

Lunch arrived and Rosemary dropped into telepathy as they ate.

Tell me what happened with the telekinesis test this morning.

As Callan answered, it occurred to her that should anyone see them during a telepathic tête-à-tête, they would be branded as weird. They had all the facial expressions and body language of an animated conversion but without a sound coming from either of them.

I couldn't make the machine match the ten-digit numbers fast enough to hold the dot in the green zone. Callan waved a deprecating hand toward the odious machines in the corner.

Don't worry about matching the numbers. Getting the numbers by clairvoyance fast enough to keep the dot steady in the green requires too fine a control for you yet. Go straight for the green dot. It's only a bit of energy on the monitor screen, and energy and matter are what we manipulate with telekinesis.

Won't that be defeating the purpose of the test?

Sure, Rosemary confirmed, her mouth pursing around a bite of sandwich, *but you need to release your paranormal powers first and rout Bianca before we satisfy Albert's craving for more statistics.*

He had me wired to an earlier version of that machine. 'Decipher the numbers with clairvoyance, and then make the machine generate matching numbers using telekinesis,' he demanded. I tried and tried for days until I was reduced to a whimpering puddle of psychic glop. Believed my psi powers were deserting me and my cushy government job spying clairvoyantly on the Russians was history. Until it occurred to me that matching those damned numbers had nothing to do with my power. Following Albert's dictates wasn't necessary.

I had that spot hopping around the screen like a ball in a tennis match, she said as she poured coffee. *Got it to play a polka, too. Albert was wild. Accused me of cheating. After that, I had no problem moving small objects like the paper airplane. Later, after more practice,*

I could match the numbers and control the spot like he wanted. Hoodwinking Albert's machine is of no consequence. Elevating your psi power is. Want to give it another try this afternoon? I can turn on the game. The electrodes aren't necessary. But don't tell Albert.

Rosemary was right. Moving the little green spot around the screen was simple, and she even managed a few bars of *Yankee Doodle* in honor of her success.

"Albert's ears must be burning," Rosemary said, with a hearty audible laugh. She seemed delighted to be subverting Albert's electronics and his plans.

When they got bored with the psi game, Rosemary brought out a lace-edged white handkerchief, shook it out to a pyramid shape and placed it carefully in the center of the conference table.

"Watch," she said, hands on hips.

The handkerchief proceeded to flick back and forth like a feather duster, moving between the empty cartons and debris from their lunch, scatting crumbs as it went. As an encore, she sailed the cartons into a trash basket sitting eight feet away in the corner.

Callan whooped and applauded and told Rosemary about her fantasy of transporting household dirt and trash out into space.

"I should have considered that possibility myself years ago," Rosemary said, dropping into vocal communication.

The handkerchief slid sluggishly across the table for a few inches when Callan tried.

"That's great! You're well on your way to having a psychic maid service," Rosemary praised her.

When they took a break for more coffee, Callan asked, "You mentioned earlier that you had a government job researching the paranormal and spying on the Russians by clairvoyance. Could you tell me about that?"

"Oh, I did more than act as Albert's research subject. Besides doing remote viewing of what was going on over on the other side of the world, I attended several disarmament talks. Saw a lot of the world that way. My cover was usually as an assistant to some official, and I sat in on the meetings. I could easily pick up the opposition's intentions, in spite of language differences, giving us a great advantage in knowing whether they were sincere in their statements or just running us around the block. I never used telepathy to probe their thoughts, which I consider unethical. However, using empathy to pick up emotions is a different matter. Just makes me a good poker player."

"Did you spend all your time on the paranormal? It must have been exhausting."

"No, not at all. I also was a damned good secretary in between the research and the spying. That was my job much of the time.

"I think my most important paranormal accomplishment was when a skinny little man showed up at our research center one afternoon. All very hush-hush, of course. He said the opposition had sent up a particularly nasty and dangerous satellite. He wanted to know if I could do anything about it.

"He pulled a sliver of metal out of his briefcase and said that it was a piece of the original satellite, but it had been removed for some reason. Felt and looked like metal foil and wasn't much larger than my little finger. He wanted to know if I could use it to locate the correct satellite, naturally not wanting me to target the wrong one. Be subtle, he insisted, no blowing it up. He didn't want an international incident. I didn't like his vibes. He didn't really believe I could do anything. Since he was telling me the truth about the situation and was truly worried about its potential for upsetting the balance of power, I said I'd try it.

"We went outside onto the research center grounds and he pointed low in the sky and said, 'It's about there right now.'

"With the metal fragment in my hand, I concentrated on the area of sky where the monster satellite was supposed to be. Found it easily enough and went inside it with my mind. Only took a moment's work using telekinesis to put a few cracks in its innards and release its power. Its lights went out. A wily job of trashing it, I must say.

"The little man must have been pleased with my efforts because he came back a few years later. The opposition was persistent and sent up two more dangerous satellites over the years. I did my patriotic duty and both of them became space junk too. I guess the taxpayers got their money's worth out of me on those jobs."

"I suspect you were underpaid, Rosemary."

"Perhaps. You know I wouldn't be surprised if you get a visit from a government man one day. So you should decide what you will or will not do for them. I emphatically stated my limits up front from the beginning of my association with the agency. I wouldn't kill for them, or rape someone's mind like Bianca does. My husband Colin wouldn't allow them to put me in danger. When seeing war and violence up close during my remote viewing trips began to upset me too much, Colin and Albert put a stop to them. They wouldn't let the powers that be hassle me about it either."

"You mentioned before that you are a widow. Colin must have been quite a guy. Would you mind telling me about him?"

"Oh, yes, he was quite a strong man, both mentally and physically. When I met him, he was head of security at the military installation where we did the paranormal research," Rosemary said, her eyes growing dreamy.

"We didn't get along at all at first." She smiled wistfully at the memory. "He believed I was weird and a dreadful charlatan. Put me in the same category as those nineteenth-century spiritualists, table-rappers he called them. Took awhile to get through to him that what I did had nothing to do with ghosts or spirits or witchcraft. After that, he started to accept and appreciate my abilities. 'You're one flaky lady, Rosemary, but one sexy babe otherwise,' he used to say.

"He was extremely masculine, with one of those straight arrow, logical minds that I love to tweak with my psychic tricks. Charming, too. Much like Albert, but without the extreme intellectual bent. Colin was the physical type. Whenever I went to a meeting overseas, he went along to make sure I was safe and that nobody bullied me. No one pushed Colin Sabin around.

"We retired eight years ago, returned home to Colorado, and expected to travel and enjoy ourselves, but he died just two years later. I live in a retirement community out east now," she said, melancholy in her eyes.

"I'm sorry about Mr. Sabin," Callan said. "It must be hard on you. How do you spend your time?"

"Naturally, I don't do golf or bridge. Golf balls just seem to naturally find their way to the hole and I always win at bridge without even trying." Rosemary shrugged her shoulders at her life. Depression had obviously settled on her.

"I do some volunteer work, but meeting you and getting involved in your fight with Bianca is the most fun I've had in ages." Her voice swiftly regained its enthusiasm and her eyes their sparkle. Rosemary's moods could change faster than the Colorado weather.

At five o'clock, when Callan said good-bye to Rosemary, she was fatigued by the concentration needed to perform Rosemary's parlor tricks but thrilled with her progress. She'd managed to avoid Sam all day too. As she drove home, she considered Rosemary and her Colin. She hoped they had loved and laughed a lot and appreciated every moment.

That night after Connor was safely in bed, and as Rosemary had instructed, she added another layer of protective aura over her house. An elaborate communion with the Earth and dancing with a whirlwind were unnecessary embellishments this time. She simply sat in a chair, quickly entered the theta state, and reinforced the aura. As prosaic as putting out the cat and locking up. For homework she tried moving a silk scarf across the dresser. The scrap of cloth barely quivered, so she fell into bed for a night of heavy sleep.

The pattern continued peacefully for the next two days. If The Gull appeared outside her house, she was unobtrusive. Callan wasn't aware of her.

* * * * *

She contrived to arrive at the office after Sam was already at work. Neither doctor entered the conference room while Rosemary and she were there. On Wednesday afternoon she was trapped in the restroom for ten minutes when Sam and Dr. Ostherhaut held an impromptu conference in the hallway outside the door. Otherwise, she was doing an excellent job of avoiding him.

Dr. Ostherhaut cheerfully wired her to the EEG every morning, and then had her practice with the biofeedback machine to deepen her theta state and improve her speed in attaining it. She played his psi game without shortcuts. She hadn't the heart to cheat by leaving out the numbers and going straight for the spot as Rosemary recommended. When she managed to hold the green spot in the dark green area for five seconds, he drowned her in a tidal wave of fatherly charisma and reminded her vividly of Sam.

Late Wednesday afternoon, just as they were preparing to leave, Callan asked Rosemary, "I've been wondering, I guess for years now, why Bianca chooses to torment me. Why did she call me 'sister, sweet sister'? Do you have a theory?"

"As to calling you sister, she may have a twisted feeling of kinship toward you as one of her own kind. She may want a psychic relative, so to speak, since she apparently killed off her blood relatives. There are few of us, psychics of Bianca's caliber or mine or yours. I've only sensed maybe three or four candidates in my lifetime. Of course, there may be others more powerful who hide from me as I hid from Bianca."

On Thursday morning Callan got careless and walked in on Sam as he was getting coffee in the small kitchen area.

"Morning, Callie." He greeted her with a pleasant but impersonal smile that he might have bestowed upon a new patient. "How's the training going?"

She gave him a brief rundown of her progress.

"Great work. Keep me posted," he said and excused himself. She felt deflated at the brush-off and his dispassionate attitude. *Isn't that exactly what you wanted?* she chided herself. *Don't whine because he gave it to you.*

At lunch that day, Rosemary added another theory on Bianca's motives.

"You know the hiatus of several years when Bianca didn't trouble you? I've been thinking about it. You were getting older and tougher. She was getting older and busier. She may have given up trying to take you over directly because she was too involved in forming her criminal organization. Controlling its brotherhood must have been a tremendous drain on her psi powers and energy, requiring constant vigilance.

"Her methods seemed to have changed from active interference to a long-term passive strategy. As a softening-up scheme, she subtly planted the seeds of moral destruction in your husband and somehow undermined your artistic ability. Then she sat back and waited for the plan to ripen. The time line fits for that idea."

"Why bother at all?" Callan questioned, perplexed by her theory. "If she considered me a threat, wouldn't it have been easier to simply kill me and have done with it?"

"The kinship angle, as I said before, the need for someone who is like herself, might be her primary reason. Possibly, she isn't aware of her true motivation. Since you didn't threaten her by honing your psychic powers, she may have felt she could be indulgent with you. Up until her trip to Colorado, at any rate."

"You could be right."

"My second idea is that she wants to recruit you as an officer in her army. She must spend an enormous amount of time, probably much of her life, in a psychic trance or in the OBE state. That's a huge energy expenditure and drain on her paranormal powers. She wants help from another psychic with her work. Someone she can control.

"If you became demoralized and depressed because of estrangement from your husband, family and friends, you conceivably could become weaker prey and more susceptible to induction into her service. Offhand, can you think of another practical reason for her actions?" Rosemary asked.

The explanation sounded plausible enough. "No," Callan answered, troubled that no other motive came to mind. "What's OBE?" she asked to avoid the subject further, since she had no way as yet to solve the enigma of The Gull.

"Out-of-body experience or astral projection," Rosemary answered. "When she appears to you as The Gull, her consciousness and spirit have left her body. The gull form is a projection of her inner image. How she perceives herself. OBE is also necessary to visit the astral plane and acquire more power."

"You're not telling me I have another paranormal skill to learn!" She pushed away from the table and stood up in agitation. Each day seemed to bring more arcane demands and problems.

"Not difficult at all. One of the easier paranormal tools to get the hang of. Nightwalking, I call it. Many people do it spontaneously just as they fall asleep. Relaxation and self-hypnosis triggers it. Have you ever had dreams of flying or visiting a place you've never been before?"

"I think so." She resumed her seat across from Rosemary. "Nightwalking. That sounds intriguing."

"It's marvelous fun. I hope you find yourself nightwalking in what is called a lucid state. That means, unlike most dreams, you have control of your actions and the overall experience. It should be easier to induce controlled nightwalking now that you've accepted your psi."

Rosemary warned her to be careful of where she went and what she did at first. A safe initial excursion was usually a visit to a familiar nearby place. Other beings encountered during OBE should be avoided until she was able to judge their temperament. At all costs her body must be safe somewhere, for example, in her bed with the room's door locked. The body must not be disturbed or moved. A silver cord rising from the head connected the astral body to the earthly body. The silver cord had infinite plasticity and would stretch into forever as far as Rosemary knew, but it was a vulnerable point. The breaking of the silver cord resulted in the death of the earthly body.

"Be careful," Rosemary insisted. "Although nightwalking is sustained by the emotions and desires, it should be controlled by the mind. Don't let feelings lead you astray."

Callan was enthralled and enthusiastic over the prospect of such freedom.

"Don't do anything rash," Rosemary warned again, "especially don't go hunting for the astral plane. When you are ready, I'll take you there. It's no place for a novice alone."

Rosemary left first that afternoon, and Callan gave her a ten-minute head start before leaving the conference room. As she approached the reception area, Sam appeared in the doorway of his office at the other end of the hall and called to her. There was no way to avoid him. Reluctantly, she went toward him.

He had shed his jacket, pulled down his tie and rolled up the sleeves of his dress shirt. His hair was rumpled as though he had been running his fingers through it.

"Can I speak with you a moment, Callie? Come into my office." His request was polite and neutral, as he stepped back and ushered her in.

He probably wants to know how long Rosemary and I will be monopolizing his conference room, she thought, feeling trapped and uncomfortable.

The office had a southwestern exposure and windows revealed the brilliant blue Colorado sky and the mountains in the distance. Bookshelves and excellent original watercolors of southwestern scenes covered the paneled walls. Across an expanse of dark burgundy carpet, a modern glass and teak desk sat with a matching console table behind.

A gold-framed portrait of a pretty, dark-haired woman sat on the console. That must be his late wife Julie, she realized. Sam hadn't talked about her much during their dinner date. Envy engulfed her for all the first times his wife had shared with him and she had not. *Get real,* she told herself. *The poor woman has been dead for three years.* She quickly looked away.

On the right, a seating arrangement of two armchairs and a sofa upholstered in a muted navy and burgundy fabric was centered on a modern, abstract area rug.

"I like your view and your art, Sam." She turned back to him.

He leaned against the closed door, his arms loosely crossed, and watched her examine his office. His grave scrutiny made her uneasy. "It's both elegant and restful," she added.

She didn't know what to say to him. Being tongue-tied in Sam's presence was a first. He was staring at her with an ardent concentration, making it a struggle to keep her eyes and voice steady. She couldn't quite identify the emotion his look was projecting.

"Did you have something to discuss?" she ventured.

He didn't answer. He moved toward her lazily, his eyes intent on hers, not pausing until he was standing only inches away. She held her breath. She'd never seen an expression precisely like that on Sam's face before. It was almost predatory.

"Sam, what...?" she questioned, troubled by the fierce sensuality she suddenly picked up from him. Under the sexual interest she caught a phantom impression, much like that she'd gotten from him on Saturday. Caution? Fear? It was gone before she could decipher it.

He slipped his hand under her hair and cupped the back of her head in his hand. His thumb stroked gently just under her left ear where her pulse fluttered. As teenagers, he had touched her in exactly that same way.

"No, no discussion," he finally answered, slowly pulling her toward him.

Surprised, her right hand found its way to his shoulder. Whether she touched him to halt the steady pull of his hand or just because she wanted to explore the muscles beneath the white dress shirt, she didn't know.

Under his woodsy aftershave, she caught his unique but forever memorable scent, his Sam-perfume, as she'd thought of it since childhood. The scent of him hadn't changed in the intervening years. She could pick him out of a dark room crowded with men just by his Sam-perfume alone. The memories associated with his particular masculine fragrance evaporated any possibility of a reasoned resistance.

His touch kindled haunting memories of long ago love and longing. As his head bent toward her and their lips touched, her arms, of their own accord, slipped around his neck. She couldn't resist kissing him back. An electric jolt shot up her spine, radiated throughout her body, and ignited her senses. Their bodies melded one into the other, fitting together as easily as they always had. It was a homecoming kiss, devouring and desperate like no other they had ever shared. The kiss softened, became a series of tender nibbles, and deepened again to a frantic, delighted exploring.

"I think that settles any questions about my real motives and wishes," Sam said raggedly when he finally lifted his head enough to speak. "Things got muddled on Saturday." He rested his chin against her temple for a moment, and then trailed kisses down her cheek to capture her mouth again. His hands slid restlessly over her back and waist, then tightened to bring her more firmly against him.

Sam's kisses are still magic. Just as they've always been, Callan thought through a haze of confusion and joy. She had forgotten the reality of his embrace. She twined her fingers in the thick dark hair at the nape of his neck and let herself dissolve into the embrace.

When Sam finally relaxed his hold, he looked down at her, his warm brown eyes sparkling, and said, "The Labor Day weekend is coming up. Will you have some time for me?"

"Sam, you can't get involved with me. The Gull..." she stuttered, still befuddled from the unexpected embrace. Gravity seemed to have loosened its hold on her, leaving her dancing on the wind, just like the night when she had first erected the protective aura around her house.

"You're not going into this by yourself. You've always been under solitary siege from this woman. You can't do it alone. I won't let you." His voice was implacable though gentle enough. He wouldn't be easy to discourage.

She started to pull away, intending to form some logical reason why they couldn't begin a relationship, but he held her firmly and kissed her again slowly and thoroughly. He knew exactly how to get to her and have his way.

"We can't go back to the past and be as we were in Apple Springs, Callie. There are too many years behind us," he said against her lips. "We have this second chance. Don't let it pass us by."

Callan stood with her hand over his heart. His was racing as madly as hers. She was too distracted to form an intelligent defense. She felt shivery, as though a delicate electrical current flowed along her nerves.

"Damn. Another patient is due any minute," he said with a sigh. "I wish we had more time."

Holding her close against his side, he walked with her to the door and opened it, not giving her time to argue. "I'll see you tomorrow and we'll make some plans."

Still at a loss, she found herself halfway down the hall. She turned to look back at him. How remarkable it was that he still cared for her. He did truly care and want to be with her. She had felt it in the hunger in his kiss, in the hard fervor of his embrace, and in the longing that poured from him as he held her.

It wasn't safe for him to be near her. Bianca could destroy him on a whim, warp his personality and turn him into someone totally foreign, just as she had done with Luke.

From the doorway he nodded, gave her his wonderful warm, crooked smile. Rejecting him, hurting him, was impossible. She hadn't the willpower or the courage to refuse his offer of help or, most of all, his passion. To put him in danger was selfish and foolhardy, but she desperately needed him to lend her backbone in the conflict ahead.

Lifting a hand in acceptance and good-bye, she turned and continued down the hall, a tornado of desire and hope, fear and guilt whirling within her.

Chapter Five

సా

That night after closing and locking her bedroom door, Callan crawled into bed and turned out the lights. She reviewed Rosemary's advice on nightwalking and decided to attempt it right away. No preliminaries were possible. She could either do it or not.

Lying on her back and deliberately relaxing each muscle, she eased into the theta pattern, let her psychic awareness roam the room and then extend outward. In the hyperaware state, the minute movements of the settling house were readily perceptible. The protective aura's iridescence glowed reassuringly from the walls. From his room across the upstairs landing, Connor's dreams unfurled, vivid with random images of baseball games and his friend Zach.

Drawing her awareness within, she cautiously moved to the edge of sleep. Pleasant shushing wave sounds filled the room, and then a low humming overlaid the waves. She wanted to get up and investigate their origins. With that wish, she found herself rolling over and standing beside the bed in a smooth effortless motion. She drifted toward the window and came to a wobbling halt. The bedroom walls shone with a pearly glow, and the breaking-wave murmur and the humming escalated. She turned and looked back.

The sleeping body on the bed was eerily still. Its respiration hardly disturbed the covering sheet. A fine silver cord, gossamer and no wider than her little finger, exited from the back of the head on the pillow. It drifted just above the bedclothes, disappeared near the foot of the bed, then reappeared near her astral feet. It flowed up her ghostly body and over her left shoulder. Rosemary had said that only six feet of the silver cord extending from either the earthly body or astral body would be visible. Any cord extending between remained invisible.

Although the unconscious physical body lay lifeless as a wax figure, she wasn't concerned about it, rather disinterested, in fact. The ethereal body she wore seemed as solid and corporeal as the earthly body, but it floated and moved with a fluid, amorphous grace impossible in a corporeal state.

She decided to check on Connor. Instantly, she was at the foot of his bed and occupying the same space as his aquarium. The glass tank surrounded her from the waist to just below her shoulders. The water felt tepid and wet. She stood stone still, afraid of what would happen if she moved. She felt solid, and instinct said movement would shatter the glass.

A vaguely ticklish sensation like a satin ribbon slithering in her chest made her glance down. A black-spotted goldfish exited from her right breast just as a yellow goldfish undulated into her left breast.

Aaaagh, she yelled, as shock sent her exploding from the tank to shoot across the room, ending up half-merged with the wall by the window. Agitated floundering sent her lurching out of the wall.

She ended up floating on her back, in the center of the room, gazing at the shadowy ceiling.

All the panicky bouncing around had left her dizzy, gasping, and with a pounding heart. As she lay there, she pondered why an astral body would have a heart that could pound or why breathing was necessary. Probably, such mundane internal processes were just a habit that the spirit carried from the earthly body. She certainly didn't intend to change them. Breathing and the thumping of a heart made her feel more comfortable in this alien dimension.

What's more, she hadn't realized that she would be able to actually feel the material world while in astral form. The ragged texture of wood and plaster around and inside her body hadn't done any harm, but the feel of the slippery goldfish in her chest was truly bizarre. Interaction with the corporeal world was disconcerting, although it didn't seem to affect an astral body. Standing in the water hadn't left her sodden, ending up in the wall hadn't hurt, and the goldfish still swam placidly in their tank where they belonged.

Even so, an astral projection shouldn't be undertaken casually. Rashly done, it could put her in some strange hot water, or as in this case, rather cool water. Rosemary's statement, "As you imagine, so shall you be," was more literally meant than she realized. After this, she'd make it a point to clearly envision a destination before traveling.

She cautiously stood up and looked at Connor. He was deeply asleep, his breathing steady, his dreams content. All the ghostly commotion hadn't disturbed him at all. Satisfied that he was safe and well-protected under the household aura, she carefully visualized her own room and was smoothly returned to the side of the bed.

What now? Up on the roof to look around, of course. Slowly. She didn't want to blast through the roof like a cannonball. This time she made the transition cautiously, slipping like smoke through cracks in the plaster, winding around wooden beams and roofing tiles without letting the materials merge with her phantom body. She was conscious of the building's substance as she passed. Plaster was pebbly, rather like whole grain cereal, wood was glossy as long as you flowed with the grain, and tile was waxy but hard-edged. It was an unsettling sensation, and more than anything else made her feel insubstantial and vulnerable, as though her essence could dissipate on a mere puff of breath.

She stood in the open air at the highest peak of the house, the roof steeply slanting away on all sides. Each red roof tile was distinctly outlined under the household protective aura. Her pearly aura extended out to the edge of the roof, adding another layer of shielding.

Looking over her shoulder for the silver cord, she saw that it still flowed from head to heels. The rest of it disappeared into the roof, presumably still connected to the body below. Reassured that everything appeared as it should, she turned back to view the area. Her hand brushed against the chimney. She could feel the gritty texture of the bricks and a greasy residue of soot.

The cool night wind skimmed her legs and pressed the softness of the nightshirt against her body, and the knobby corrugated tiles scored her bare feet when she settled firmly on the roof. The persistent wave beat and subliminal humming continued as a comforting background to the ordinary night sounds. The cricket choir rasped through the night. The muted whisper of the breeze and the thrum of a loose drainpipe vibrating in the wind confirmed hearing as well. The throb of a car's engine and its headlights drew her attention as it turned into a cul-de-sac to the east.

The darkened neighborhood was silent, mysterious and remote. Homes, streets and empty fields stretched before her, and the radiant city lights marched to the horizon until they vanished into the eastern plains. She pivoted to face the mountain range that dominated the western skyline, its bulk more sensed than seen in the darkness. Lightning flickered in the far northwest and a few shredded clouds raced across the sky and covered the stars that rode high above the mountains. More than likely, there could be rain somewhere in the city by morning.

She allowed herself to float up a few yards in giddy lightness and freedom. Vertigo fortunately wasn't a problem. The experience seemed familiar in some inexplicable way. Her heart pounded and her breath came faster with excitement, and a film of sweat coated her forehead. Some spirit she was, sweating and panting like that.

After a pause to wipe the back of her hand across her forehead, she flapped her arms up and down. The movement threw her off balance and tipped her into a floundering roll. When she struggled to right herself, her legs sank up to the knees in the roof. She'd lost her concentration and had tripped on the earthly world again.

Okay, doing ridiculous acrobatics is fascinating but isn't the purpose of the expedition, she chided herself as she retracted her legs from the roof. *Do the homework. Rosemary said nightwalking was important, the gateway to the astral plane. The first time out should be a cruise around the neighborhood or a visit to a familiar place.*

Where to?

A visit to her family in Apple Springs was a possibility, but it seemed too distant for a first excursion. Then she knew who she wanted to visit most of all. Sam. Since he had kissed her that afternoon, she was impatient to see him, although a relationship with him was against her better judgment.

Where is he? He said he lived a couple of miles further southwest. She turned to face in that direction and caught a sense of him there. Rising a few feet above the roof, astral light enclosed her like a soap bubble as she floated on the breeze. She glided south, upright and inclined somewhat forward, arms held loosely at her sides.

Stephanie would have a valid reason to call her Mighty Mouse now! Connor would dearly love this flying. Superman sans cape! In merriment, she assumed the position, parallel to the ground and arms outstretched. For fun, she swooped up a hundred feet to gain some space, arched her back, and did several lazy, tight back loops, then gently floated back down. Not bad, but the Superman pose was absurd. She wasn't moving much faster than her normal jogging speed. Resuming her previous upright position, she proceeded sedately on through the night, toes pointed demurely downward.

As she approached the outskirts of the subdivision near the main thoroughfare, she glanced down at her nightwear and giggled. The nightshirt, a birthday gift from Connor, was actually an oversized, faded orange T-shirt, adorned with the Denver Broncos' horse head logo on the front. The clingy knit was laminated to the astral body like plastic wrap. It certainly wasn't suitable for impersonating Superman or gliding through a moonlit night to visit a male friend.

She recalled Rosemary's declaration again, "As you imagine, so shall you be." Okay, the occasion called for something romantic and flowing, like the sexy teal dress from Saturday night. She floated to the top of a pine tree, wiggled her toes against the prickly needles, closed her eyes and concentrated on the look and feel of the dress. Silkiness caressed her skin and looking down, there was the teal gown, shimmering in her astral glow.

The dress was bias-cut, an unadorned fall of dark teal silk crepe. She knew that the color, dark blue shadowed with forest green, gave her gray eyes a blue-green cast and deepened the golden cast in her hair that was the color of brown sugar. Skimming the breasts and hips, caressing the waistline, it flowed into a slight flair above the knees. As she moved, it shifted enticingly, clinging discreetly here and there. The delicate straps looked too insubstantial to defeat gravity and gave the impression the dress might float away in a modest breeze.

The fabric felt marvelously sensuous, like being stroked with a mink mitten. It wasn't just how a dress looked, she believed, but how the fabric felt against the skin that made of women feel awesomely sexy. The way this looked wasn't half-bad either. *An inspired purchase*, she decided. Considering what happened that afternoon, it apparently had had more effect on Sam on Saturday night than she realized.

Maybe it should be longer. The dress obligingly stretched to ankle-length and flared out in the night wind. *Perfect!* She got a bearing on Sam again and with increasing speed flew on, enjoying the cool wind and the satisfying flutter of the dress against her legs.

Slowing to get her bearings, she drifted toward a street curving southwest, where the houses appeared larger and more luxurious than those in nearby neighborhoods. He was somewhere in the vicinity.

Ahead on the left, an old man in a plaid bathrobe and bedroom slippers shuffled down a driveway, a roly-poly dachshund on a leash preceding him. A silver cord trailed from the back of the man's head like a lengthy ponytail. A pearly light radiated from him, enclosing the dog in its luminescence.

Curious about the fellow nightwalker, she landed on a tree branch extending over the house's lawn. The old man and the dachshund reached the end of the driveway where the dog lifted a leg and watered some shrubs. The nightwalker and canine companion abruptly disappeared, only to reappear again at the door of the house. They advanced down the driveway again to visit the same bush.

The old man looked blank-eyed and mechanical. Obviously, it was a non-lucid astral projection. The dog was probably a figment of the man's dream, unless animals also nightwalked. She wondered if the man was tired in the mornings from walking the dachshund all night.

Spiraling away from the branch, confidently gaining some altitude, she aimed for where the street curved south again. A few blocks farther a red brick house on the left with dormer windows and a deeply recessed front door drew her interest. A low red brick wall edged the sidewalk, curving to follow the driveway. Massive pines and numerous shrubs and flowerbeds graced the front lawn, and more trees loomed in the back. She swooped in and landed on the overhang above the front door.

Sam was in this house, alone and quiet. She paused for a moment to consider the ethics of invading his privacy. She wouldn't stay long. *Just a quick peek and a wish for pleasant dreams, so this special first trip won't be wasted.* Sliding through the fan-shaped window above the door, she entered a parquetry-floored front hall.

Aura light showed a grand foyer barren of furniture or decoration except for an ornate chandelier hanging from the vaulted ceiling two stories above. Arched doorways opened onto dark rooms on either side. A center staircase rose in a stately curve to a balcony lined with windows on the second floor. Two sets of French doors guarded the back of the hall. The place was palatial. Sam had done himself proud.

His presence called to her from the rear of the house. She glided across the foyer and went through a door on the right. A single lamp burned. He lay asleep in an overstuffed chair with stockinged feet propped on an ottoman. The lamp beside the chair shone on an open book in his lap but left his face in shadow. His right hand rested between his thigh and the chair arm, the other hand lay on the padded chair arm, palm upwards. He still wore the white shirt and gray suit slacks from that afternoon. A tie lay in a crumpled heap on the side table. His unbuttoned shirt gaped open, exposing his chest.

On impulse she curled up her legs and slithered, weightless as a dream, onto his lap on top of the book. She was surprised to find herself there. She hadn't intended to do anything except look at him for a moment from a safe distance. Freezing, she studied him intently, worried that she might have disturbed him. He continued to sleep with his head tipped back, face in profile and mouth relaxed.

The chance to really study him was irresistible. For nearly a week, she'd wanted to thoroughly study his subtlety-changed features. She couldn't seem to get enough of him. With the mature creases of his face smoothed out in sleep, he seemed more like the young Sam, and not the alien, mature man he had become. She studied the line of his jaw, the contour of his full lower lip and the thick, stubby dark lashes edging his closed lids. Reaching out, she slowly traced the prickly beard darkening his cheek.

Her fingers trailed downward to caress his neck and on to explore the muscles of his shoulder. His skin was warm and smooth and the intimate feel of his flesh sparked a glow at the base of her spine. Emboldened, she recklessly threaded her fingers through the mat of hair on his chest, letting her fingers trail down to his belt buckle. He seemed undisturbed by the ghostly fondling, so she nuzzled her face into the curve of his neck and rested there for a moment, content with his sleeping company.

Sam mumbled in his sleep and turned his head toward her. The temptation to do with him as she wanted was irresistible. She pressed light kisses along the curve of his jaw and cheek and moved up to brush his eyelids with her lips. The movement of his eyes under her mouth revealed that he was dreaming, and she caught fleeting erotic images of kisses and fondling. With herself as the other participant, she hoped.

She cautiously kissed his mouth, slipping a hand behind his neck, much as he had done to her that afternoon. She lingered there, savoring his sleeping mouth with deepening kisses and strokes of her tongue across his lips. Her aura flared into a salmon-pearl rainbow around them, fading to a cameo pink in the far corners of the room. He tasted and smelled so good, so familiar. Long ago, together, the two of them had learned how to kiss. Now he was physically different, bigger and harder, with more sharply defined muscles. It made him exotic.

She'd never really forgotten him and realized how much she had missed him over the years. She stroked the short soft hair at the back of his neck.

He stirred restlessly, so she warily sat back and watched his face. Could he feel her weight or her touch? He ran his tongue over his lower lip and smiled faintly. His right arm lifted lazily from beside his thigh and flopped onto the chair arm.

Oops! He's waking up! She tensed, prepared to bolt for the safety of the night. He probably wouldn't be able to see her, but he might sense her presence. Besides, it seemed bad mannered to gawk at him this way.

A sharp pain lanced through the back of her head. Sam vanished and a kaleidoscope of shrieking colors sucked her into a vortex. The colors had faces that leered and voices that gibbered. Spinning, falling through the tunnel, disorientation was complete. No Sam, no starlit night, no up or down, no body, just a mad whirlpool of brain-exploding colors that mocked and shrieked.

She groped for something to mentally anchor herself, to stop the headlong descent down the nightmare funnel. There was nothing to grab. Faces and voices flashed by, savage and untouchable, forming a lost world of mania that she couldn't link with.

Darkness exploded around her, obliterating the insane tunnel. Suddenly there was weight on her, and her senses rose up and crushed her. It hurt through and through, as if one of the mountains were crushing her.

Cricket sounds and the humming of the night wind assaulted her ears. The sheets against her body felt like sandpaper abrading her skin. There was a bitter, acrid taste in her mouth. Worst of all was the odor of rotting onions and fish, general garbage, and decaying tropical flowers. She gagged and opened her eyes to a wavering dimness. She was back in her room in her earthly body, which had curled into a fetal position.

Her muscles twitched. Terrified, she struggled for breath and fought down nausea from the rank smell and the savage termination of her astral projection. Her astral body shifted from her earthly body and back again as it struggled to realign itself properly. Although her orientation oscillated wildly, she sensed the presence of another being in the room.

You will not slobber over that male! He's never been for you! a voice bellowed in her mind.

Callan fought to focus her eyes. The illumination in the room was a murky haze reflecting a dim aura. Her protective aura drifted in the room like shattered pieces of a rainbow. She could barely make out a huge blackness hovering near the ceiling.

You tried to keep Us out! an angry mind-voice screeched. *Puny rebellion such as that, my sweet innocent one, deserves the punishment you have just received.*

She lay huddled, shuddering under the bedclothes, unable to either vocally or telepathically deflect The Gull's assault.

Her vision cleared further, allowing her to see the hovering monstrous shape. A bird form spread across the ceiling, wings blending into the walls. Spectral feathers rustled and fluttered in agitation. Whirling sapphire eyes pinned her to the bed, cold with malignancy and hot with power. The flattened gull head stretched toward her, and the down-turned hooked bill jerked with predatory menace at her face. The foul stench of decaying onions and fish nearly sent her into unconsciousness. Panic and nausea crushed her into the mattress.

The roar in her mind moderated to an accented feminine voice that continued regally.

Your dreams and psychic vigor have always been so stimulating, my dear little one. We have fed on them for many years. They are so tender. They have surely provided Us with much amusement. A splendid future can be mapped out for you, sweet sister. What can We make of you? A great courtesan perhaps? Influencing wealthy and powerful men in many countries? You do seem to appreciate the male of the species, ape-like and unawakened as they are.

As The Gull's litany spilled over her, Callan groped for the fragments of her scattered psychic power. They eluded her, fleeing her mental grasp like terrorized ants on a demolished anthill.

Or a power standing beside Our throne, perhaps. Would you like that? We have much to teach you.

The voice of The Gull battered at her mind. The sweet, crooning voice made Callan's teeth ache.

Yes, a future as Our trusted lieutenant with all your many talents at Our command will be most appropriate, We think. You will make a fine captain of Our new North American operation. What a splendid future you can look forward to.

Please, please, Callan begged silently, deep within her mind. She didn't know who she begged. Pleading with The Gull, she instinctively knew, would only deepen her peril. There was no mercy in this insane spirit. There had certainly been none for Bernie Rabney.

In desperation, she cautiously sought strength where she could find it. Reaching down, down deep, into that otherworldly place she had visited only days before, she forged a surreptitious tap into the life energy of the planet. She sought the resilience of growing green things upon the land, drew upon the potency of Earth's burrowing and striding life, and siphoned a minute portion of the power from the world's aura.

The force had to grow large enough to be effective. Just a little longer. An ill-timed, feeble burp of psychic power would only irritate The Gull. She let the energy seep into her. Taut with tension and horror, huddling unmoving in the bed, she harbored the power like a treasure within her mind.

The Gull seemed unaware of her furtive gathering of psychic energy. The wings slipped in and out of the walls and ceiling as she lazily fanned them. With each down stroke, the onion, fish and flower stench choked Callan. The Gull's astral self stank unbearably.

Formalities must be adhered to, mustn't they, my dear? The Gull continued haughtily in her imperial voice. *The question asked and a fitting answer given, must they not? A proper contract between Us. Will you, sweet sister? Will you? Fame, fortune, life as you cannot imagine. Accept and it will begin!* As The Gull's head lowered, the weight of its telepathic demands pressed mercilessly upon her exhausted mind and body.

No! No! I won't! Get away! The pressure couldn't be endured any longer. She released the full force of the Earth tap into The Gull's face. The eruption was so adamant and explosive that the great bird's head flinched back to merge with the ceiling, dimming the sapphire eyes for a moment.

After a pause, the gull head slowly lowered until it was inches from her face. She held on, keeping the Earth power before her like a warrior's shield.

Very well, my sweet, sweet dear, you will come, yes, yes, you will come. Easily now or hurtfully later, the voice hissed. The stink of the creature was stifling. Rimmed with red now, the eyes spun faster and faster.

The frailty of others will persuade you to become agreeable to Our generous offer. That is a very tasty boy-dumpling in the other room. Remember that. You may regret your ill-advised refusal.

The apparition dissolved and the muddy aura faded, leaving the room in untainted darkness.

We will see to it, came a faraway whisper.

The resonance of the words left an unearthly throb vibrating through her being. She was cold, so cold, as if her bed was an Arctic ice floe. She lay sharply awake, shivering, wounded in body and spirit, and probed the now empty room with staring eyes and a fearful mind until the sun rose.

* * * * *

"Why isn't she here? Why didn't somebody find out? Well, answer me!"

Callan heard Rosemary's strident voice as she approached the conference room the next morning. The three clustered by the conference table, with Rosemary glowering at Sam and Dr. Ostherhaut. Her message earlier to Dr. Ostherhaut, letting him know she couldn't make it until ten o'clock, had apparently alarmed only Rosemary.

As she leaned weakly against the doorjamb, gratitude for their assistance filled her along with an equal amount of remorse and guilt over the danger they could face for aiding her. They were the only help she had. There was no one else she could turn to and nowhere to run. At that moment, she longed to throw herself into their arms and unburden herself with hysterical weeping.

"Sorry I'm late."

Dr. Ostherhaut looked more curious than concerned at her appearance. Sam dropped his pretense of polite attention to Rosemary's temper tantrum and let his alarm emerge the moment he saw her. He hurried toward her and engulfed her in an embrace.

"Callie, are you okay? What happened? You should have called me," he said gravely, tipping her face up to his. "You're so pale."

Rosemary rushed forward, grasped her hand, and gave it an impatient little shake. "Bianca got through to you last night, didn't she? What'd she do?"

"I'm sorry if I've caused you worry, Rosemary. I should have let Dr. Ostherhaut know what happened."

Arm around her waist, Sam pulled her against his side and walked her to a chair. He squatted down by her and rested a hand on her shoulder. She knew he could feel her tremors. Rosemary and Dr. Ostherhaut looked expectantly down at her.

She hadn't stopped shivering for a moment since Bianca's assault the night before. The muscles of her arms, legs and back had twitched uncontrollably, leaving her sleepless. The pain of the muscle spasms was endurable, but bearing her lonely fear through the long hours of darkness left her hopeless and weary with stress.

Early in the morning Connor pounded on her door and demanded to know why she wasn't up yet. He said she looked "as bad as Zach's bullfrog after they'd left it out in the sun too long." He was sympathetic but matter-of-fact when told she'd been sick during the night. He'd brought her tea and toast before catching his ride to school with Stephanie and Zach. She was so shaky and nauseated that she spilled half the tea and left the toast untouched.

The intermittent muscle spasms almost kept her from dressing and driving to Sam's office, but she fought the tremors, determined that Bianca would not stop her from going where she wanted. She craved the sanctuary of Rosemary's protective aura around Sam's office. She had no energy to reconstruct the one around her house. The effort to remain alert and in control of the car exhausted her reserves of strength. Remaining upright for much longer might be a problem.

"I tried nightwalking last night. The Gull yanked my chain, so to speak," she said. Considering what she had been doing just before Bianca's interruption, she hoped her face wasn't broadcasting a guilty expression. "I rebounded back into my body and Bianca was waiting for me. Feathers, beak and all. Made me an offer of employment. Threatened me—and others too—when I wouldn't accept. You were right, Rosemary, about her motives. She wants a submissive psychic lieutenant. I've been disoriented since and can't seem to stop this shaking and twitching."

"Damn! The protective aura was in place?" Rosemary asked.

"Yes, but she shattered it."

Rosemary dropped into a chair and said, "She's stronger than I estimated, penetrating such a heavy protective aura. She probably used telekinesis to jerk your silver cord and caused the astral projection to terminate violently. The resulting psychic displacement can cause shock. Albert, you should check her over."

Dr. Ostherhaut had been silent, observing her while she spoke with the others. "Indeed. I think we can relieve those spasms you're having, Callan."

Sam said nothing, simply scooped her out of the chair and carried her from the conference room. She gasped in surprise but then relaxed, resting her head on his shoulder. It was the only moment she had felt safe in the past terrifying hours. She knew the feeling of security was an illusion. There could never be safety anywhere for her, especially in Sam's arms, until Bianca was defeated.

* * * * *

Her awakening was slow and luxurious, much like those long-ago summer mornings as a child when there was ample time to linger in a dream or create a fantasy around the potential in a carefree summer day. She savored now a daydream of

Sam's arms around her and let it flow into a vision of happiness and passion between them. The images slipped away as insistent reality pressed on her. Dim sunlight edged the draperies on the windows across the room. She was on a couch with a blanket covering her.

"How are you feeling, my dear?" Rosemary's question brought her fully awake.

"Okay. At least I've stopped twitching. What time is it?" She pushed aside the blanket, sat up and ran a hand through her hair.

"It's about three. I heated this soup when you started waking up. Can you eat?"

"I'm starved. I can eat it and anything else around." She began to stand up.

"Stay there," Rosemary ordered. "I'll bring it over. There's a chicken sandwich too. How about coffee or a soft drink."

"All of it, please. You've been here since this morning? I appreciate you taking care of me like this."

"I wanted to make sure you would come out of this all right." She placed the food on a side table by the couch. "Eat while we talk. I must say you've rebounded from an experience that would totally incapacitate most people for some time. I had an out-of-body trance interrupted once. Down and out for three days. Eat now."

As she complied, with telepathy she asked, *Is OBE really necessary? It seems too dangerous to use without a desperate reason. It leaves you unguarded and open to attack. Although it was exciting, I'll admit, until I snapped back. It was like the Rocky Mountains had fallen on me when Bianca pulled me in like a hooked trout on her fishing line.*

I'm glad you've kept a sense of humor through all this. Rosemary chuckled a little underneath. *Oh, yes, OBE is vital. You must use it to gain sufficient power to put the kibosh on Bianca's little game.*

How? Why?

You haven't time to take leisurely lessons in the art of the psychic. What I've taught you is hardly more than a few paranormal parlor games. Your talents must be sharpened as fast as you can manage. I don't know how long we have. What takes years of effort, you need to learn practically overnight. Bianca won't wait for you to catch up. The disquiet and fear in Rosemary's eyes confirmed that she was scared too.

You don't have much hope that I can survive this, do you Rosemary?

Of course I have hope! If I didn't, I wouldn't help you. I'd just advise you to submit to The Gull. At least you would be alive under her rule. You must believe you can overcome her with a little more power and training. To get it in a hurry we must go to the source, the astral plane.

That means OBE and nightwalking, Callan concluded.

Right. It's the only way I know. Maybe you will discover someday how to draw power directly from the astral plane without abandoning the earthly body to go there. Will you be strong enough to go tonight?

Callan had finished the food and answered vocally. "I'll be hardy enough."

She searched Rosemary's face for the boldness she had come to know over the last few days. All she could see there was a rather tired woman past the time of plentiful energy.

"Rosemary, you don't have to do this. I know now how dangerous The Gull is. There are already too many people that I care about that she can hold hostage. I don't want you to be one of them. Isn't there a way to help me and remain clear of this mess?

"No. I can't remain underground anymore. I feel this challenge is a moral obligation on my part. I believe what I've learned through the years I can condense for you in a few trips to the astral plane. There are no maps or instruction manuals. Please believe that I do have ways to protect would-be hostages from Bianca. But I'll have to show you. Besides, life's been dull lately. I could use an adventure!"

Callan had no option but to accept her aid. Together they reconstructed Callan's shattered personal shield, and with

Rosemary's help, it was thicker than grandma's crystal cake cover. They confirmed the time for their nightwalking trip before Rosemary left.

Callan freshened up in the office restroom. Her slept-in pantsuit looked as though it had been retrieved from the bottom of a closet. Her hair had lost its bounce, and there were dark smudges under her eyes. A touch of makeup didn't help much. In spite of her appearance, she went to inquire for Sam at the reception desk. After a short wait, he ushered out a patient and hustled her into his office. He was wearing his serious doctor face, Callan noted, as he stopped her in the middle of his office to take her pulse and scrutinize her face.

"You're good," he said, and pulled her into his arms for a kiss that left her almost as wobbly as when she had arrived that morning.

"Do doctors usually take a woman's pulse before they kiss her, Doctor Cavendar?" she drawled when he relaxed his hold a little. "Though that's quite an effective restorative you prescribe."

"You're well enough to be impertinent, I see." He nuzzled her neck and kissed her again. "You taste good—like chicken sandwiches. Makes me want to eat you up."

"I'm a big girl. You don't have time before your next patient. Besides, I want to ask you to a picnic with Connor and me. Sunday at 10:00. I'll bring the food. How about it?"

"Best offer I've had in seventeen years," he said.

They made good use of their remaining time.

Callan was left with only a few minutes to outline her and Rosemary's plans for that night. He frowned at her report.

"Boy, do I feel useless. I can't protect you or even help much. Can't even be with you when you go tonight. Call me at the slightest problem," he instructed, his voice uncompromising. "I'll come. You've gotten too damned independent since you grew up. You used to ask for my help all the time. Promise you'll call."

"I promise. Don't worry, Sam. Rosemary will be looking out for me," she reassured him from the door. "You do help, a lot."

The prospect of spending Sunday with Sam lessened the weight of fear and worry she'd been accumulating in the past days. Bianca, be damned! She wouldn't cower in her house like a rabbit waiting for the wolf to break down her door.

Chapter Six

✇

Callan, Callan! Hey! Come fly with me!

Drifting in a timeless moment between the theta state and sleep, Callan heard Rosemary's voice calling her. The sound of waves beating against a shore and the deep-toned background hum washed through her bedroom. With a gentle push against the resistance of her earthly body, her astral self broke free and stood by the bedside.

I'm coming, she sent ahead as she rose through the roof of the house and sailed into the night.

Down here.

A much-changed Rosemary stood below on the roof of the front porch, her aura dispersed around her like aqua and pearl footlights. She stood jauntily, hands on hips, feet planted on either side of the peaked porch roof. In her astral form, Rosemary appeared no more than twenty-five years old. A brown leather bomber jacket, trim tan jodhpurs, and knee-high boots graced her slender, regal figure. A long, fringed, white silk scarf looped around her neck, and a cascade of blond curls curved over her shoulder. Her astral eyes glowed a vivid turquoise, unlike her faded-blue earthly eyes. She resembled a glamorous, old-fashioned fly girl.

Really sharp nightwalking costume, Rosemary. Do you have one of those leather flying helmets, too? Callan asked as she touched down beside her. She couldn't resist kidding Rosemary a little about her choice of astral apparel. It further illustrated her ingenious, mercurial nature.

Thanks. No helmet. They give me helmet hair. Now don't tease me, child. After all, we must all indulge our little fantasies now and then, she answered in her usual intrepid style.

That's a fabulous outfit, she went on, expertly turning the subject back to Callan. *You look like you stepped out of a 1930s romantic comedy. Where's your feather boa? I bet I know where you went last night on your maiden nightwalking excursion,* she added with an arched eyebrow and a wink.

Callan looked down at her flowing teal dress. Was her telepathic control so weak that all her thoughts and feelings were transparent to Rosemary? Or had she been doing a little unauthorized astral snooping? That possibility was appalling. She'd trusted Rosemary and didn't think she would violate the code of the mind's sanctity. She hadn't told anyone where she'd gone on her first nightwalking expedition, just that The Gull had interrupted it. Probably, her unsettled emotions over Sam were oozing out all over the place, and Rosemary had just picked some up and made a good guess. Even so, she wasn't comfortable with the idea that her mind and emotions could be easily scrutinized or deduced.

Feather boas tickle, she finally shot back, flustered.

Rosemary chuckled. *As I remember, that's not all that tickles! Let's get this mission started,* she said, as she bent her knees and launched herself straight up into the sky. Callan lifted after her, skirt fluttering in the night breeze. She hoped her blush hadn't shown up under astral light.

High above her house, the starlight-silhouetted mountains still loomed over them. City lights spread out below them in a panorama from the foothills to the plains. To the south, she saw the lights of Colorado Springs and to the north the glow from Fort Collins. Smaller upland towns showed as rosettes of light cradled in the folds of the mountains. Cars moving on highways connected the city and mountains with a web of lacy light-traces.

Tell me about the astral plane, Rosemary, she requested, curious about their destination, as they flew higher and higher.

Rosemary explained that the astral plane was the junction point for the exchange of life energy between the creative impulse of the universe and living things on Earth. All sentient beings had pillars of light on the astral plane. Highly evolved souls or old souls who had lived many lives had pillars that nearly reached the high astral realms. All pillars, no matter what their size, displayed coloration that revealed their earthly personalities, talents and spiritual tendencies. The pillars also provided a history of the soul, with the present life represented at the bottom. Next up, another band illustrated the previous life, and above that another one and so on, in order, until the very first life, which appeared at the top. The largest pillars, belonging to the wise old souls, tended to attract a flock of immature souls rather like chicks clustering around a mother hen. Bianca was an example of a rare psychic, like Rosemary, who had gained access to the dimension, using it to enhance her psi powers.

So, the pillars are rather like a map of the soul? Callan asked.

That's an apt description.

How did you first come to the astral plane? Callan questioned.

My mother brought me here as a child. She bequeathed me this outfit before she passed away. She was a great admirer of Amelia Earhart. Psychics have run in my family for generations, usually from mother to daughter, or sometimes from grandmother to granddaughter.

What are we going to do tonight?

They paused, and at their high altitude, the night sky was crowded with stars, and under the moon's brilliant radiance the city lights had faded to a diffuse glow.

We're going to search out your pillar of light on the astral plane. Then we're going to place it next to a guardian where Bianca can't get at it, much as I did with mine long ago. If she can't get near it, she won't be able to alter your talents or basic nature. Then each night we'll search for the astral pillars of each potential hostage and take them to safety too. It won't protect them, or you, from a physical attack on the earthly plane, but it will prevent occurrences like what happened to your former husband. Unfortunately, we can only make one trip per night since more would put a serious strain on the earthly body.

What about my art? Can we fix it so I can paint again?

We'll counteract any distortion of your natural talents or personality tonight. This trip we'll enhance your psi powers too, give you more control, and let you activate them more easily. There'll be less strain on you.

Connor, and Stephanie and her family, and my folks back in Apple Springs and Sam will be safe from Bianca? Callan asked again, doubtful of Rosemary's claims. *Sounds like almost an impossible task.*

It's a huge job, yes. We're going to be extremely busy the next few nights getting them settled. Here, we're almost there. Take my hand. Don't let go. Our auras must meld when we make the transition.

As they joined hands, their astral lights contracted, forming compact ovals around them and blending at the sides where they touched. Callan's aura flared salmon pink where it merged with Rosemary's aquamarine emanation.

Callan, Rosemary called her to attention, *stay close to me when we are on the astral plane and be aware of your surroundings. Stay focused. It's no place for the unwary or the uninitiated. An entity on the astral plane may react like its counterpart on the earthly plane if it's annoyed.*

Have you been attacked?

I've been stalked and once something pounced on me. I wasn't watching where I was going and blundered into it. Felt like the spirit of a big cat. A lion is still a lion up here, as far as it's concerned. A beast has energy even if it doesn't have claws. It tried to suck up my life force. Scared the hell out of me. So don't mess with the astral animal kingdom. We're at the transition point, Rosemary warned suddenly, tightening her hold on Callan's hand.

They were so high in the sky that the city lights below were no more than a vague glowing band across the Earth. Only the stars and moon were sharp and unchanged. Callan searched the emptiness around them for a difference in the atmosphere. She was beginning to be a little scared of what the astral plane would throw at her. From Rosemary's description, it sounded uncanny and more than a little dangerous.

How do you know this is the way? It seems no different than any other point in all this space, she asked.

Clairvoyance. I feel it. There's a density…a compactness about this space that I sense. This is where my mother brought me on my first trip. There may be other gateways to the astral plane, but it's the only one I know of. Bianca probably has another way in. Once you have been through this transition point, you should be able to find it clairvoyantly again and enter without me. Do you sense it? Mark it well. Telekinesis triggers the opening of the portal. Link with me and feel how I do it. Hold tight. Here we go!

She felt Rosemary's mind expand outward, seeking. After a moment, Rosemary's telekinesis found and encompassed something as fluid as water, incorporeal and unfathomable, and boundless as the night sky. The sky winked out, replaced by a whiteness flecked with black.

Rosemary pushed outward with her mind, against the gateway, much as she had done when making her handkerchief flit across the conference table. This effort was infinitely more forceful, as if she were striving to shift a multistoried office building with her will alone. Then a whirlpool, blazing with rainbow colors, reached out and seized them. Rosemary's mind pulled back to a narrow focus, and they were standing in a world of opalescent splendor.

Overhead a low sky rotated through a spectrum of color, from azure, apple green, primrose yellow, petal pink, to deeper shades of sapphire, scarlet and chrome yellow at the horizon. The tints shifted with never-ending serpentine grace, throwing an aurora borealis effect over the fleecy white landscape.

From horizon to horizon, the terrain was in constant motion. Although the tepid air was still, a knee-high alabaster fog shifted and curled around them, then billowed upward, condensing into flat sheets that coiled into funnels and then spun off to disappear at the horizon. A clear white light fell over the place, infiltrating each fold and eddy of the mist, leaving no place for shadows to hide. The drifts of vapor held a tinge of the sky colors within their folds and changed hues with each billow and surge, as if she walked within a sunset.

White hillocks like heaps of whipped cream pushed up randomly through the fog, and in the distance, a long chain of mounds formed a range of milk-white foothills. Spotted across the terrain, separately and in groups, motionless white poles and angular shapes rose from the undulating land, their tops sometimes crowned with more of the lacy, shifting cloud stuff. They too were blushed by the multicolored sky.

Despite the constant movement, the place had an eerie stillness about it. No murmur of wind or insect hum or animal call disturbed the quiet. No fragrance of growing plants or damp earth or the tang of dust scented the air. The place would have felt sterile, but in the thick quiet, Callan felt watched. A multitude of life inhabited the place, she sensed, and it spied from shrouded hiding places. It made her neck prickle.

Rosemary pointed at a group of the tall angular shapes and said, *Those are trees or bushes of some kind, and much of the movement under the mist is the life force of smaller animals. The larger animals extend above this soup and you can usually see them coming. The wildlife and plants here don't duplicate their earthly forms exactly. Since the animals and fauna aren't sentient, they have no personal comprehension of exactly how they look. Perhaps only a spatial awareness of size and function. So they only project an indefinite appearance. They can't manifest as fully as we can. You'll find too that they aren't grouped here according to earthly geography. A polar bear and a Bengal tiger may inhabit the same territory.*

What's down below? Callan asked, pointing to the fluffy shifting mist under their feet.

Never got around to exploring down there. Maybe aliens from another planet.

Oh, come on. Maybe it's just fish.

Hey, this is the paranormal, remember? Don't expect the ordinary or logical. Don't tell me Albert's infected you already.

Right. Aliens seem reasonable.

Look over there, Rosemary said.

A few yards in front of them the ground cover bulged and surged and a foot-wide stream of brighter mist coalesced and moved toward them, shimmering with a myriad of tiny sparks.

Let's move out of the way. Rosemary drew her back and aside from the advancing mass.

What is it?

Rosemary considered it for a moment and replied, *Feels like the life force of a swarm of insects, locusts or ants.*

The sense of innumerable sparks of life fluttering and crawling made her skin tighten and her toes curl.

Dangerous?

Could be, but I don't want to find out. Would you want millions of little astral insect feet marching over your body? Rosemary gave an exaggerated shiver.

Callan pulled her bare feet well up out of the fog and under her skirt. The astral swarm ignored their presence. It was definitely a multi-legged life form sweeping past.

Maybe I should wear shoes.

Wouldn't hurt. Wiggling toes might be enticing, almost like worms on a fishhook, to some dwellers in the mist. Rosemary's expression was carefully deadpan.

She was undoubtedly exaggerating a bit. Callan didn't know her well enough yet to tell for certain when Rosemary was serious or when she was just kidding. To be cautious, she created a pair of high-top athletic shoes in a teal color to match her dress. As an afterthought, silver lightning bolts appeared on the sides. She lifted her skirt and stuck out a waggling foot to show off her handiwork.

Funky. I like your style, Callan. Your nightwalking outfit suits you.

Thanks. So, where's my pillar of light?

I don't know. You'll have to find it. Rosemary turned to her right and pointed behind her. *My pillar is right over there next to my guardian's pillar.*

She hadn't noticed the group of pillars perhaps a mile away. Distances would be hard to judge here with the air so clear and with the landscape and sky in constant motion. The pillars were huge, spearing up through the ground fog like ice obelisks gleaming under winter sunlight. One column was so tall it merged into the sky, and it was the focal point for what she realized must be a grove of the massive shafts.

Oh, how beautiful! Can we go see them?

Yes, they are magnificent, Rosemary agreed. *We'll see them later. Right now, let's find your pillar. I suggest you focus inward and cast about mentally for it.*

Callan closed her eyes, drew within and focused, then expanded her awareness into the white world around her, searching for the essence of herself. A few moments scanning brought a strong urge to move ahead and to the left of Rosemary's grouped pillars.

There! It's over there! she said, pointing in the direction of the pull.

Let's move. Watch your feet!

Holding hands, they lifted above the ground cover and glided in the direction Callan had indicated. Their trailing toes left parallel tracks in the mist that disappeared as the life-filled vapor swirled and erased all evidence of their passing.

How big is this place, Rosemary?

Infinite, it seems. I've never found the end to it in all the time I've been coming here.

Since it's so vast, why don't we just wish ourselves over to my pillar?

Instantaneous astral travel here is dicey. The erratic nature of the realm throws you off course. The geography shifts unexpectedly, and you can find yourself far from your intended destination. It's more reliable to take a heading and jet over like this.

Rosemary's home pillars passed on their right, still indistinct in the shifting mist. Angling steadily toward the left, they pushed on.

They detoured around scattered hillocks, once nimbly hopping a dozen small blobs of luminescence that circled low in the mist. Callan caught the essence of duck as they passed over. They gradually picked up speed, and scenery flashed by in a blur.

There it is! she declared, as they slowed to fly between two large mounds that had risen abruptly in their path. A pillar sat in solitary splendor in a hollow on the other side of the mounds.

In its lonely glory, it reached more than halfway into the ever-changing sky. Small teardrop-shaped clouds in pastel hues drifted around its top. The swan white pillar was banded with pearly hues of pink, from melon to a delicate shell for a dozen feet up its body. It glowed with an interior luminescence. The colors did a lively dance, rotating and folding in on themselves in an endless wave pattern. The design, still in predominantly rosy hues, gradually changed to a simpler spiral pattern at about the twelve-foot mark. The pattern changed again above that section. Rosemary said a pattern change indicated a previous life.

It looks like all the petals from a rose garden were dumped in there. I like it! Callan exclaimed with pride.

Indeed it does. Rosemary began to circle the pillar. *You should be pleased. The pinks indicate that your spirit harbors abundant love and generosity, ample intuition, and a talent for communication. Although I could have told you that just by looking at the aura around you. You're well on your way to becoming an old soul.*

Peering closely at the pillar, Callan saw random dark areas sprinkled through the wave pattern. *What are these tan and brown spots?* she asked.

Character defects. Sins, possibly. Everyone's pillar has some. After all, this isn't heaven and we aren't angels. Oh my, would you look at this generous patch of crimson? That particular shade shows you have lots of physical vitality and an abundance of sexuality, Rosemary said, as she tracked the revealing crimson around to the back of the column.

What was it with both Rosemary and Stephanie? They both had the same annoying habit of commenting on her personal concerns. A personal wisecrack in return would just encourage them to embellish their remarks. She was no match for either of them in the verbal combat department.

Come look at this side, Rosemary called.

Aware that they had dropped hands and their auras no longer touched, Callan hurried to join her. Their auras sparked and then blended when she hovered beside her. She saw that her pillar displayed other colors besides the pinks and the splash of incriminating red.

Here, Rosemary said, as she fanned away the fog and pointed to an area just barely visible above the knee-level mist. *See this patch of cerulean blue? That particular shade indicates a person of great creativity. Bianca has left her dirty little fingerprints on it. That dark gray line around the blue is her separating your artistry from the rest of your spirit. See there*, she exclaimed, pointing at the base of the pillar, *that aquamarine sweeping up into the cerulean blue indicates your psychic powers. From that arrangement, it would appear that your creativity grows out of your psychic talent. See that gray slash over the aquamarine? She's fenced your psychic ability off too, along with your creativity. No wonder you abandoned your painting and were reluctant to have anything to do with the paranormal.*

As she traced the blue mark shaped like a big daisy, Callan saw that the ragged scar below it continued completely around the pillar, severing the four-foot-wide band of aquamarine from the cerulean blue and the rest of the flowing colors. It looked as though someone had gouged wet clay with a finger. Tentacles of aquamarine had broken through the gray lines in many places, as though the psychic band had overgrown the barrier Bianca had erected.

As she understood the enormity of the violation, anger surged through her, and the pillar's colors flamed red in response. Her fury left her feeling enervated and cold, and she shivered in reaction.

How do I fix it? she asked grimly, reining in the rage. The pillar lost its fiery glow and subsided into hues that were more temperate.

Touch the defaced areas and heal them. Smooth out the gray by thinking of wholeness, happiness, and the fulfillment you experience when you paint.

She caressed the blue daisy patch as if it were her infant. The pillar was as warm and pliant as human flesh, and she recognized the essence of her own emotions flowing under her fingertips. As she proceeded around the pillar, smoothing and obliterating the profane gash with firm strokes, serenity filled her. The long-missed yearning to paint, to birth into the world her own particular vision, permeated her once more, filling the void within that she had denied and repressed. For the first time in years the craving to use her talent swelled in her and she shivered with the euphoria that came with it.

This feels as good as Sam's kisses, she thought, then squelched it before Rosemary heard her. She continued on smoothing and stroking until the gray slash mark was erased from the cerulean and the aquamarine.

She faced Rosemary and said, *Thanks. This is an incredible gift. I suspect I will eventually have much more to thank you for.*

You're welcome, my dear. Shall we proceed to move this fine spirit over among its friends, she suggested, gesturing in the direction of the pillars they passed earlier. *On the astral plane, there is strength in numbers and in kindred.*

Callan tipped back her head and gazed upward. She could barely see the top of the pillar. *It's pretty big. Can we hire a crane locally to move it?* she asked.

Sorry, only you can move it. At Callan's snort of incredulity, she added, *it will follow along easily enough. Take your silver cord and wrap it around the pillar twice, clockwise, until it's lassoed.*

You're the boss.

Callan reached over her shoulder and found the silver cord. It felt smooth and warm in her hand and seemed to pulse with the rhythm of her heartbeat. She was still surprised she could feel a heart beat while in astral form. She pulled the cord over her shoulder and threaded a six-foot length through her hands. As she touched the hidden portion of the cord, another six-foot length became visible, followed by another and another. After measuring off more than forty feet of cord from her head, she approached her pillar and pressed the end of the visible length against it. The cord stuck and momentarily flared in the pinks of the column. As she circled the pillar twice to secure the cord, happiness surged through her. With it came a strong essence of herself, with the addition of some attitudes and abilities that she had never been aware of. Those particular surprises would have to be sorted out and explored in a more conventional environment.

Okay, what now? she asked, still half believing that Rosemary was playing an absurd joke on her.

We'll just move ahead. It will follow along easily enough.

Callan cautiously stepped back until the silver line was taut. The pull on the silver cord caused her no discomfort, unlike Bianca's jerk the night before. The pillar lifted easily and floated above the mist, seemingly weightless, looking much like a giant redwood on a leash. The sensation was rather like working a well-toned muscle.

They moved at a careful, leisurely pace as Callan guided her cargo between the mounds. Clearing the pass, they flew at a moderate speed and altitude toward the territory of the guardian pillar.

The outer area around the guardian pillar was crowded with obelisks of various heights, a few no more than a dozen feet tall, the equivalent of one lifetime, Rosemary said, to those the size of a ten-story building, which seemed to be about average. Unlike the massive pillars that remained grounded, the smaller citizens drifted randomly and slowly with the ground mist although they stayed within the periphery of the larger ones. On some of the smaller pillars, the colors lacked clear patterns, and browns and grays were more dominant.

Whose pillars are these? she asked Rosemary.

I don't know. They could belong to anyone. If I accidentally came upon the pillar of someone I knew and cared to explore it, I might recognize it. Otherwise, pillars are anonymous.

They wove cautiously through the throng, Callan maneuvering her column carefully. Her pride in her own marker took a nosedive when she got a clearer look at the guardian pillar in the center. A behemoth, at least thirty feet in diameter, its top brushed the multicolored sky. A pure opalescent white, the column glowed with a pure inner light. It was tinged with a violet and indigo flame pattern as far up as she could see.

Wow, I'm impressed! What's the significance of the violet and indigo? Do you know who this pillar belongs to?

The violet indicates that this individual has the qualities of purity, enlightenment and a protective spirit, compassion, I suppose. The indigo signifies spiritual awareness and strong morality. Also, a unique understanding of the emotions of others. Empathy, you would say. The yellow-gold outlining the violet says this person is highly intelligent. The various subtle hues have more specific meanings.

Rosemary stuffed her hands in the pockets of her jacket and turned to study some small columns nearby.

Whose is it? Callan drifted back a few paces and craned her neck to view more of the magnificent pillar.

Rosemary's reply was indistinct.

Pardon me, I didn't hear you.

I said, it's Albert's.

Dr. Ostherhaut's! You've got your pillar under the protection of his? I don't believe it! A giggle escaped her before she could squash it. *Let me see yours!* she said.

Rosemary whipped around to face her. *Don't you dare tell Albert about this!* she flared up. Her face was flushed and her eyes snapped. *He'll give me one of his smarty-cheeky grins. I'll never be able to face him if he finds out!*

Dr. Ostherhaut is so kind and has a charming smile, Callan answered. *It warms the heart.* She flapped a hand at his pillar as if asking how Rosemary could be reluctant to confide in such a paragon.

That's the problem! Rosemary snapped, as she stalked toward the right side of Albert's pillar. *I'm around here if you want to see.*

So that's the way the wind blows, Callan thought, as she hurried to place her pillar to the left of Albert's, close but not crowding him. She unwound her silver cord and hurried after Rosemary. She thought about what kind of relationship the two older people had or had once had.

I won't tell. I'm sorry I laughed, she said to Rosemary's rigid back.

I know. Rosemary turned, smiled and put out her hand to grasp Callan's. *Your kindness comes naturally, like Albert's and Sam's. Not like me. I have to work at it all the time. Don't feel sorry for me. Albert and I've been together before in other lives. Father and daughter, sister and brother, once even married. That was a debacle for me though! This time we're just friends. In this life there was Colin for me. If you're ever curious about your past lives, touching higher sections of your pillar will give you a glimpse. I warn you though, lives in those olden times were sometimes short and brutish and sad.*

Callan considered the idea of exploring what had happened to her long ago. To spy on her past lives? To watch someone who was essentially herself live, love, and then die? The idea gave her a shiver of revulsion.

No, thanks, I don't want to know. The problems of one life are enough. Dismissing the idea, she looked over Rosemary's pillar.

The obelisk sat close to Albert's and was about the same size as Callan's. Rosemary stood silent, withdrawing again as she watched Callan inspect it. The background tint was a creamy ivory underlying a vivid spiral pattern. All the astral shades, pinks and reds, blues and violets that Rosemary had identified earlier embellished it, although no one color predominated. Embedded in the wide band of aquamarine signifying the psychically talented at the base, the colors twined upward like ivy wrapping a trellis. It was a complex design, as though it had been taken from a garden depicted in a medieval tapestry. Callan noticed green and orange accenting the other tints and asked their significance.

Green means a love of prosperity. The orange shows a strong emotional nature along with courage and confidence, Rosemary answered matter-of-factly.

Callan regarded Rosemary for a moment then looked back at the pillar. *You have an abundance of fine qualities, in fact, all of them. I like the unusual pattern too. It indicates great individuality and vitality. I'd say it reflects you very well. What a great abstract painting it would make!*

Nice wallpaper, you mean.

No, I don't. You don't need to feel your soul's lesser than Albert's or anyone else's, if that's the way you've been feeling.

I suppose I should be glad it isn't boring or full of muddy browns and ominous blacks, Rosemary conceded, her impudent grin struggling free. *Albert would feel duty-bound to straighten me out!* They laughed with the easing of the strain between them.

I must confess that my pillar is not that of an enlightened one, nor is it as small and chaotic as some of the immature who have lived fewer lives, Rosemary added with a wan smile. *I'm still a spiritual adolescent, I'm afraid. Since I'm not wise or powerful enough spiritually, I hide my pillar, which divulges my paranormal power, within Albert's territory. I'm protected by its radiance and obscured by its attending chicks, as I think of the young souls. The corrupt dark ones, like Bianca's, won't get too near the highly evolved soul-pillars.*

Let's go home now, Rosemary said with a tired sigh. *We'll come back tomorrow night with Connor.*

Rosemary led her up into the swirling multicolored sky and some distance away from the clustered pillars. With their auras overlapping, she initiated the transition, and they arrived back in their own familiar starry sky.

As they drifted leisurely downward Rosemary warned her, *Don't go there too often, Callan. Visiting the astral plane augments your paranormal powers, but while under its influence, much of the life force is diverted from your earthly body. In the picture of Bianca that*

Albert showed us, did you notice how small she was? How childish her figure? She's probably spent so much time on the astral plane that her body never received enough life force to grow and mature.

In my own case, as a youngster and then a young woman, I think I came here too often and explored too long, she continued. *Perhaps that's why I never had children. My earthly body hadn't the strength to nurture another life. So, if you want more kids and good health, avoid frequent or prolonged visits to the astral plane. Nightwalking on the earthly plane is okay. It isn't detrimental to your physical body at all. People do it regularly without harm.*

They said goodnight floating above Callan's house. Before returning to her bedroom, she extended her awareness to check on Connor, the Ellisons' house next door, and surveyed the neighborhood for anything suspicious. Unlike the night before, all seemed peaceful, so she slipped gratefully back into her body and let its sleeping serenity claim her.

As she drifted on the edge of sleep, she theorized why her pillar had been isolated, set off in the wilderness with no others for company. The passing question submerged into increasing lethargy. Her last coherent thought was a wish for a day of peace from Bianca's machinations. It seemed so long since she felt normal and serene. Deep down where the precognitive instinct dwelled, something mocked with snickery laughter at her wish.

Chapter Seven

ℰᴓ

As she looked out the bay window of the kitchen just after dawn on Saturday, Callan felt as if she had drawn down the astral plane and released it over the Colorado landscape. The morning was cool with low-hanging clouds and dampness in the air. After weeks of bright, arid August days with only quickly evaporating showers to provide relief, the contrast was refreshing. The sluggishness that remained from her lengthy trip to the astral plane and semi-sleepless night reminded her that she had been neglecting her workouts lately. She felt out of shape. Even under normal circumstances, without regular exercise her body had a tendency to slump and lose its vitality. Maybe a run would perk her up.

She hoped Rosemary had exaggerated somewhat about how too many visits to the astral plane depleted the body's life energy. If she hadn't, what mental and physical condition would they be in after making nightly trips to the astral plane? Only one trip a night allowed, Rosemary decreed. She would gladly pay the price, but Rosemary probably couldn't endure many more trips to the other dimension. Would Bianca be so negligent as to allow them time to get everyone to safekeeping by Dr. Ostherhaut's pillar? Not likely. Without a doubt, Bianca would soon be all over them like a swarm of mosquitoes.

Clairvoyance had proven useless on the most critical of questions. From Bianca's point of view, who could she threaten that would coerce Callan into joining the Brazilian's organization? Connor obviously would be the primary objective, but he would go to the plane tonight. After that, under Bianca's perverted logic, who was likely to become her next victim? In what order should Callan rank loved ones for escort to the astral plane? Her parents and brothers and their wives and kids back in Wisconsin were in jeopardy. Stephanie, Matt, Zach and Katie, along with Sam, were potential targets. Other old friends scattered all over the country could eventually be taken over or injured. How, for heaven's sake, would they take an infant like Katie to the astral plane and get her to move a pillar of light?

Bianca might give up her psychic intimidation and simply follow the gang-style method of kidnapping or murder. She hadn't hesitated to use common physical violence to murder Bernie with her own hands. Stealing minds, holding hostages or destroying bodies offered endless options. She'd considered becoming Bianca's willing zombie but rejected the idea, as it ultimately offered no safety for the others. It would only put them in more danger—from her. Dr. Ostherhaut had said that entire families had been drawn into Bianca's criminal organization. The future seemed hopeless.

Even if she could disregard the well-being of everyone else, and Connor and she cowered in their house under her protective aura day after day, her money wouldn't last forever. She had to work. Of course, Connor would never stand for such imprisonment. Neither would she.

Since Sam had thrust himself back into her life, she wanted to explore a relationship with him. Her newly released creativity generated a yearning for a sketchpad and pencil that had been nagging at her since she woke up this morning. Bianca could be thanked, in a roundabout way, for the return of Sam to her life, but Callan would never forgive her for the theft of her art. The roll of Bianca's crimes grew longer by the day, and thinking of any one of them left her trembling with outrage.

Fight back, day by day, and live free, it was the only option for now. She'd fight and block Bianca and frustrate her in any way she could, one day at a time. She'd stop looking over her shoulder and take the offensive. How to accomplish that? She didn't know. Her intuition questioned what was at the heart of The Gull, and why Bianca chose to appear in that form. What was her weakness? If only there was a deeper knowledge of the paranormal, because, as things were now, her so-called powers were decidedly inadequate. Time was running out.

Awake earlier than usual on a Saturday, Connor wandered into the kitchen. He agreed to a morning run, and she was relieved that she didn't have to persuade him to go. With Bianca's threats hanging over them, leaving him alone in the house was risky.

As usual, if an activity was competitive, Connor was an enthusiastic participant. His goal was to run his mom into the ground. As they approached the golf course on the return leg of their run and headed eastward for the last mile home, she believed he might get his wish this morning. She'd begun to feel the exertion. Connor passed her easily and sprinted ahead. She called out for him to wait.

When she caught up, he said with a self-satisfied grin, "What'd I tell you about eating those yucky hamburgers? Spoils your wind," Connor said in a smirky voice.

"Does not. I was sick this week, remember, and missed my workouts," she wheezed, hands on knees as she caught her breath. "Give me a few days, and I'll be back in stride. Then look out, macho man."

"Meat eaters stink, too. Like dried blood and rotten dead things," he said.

"I don't stink!" she exploded. "You can stick your goofy opinions in your ear, for all I care!"

"Admit it, Mom—you're just a nasty old carnivore."

"I'm not! And I'm not old either!"

She took a deep breath to cool her exasperation. He'd needled her into overreacting, again. She was acting more like an eleven-year-old than he was and in the process fast losing her maternal dignity.

"And your arteries turn into slimy, fat-clogged organic drains, that's what," he kept on. "Disgusting." His impudent, superior grin would provoke any red-blooded American mother.

"I don't care. I want a hamburger! Right now!" Callan yelled at him, turning and stalking ahead.

"Oh, gross. We haven't even had breakfast yet."

"Whatever, Connor! I just can't stand another of your gawdawful bean sprout sandwiches."

"If you don't eat any more disgusting hamburgers, you might outrun me. They're probably what made you sick!"

"Oh yeah? Can it, why don't you? You're getting to be a fanatic and a pest."

"Race you the last mile home," he said as he came up to her. "If I beat you, you'll take out the trash next week instead of me."

There it was again, his unquenchable need to compete and win. He saw everything in life as an opportunity to show his superiority. It had to stop.

Her longer legs usually gave her the advantage, but he had a good chance of outrunning her if she was winded. Callan wiped sweat from her face with the back of her hand and scowled at him. That unhealthy obsession to win, more than his belittling remarks about her diet, made her say, "You're on!"

* * * * *

Later, as she sorted laundry before leaving for the gym and self-defense class, she questioned whether she should have let him win. She'd taken full advantage of longer legs and a second wind. After losing the race, the usual sulky anger surfaced on his face and remained through breakfast. He was upstairs now tending his hurt feelings and cleaning out the aquarium.

She finished sorting T-shirts, underwear and white athletic socks from a large stack and lifted an armload to fill the washer. A sock tumbled off the top of the pile and fell between the wall and the back of the washer. There was no room to get behind the appliance and retrieve the sock. To retrieve it, she'd either have to heave the washer out of its stall or go upstairs, get a wire coat hanger, straighten it, crawl on top of the washer and hope to hook it out. What a nuisance for one lousy sock! But a sock wasn't that much heavier than a handkerchief. Time to give the telekinesis another tryout. Maybe it could be useful for something besides dusting the furniture or opening a celestial gateway.

Closing the door to the laundry room and leaning against it, she took a deep breath and stared at the concrete wall next to the hot water heater. When the trance state took hold, she looked at the washer out of the corner of her eye and thought about a dirty white sock with a ribbed cuff and grass stains on the bottom.

The sock sailed up from behind the washer and landed at her feet. With a grin she mentally grabbed it, along with three pairs of shorts and a T-shirt, and stuffed them in the washer. A bigger bunch followed. Then the last of the pile cascaded in. Putting in a scoop of detergent took more concentration, but she managed without spilling much. A mental twitch slammed down the washer lid and the timer set itself. With a cerebral pull of the dial, water began running into the machine.

"Cooool," she crooned, as she left the laundry room and went to see how Connor was doing with his aquarium cleaning.

After gym and class, to appease Connor, they picked up a quick lunch of vegetarian submarine sandwiches. Then they spent the afternoon running errands in the rain.

They made a stop at the dry cleaners and at the liquor store for wine to take to the picnic. Before heading for the supermarket, she made a detour to an art supply store for a sketchpad, pencils and chalk. The paints, easels, canvases and other supplies lured her. She fended off the temptation to rummage about and fill her car to bursting with art goodies until another day when she had time to browse and indulge herself.

Late in the afternoon in the crowded supermarket, she scolded herself for not doing the grocery shopping before the holiday weekend crush. More laundry waited at home, along with cooking for the picnic. The line for the cashier barely crawled forward.

After unloading and putting away their purchases, dinner was late. Afterwards, Zach phoned Connor to suggest some soccer practice in the Ellisons' backyard. Stephanie and Callan had decided the boys should stay close to home and under the watch of one of the adults. Although the boys usually walked to and from school, Callan would now take them in the mornings and Stephanie would pick them up. When the boys objected to the new restrictions, their mothers pointed to the Rabney murder as an excuse for the closer supervision.

Callan seasoned a chicken and put it in the oven to slow roast. Cold chicken wouldn't be as exotic as the pheasant Sam had ordered at Carlotta's the previous Saturday night, but acceptable for a picnic. Salads from the deli would have to do for the remainder of the meal. She wasn't in the mood for elaborate or extensive cooking. The chicken would roast without her presence, so a visit with Stephanie seemed a good way to get her mind off Bianca.

Steph was cleaning up the dinner dishes. Her kitchen faced the backyard, so Callan could check on Connor as she dried pots and pans. Stephanie had a polite, interested expression when she described Bianca's attack during her first nightwalking trip, leaving out her visit to Sam, of course. A skeptical eyebrow rose at the description of Rosemary's astral plane.

When she told her about doing laundry with telekinesis that morning, Stephanie demanded, "Okay, fly girl, I want to see you do it. Sorry, but that's too much to accept without a demonstration. Let's go."

They crowded into the tiny basement laundry room and shut the door. Stephanie squeezed between the water heater and the wall, and Callan leaned against the door. A basket of Katie's laundry sat in front of the washer.

"There it is. Have at it." The furrow between Stephanie's eyes contradicted her nonchalant expression. Callan didn't blame her for being skeptical.

Getting into the trance state was becoming easier and faster each time she did it. Up popped the washer lid. A clump of

Katie's coveralls, playsuits and nighties sailed up and tumbled into the machine. The remainder of the clothes followed in a cascade.

"How much detergent and what temperature?" Callan asked, momentarily surfacing from the trance.

A slack-jawed Stephanie mumbled, "Warm…one scoop."

Callan flipped open the detergent box and made the measuring scoop dig into the powder. Breathing deeply and with eyes half shut in concentration, she floated the scoop slowly to the washer and dumped it in. The lid closed without slamming, the dials spun, and the water began running.

"Laundry by telekinesis," she said, rocking back on her heels. "One night on the astral plane and I'm hot."

"I'll be damned! I don't believe it. You know, you could become rich and famous as a magician."

"Nope. I'm leaning toward starting a telekinetic janitorial service."

They returned to the kitchen where Stephanie began absentmindedly re-wiping her spotless counters. Callan stood near the kitchen table watching her. Stephanie was more disturbed by her demonstration than she let on. Would she reject their friendship because of the weird things Callan could do?

To break the uncomfortable silence, and discover how Steph was feeling about her now, Callan finally said, "I can move things with my mind. Visit the astral plane. Talk telepathically with Rosemary, and occasionally prevent a tragedy. I still don't have a notion how to fight off The Gull and get her to leave me alone. What am I going to do?"

Stephanie paused in her wiping and looked at her pensively. Her usual quick response to a request for advice was not forthcoming, and its absence troubled Callan.

"I'm sorry, Steph, I didn't mean to dump on you."

"You have such fascinating problems, Mighty Mouse." She precisely refolded a dishtowel and hung it up.

Matt Ellison ambled in with a sleeping Katie draped over his shoulder. He was tall and lean and his wife barely came to the middle of his chest. His straight black hair was sleek in contrast to Stephanie's untamed cinnamon mop. He was quiet too, where she was outgoing. They were complete opposites, which could account for the attraction between them, but Callan sensed they matched in some other enigmatic way she hadn't figured out yet. His rather stern, sharp-hewn features disguised that he was one of the most kindhearted men she had ever met, except for maybe Sam and Dr. Ostherhaut.

After greeting Callan and getting a soft drink from the refrigerator, he looked pointedly at them and asked, "You two been hitting the beer again?"

"Smartass. Women's business. Beer's a good idea though," Stephanie said, shooing him away from the refrigerator. The underlying tenderness in her voice didn't match her words.

"Don't let her get you fried, Callan," he said, his black eyes teasing. As he retreated from the kitchen, she felt a bleak envy at Stephanie's good fortune in having Matt's love.

"No beer for me, thanks," she said when Stephanie waved a bottle at her. "Makes me sleep too deeply. I wouldn't be able to wake up when Rosemary comes to nightwalk. You're lucky to have Matt, you know," she added. Her envy probably showed clearly in her voice and on her face. "I hope you appreciate him."

"I appreciate him every chance I get. By the way, how's the studly doc? Any progress there or are you still giving him the evil eye?"

"You were right about our date. Thursday afternoon in his office, we straightened out the misunderstanding."

"Great. Is he ripped?"

"What? Of all the nerve! That's the most outrageous, personal thing to ask…" Callan stammered. She was appalled at the question. Sometimes Stephanie pushed their friendship all the way. She needed to put her foot down about some subjects.

"No, no, it doesn't mean what you're thinking," Stephanie waved her hands in the air, hardly able to get the words out around her giggling.

Considering Steph's reaction, Callan realized she must have an extremely puckered-up, offended expression on her face. She had gotten to her again. "So what does it mean?" she asked warily.

"Ripped means great abs, as in a washboard stomach. Didn't you know that? You spend time in a gym."

"No, I've never heard the term."

Her pique had begun to subside but she was still uncomfortable over Stephanie's question. She looked back on her astral visit to Sam and their embraces in his office, searching for a definite answer to Stephanie's question, if only for herself.

She hadn't really explored his anatomy that much.

"You don't know if he's ripped! Mighty Mouse, you're such a Puritan. Didn't you try out his shrink couch? Don't you know that a muscled tummy shows a man has initiative and isn't a slacker?"

"Darn it, Steph, don't rush me!" she objected, rattled under the brash questioning.

"Darn it? Is that the best you can do for a swear word? You really should expand your adult vocabulary. Say 'damn it' like a grownup. Go ahead, try. It relieves a lot of tension." Stephanie was on a roll.

"No can do. I never got in the habit of cursing. Profanity isn't used in my family. I don't intend to start now. Why don't we change the subject?"

"Okay. We're grilling steaks tomorrow night. You, Connor and Sam are invited. I want to check this guy out and see if he's good enough for you."

"No way, Mommy. Not when you're planning on jabbing him in the stomach to see if he has character."

* * * * *

That night, Callan in astral form was waiting when Rosemary appeared outside her window.

Hey, Callan, she heard her call, *open up.*

Callan concentrated on creating an entrance in the protective shield around her house. The ragged edges of the lopsided rectangle sparked and glimmered when it opened in the bedroom wall. After Rosemary entered, she let the opening fall shut.

Hi. Connor's over here, she said, moving through the bedroom door and then through his.

Connor, sleeping on his stomach, had tossed aside his covers. Instead of pajamas, he wore a faded blue T-shirt and a pair of gray sweatpants that he'd hacked off above the knees. The T-shirt was twisted under his armpits and the sweatpants had slipped below his hipbones. His perfectionism didn't extend to his nightwear.

So how to we get him to release his astral body? Callan asked as they floated beside his bed.

Coax him out. Talk to him telepathically. Entice him with something that would interest him. He's dreaming about baseball. Invite him to a game. He'll follow his mother.

Connor, you're late for the ball game. You don't want to miss it, do you?

The protective aura around Connor expanded slightly, and under it his astral body stirred restlessly then relaxed inward.

Come on, Connor, let's play ball! The wave sound and low-pitched humming filled the room. Connor's astral body slipped halfway out and then back in again. Callan could sense his dreaming eagerness to get into a ball game.

Try again, Connor, she urged, with a more insistent mental nudge.

With a flutter and then a rush, his astral body stood beside the bed. His silver cord was attached somewhat lower than

Callan's or Rosemary's, emerging just above the neck, unlike the high-pulled ponytailed look that the women wore. His aura was a bright blue tinged with yellow gold. Connor was as blank-faced as the old man Callan had seen walking his dog, and his vacant stare gave her a shiver of uneasiness.

His T-shirt was still bunched up under his arms in defiance of gravity, and the sweatpants hung dangerously low. Callan tugged the T-shirt down and the pants up.

Well, at least his flying outfit is comfortable, she commented, slightly embarrassed. *We're ready to go.*

Okay, one of us on each side of him. Hold on to his arm, Rosemary said, as they rose through the roof and headed for the transition point with Connor's astral body gliding between them. Callan caught a fragment of his dream as they flew. He was driving their car to a game.

As they neared the transition point, Rosemary said, *See if you can locate the portal. I want you to open it for practice.*

Are you sure that's a good idea? With Connor along I don't want to end up in the wrong dimension. Such as further south or something.

Don't worry. Join with me. I'll take over if necessary. Hold my hand across Connor and enclose him in our auras.

At the touch of their hands, the auras flared and Connor's astral bubble compressed between them.

There's the transition point, Callan said a moment later. She could feel the strange density of the space as if the entrance had a connection way back in her mind. It pulled and tickled.

Correct. Remember how to open it? Enfold the gateway, then pull as hard as you can with your telekinesis.

Callan, grateful for Rosemary's protective mind hovering close beside her own, encompassed the transition point and pulled with all her strength. White flecked with black filled the universe, then the whirlpool of spinning colors sucked them in, and they materialized on the astral plane.

The place seemed unchanged since the previous night. The white ground mist undulated across the landscape and the sky flashed with aurora borealis colors. She was more sensitive tonight to the teeming life inhabiting it. The crowded feeling was almost suffocating in its density.

She had brought them west of the hillock just beyond Dr. Ostherhaut's pillar. It rose above the mound, looming over the landscape like a colossal lighthouse. They dropped hands and let their auras expand to their natural oval shape.

Now what?

Encourage him to locate his pillar of light. Just talk to him. Tell him to find it, Rosemary said. *People are extremely suggestible during non-lucid nightwalking.*

Callan moved in front of her son and looked into his eyes. They were still eerily unfocused.

Connor, find your pillar of light. It's big, wonderful and full of pretty colors. Do you know where it is?

He seemed to rouse from the dreamy state and looked at her with awareness. He smiled slightly and his eyes moved to take in the scene.

Rosemary, I think he's waking up!

Rosemary examined his face and shook her head. *Not really. He's just become more aware of his surroundings, but he remains in a hypnotic state. Tomorrow, he may remember a vivid dream, but right now, he isn't really capable of independent action since he didn't enter the astral plane in a lucid state. Ask him again.*

Connor, think about your pillar of light. You know where it is. I'd like to see it.

After a moment, he glided forward hesitantly, then turned to the left and began heading in the direction Callan had begun to think of as north. He unexpectedly picked up speed and zoomed ahead, rapidly leaving them behind.

He never walks if he can run, she said. They hurried to catch up.

They traveled at a speed that blurred their surroundings, but the trip was long and she felt as though they were traversing a continent. Meeting a herd of life forms that bounded above the mist and across their path, they had to interrupt Connor's headlong flight while it streamed by. They dodged other life forms, solitary wraiths and others in family groupings, during the journey.

Connor led them into a vast tract of the lacy white tree forms. When they attempted to fly over the area, Connor refused to lift and they were forced to plunge into the white woodland.

Callan immediately sensed an increase in life energy. The area was thick with ghostly underbrush, and she could feel the hordes of creatures crawling and burrowing under the concealing ground mist and foliage. Although the spectral vegetation gave way easily before them, she disliked the suffocating feeling of the massed life forms.

This is a swamp, Rosemary. If he isn't capable of independent action, why are we slogging through this place?

You're not getting your feet wet, are you? Don't complain. Always remember to follow your instincts and intuition while in the psychic realm. If Connor wants to go this way, we go.

Callan refrained from mentioning that in Connor's case he was probably simply enjoying the adventure and the challenge, lucid or not.

The oppressive foliage began to thin out and they entered a clearing. A ghostly form lunged from the undergrowth. It was log-shaped and massive. The pointed front end suddenly separated horizontally into a gaping mouth.

Callan reacted. With a squeak, she grabbed Connor and shot up into the misty branches of a tree form. Down below, the white beast shook its front end wildly back and forth, bellowed and charged Rosemary.

Rosemary stood her ground, swung her booted foot at the creature, and connected with the snout end. The thing promptly turned and lurched into the undergrowth. With a whoop of triumph, she added another kick to its backside.

Later, alligator, Rosemary crowed and waved as its tapered rear end vanished into the mist.

She looked around, spied them in the tree and flew up to hover just below them. Connor grinned down at Rosemary. She grinned back and gave him thumbs-up. Obviously, they were two of a kind and both were enjoying the escapade. Callan wasn't.

Her aura had turned an ashy blue shade that likely reflected the hue of her face. That astral beast could have taken a chunk out of their life forces. What had possessed her to bring Connor to this place? There must be another way to protect him from The Gull. She anxiously scrutinized the area below for more white menaces.

You can come down now, Rosemary said, tugging on her hem. *A boot in the snout will discourage most beasties here.*

Callan realized how ridiculous she must look. Her high-tops were pulled up under her long skirt like a ninny scared of a mouse. Her eyes felt owl-sized. Connor was tucked under her arm like an oversized football, with his bare legs and feet floating up behind them.

No! That thing might come back. We're not ending up as some astral critter's lunch!

Astral spirits don't eat. Have you felt hungry or thirsty while in astral form?

No, but I don't care. They might bite. We're outta this swamp now!

They went up. Callan didn't release Connor until they were well above tree level and over a clear area.

After a time, they caught sight of a circle of pillars directly ahead. They slowed as they drew nearer. She wondered if Connor's pillar was among them. A medium-sized pillar near the perimeter began to spin on its base. A whistle like that of a giant spinning top issued from it.

What's that pillar doing? Callan asked, halting Connor's drift. The rotation of the pillar increased until, as they watched, it became a blur of rainbow light. Rising slowly, the pillar hovered above the ground fog and then lumbered into the sky.

What's happening? she asked again.

Death, Rosemary answered simply as she rolled over on her back to watch the ascent. *Look, see the ghostly figure overtaking it? That's the soul returning home.*

Above them, the column now resembled a spinning, hollow cylinder. Callan saw a phantom shape, hardly more than a blurry stick figure, approaching the bottom of the retreating pillar. As she watched in awe and trepidation, the amorphous figure vanished into the tube, which then plunged into the whirling peacock sky and disappeared.

At the death of someone on Earth, Rosemary explained, *their pillar rises and forms the long tunnel leading to the hereafter that so many people have described during a near-death experience. I've seen these pillars rise hundreds of times. I've also seen the birth of a pillar of light. When you are born, the pillar descends from above and takes its place on the astral plane for the duration. It's a spectacular sight, especially when a massive column of an ancient soul returns for another life on Earth.*

Callan felt privileged for the experience, but also as though she was a snoopy tourist watching a sacred native ritual in some distant land.

Connor stirred restlessly and began moving ahead again, bearing to the right. Callan and Rosemary fell in beside him and bracketed him within their astral shields.

After a few more minutes of travel, about two dozen pillars appeared in a deserted flat area unmarked by any hill mounds or tree forms. Connor threaded his way through the throng. In the center was a pillar, the largest of the lot, which appeared to Callan to be comparable to her own in height and circumference. On reaching it, Connor gently stroked its side and lightly traced a deep apricot patch overlaying the basic eggshell white of the column. His face flushed with pleasure. Connor had found his pillar of light.

Its overall pattern was an overlapping plume design with the apricot outlined in the brilliant yellow-gold of intelligence, interspersed were various shades of orange. She remembered that orange indicated courage, strength and confidence. The green of prosperity accented the majority hues of orange and yellow-gold. She hadn't realized it before but he and Rosemary shared many characteristics although in different proportions. None of this was surprising or revealed anything she didn't already know about Connor.

There was an aquamarine band indicative of psychic power near the base but it was less than a foot wide. Connor had inherited some of her paranormal abilities, but she had no idea how powerful they were or how they would manifest themselves. Moving closer, she caught the essence of her son like a perfume of the mind.

He's definitely his mother's son. Just look at this big crimson patch, Rosemary said with a chuckle from the other side of Connor. *He's going to be a devil with the girls in a few years.*

She ignored this comment as she had ignored Rosemary's remark about her own red patch.

Connor remained transfixed by the apricot area he originally touched. Callan looked closer and noticed a dappled swathe of brown and ash-gray across several of the plumes.

Rosemary, come look at this. Why is his column marked? He's too young to have developed any vices or committed any major sins.

Connor had noticed too and was scrubbing at the gray-brown spots.

Does he have any unusual problems?

Callan hesitated, then said, *The last couple of years he's gotten very competitive and wants everything around him to be perfect, everything under his control.*

That's probably it then. Extremely negative personality traits are revealed here at any age. The spots will fade if the person overcomes the difficulty.

Sam was going to have a new patient soon, Callan decided. It was past time that the problem was confronted head-on. She didn't like the marring of his pillar any more than Connor did.

Fortunately, the column was otherwise unmarked. Bianca hadn't paid a visit here.

Get him to wrap his silver cord around the pillar, Rosemary instructed, obviously tired and impatient. *It's a long way back to Albert.*

Although there was no trouble getting Connor to lasso his column, even without detours through swamps, the return trip took much longer as they couldn't move as swiftly with the pillar bobbing along behind.

With a sunny smile, Connor pulled steadily and frequently turned to look back at the pillar. Shortly after they started out, several of the smaller companion columns that had surrounded Connor's pillar began to move, apparently attempting to follow. Although they fell behind, Callan caught an occasional glimpse of them on the horizon. If they managed to track Connor across the great plain, Dr. Ostherhaut would have more souls to guard.

They finally approached Albert's home territory and began to circle the nearby mound. Rosemary stopped and scanned the plane behind and the horizon.

Something's coming. I don't like the feel of it. Keep Connor moving, she said warily, motioning them ahead as she studied the horizon.

Callan caught Connor's arm and hurried him along. A sucking sensation filled the atmosphere as though something was pulling at her life force. Glancing back, she saw The Gull materialize at the horizon and dive toward them like a black arrow shot from heaven. A gray aura rippled around the massive bird and ebony light shot from it to strike the mist below. The white clouds bellowed into streamers and huge clumps spun across the ground like boulders.

It's going to try to cut Connor's cord, Rosemary shouted, watching The Gull's downward plunge. *Watch out at your end!* She positioned herself like a goalie near his cord where it looped around the pillar.

Hurry, Connor! Callan shoved him ahead. Floating backwards to keep an eye on the action, she kept close to his back to guard the six feet of cord extending from his head. If they could get around the mound to Dr. Ostherhaut, they'd be safe. Her heart slammed against her astral breastbone. A flesh and blood body wasn't necessary to feel the effects of terror. She was shaking all over with an adrenaline rush.

The Gull flew straight toward Rosemary in a flat dive. Rosemary was a moment away from being ravaged by the vicious hooked beak and claws. At the last second she threw up her hands. A balloon of clear light burst into the path of the plummeting gull. Unable to swerve quickly enough, it plunged headfirst into the glowing bubble. With a scream, it sheared off and reeled into a flat spin over the milky ground cover, its flapping wings churning the mist into froth.

Callan turned back to Connor and yanked at his arm. He was starring at the black bird, both fascination and anxiety bleaching his tanned face. She urged him onward.

They had gone no more than a few feet when Rosemary cried out another warning. Callan stumbled and dropped Connor's arm in her hurry to turn around. The Gull had come out of the spin and returned to attack. Shooting toward them with wings folded back along the body, the neck stretched taut, it was a black torpedo. The bird head had disappeared, engulfed by the distended sapphire eyes. Their wrath was trained on Connor. An infuriated squawk shredded the air.

He's Ours or he's dead, came a shrill mental voice, embedded within the screech of the bird. *The little bastard's Ours. Just like his father*. The telepathic voice pierced her head with a sharp pang not unlike that caused by a frosty drink on a hot day.

In a panic, Callan clumsily knocked him facedown into the ground mist and enclosed him in her astral shield. Facing outward, she stood crouched over him ready to defend him. Exactly how she could protect him she didn't know. One telepathic jerk of a silver cord, and another pillar or two would make their death voyages tonight.

A rumbling vibrated through the mist, and then a brilliant violet sphere appeared behind The Gull. Concentrated life force radiated from it. *Power without heat*, it hissed overhead like an angry serpent. The basketball-sized sphere streaked toward the bird. It hit with a flash. A scream of terror split the atmosphere. The Gull, wings flapping uselessly, sailed over a nearby hill mound.

Callan couldn't move. Her astral knees shouldn't quake, but they did. The attack had ended so suddenly that she felt disoriented and still frozen with fear.

Rosemary appeared beside her. For a moment her face seemed transparent, the older earthly woman showing plainly beneath the young face.

Are you two okay? she asked, reaching out to grasp Callan's arm.

She helped her upright and quickly checked her cord. Grabbing Connor by the waist, she set him on his feet too. His cord was undamaged. His pillar had floated ahead until arrested by the tethering silver line. He gazed around, obviously bewildered and scared.

Albert sure let her know who's king of the hill around here! Rosemary boasted after finishing her inspections.

That light ball came from Dr. Ostherhaut?

You bet! Good old Albert let off a little life energy charge. An old guardian spirit won't tolerate Bianca's kind harassing their young ones. She was awfully stupid and arrogant to try something right under Albert's nose. The woman's an idiot. Taking a big shot of life energy could have disassociated her astral body. Her earthly body would languish in a coma until it died. Luckily for her, Albert isn't vindictive. He barely singed her tail feathers. She'll be rattled for a while and won't try that again soon. Not close to Albert anyway.

What was that ball of light you threw at her?

I just extruded more astral shield and threw it in her face, but she zigged by. I couldn't generate another quickly enough to get her. If she'd hit it head-on, it would have bounced her back into her earthly body so hard that she'd be twitching for a week. In comparison, what she did to you the other night would be trivial. I'm not benevolent like Albert.

I tried to protect Connor with my shield, but I don't think it would have stopped her, Callan said, still shaken by the encounter. *I don't have enough power in me yet.*

As they moved slowly forward again, Rosemary said, *Our next lesson will be drawing energy directly from the astral plane. The process isn't much different from what you did to draw energy from the Earth's life field. So far, you've simply assimilated the background energy of the astral plane by spending time here. The mounds situated all over the plane aren't just scenery. They are condensed life energy, rather like storage batteries. Don't try to walk through one. There's a line between gaining ample power and a dangerous overload.*

As the women talked, Connor drifted back into a dream state. Callan had to tug him forward. His pillar followed along. When they reached the crowd around Dr. Ostherhaut, he had to be guided to prevent him from colliding with the surrounding pillars. A dozen feet from the guardian, Connor once more snapped out of his dream state. He moved eagerly toward it, stopped a few feet away and gazed up in wonder.

Where'd you like to put him? Rosemary asked. From the contented look on her face, standing close to Dr. Ostherhaut's pillar gave her pleasure too. Callan noticed the serenity surrounding it and took a moment to soak up some of the ambience.

On the other side by mine, Callan answered as she took Connor's arm and led him forward. Her kid would have her protection on the astral plane too. After some maneuvering, they settled his pillar six feet from Callan's. This time, without help from his mother, Connor unwound the silver cord from his pillar. When he finished, he stood tracing and stroking the colorful pattern adorning its sides. In relief that he was safe from Bianca's spiritual vandalism, Callan grinned at Rosemary.

Rosemary grinned back. *A good night's work. Let's get home. Keep a sharp eye out for Bianca. We've got a long way to go unprotected. I don't think the sneaky bitch will try anything more tonight, but with her kind you never know.*

Callan longed to call it a night. She wouldn't have the energy to fight if Bianca attacked on their way home. If she didn't get some rest before the picnic tomorrow with Sam, she'd be too droopy with exhaustion to do more than settle under a tree and fall asleep.

Connor had other ideas. He clung stubbornly to his pillar until allowed to stroke it all the way around its circumference. Then he lapsed once again into the non-lucid state. Cautiously, they led him home, their astral eyes and minds alert for signs of the black nemesis that haunted the otherworldly plane.

Chapter Eight

❧

Rosemary is right, Callan thought the next morning. *Bianca is a devious, loathsome bitch, and I'm thoroughly sick of being on guard against The Gull.* Resentment of the disruption in her life gave rise to the purest malice she had ever felt.

With any luck, Bianca would be recuperating today after her run-in with Dr. Ostherhaut last night. She might get a tranquil day with Sam, without the unsettling intrusion of a huge black gull. During the past week's crisis, she dared to be with him for only minutes. Time to simply enjoy his company, to begin to truly know the adult Sam, seemed a luxury beyond her reach while they lived under The Gull's shadow.

As she was putting the last of the food in the ice chest for the picnic, Connor ushered Sam into the kitchen. Today, Sam looked just as sexy in his jeans and stonewashed blue denim shirt as he had the previous Saturday dressed up for their dinner date. His shirtsleeves were rolled up to his elbows, showing corded forearms. Well-developed forearms on a man were one of her weaknesses. It made her feel as though there was a shortage of oxygen in the room.

She suddenly wondered if an occasion to answer Stephanie's impertinent question about the state of Sam's abdominal muscles would present itself that afternoon. If Connor hadn't been there, she might have attempted to find out immediately. The absorbed roving of Sam's eyes over her body indicated he wasn't adverse to some mutual exploration.

"Here's Sam, Mom," Connor announced with a grin. He had taken an instant liking to Sam when they met last Saturday outside the gym. Of course, Sam, had done all he could to charm the boy.

"Yes, he certainly is," she answered, hearing her own voice go sultry in welcome. She hadn't intended to sound so warm. To divert attention from the flirtatious tone, she said briskly, "Let's go. I'll pull the car out if you gentlemen will bring the ice chest and picnic hamper out front to the driveway."

Picking up her car keys and tote bag, she headed for the kitchen entrance to the garage. As she pushed the button to raise the garage door, she heard Connor say to Sam, "She's getting her beast."

After backing out their transportation, she got out, stood beside the door and waited for the two males. Would Sam remember?

"What'd I tell you, Sam?" she heard Connor say as they came down the front walk. "It's a big metal freak."

Sam gave an appreciative whistle as he came up. Callan's 1959 Chevy Bel Air was nearly seventeen feet long, painted two-tone with an ivory roof and the body a feminine, metallic, pinkish-mauve. Aunt Noonan had called the roof "India Ivory" and the mauve "Dusk Pearl." When she was six, the colors and their names had caught her fancy.

The Chevy boasted a massive chrome grill and bumper. A heavy chrome stripe began at the headlights, continued across the doors, to divide into a y-shape on the fenders. More chrome defined the sharply edged rear fins. Stainless-steel wheel covers accented the white-wall tires. A spotlight jutted up on the driver's side, and the radio antenna flew a small United States flag. Finish, chrome, and glass flashed and sparkled under the late morning sun.

"It's your Aunt Noonan's Evelyn, isn't it?" Sam asked. "It used to be on blocks in the barn at your folks' place. I would find you down there, sitting behind the steering wheel. You'd pretend to take me places."

Sam appreciatively ran his hand over the front fender's satiny finish, set the antenna vibrating with a flick of a finger, and cupped the spotlight in his hand. Heat flared in the pit of her stomach and danced along nerve endings. Jealousy over his attention to Evelyn flashed through Callan. When she understood watching Sam fondle Evelyn caused the emotion, she couldn't believe it. *Get a grip, woman.* If he kept touching the car like that much longer, she'd likely slap his hands away.

"Dad and my brothers restored it and gave it to me for my college graduation," she explained. "I couldn't leave her behind in Apple Springs. Let's get going!" She couldn't watch him stroke the car another moment. It made her feel like a voyeur.

"It's an ugly gas-guzzling monster, and she makes me ride in it," Connor complained as he crawled into the backseat. "When it backfires, it sounds like an elephant farting. Why can't we take our regular car or Sam's BMW? It's cool."

"She does not backfire!" Callan objected hotly, hands on hips as she glared through the side window at him. "And watch your mouth, young man. Especially since I know you're just trying to get me riled."

"It does too fart. All the time!" Connor was mulish in his insistence. There was no teasing light in his eyes, just obstinacy, but she couldn't really believe he was totally negative about Evelyn. Then again, she couldn't be sure. Connor had changed so much the last couple of years.

"Kids!" she muttered under her breath, and marched to the car's rear end to open the trunk.

Standing by the passenger side, Sam was trying to swallow his laughter and in the process was close to popping the buttons on his tight shirt. It would serve him right for finding the situation amusing, even though flying buttons would certainly provide revenge, distraction and entertainment for her. He was a shrink for crying out loud, but all he did was snort and cackle! Why didn't he step in and help ease the situation? He certainly must have a lot of experience in handling parent/kid conflicts. Although, to be fair, she would probably resent unsought advice or interference.

Sam walked to the back of the car, and as they loaded the picnic things, his chuckles ran down, but from his grin it looked as if guffaws could break out again any second. He gave her a brief sympathetic glance and pat on the shoulder as he turned away to get in the passenger side. Apparently, she'd get only meager sympathy for the problems of raising a pre-teen son. That pat wasn't much. Then again, maybe it was. It gave her lavish goose bumps.

* * * * *

As they pulled onto the main thoroughfare heading west toward the mountains, Callan told Sam about the classic car club she had joined the previous year. They were going to a club picnic. Usually, a club activity was some sort of parade or car show, but classic car owners also simply enjoyed driving their vehicles somewhere.

At a stoplight, a late model sporty-looking car pulled up beside them in the center lane. The occupants, two young men in their late teens, stared openly at Evelyn. The passenger made a comment to the driver and they both laughed, obviously mocking the Chevy.

Evelyn usually drew wolf whistles and admiring looks, but occasionally the ignorant made snide comments about her size, heavy chrome or age. Such ridicule always brought out the demon in Callan. Evelyn was beautiful and classy and no smirky teenage would get away with belittling her.

Connor released his seat belt and scooted forward to lean over the back of Sam's seat. "Watch this. See that funny-looking grin on her face? She's showing all her teeth, isn't she?"

"Sure is," Sam said mildly. He sounded like he wanted to say more but was prudently holding back. His natural tact would probably be strained to the limit today.

Callan knew she had a wide, rather fixed smile. She had caught glimpses of it in the rearview mirror before when encountering the rare derogatory reaction to Evelyn. She concentrated on staring straight ahead, tapped her fingers against the steering wheel, and waited for the light to change. It wouldn't do to lose her cool again in front of Sam.

The teenagers' contemptuous stares were searing a hole in Evelyn's shiny paint. She could feel it. They couldn't be allowed to get away with it. Slowly, she slid her sunglasses up, turned toward them and gave them a haughty facial challenge of raised eyebrow and curled lip. They wouldn't be able to ignore that message.

Regally, she raised her chin, lowered the sunglasses and turned to stare eagerly over the big steering wheel. The artificial grin on her face felt as stiff as a plastic Halloween mask. She revved Evelyn's engine to a throaty rumble. Out of the corner of her eye, she could see that the driver had gotten the message.

The light changed to green, Evelyn's engine roared, her tires squealed and the acceleration thrust Connor back into his seat.

"Eat her dust, hotshots!" Callan crowed, and slapped the steering wheel in triumph as they shot across the intersection.

"Got 'em, Callie," Sam reported with a whoop. Looking back, he added, "They've barely cleared the intersection."

With style and an antique but powerful engine, Evelyn had taken her revenge on an ignorant smart aleck in a late model, generic car.

"Oh, gross, another monster lover. You're going to get arrested for drag racing one of these days," Connor complained, practically in Callan's ear. "How'm I supposed to get you out of jail?"

He was serious. Blatant peevishness and condemnation came from the backseat, as thick as astral fog in the car, overlaying the moment. Connor's staid disapproval was derailing the fun and neutralizing the moment.

Rotten kid. Sometimes he's a real pain in the patootie. She took a deep breath to cool her exasperation.

His attitude toward anything even marginally against the rules had originally been only a minor irritation. She understood that it was just his way of trying to control his environment, but lately it was getting out of hand. Exactness and perfection were commendable and necessary in many situations, and so, of course, was obeying laws. However, those ideals shouldn't include studiously picking lint off an old pair of athletic socks as she had caught him doing the previous week. Or becoming irate over a low-key challenge at a stoplight.

She glanced at Sam and saw lingering amusement at what she had done. Back in tiny Apple Springs, drag racing was an honorable sport. The surge of the car seemed to have cut the constraint between them and for the moment created a link back to when they were young and in love. She didn't know what to say to Sam as the atmosphere thickened, and she certainly didn't want to get into a row with her son.

He already had his seat belt back on, as the law dictated, so she couldn't tell him to do it. Completely ignoring his tirade would cause maternal loss of face. To reestablish her parental authority and as a way of letting him know she wasn't exactly delighted with him either, she said dryly, "Deal, Connor. Deal."

* * * * *

They arrived at the park in the foothills without further challenges to Evelyn's honor. The parking area held a dozen classic automobiles. Highly polished paint and chrome glittered under the midday sun. Callan parked between a pristine black Model-T Ford and a vintage dark green Jaguar sports car.

"The owners of these cars would be glad to tell you all about them, Sam," Callan said as they got out of Evelyn. "Some people recognize class and quality, unlike some I could name." She pointedly looked at Connor as she said it. Not long ago, he had liked Evelyn. In a few years, Connor would be nearing the age of the teenage boys in the sporty car. She wasn't looking forward to an increase in his negative attitude toward Evelyn, or living with his obsessions.

Connor didn't seem to hear her comment. His attention was solely focused on a soccer game being played in a field adjacent to the picnic area. He ran ahead as the adults unloaded the picnic hamper from the trunk.

Callan greeted several people as they made their way across the recreation area, introducing Sam to a few friends as they went, while keeping an eye on Connor. They found an empty table shaded by a grove of aspen trees near the park's small reservoir. At the edge of the field Connor had joined some boys. He had brought his baseball, glove and bat in anticipation of some action that afternoon.

Sam helped spread a blue-checked tablecloth across the rough planks of the table, and she opened the ice chest and set out soft drinks and a bottle of wine. Sam was examining the wine when a tall, wiry man in his mid-forties dressed in a green knit golf shirt and matching checked pants, sauntered up to the table. His receding black hair was slicked back and sprayed so rigidly that the light breeze that ruffled the leaves overhead didn't stir a hair.

"Callan, so glad you could make it today," he said, pronouncing each word as though he resented its escape from his lips.

Callan noticed that Sam had a pleasant noncommittal expression, the one she recalled he used when he was annoyed about a situation and wished to conceal the fact.

"Hello, Eddie. I'd like you to meet an old friend of mine, Dr. Sam Cavendar. Sam, this is Eddie Chudy, treasurer of our classic car association."

As the men shook hands, Eddie said, "Glad to meet you. I'm the Chudy of the Chudy Car Washes here in the metro area. You've heard of them, I'm sure."

"Yes, I believe I've used them," Sam said graciously. His face was still bland.

Eddie glanced past Sam toward the playing field, then said, "Nice to meet you, Sam. Hope you can make it to our next club business meeting, Callan." He abruptly turned and hurried toward the parking area.

"Eddie saw me coming and ran to check his Model-T," Connor crowed as he came up. "You didn't agree to go out with him, did you, Mom?"

He sat down on a bench and reached for a soft drink. Callan took plates and utensils from the wicker basket. Sam sat across from Connor and began opening the bottle of wine.

"No, young man. Not that it's any concern of yours."

"Old Chudy is sweet on Mom. Always trying to get her to go out with him," he informed Sam.

"So how do you feel about your mom dating?"

He asked so casually, as if the question was no more important than Connor's preference in soft drinks, but Callan suspected he was fishing for information about her social life. Dating activities in particular. That he would ask Connor such a leading question in front of her surprised her at first, but then exhilaration bubbled through her. Was he worried about competition?

"Okay, I guess," Connor answered seriously. Eyes downcast, he gave his reply some deliberation, knowing a man in his mother's life could have vital consequences for him. After a moment, he said slowly, as though he were reluctant to really think about such a situation, but knowing he needed to be fair, "Zach says our moms aren't old. No wrinkles or gray hair yet. So, I guess, since Mom's divorced, it's okay. But I hope she doesn't go out with ol' Eddie!"

"Don't you like him?" Sam asked, with a sidelong glance at her. She decided to ignore being talked about as if she weren't there and began removing containers from the ice chest. Sam's questions and Connor's answers were certain to be enlightening.

"Nah. He doesn't like me. When he sees me, his nostrils suck in real hard. Looks like he's got an invisible clothespin clamped on his nose. I touched his Model-T at the Fourth of July picnic and his nose sucked in so hard I thought I heard it break."

"Connor," Callan jumped in, "you're exaggerating. Be fair. You got fried chicken grease on it. Deliberately, I suspect."

"I did not! Besides, it was only a little smudge. He carried on like I'd slammed it with my bat. Don't you think that's kind of silly, Sam?"

Callan stopped fiddling with the lunch containers and studied Sam, curious how he would handle Connor's question. Would he give a righteous lecture on the sanctity of private property and the importance of another's feelings?

"Callie, by any chance is that fried chicken you have in that box?" he asked with a beatific smile.

* * * * *

"Are you trying to bewitch my son, Sam Cavendar? Or corrupt his morals?" Callan challenged after lunch, as they hiked up a switchback trail to a ridge behind the park. "The look on his face when you asked me about the chicken!"

Connor, involved in a baseball game, had declined to go with them. He was in the charge of Mrs. Halloway, owner of a silver 1950 Cadillac and sharp-eyed mother of three boys also playing in the game.

"Oh, I'm guilty all right. So I want him on my side. Can't blame me for that. Connor's a great kid. Honest, straightforward, protective of his mother. Too smart to let her date a car wash magnate." He took Callan's sketchpad away from her and tucked it under his arm. "I'm glad to know that you're not letting old green bean Chudy carry your books home from school."

"Come on, Sam," Callan said, snatching back the sketchpad. "Since meeting you, I feel like I've entered a time warp and gone back twenty years. It's hard enough keeping things straight, what's now and what was then. Don't confuse things more."

"Maybe things haven't changed as much as you think. I'm still the same big-nosed, homely kid. Fascinated by people and what makes them tick. Still charmed by a certain young lady. Same as back in Apple Springs."

"You were never homely! You were the best-looking guy in town."

"Hah! Thanks, though. You were the only girl who believed that. You'll never know how much you did for my callow male ego."

"You're welcome. Glad I could be of help," she answered.

The path narrowed and grew steeper, and it was an excuse for not continuing the discussion. Better to let the past go and explore future possibilities. Following him up the trail, she considered his confession and what it signified about their present relationship, if The Gull allowed her to have a future.

Beyond the boulders, the trail continued on, winding along the top of the ridge, but shortly a small grassy glen opened out on the left, snuggled between a deep ravine and in a fold in the hill. A ring of tumbled boulders offered seats and encircling pines gave shade from the fierce golden afternoon sun. A chipmunk scurried over the rocks and disappeared up a tree at their approach.

"Let's stop here," Callan said. "I've been dying for a chance to do a little sketching."

Sam selected a smooth-sided rock in the shade, stretched out with his back against it, and laced his fingers across his ribs. She perched on a nearby rock and opened the sketchpad to the first unblemished page.

More than fifteen years had passed since she had done more than doodle while on the phone. Would any talent or skill be left after so long? For a moment she hesitated, afraid that what had been so casually taken for granted long ago would have irrevocably decayed in the intervening years. If nothing were left, the loss would be hard to bear again. Only one way to find out. Sam's long form offered familiar inspiration. He posed for her, head tilted back against the boulder, watching clouds move across the sky. She had sketched him this way many times during their excursions into the woods outside Apple Springs. Taking a deep breath, she pulled a soft-lead pencil from her pocket and began.

A few minutes later, the head and shoulders sketch of Sam was done. She was amazed at the results. Her hand hadn't forgotten what to do. Surprisingly, her technique hadn't diminished, as if, even tucked away in hibernation, her style had matured and continued to evolve without her conscious guidance.

Sam regarded her for a moment then held out his hand and said, "Could I see it, Callie?"

She moved over and set beside him, her hip brushing his. Was her estimation of the drawing accurate or just wishful thinking? For a moment she didn't want to expose it to his criticism. Handing him the pad, she waited, muscles tight, as he studied the sketch, and his spontaneous grin and nod of approval produced such a deep relief and satisfaction that her eyes misted.

"You've still got it." He carefully set aside the pad and reached for her. "Now it's my turn for your undivided attention."

Sam drew her against him, chest to breast, with her face nestled in the curve of his neck. His arms wrapped around her firmly, and he dropped a kiss on her temple. She hugged him back and snuggled deeper into the embrace. The muscles of his chest, shoulders and arms felt as solid as the rock he leaned against. Sam-perfume enveloped her like a moss bouquet and sunlight on water.

His hands caressed and kneaded her back. Her shirt, knotted at the waist above her jeans' waistband, slipped up, and his fingers unerringly found her bare skin to stroke. The embrace left her both languid and soft with contentment, melting and needy with desire. It had been years since she had been held with such simple, complete tenderness.

"Sam-perfume," she murmured against his neck.

"Ummm?" he questioned and stirred, molding her tighter against his chest, as he dropped delicate kisses across her cheek, ending with her shirt collar pulled back and his lips nibbling at her neck, his tongue wetting her skin with delicate traces of fire. His hand slipped up to cup the side of her breast and almost frantically, he transferred back to her mouth and began enthralling her with slow-moving, demanding lips and tongue. Fierce tremors shook her, whirling her into a vortex where there was no bittersweet past and no need for tomorrow.

She didn't know exactly when he stopped kissing her and just held her, rocking her gently in his arms, his cheek pressed against her hair, his breathing uneven.

If he had continued, she wouldn't have stopped him. As teenagers, he was always the one to call a halt to their petting before they went too far, saying he loved her too much to put her at risk. He wanted more for them than furtive sex. They would wait until they were older for their first time, and had the maturity and resources to handle any consequences. Their first times had passed and each of them had shared it with another.

He had been right, then and now, but each denial had taken something out of her, leaving behind a residue of bitterness at its necessity. One more denial was too many, and the rage and disappoint clawed like a snarling animal in the pit of her stomach, the same reaction she'd felt long ago.

She wanted to pound his chest in frustration. Instead she clung to him, letting him rock them, afraid to disturb her precarious emotional balance by even taking a deep cleansing breath or moving away. Fear of the desire roaring through her kept her silent and tense in his arms. Her self-control and her self-respect could be easily forfeited under an unwise move or a light caress.

The disobedient, painful ache in her middle subsided gradually as she sought calm and an end to the agony of craving. Rigid in his arms, her empathetic perception picked up his emotions and she knew his struggle for self-command was equally as vicious and tormenting as her own. She could only wonder at his control. Suddenly, under the waning passion, she caught another emotion flowing like an underground river within him. Caution, a disquiet that she couldn't quite decipher. The trace emotion disappeared as quickly as it had come, leaving her wondering about its origin. It felt somehow connected with her, but she'd never given him reason to fear or distrust her.

After a few more minutes, his fierce embrace relaxed. She scooted away, putting a few inches between their bodies although her head remained lightly resting against his shoulder.

In a low, serene voice he said, "I remember the first time I held you like this. We were ten. Your mom let you out of the house after several days in bed with a bad cold. You were supposed to stay on the back porch, but we sneaked away and headed for the woods. Do you remember?"

Callan recalled that day. It had been wonderful to see Sam after being cloistered in her room for days, and stepping out into the sun and running across the pasture to the line of trees beyond seemed the essence of freedom. "I remember," she whispered.

"It was early spring, the sun was shining, but a chilly wind blew out of the north," Sam went on. "By the time we hit the trees, you were cold. Tired out and wheezing. There was a sunny sheltered place nearby in a circle of rocks, much like here. We sat down, just as we are now, chest to chest. I pulled my jacket around you and you rested your head against my shoulder, like now. Then you fell asleep.

"Your nose was red and peeling. Cold too. You sniffled against my neck. You smelled like the Vicks VapoRub your mother rubbed on your chest."

Callan grinned at the memory of her mom's remedies for a cold. The memory of the pungent smell brought a flash of deep nostalgia for childhood days in bed with books, sketch pads, a box of tissues, and her mom's ever-present chicken soup drunk from a large mug. Sam hugged her tighter, eliminating the few inches she had put between them and went on.

"While you slept, I watched the clouds and listened to the birds. I liked holding you. You were my best friend, and protecting you, helping you, was satisfying in a way I had never experienced before.

"Sometime during that hour by the rock, I knew way down deep that I wanted to be a doctor when I grew up. That I'd never be happy doing anything else. You were my inspiration in more ways than you know."

"What do you mean?" she asked, uneasy with where this was leading.

"I suppose, in some unconscious way, the wonderful things you could do with your mind made me realize that anything was possible, even for a homely kid from a little burg like Apple Springs. Besides, you were always with me when I had a revelation about other people or myself or when something profound happened to me. You gave me many firsthand examples of the marvels in this world and an inkling that I wasn't limited to what Apple Springs had to offer. I could go out and contribute somehow."

She tilted her head and looked into his eyes. He gazed back with just enough amusement behind the copper glow in his eyes to let her know that he understood the revelation was rather weighty for a young boy. He was scared that she'd laugh at him.

She wouldn't laugh. He had either given her the most sublime tribute she had ever received, or another example, in a long line of such instances, of being set apart as an outcast. She didn't want to be too blunt and point out that negative, so she said simply, "Thank you, Sam. Maybe you give me too much credit for what would have happened whether or not I had been there."

"No, I don't think so. You were always my oracle."

She didn't know what else to say, so for a moment she looked back at him, wondering how deep his feelings went for her. Were they nothing but stale leftovers from their shared past? Or, even if they were, could something more lasting be built on that foundation?

The sun had lowered to a hand's width above the mountains, and of the same mind, they rose and brushed pine needles from their clothes. She retrieved the sketchpad and walked beside him back to the trail.

Just before the first turn in the trail the air suddenly felt thick and clammy. A presence hovered nearby, evasive and menacing, but definitely there.

"Wait," she cautioned. "Something's wrong."

Sam scanned the area, shook his head and looked back at her, puzzled. "What is it? What's wrong?"

She slipped down to the theta level and let her awareness expand outward to take in the clearing behind them and the trail ahead. A sinuous serpentine shadow, primitive at the core, moved across the surface of her mind. Narrowing her mind focus, she tracked the elusive presence to a tumbled rock pile at the base of the left-hand boulder next to the trail.

"Rattlesnake." She pointed to the shaded area where its diamond-patterned, gray-brown length lay camouflaged atop a rock. In passing, they would have come within a foot of the rattler, and its rock perch was at thigh level, perfect for a strike.

"Shall we look for another way down?" Sam asked. "I don't want to kill it just so we can get by."

"Let me try something I learned yesterday."

Callan dipped down into theta again and reached with a tenuous mind probe for the snake. At first touch, the undulating suppleness of the serpent made her flinch in disgust. It reacted to the probe, and the diamond-shaped head swept upward and a buzzing warning followed. She caught her breath and jerked back.

She reached out again reluctantly and with her mind examined the cool dry skin and the whippy pliancy of its body. When she thought she could bear the feel of it for longer than a second, she imagined a tentacle wrapping around the agitated snake at midpoint. Sensing the mind grasp, it writhed and struck at empty air. Lifting quickly, she transported the thrashing reptile over the top of the boulder and above the brush-filled ravine behind. There were cushioning bushes below. She released it. It made a soft rustling noise dropping through the leaves and branches.

"I hate snakes!" She rubbed her hands on her jeans then pressed her fingers against her temples. "How do I get the snake feel out of my head? I can't take my brain out and wash it!"

Sam was looking at her, fascinated and obviously discomfited, with overtones of wonder on his face, much like when he discovered that Rosemary and she were conversing telepathically. The look set her apart from him, and she loathed the idea he might find her freakish. Having him think of her as awesome in any way would be just as bad. *Different, apart always, different*, her mind chanted.

"Don't you dare look at me that way, Sam Cavendar!" she said, poking him hard in the midriff with her forefinger. He twitched at the jab. She didn't want to be his oracle or inspiration. The idea made her furious.

"I'm Callie, just a woman, and no different than I've ever been. Remember that! And get that impressed look off your face right now!" She poked him again.

"Sorry. I've gotten used to paper airplanes flying around, but flying snakes will take time." His expression cleared and he grinned at her. "I'll bet that poor snake is making tracks for the Mexican border."

She grinned back, her anger dissipating, glad that he was resilient enough to recover quickly. If they were to continue to be friends or anything else, he would just have to get used to a few little anomalies occurring now and then.

She started to tell him how she had done her laundry the day before, but a furtive prickle flickered across her mind. The mental touch winked out abruptly. Only Bianca caused that irritating itch. She placed a detaining hand on Sam's arm and slipped partly into a guarded theta state. She smelled rotting onions. It was the black gull's calling card, and often preceded its appearance. It was somewhere nearby. Although she searched for further evidence of it, the path and hilltop were suddenly blank psychically.

Had the psychic touch been just a quick check on her whereabouts or a forewarning of something more serious? How long had Bianca been spying on them that afternoon? What had she seen? Before sensing the rattler, everything seemed normal. If Bianca saw the snake levitate, it would reveal the extent of Callan's emerging telekinetic power. Even worse, if Bianca had spied on them during their embrace, she would realize Sam was more than a casual friend. The violation of her privacy and the possible danger to Sam caused her heart to pound faster than during her contact with the rattler.

"What's the matter, Callie? You're so pale." He put his arm around her waist and pulled her closer to his side.

"I guess I've just realized what I did a moment ago. The Gull was here too," she whispered, as she jerked away and headed down the path. "Let's get back down. I shouldn't have left Connor."

For the remainder of the afternoon, Callan kept Sam at a distance, not letting him hold her hand as they walked back to the park from the ridge. At the quizzical expression in his eyes at her standoffish behavior, she whispered, "She might be watching, so we've got to act casual."

He obviously didn't agree with the implication that he needed protecting, but didn't pursue the subject and let her alone.

* * * * *

They returned to her house just as the sun touched the tops of the mountains. Connor, as usual after one of his athletic contests, wore a good portion of the Colorado terrain. He'd resented sitting on the picnic tablecloth on the way home so as not to soil Evelyn's mauve and ivory upholstery. He went upstairs for a quick shower before going to the Ellisons' for dinner. Sam followed her into the kitchen.

He leaned against a counter, somberly watching her unpack the picnic hamper, and then said, "I'm not up-to-date on what you and Rosemary have been doing. The snake stunt shows you're incredibly more powerful than when you were a kid. Would you tell me what's been going on, and why you backed away from me, both physically and emotionally, this afternoon?"

"I'm sorry you felt rejected, Sam." She put a handful of utensils in the sink and faced him. "I wasn't playing games. I sensed Bianca lurking, spying on us. I don't want her to zero in on you as a possible hostage. We're safe enough here in my house and can talk freely. I've got a thick astral shield around it."

Sam shifted position against the counter as though the idea of some paranormal power hanging over his head made him uneasy. A sudden undercurrent of wariness emanating from him made her skittish as well.

Maybe, like Dr. Ostherhaut, he upheld the terrestrial over the otherworldly, emotionally unable to accept a reality so radically outside the commonplace. For a moment, Callan felt disappointed that he was in any way inflexible. He'd never be comfortable around her if he was. No matter what Sam's feelings about her abilities or situation, he must have the facts as she knew them, however unconventional they might be. Let him make his decisions based on her new reality. Otherwise, they could never have an honest relationship.

"You've got to remain distant from me, stay neutral and distant in this war," she continued, determined that he understand the danger he might face from an association with her. "Rosemary and I think it's likely Bianca will threaten or even try to harm my friends and relatives to force me to submit to her."

"You believe she might zero in on me?"

"Yes, if we spend much time together or she sees us like we were this afternoon on the ridge. I should never have let you come near me. I wouldn't blame you if you left right now. In fact, that might be your best bet. I could lose, you know. One way or another, I don't expect this struggle will take much longer."

"You're not going to lose, Callie. There's no chance of me leaving either." He pulled her into his arms, brushing her hair away from her face and kissing her temple. "You're not facing this woman alone anymore. We'll be casual and platonic in public and not give her a reason to bother with me. Remember, she never pulled anything on me back in Apple Springs, and we were together constantly for years. Maybe I'm immune to her psychic exploitation."

He was right. The Gull had never threatened him. Callan wanted to believe in everything he said. "All right. If you're willing to take the risk."

He grinned and pulled the wine from the open cooler. "Why don't we finish this before Connor comes down? You can tell me all about the astral plane and what you and Rosemary do there. Are non-psychic tourists allowed?"

"Maybe."

The idea of escorting Sam to the plane, sharing the place with him, seeing how his pillar was marked, sent a jolt of both excitement and dread through her. Would his pillar reveal some abysmal flaw in his character that would destroy her perception of him? That kind of intimate knowledge could provide the answer to his strange subterranean feelings toward her, but could also forever bar a future together.

Chapter Nine

ЮЭ

"...and it must have been the North Pole because there was snow around and all these huge trees with colored lights. Mom and me and this other lady, we got one and I pulled it a long way to where a bunch of others were. Before we found it, we went through this white swamp and got attacked by a white rhino..."

I thought it was an alligator, Callan reflected, listening to Connor telling Zach about his interesting dream the night before. At least Connor's trip to the astral plane hadn't been a nightmare for him.

"Then this big black jet tried to strafe us, and then this humongous Christmas tree shot a missile at it ..."

Zach, who looked like his father but had his mother's temperament, tolerantly listened to Connor's tale.

From the Ellisons' patio, Callan looked up at the stars and knew an intense feeling of well-being. The evening air was cool and mellow in contrast to the baking heat of the day, and soothed the slight sunburn on her cheekbones acquired during the picnic. Many of those she cared for were close by — Connor and Sam, Stephanie and her family. The two boys slouched at the patio table, pursuing crumbs around the bottom of the brownie pan. Stephanie sat next to her in a wicker chair with a sleepy Katie in her lap. Inside, Matt and Sam had Matt's fossil collection spread out on the dining room table. According to Stephanie, Matt only bored people he liked with his collection.

"Callan? Hey, Mighty Mouse, where are you? Is something the matter with your finger?" Stephanie asked, interrupting her woolgathering. "You keep rubbing it."

"It's sore. I don't know what I did to it. Must have gotten a stranglehold on my sketching pencil this afternoon."

It occurred to her then that if she had tightened down on the pencil hard enough to cause a sore, cramped index finger, she wouldn't have been able to draw as fluidly as she had. Then she remembered poking Sam above his belt buckle after moving the rattlesnake. He hadn't flinched much and there had been no give to his middle, although she'd given him a considerable jab. She began to chuckle.

"Share the joke. Some powerful picture you drew to give you a sore finger. By the way, what did you draw?"

Fighting snickers, Callan choked out, "Sam."

She could imagine what Steph would say if she found out Callan had an answer to the condition of Sam's abdominal muscles. She remembered her initial misunderstanding of the term "ripped". He was that all right, enough to give her finger a major charley horse. If Stephanie found out her method of discovery, her derisive, outrageous comments would likely attract the attention of Connor and Zach. A full-bodied laugh burst from her. She couldn't hold it in.

"The drawing must be naughty. That was the most wanton laugh I've ever heard from you. I want to see what you drew. You're holding out on me."

"I wasn't laughing about the sketch."

"If you're going to be stingy and not tell me what's so funny, I'm putting the wee one to bed," Steph commented, with one of her knowing sidelong glances. "I'll get it out of you later," she threatened, heading for the house.

"You're welcome to try," Callan called after her. "I'll clear up the last of the dishes for you."

She retrieved the brownie pan, which the boys had scoured so thoroughly it looked as if it had already been washed. Together, the three of them collected the last of the scattered glassware and plates and put them in the dishwasher.

After they finished, she was relieved when Connor challenged Zach to a game on the Ellisons' computer. They ran off to the basement. If they had chosen to kick around a ball on the lawn, she would have had to watch them and she didn't want to. She felt vulnerable outside after dark. Since the coming of Bianca, she felt secure only inside under a strong protective aura.

"Sam has offered to show me a new area for fossil hunting," Matt told her when she entered the dining room. Sam looked up from a rock he was examining and smiled, with all the wattage of his charm behind it. Warm coils of desire traveled through her. She reminded herself that it wouldn't be wise to fall totally under that impressive charm. He was still an unknown quantity. Furthermore, a remnant of distrust from the fiasco of their original parting still lingered. Wise or not, she yearned to snuggle into his lap, nuzzle his neck and explore various parts of his anatomy.

"Would you like to see my fossil, lady?" Sam asked with a suggestive wink.

Blatant flirting from Sam was certainly a novelty. Shy and serious, he hadn't been inclined toward provocative comments or even subtle come-ons during their teen years. The eroticism he was projecting now certainly wasn't bashful.

"Sure would," she said, putting all the seductive invitation that she could muster into the answer.

They weren't naïve teenagers anymore, so perhaps this was a sign that he wouldn't keep up the too-respectful, worshipful attitude he'd displayed on the mountain that afternoon. When the time was ripe to take another step together, undue reverence could form a barrier. Eventually, perhaps he would explain his actions long ago and give her something to understand and live with, so the trusting bond they'd had as kids could blossom again.

She rested her hand on his shoulder and gave a squeeze to the hard plane of muscle. When her finger twanged in complaint, she almost laughed aloud. Sam looked up at her, the lines around his eyes deepening and slanting upward, and put his arm around her waist, his hand resting on her hip, and pulled her closer to his side.

Matt ignored the by-play and enthusiastically showed her his newest acquisition, a sliver of rock bearing the imprint of a delicate fern-like plant, and then followed up with a lecture on its likely genesis.

As she listened to him, disquiet crept in and the serenity of the evening slowly vanished under the blank gaze of the darkened dining room windows. The nervousness grew into anxiety and the warmth of Sam's arm around her didn't dispel it. Stephanie seemed to be taking a long time putting Katie to bed.

"The fossil is fascinating, Matt. Thanks for showing it to me. I'd like to use the design in a drawing sometime. I'm going upstairs to see what's keeping Stephanie."

Something had invaded the house. It was insidious and dangerous. She had to get upstairs. When she pulled away from Sam, he looked quizzically at her and frowned.

"Callie?"

Matt didn't look up from replacing his fossils in their proper slots. "Tell her I'm about to cut the apple pie. If you don't hustle, the guys will finish it off without you," he said.

"We'll be right down," she replied, shaking her head at Sam. Before he could question her further, she hurried toward the foyer and the stairway.

"Steph?" she called softly, pausing at the top of the stairs. The hallway was shadowy, lit only by a faint spill of light from Katie's open bedroom door at the end of the passage. The agitated swish of tree leaves in the rising night wind invaded the hall. The draft was cold and musty. The intensifying rustle from the trees obliterated the chirrup of the crickets.

As she cautiously moved down the hall, her newly honed clairvoyance opened to encompass the house. It focused on

Katie's room. Bianca's mental scent emanated from the room like moldy onions, rancid and cloying.

The familiar mental itch and pressure hit hard. A pool of burning oil expanded behind her eyes. The hallway vanished in a white corona like multiple flashbulb explosions. She gave a soft cry of pain and blundered into a wall. Clinging to it for support, she fought the headache that was hammering her to her knees. It was impossible to draw a breath around the pain. Nothing The Gull had ever done had hurt so hellishly. It drove out her alarm for Stephanie and Katie and smashed her determination to protect them. A titter worked itself around the pain in her head.

Then the sugary voice of The Gull said, *Ah, poor little sister, you are so stubborn. Are you having fun playing with your puny childish power, little one? Enjoying your new toy, are you? Remember, I warned you about the fragility of others. We can take everyone you love. One by one. Until you are all alone. Then you will come to Us, grateful for Our love and comfort. We'll be waiting, dear sweet sister.*

The agony in her head retreated to a dull ache. She gasped for breath and moaned in relief. Her sight returned on a dark wave that washed away the white light. The Gull was gone. She didn't know how long she had stood there frozen with the pain. What had The Gull done to Steph and Katie? She pushed upright and lurched the last few feet to the bedroom doorway.

"Steph," she croaked out, terrified by the myriad forms of damage Bianca could execute on unprotected minds.

Only a small Donald Duck lamp on the dresser lighted the room. The window was open a few inches and the curtains fluffed inward on a cool breeze. Stephanie stood unmoving by Katie's crib, her back to the door, arms lax at her sides. Her head drooped as if she stared down at the baby. Callan crossed the room and grasped her arm.

"Stephanie, are you okay?"

She didn't move or lift her head. Katie lay on her stomach, her breathing slow and even. Callan reached out to the baby with a brief mental probe. Katie was unscathed and in a natural sleep.

Gently, Callan turned Stephanie toward her and with a finger under her chin lifted her head. The eyes were open and stared unblinking, without recognition. The faint freckles scattered across her nose and cheekbones stood out against chalky skin. Callan brushed the surface of her mind with a light touch. All the intelligence, dry wit and generosity that formed Stephanie's personality had vanished. The spirit that motivated this body was nowhere in evidence. The blankness of her mind and the vacancy of the staring eyes ravaged Callan with guilt and grief.

"No, Stephanie," she moaned. She had been harmed simply because she was Callan's friend.

Stephanie's body sagged, and she slipped a supporting arm around her waist. As her head lolled on Callan's shoulder, she caught a faint panicked wail, seemingly from light years away, and recognized her friend's cry. Bianca hadn't destroyed her mind, only somehow blocked it from the unresponsive body she held.

Stephanie? Callan sent out a questing thought but the wail continued, a telltale wisp echoing faintly in her mind.

An urging, guiding arm was enough to get Stephanie to walk to the rocking chair by the window. Pressure on her shoulders caused her to sit. Her head dropped against the rocker's high back. When Callan knelt in front of her, she stared unseeing past her left shoulder.

Callan had never deliberately tried to read another's mind, only picking up fragmentary thoughts spewed out during emotional storms. Her telepathy practice with Rosemary had been a mutually agreed upon conversation. They hadn't delved into each other's inner psyche. The idea of invading Stephanie's mind was repugnant, but it couldn't be avoided if she was to discover precisely what Bianca had done. It must be done quickly, before one of the men came searching for them.

All her psychic power would be needed. She deliberately slowed her breathing and struggled to find the deepest theta state. Her fear and worry kept impeding her concentration, but finally she felt the third eye form on her forehead, the indigo vortex whirling outward from her inner cosmos to connect with the outer universe. Its vigorous pulsing whisked away her near-hysteria and left her clairvoyance and telepathy raw, sensitive and all-enveloping.

A hand on Stephanie's cheek brought the blank eyes to a level with her own. She focused the power of the third eye on the empty brown eyes and glided into Stephanie's mind as effortlessly as carving a slab of softened butter.

A lackluster gray plain spread infinitely around her. A few yards ahead, a black wall bisected the plain from leaden horizon to leaden horizon and rose into a featureless murkiness overhead. It appeared to have been constructed of bricks made of some satiny material that shimmered like a black pearl. The faint sobbing was clearer now but seemed to come from all directions.

Diffusing the focus of the third eye, she ranged outward in search of the spirit that she knew as Stephanie. Only the bleak expanse of wall and the hollow wail filled the void that had been a vibrant mind. She cast about, following the wall to each side for what seemed like miles. It appeared to extend forever.

Finally, she soared above it, hunting the source of the ghostly cries. From that perspective, the wall was actually a narrow vault that meandered over the plain. There was nothing else but the featureless, endless wall, and there was no entrance that she could see, so she returned to her starting point. The cries were definitely coming from inside the vault. Had Bianca destroyed Stephanie's intellect or only imprisoned it within the serpentine vault?

The smooth surface was hard, cold to the touch, with no fleshy give to the surface. It radiated terror. She snatched her hand away. Cautiously, she again lay her hand against the stone, ready to retreat if the terror seemed inclined to overflow into her. The horror remained encased in the wall.

With a focused beam of telepathy she called, *Stephanie, Stephanie! Answer me! Where are you?*

The call slid off the polished surface and dissipated around her. How could she get in? She dared not use telekinesis within a fragile physical brain to break the barrier. Frantic in the forbidding emptiness and silence of what had been her friend's lively mind, Callan withdrew to the quiet bedroom. She had no notion how to deal with this catastrophe.

Katie whimpered in her sleep. Callan flinched at the small mewing sound in the strained hush of the room. The murmur of the wind outside seemed unnaturally muted. Time was short. Soon Matt would come looking for them. He mustn't see his wife like this. Losing Stephanie to a strange catatonia would devastate him and their children. At the sight of her condition, he would certainly call the rescue squad. Conventional medicine would have no remedy for this state. Stephanie would be condemned to molder in some institution.

Rosemary. She must have some arcane knowledge up her sleeve to restore Stephanie. Callan had never tried to contact her telepathically from such a distance. She didn't even know the range of her telepathic ability. It was another of the many things that they hadn't gotten around to investigating. She made the third eye spin faster on her forehead and the flickering sapphire light painted the walls of the room.

Rosemary! She launched her mental energy toward the southeastern suburb where Rosemary lived. *Rosemary, help! Please answer!*

Callan, turn down your volume, child. No need to scream. What's the matter? came the reply, in Rosemary's usual steadfast mind voice.

Bianca did something awful to Stephanie. She's blocked away her mind. I can't find her anywhere. She's like a zombie. We've got to do something right away. There's a black vault in her mind, she's in there somewhere and I can't get in. What should I do?

That sneaky bitch. What's she done now? Rosemary's astral presence filled the room. Callan was so startled at her sudden appearance that she nearly screamed.

Okay, Rosemary instructed, *let's get back in there. I'll piggyback with you.*

Callan refocused her third eye and entered again to stand before the intimidating black vault. Rosemary appeared beside her, dressed in a long, flowing flowered robe. She hadn't bothered to assume her usual Amelia Earhart persona.

I heard Stephanie cry out right after Bianca left, and I keep hearing her. I think Bianca's walled her up behind that. Feel it. It's as if all of Stephanie's fright is there. I tried reaching her with telepathy, but it didn't work. She doesn't hear me.

Rosemary touched the wall. *You're right. Her spirit's left the body and withdrawn behind it. The wall is constructed from Stephanie's fears. Only Stephanie can tear it down.*

So how do I get her to do that? Callan snapped. *I haven't even been able to get her to speak to me.*

Remember the psychic healing I did for you the day we met? I coaxed you into relaxing first, and then helped you to heal yourself. Much of psychic healing is self-healing. Touch the wall, send calm and reassurance to Stephanie. Then help her dissolve the barrier. Easy now. You're not drilling for oil, you know.

Callan was doubtful of the vague instructions, but did as she was told and placed both hands on the vault. It was hard to keep them there as fear seeped into her hands and flowed into her own mind.

Steph? She sent a gentle wave of reassurance against the barrier. The stone at first repelled her repeated calls but gradually began to absorb her entreaty like a huge black sponge.

It's me, Mighty Mouse. I've come to take you home to Matt and the kids. Don't be scared. I won't let anyone hurt you. Be calm and reach out to me. Please, can you do that?

After what seemed an interminable time of repeating the call and beseeching Stephanie to come out, the diamond-hard bricks under her hands warmed, or a least seemed less icy. Encouraged, she continued, as Rosemary waited patiently by her side.

I'm here, Steph. Come to me. Everything will be okay, I promise.

On and on she cajoled, directing the power of her third eye through her hands to soften and penetrate the resistant mental blocks. It would be easier to coax a frightened child from a hidey-hole. Slowly, the terror lessened where her fingers lay splayed, and she sensed a wary, childlike questioning from within the vault.

Yes, Steph, it's me, Callan. You can come out now and we'll go home. It's safe. Here, reach out to me…take my hand. Callan felt Stephanie's presence nearby and delved eagerly back, pleading for her to come out, extending the power of her third eye farther into the breach.

Suddenly, from beyond the barrier, Stephanie's mind touched hers and she gently caught it.

I have you, Steph. Let the wall fall. You don't need it anymore.

For what seemed another eon, Callan felt her uncertainty and fear, but finally the vault dissolved into glittering black sand drifts. The sand contracted into whirlwinds that spun across the empty plain to disappear over the horizon.

Stephanie stood before her, gripping her hands. Tears flowed down her face. Callan had never seen her cry before. That Bianca could make her feisty friend cry in fear enraged her, and she wanted very much to pound something. Quickly, she reined in the emotion, not wanting to alarm Stephanie. Catching sight of a strange woman, Stephanie flinched and stepped back.

This is Rosemary, Callan quickly reassured her. *She came to help.*

Stephanie managed a polite nod, which Rosemary returned. Steph immediately turned back to Callan, grabbed her shoulders and stammered out, *The Gull! Its beak and head came through the bedroom wall, right above Katie's crib. It was huge! The awful eyes! I saw it eating us—in my mind—pecking and ripping us to pieces. Oh, god, I believed we were going to die, torn up by the sharp beak! I've never been so scared! I was all alone in a dark place for such a long time...then you came. Is Katie all right? Where are we?*

Katie's fine, and we're inside your mind, Callan informed her.

Really? Stephanie looked curiously around as she wiped away tears with the back of her hand. *This is weird. Not very busy is it? I supposed I had more in my head than all this vacant space.* Her sense of humor was returning along with her aplomb.

Your spirit retreated into the primitive part of your mind that holds primal fears. There is no intellect here, Rosemary explained. Callan noted that she had assumed an uncharacteristic, seer-like dignity.

Oh. Well, that's a relief, Stephanie answered in an ironic tone. *Are you two going to put the whammy on bird girl soon? Being sent to a dungeon in your own head is really scary and annoying. Can't you pluck her tail feathers?*

Soon, Callan promised, *she'll be as bald as a Thanksgiving turkey. Baked a nice shiny brown, too.*

Roasted in hell, I hope, she answered, jamming her hands into the front pockets of her blue denim jump suit. *So, how do we get out of my head?*

We jump out through your eyeballs, silly.

Stephanie's mouth dropped open.

Gotcha! Callan felt smug and then ashamed for teasing Steph at such a time. Stephanie's derisive snort and appreciative grin were a relief.

Rosemary cocked an eyebrow at their banter but only said to Callan, *I think an extra-protective aura over Stephanie, her family and her house is in order.*

I'll take care of it right away.

I'll meet you later for the trip to the astral plane as usual. Let's get out of here. Rosemary moved to Stephanie's other side, and their astral shields enfolded her spirit. Gently, they led Stephanie's essence away from the primitive mind and let it unfold into the whole of her body.

Callan opened her eyes to find Stephanie, fully cognizant, staring back at her. Rosemary's psychic presence was gone.

To her surprise, Sam squatted beside the rocking chair, the fingers of his left hand holding Stephanie's wrist and his right holding Callan's. His eyebrows were drawn down in worry, but after studying them both intently, he relaxed, dropped their wrists and sat back on his heels.

"Your pulses are back to normal," he said. "You two scared the hell out of me. When I walked in here, the room was filled with a blue light. Like being underwater. You two were spaced out — gone. What happened?"

He stood and stepped back from the rocking chair. Stephanie started to answer him, but Matt appeared in the doorway.

"The pie's cut," he announced.

When he saw Stephanie's drawn face, he joined Callan beside the rocking chair and exclaimed, "Honey, what's the matter?"

Callan moved back to give him room and let Stephanie provide whatever explanation she believed appropriate. She went to check Katie again, caressed her back, grateful for the unformed, peaceful baby dreams radiating from her. She summoned another radiant protective aura to cover the original one surrounding Katie.

Stephanie observed Callan's attention to the small sleeping body and distractedly answered Matt, "I think I'll pass on the pie. I'm feeling a little queasy. Ate too much dinner and definitely shouldn't have had that second beer."

She got up somewhat unsteadily and went to check on Katie too. Accepting Callan's affirmative nod that all was well with the baby, she turned to the others and said, "Let's go downstairs before we wake her up."

Only Matt was truly appreciative of the apple pie. Sam's questions remained unanswered and he seemed preoccupied, and like Callan, he only nibbled at the pie. Her head still ached.

She felt sick to the bone, and worried over Bianca's attack on Stephanie. What would the woman do next?

It was after ten o'clock, and the evening had lost its luster. Callan, already weary after an eventful day, had another trip to the astral plane ahead of her. Stephanie was still pale and obviously needed some rest. Time to call it a night.

On her way to the basement to summon Connor, she paused on the stairs, descended to the theta level and threw the strongest protective aura over the house that she could manage. The place now had two layers. When Zach and Connor passed her on their way up, she gave Zach a friendly pat on the back along with another incandescent aura too. Matt wasn't a hugger, but at the front door, a brief neighborly handclasp was sufficient to drench him with his extra share of aura. Stephanie got a quick hug, a thank you for a delicious dinner, and her own generous layer of shield.

While Sam and Matt were exchanging goodbyes, Callan was able to whisper to Stephanie, "Sleep well. Don't worry. I've got you so covered that not so much as a feather'll get in here."

Only then, as she reassured Stephanie, did she admit to herself the facts of the situation. In the upstairs hallway, Bianca had rendered her psychically and physically helpless.

The defensive shields over her friends had been penetrated effortlessly. Her own protective aura had been worthless against the power of The Gull. Pain from Bianca's assault lingered, sharp as phantom ant bites in the corners of her mind. Exhaustion and the ache in her head, along with the realization of what might have happened tonight, nearly sent her to her knees.

Chapter Ten

❧

The Ellisons' door shut behind them. The front porch shimmered under the aurora borealis glow of the protective aura Callan had cast around the house. To her eyes it was brighter than full moonlight, easily eclipsing the dim porch light and extending across the lawn almost to the street. The streetlights glowed feebly under its brilliance.

The potency of her spell should have reassured her of the Ellisons' safety, but after Bianca's penetration of her own aura earlier, Callan knew that any confidence in her paranormal powers and competence was absurd. She had no right to tell Stephanie that she and her family were safe from The Gull. No right at all. She'd told a whopper of a lie.

Connor ran down the steps and started across the lawn toward their house.

"Wait, Connor," she called, not knowing what lay concealed in the darkness beyond the illuminating aura light. In an unguarded moment, The Gull could materialize out of the night and attack him.

Connor stopped at the outer range of the astral glow and turned to look back at them. As she and Sam started down the steps, she stumbled in exhaustion, drained from strengthening the Ellisons' protective auras. Sam caught her around the waist, and cold and weak, she leaned into him, craving the incorporeal psychic sustenance that blazed from his muscular body. Without the support of his hard arm, she would have tumbled down the steps to land in a sloppy heap at the bottom.

"Callie, are you okay?" Sam whispered, as he drew her even closer against his side, his tight hold hovering on the edge of pain. "What in hell went on in there tonight?"

"Not hell, Sam. The Gull. Get me home and undercover. The aura there is better than nothing." Her heart was thumping in dread of the eerie shadows around the other houses in the cul-de-sac. Bernie Rabney's house, blotted out in a pool of darkness, appeared as a formless black hump. Sam said nothing more but eased his hold and walked her across the lawn to where Connor waited.

Connor's frown when he saw Sam's arm around her said he felt their intimacy was inappropriate. Connor appeared to enjoy having Sam around, but he needed to accept that there would be physical contact between the two adults. Problems large and small were cropping up faster than she could handle them.

Callan openly leaned against Sam, her arm also around his waist. Might as well begin acclimating Connor to the idea of them touching. If she was lucky enough to get rid of Bianca and had a future of her own choice, she wanted the freedom to explore a relationship with a man, even if it didn't turn out to be with Sam. Since his appearance a week ago, she had come to realize that she had been bypassing that aspect of life for too long, concerned how it would affect her son.

With a sigh, she put her free arm around Connor, including him in their march across the lawn and up their porch steps. The house still glistened with the protective aura that she had renewed early that morning before the picnic.

As Connor opened the front door with his key, Callan asked, "Did you have fun today, Connor?" A quick clairvoyant scan of the house as the door opened revealed no trace of Bianca. Perhaps the woman wouldn't bother with an empty house.

"Yeah, it was great, Mom." Connor stepped through, held the door for them, shut it and engaged the deadbolt. He turned and beamed at her, then included Sam in his cocky grin. "Except for having to ride in the beast. Running off ol' Eddie Chudy was fun," he added with a one-shouldered shrug, giving his key an impudent toss in emphasis. "A guy's gotta look out for his mom, don't you think, Sam? Make sure she doesn't take up with any unsavory characters."

"Oh, don't be such a pill," Callan said, exasperated with him all over again, although not for the comment about Eddie Chudy. "You know you're proud of Evelyn."

"I won't forget this afternoon soon," Sam said, with a husky chuckle as he held out his hand to Connor. With a wry, adult coolness, Connor looked straight into Sam's eyes and firmly shook hands. Callan wondered what subliminal masculine message they exchanged in that moment of enigmatic camaraderie. All that she could pick up was a low-key friendliness from Connor and the usual emotional warmth projected by Sam. Connor's momentary hostility toward Sam seemed to have dissipated. Males were so weird sometimes.

"Me neither. 'Night, Mom...Sam." He headed upstairs to bed without benefit of the tactful suggestion that Callan was prepared to deliver.

She envied Connor his destination. She felt grubby after a hot, active day and wanted a shower and twelve hours of restful sleep undisturbed by nightwalking or a pseudo-feathered adversary. The first wish would be easy to acquire a little later, the others wouldn't be, possibly for days to come, if ever. Meanwhile, Sam stood in her foyer looking expectant. There was no avoiding this interrogation.

She wished she could simply take him upstairs for reassurance as she slept without the question and answer session. The companionship of a warm strong body beside her would counteract the terrors of the night, although the feeling of security would be an illusion. If Bianca shattered the protective aura around the house, Sam would have no defenses against her.

She reluctantly led the way into the living room. "Okay, Sam, ask your questions." She had little defense against a determined Sam with something on his mind.

They sat on the sofa, Sam in one corner, Callan in the other. "I saw a blue light in Katie's room. What was it?"

That was an easy question, although the answer might startle him. She didn't want to talk about what happened earlier, but he wanted an answer now. It was still too raw and chilling in her mind.

"You saw the psychic glow from my third eye. When I call it up, it radiates a deep indigo. Only someone gifted with psychic abilities could have seen it. Rosemary was right, Sam, you have psychic talents yourself. You picked up the vibrations of our telepathic conversation in the conference that first day, too, remember? Then, there is your unique empathy with people, the uncanny way you've always perceived others' feelings, understood their motivations."

He drew a hand over his face and crooked an eyebrow at her. "I've always believed I was devoid of anything psychic. I never realized getting along well with people was exceptional. The concept of my personally having atypical senses is weird, to say the least. I'm just an ordinary guy. I've only recently come to think of a psychic as being in the same category as an exceptional athlete or a gifted artist."

"One thing you are not, Sam, is ordinary." Keeping the conversation on his psychic abilities would distract him, although it was only fair that he should be cautioned about Bianca. Right now she couldn't even save herself, much less him. She was terrified. Warning him would probably scare him to death and send him running. The only thing she could do was keep talking and hope Rosemary would have some ideas when they met later.

Callan sank deeper into the couch and forged on. "Rosemary says that Dr. Ostherhaut is clairvoyant and has a large measure of empathy, like you, but refuses to admit it. Using it, even subconsciously, makes him unusually effective as a doctor. Scientific and linear thinking has corrupted him, she says, and doesn't give credit to his mystical side. From what I've seen on the ethereal plane, she is absolutely right about his spiritual and paranormal power. You should cultivate your talents and not dismiss them just because they're not easy to measure scientifically."

Sam's mouth twitched. Obviously, he was suppressing amusement at her lecture. He made no reply to her suggestions. Instead, his hand shot out, caught her wrist and tugged gently, urging her to his end of the couch. She went willingly and let him gather her into his arms. Reclining against him, chest to breast, they were in the same position as that afternoon on the ridge.

"Never mind my third-rate psychic abilities, Callie." He removed the clip securing her hair at the nape of her neck and ran his fingers through the strands until it was loose and full. When he began to caress and massage her shoulders and neck, Callan sighed and settled fully into his arms, feeling like sweet chocolate melting in the sun. The headache was lifting. She put her arm around his waist, snuggled her face into the curve of his neck and inhaled his rainwater scent. Even after a day in the sun, he still smelled fresh. Maybe his body reflected a clean spirit. She'd have to research that subject.

He kissed her forehead and said, "Okay, now that we're comfortable, tell me what went on over there tonight? The third eye…you and Stephanie like waxwork figures? You both looked haunted when you came around. It was the eeriest thing I've ever seen."

He continued to stroke her neck and back. He hadn't been sidetracked in the slightest. With him still on target, there was no use avoiding the issue.

"The Gull paid Stephanie a visit. She forced Stephanie into a fear-induced trance. Bianca ambushed me with a headache when I went upstairs. Nearly knocked me out. Rosemary and I managed to retrieve Stephanie though."

His caresses were making it difficult to form a coherent narrative. She ended with her primary fear, whispering it into his neck. "Since she can break through my personal aura and incapacitate me, I have no defense against her. She can probably shred the protection I've put around our houses and get in. If I lose this war, everyone I love, you, Connor, the Ellisons and other family members could join me as Bianca's slaves."

Putting him first in her list of those she loved had just slipped out. She was glad. Prudence and courting games didn't seem important under the threat of annihilation. The vague misgivings she'd harbored about him had vanished. The reason he had dumped her was still unanswered, but she sensed no deceit in him now, only esteem for her and a deep affection.

His desire had grown over the minutes they'd been cuddling. It surged now through his body, mounting and ebbing repeatedly, igniting her own passion as she had related the evening's action. Outwardly, Sam seemed completely in command of himself, holding her gently while fingering her hair, caressing her cheek, asking an occasional question. If his feelings for her weren't love, they were certainly close. An opportunity to tell him how she felt might never come again. She tilted her head back to look into his face.

In the lamplight, his eyes glowed like antique bronze. Although he hadn't reacted outwardly to her declaration, she knew he had heard her statement and understood the implication. His heartbeat had quickened when she'd included him with those she loved. Maybe he was only reacting to his own jeopardy. No, there was worry in him for her, but she could discern no fear or panic.

Passion, tenderness, and yes, love cascaded from him as clearly and as vibrantly as his own scent, his Sam-perfume. She wouldn't probe his mind, but she was certain of what he felt for her. Still he was silent. His reticence was puzzling. All of a sudden, under the passion, she caught a buried flash of sorrow, edged around with caution and doubt. He still had some negative emotions about her. The realization made her feel hollow and hopeless. Then again, it could be caused simply by lingering guilt over abandoning her years ago.

"You won't lose this war, Callie love," he said, before she could get a deeper impression of the emotions uncoiling from the depth of his psyche. "If I have any clairvoyance at all, it's telling me so now. Remember what I told you this afternoon on the hill? How you were always my guiding oracle?

"I always felt that way about you," he continued. "Because of this otherworldly strength in you, I always believed that your decisions were unerring, guided by something mystical. Destiny, perhaps."

"Nobody's infallible. That's ridiculous," she protested, sitting up and pushing away from him, flustered by his confession and knowing that he didn't completely trust her, in spite of his words. "I'm no oracle. You put an unfair burden on me."

"I'm sorry, but I know you'll win over The Gull, because you must." His sincere belief glowed in his aura. It felt reassuring somehow, although she couldn't believe in it. "Never doubt that you have the strength. You're not alone either. You have Rosemary and me, although I'm obviously ineffectual in this situation. I wish I could wrestle the villain to the ground for you. Would you feel safer if I stayed the night? I can bunk down here on the couch."

She nailed him with her eyes and said with sarcasm, "If you ever spend the night, you won't be down here on this couch!"

His eyes sparkled with sensual pleasure, and he brought her back into his embrace, kissing her so thoroughly and expertly that it seemed her astral spirit might break loose of its own accord and fly. Enthralled, she let a segment of her mind slip away to float free.

Shimmering like a net made of diamonds, it rose from the house and spread itself upon the night wind. She called upon Mother Earth to again bequeath her the power of creation. As the ethereal music box played its delicate tune, the spangled net gathered the power, sensuous and fertile, and she welcomed into herself the mother's bounty. With it she raised a pulsing, mighty astral shield about Sam, unlike any she had ever created.

When awareness flowed back, she opened her eyes to find Sam staring at her, a grimace of shock and pain on his face. His body was rigid and his fingers dug painfully, convulsively into her back. The magnitude of his desire was horribly unnatural. The evidence stabbed her hip like a bar of iron. Channeling that much creative power while in his arms was foolhardy. Along with the protective aura, she had unwittingly unleashed the primal sexual element of the Earth's energy field. Untamed, it had overflowed, out of control, into Sam.

The compassionate, self-controlled Sam was gone — submerged in primitive lust, held in a rut no different than that of an animal. It was as terrifying as a rapist with a knife at her throat. Sam's masculinity had never frightened her before.

In panic she strained against him, shoving hard against his shoulders. He ignored her struggles, his hands tightening on her waist painfully. His face hardened, menacing wildness in his eyes. He wanted to keep her, to possess her, as only a female body, without recognition of who she was.

She had wanted him, but not this way, not compelled by a surfeit of erotic force drained from Terra herself. Sam would find having his mind and control ripped away appalling. He might never forgive her. His arousal was blind madness and its overflow snared her as well. In response, an animal growl crept into her throat, and she wanted to fall upon him and let lust drive out the shadows and terrors of the night. She forced the compulsion back, shoving it into the stream of Earth energy she had so foolishly summoned.

"Sam," she called. *Sam*, she sent telepathically, along with the essence of her own life force. She added memories of him, his face as a young boy and the loving words he had spoken this afternoon on the hill. He caught at the memories, as anchors in the struggle for mastery, and battled to purge the savagery within. His hands gradually relaxed and with a twist she slipped free.

She scrambled to the other end of the couch to sit with knees pulled up and arms wrapped around them. Breathing with ragged gasps, he slumped forward, elbows on knees, and head bowed.

"What happened?" he finally choked out. He didn't look at her.

"Earth magic. I wove an astral shield for you, using the Earth's energy field. I wanted to give you strong protection from Bianca." Guilt pecked at her at what she had done.

Minutes passed as he sat hunched forward, not responding to her explanation.

"Hold your hand up toward the lamp. Can you see the shield?" she finally said, wanting to relieve the tension in the room and to somehow justify, to lessen, the horrible violation she had subjected him to.

Lifting his trembling hand sluggishly, he held it against the lamplight. The astral corona extended nearly a foot from his fingers, scintillating with rainbow light.

"Let your eyes go out of focus," she instructed. "It's easier to see."

"I think I see it, but it might only be my imagination." He rubbed a hand across his forehead, removing a film of sweat and lowered the hand again to his knee, obviously still in distress.

"Not imagination. It's real and the only protection I can give you right now." She was almost babbling with guilt and embarrassment. Sam didn't appear to hear her. The room felt airless, and her disordered emotions felt oppressive, crowding around and smothering her.

"I'll take Stephanie and Katie to the ethereal plane tonight," she hurriedly went on, afraid of the silence. "They're in the most danger right now. After them, I suppose Matt and Zach should go tomorrow night. You need protection too. So do my mom and dad and brothers. Who should I pick to go next?"

Sam glanced at her for the first time, his eyes drained and flat brown. He appeared to clutch at the logical question as a diversion. "Take the Ellisons and then your immediate family. With her Latin heritage, Bianca probably attaches greater significance to blood kinship. I can wait. Since I appear to be only a casual friend, she'll take her time getting around to me."

"I wish I could believe that," Callan said, relieved that he was regaining control. "The protective aura marks you. Bianca won't miss its meaning. I couldn't let you leave here tonight without something. Not after what happened at the Ellisons'."

"Speaking of leaving, I'd better get going while I can still move." He awkwardly stood up, still slightly bent over as though straightening to his full height would break his spine.

Callan followed him into the foyer. Remorse and mortification lashed her for subjecting him to such a humiliating ordeal. She had broadsided him with not only a declaration of love, but runaway sex magic. She was an idiot and a wretched tease and wouldn't blame him if he never came near her again.

When he gripped the door handle, she panicked and burst out, "I'm so sorry, Sam. I didn't mean to do that... I was only..."

Sam turned back to her and said distantly, "Don't worry, Callie, I'm okay." A vague smile crossed his mouth.

"I never meant for that to happen. Please forgive me, Sam."

"I haven't been ruined. Believe me, it was quite a turn-on— riveting, in fact." A glimmer of humor surfaced in his eyes. "Be careful though. If that energy got totally out of control, it could incinerate a man, along with you. Call me if you need me. Take care." Then he was gone.

Callan stood staring at the closed, blank door, her hands clenched into tight, bloodless fists. With slow jerky movements, they rose and the knuckles ground sharply into her cheekbones.

"Oooh shit!" she wailed to the empty foyer.

* * * * *

After midnight, Callan's astral projection stood at the foot of the bed and looked down at her earthly body. In her astral eyes, it seemed small and vulnerable in its exhaustion, lying so still, its breathing nearly imperceptible.

The tousled, newly washed hair, crowned by the halo of silver cord, seemed glossier and prettier than when she saw it in the mirror. The nose appeared more pert and less prominent than she had believed, but she hadn't realized before that her chin looked so stubborn.

The impersonal appraisal was moderately interesting, better than dwelling on the debacle earlier with Sam, but of no actual importance. Time to go. She wasn't sorry to leave that poor, worn-out piece of flesh behind for a while.

Callan willed herself outside her bedroom window as Rosemary materialized above the Douglas fir on the front lawn. Her arms were akimbo as she hovered and studied the protective auras covering the Ellisons' house and Callan's.

I can hardly tell these are houses. What did you do? Suck up all the Earth energy in the western hemisphere? she asked.

Not quite. Besides, after the night I've had, I need all the protection I can get.

Got man problems too? The wise aqua eyes in the young face narrowed with amusement and some sympathy.

I don't want to talk about it, so don't pick, Callan snapped back. *What's the procedure tonight? At the rate we're shuttling people upstairs, it'll be Halloween before it's finished. One person at a time is hopeless. Plus my paranormal powers aren't adequate. I forgot to tell you that Bianca broke my protective aura when she got Stephanie. Gave me a headful of boiling oil, while she was at it. Furthermore, I still don't know how to make her stop.*

Callan looked away, ashamed that she was taking out her frustration and fear on Rosemary, who was putting herself in jeopardy for her benefit.

I'm sorry, Rosemary, she said, looking squarely back at her friend. Rosemary seemed unperturbed about her outburst. *I'm scared and still so ignorant. Not even a half-baked psychic yet.*

Rosemary studied Callan for a moment, then said, *You're right to be scared. If Bianca broke your protection, she's tapped into extra power. You'll have to go to the source too. The ethereal plane has enough energy to defeat Bianca's army, although it's dangerous to take too much on at once. Overdone, it can have a harmful impact on the body.*

So what! I have no choice! I'm sick of being Bianca's equivalent of popcorn and a movie! After moving Stephanie's pillar of light tonight, can we do it, whatever it is? We have to take Katie with us too. We can handle both of them, can't we?

Certainly. It's a good idea to start taking them in pairs whenever we can. Let's get at it.

In accord they flew toward the Ellisons' house, where Callan opened a doorway in the protective shield, and they entered Stephanie and Matt's bedroom.

One glance at the bed sent Callan's eyes skittering away. Matt was naked. If he hadn't been curled spoon-fashion against Stephanie with an arm snuggled around her waist, he would have been totally exposed. Matt then rolled over onto his back, and she swallowed a gulp and felt her face grow warm. What else could she expect? Embarrassment was only justice if a person invaded someone else's bedroom in the middle of the night.

This is a horrible invasion of their privacy, Callan mumbled, as they drifted closer to the bed. She kept her eyes fastened on Stephanie's face and away from Matt.

Can't be helped. Go on, coax her spirit out. Rosemary seemed unperturbed by the ethics of the situation.

Callan's tactic to entice Stephanie's astral spirit was much as she had done with Connor, only this time she said that Katie wanted her mother. Stephanie's spirit promptly slipped from her body with an audible pop and stood by the bed. Her eyes were open, and the vacancy in them was similar to her catatonic state earlier that evening. Their strangeness gave Callan a queer shivery feeling.

Stephanie's silver cord draped over her left shoulder, gradually fading into the floor. Totally unlike her usual daytime wear of practical denim, she wore a short, diaphanous sea-green nightgown. Emphasized by the revealing gown, her figure was even more voluptuous than Callan had realized.

Oh, jeez, Callan said with a gulp, as she saw her friend's scanty nightwear, *she can't go out nightwalking like that. Where's her robe?*

She spotted a long cotton kimono lying across a chair and recreated it on Stephanie's astral form, with the belt snugly tied around the waist. Rosemary, looking on with a bemused expression on her face, said nothing.

I just thought of something. What if Matt moves and disturbs Stephanie? Won't that cause her astral spirit to snap back here? Callan asked, remembering Bianca's painful termination of her own first nightwalking attempt.

No, she's used to having her husband beside her. Unless he shoves her out of bed or tries to violently shake her awake, his movements will make no impression on her. Married couples nightwalk all the time without ill effects. Let's get the baby.

Callan and Rosemary, with Stephanie between them, appeared beside Katie's crib. Katie, in her yellow terry sleepers, slept on her stomach, her knees pulled under her and her bottom in the air. Stephanie stared straight ahead, across the crib, engaged in a dream of her own.

What now? Callan asked irritably, emotionally spent from the problems of the day. *How do we coax the astral spirit of a baby? What will move her?*

Her mother, of course. Really, Callan, you must learn to take more initiative, rely more on your common sense and intuition in these matters, Rosemary answered with dry exasperation.

Sorry.

She seemed to have spent the last few hours doing nothing but apologizing to her friends.

Katie, mama wants you to go bye-bye with her, Callan said to the baby in a barely audible mind whisper. Katie stirred and removed her thumb from her mouth.

Katie, Katie sweetie, come to mama.

Katie's astral spirit detached with a whoosh and stood by the crib's railing. Her black curls were flattened on one side. Looking from one to the other, the tiny spirit seemed fully awake and aware of them. Callan ruffled the curls so they stood out around Katie's face. She smiled, displaying her front baby teeth, and held up her arms.

Pick up Katie, Callan said to Stephanie. Stephanie obediently held out her arms, and the child rose from the crib to settle into them. Katie looked around the room as if expecting some entertainment, then popped her thumb back in her mouth.

See, easy isn't it? Since they're not long from the spiritual state, babies are natural nightwalkers, Rosemary commented, as they guided Stephanie back to the master bedroom overlooking the cul-de-sac.

Callan reopened the protective shield and ushered Stephanie through into the night. Suddenly, Rosemary wasn't on Stephanie's other side. She glanced back to check on her.

Rosemary's head and shoulders were behind the bedroom wall, invisible, while her hips, legs and silver cord floated free outside.

Whoa! The pecs and buns on that fella! Callan heard her say.

This was contemptible! Scandalized, she let go of Stephanie, grabbed a handful of leather jacket and gave a yank.

Rosemary, cut that out! she yelled. Rosemary's upper half popped from the wall. *You're disgraceful! Ogling Matt like that!*

Rosemary turned to face her, casually straightening the white silk scarf around her neck. The protective aura around the house flowed shut behind her. Rocking back on her heels on empty air, she hung her thumbs from the front pockets of her pants.

Honestly, Callan, you're such a prude, Rosemary said sardonically. *Sometimes, I think you're the old lady instead of me.*

Stung, Callan retorted, *I am not! I just respect other people's privacy.*

189

That's a load of crap! I see in your mind a picture of that young man half-naked! You can't fool me, I'm psychic.

He mows his front lawn with his shirt off! I can't help but see him if he parades around in public like that!

Oh sure, gawking out your kitchen window, getting an eyeful is more like it!

You stay out of my private thoughts! What would Stephanie think if…where's Stephanie?

Callan whipped around, scanning the area. Stephanie, with a beaming Katie peering back over her shoulder, passed over Bernie Rabney's house and moved steadily eastward.

Chapter Eleven

ɛɔ

Catching up with Stephanie and Katie was immediate, closing the rift between the two psychics was less so. A frigid silence held until they were hovering above the astral plane.

Callan, my dear, I apologize for what I said earlier.

Now was no time to hold a grudge. *I'm sorry too,* Callan replied.

I should have realized, but spending too much time on the astral plane causes our mutual irritability, Rosemary added.

Callan didn't believe that the effects of the astral plane explained Rosemary's uninhibited scrutiny of Matt's physique. She obviously still appreciated a handsome man and she hadn't precisely apologized for ogling Matt. Flaunting that admiration could be laid to nightwalking fatigue, perhaps. Rosemary's astral projection was young and sensual and maybe that reflected her inner being. If Stephanie knew about the incident, she would give that astute grin of hers and say Rosemary had good taste in men, and laugh heartily. And who was Callan to guard Stephanie's husband? Rosemary was right—she was a prude and a hypocrite. She had enjoyed looking at Matt's muscular body just as much as Rosemary had. Neither of them were saints.

I feel wonderful in the astral state, Callan said. *Are you saying that underneath I'm tired?*

Oh, yes. The astral body will feel superb, but your judgment becomes unreliable.

I assumed I was just worried and scared all the time. Although my judgment certainly has been shot lately. You wouldn't believe what I did to Sam tonight.

Rosemary chuckled a little, though with a weary undertone. *I can imagine, considering the Earth energy you pulled in. Remember, the astral body may feel strong, wonderfully light and free in its limitless energy. But the astral body and mind, along with the earthly body, can begin to degenerate without sufficient recuperative time between trips.*

I can't stop coming here for even one night, Rosemary. If I do, someone I care for could be destroyed. Why don't you take a break? I can do shuttle duty by myself. I've got the opening of the gateway and basic nightwalking down pretty good.

Frowning, Rosemary considered as she absently instructed Stephanie to find her pillar of light. Stephanie was still blank-faced but obediently turned and headed in a southerly direction. Held in her mother's arms, Katie, thumb in her mouth, was alert, looking about at the scenery, and seemed to be enjoying the ride. Unlike Connor the night before, Stephanie proceeded at a fast, straight pace, going up and over any incorporeal wildlife, tree forms and energy mounds in their path.

You're right. It's time for you to go solo, Rosemary finally answered, as they sped over the astral plane. *I've loved being with you, flying with you and teaching you this past week. But my earthly body isn't what it once was. It would be prudent of me to do as you say. We can still meet on the earthly plane for your training.*

Good. Learning about my peculiar talents and sharing this adventure with you has been fascinating, but I don't want you becoming ill because of this. I can never repay you for what you've done. By the way, I've got a question I've been meaning to ask about.

What's that?

Do you know where Bianca is? Physically, I mean.

In the mountains, northwest of Denver. At a guess, between seventy and a hundred miles away. I could find her easily enough if I wanted. You could too. You aren't considering tracking her down and forcing a confrontation are you?

The idea had crossed my mind. I can't live with the tension much longer. Something's got to be done about her.

Don't push it, Rosemary cautioned sharply. *Avoid a battle as long as possible. Let her instigate the showdown. You haven't enough experience on the psychic level to formulate a strategy against her. Each day you spend gaining power and learning your craft improves the odds. With some time, you will acquire the flexibility and cunning to respond to whatever she throws at you. You also have more physical strength than she does. Her earthly body is fragile. That's an advantage for you. If necessary, you can channel more power and simply outlast her. Don't discount your corporeal vitality.*

Okay. I'll do as you say since I'm still pretty inept as a psychic. I'm going to be sweating out every minute.

Not up here, Rosemary said with a musical laugh. *Astral bodies don't sweat.*

Stephanie had slowed their pace across the plane.

Look at that! Callan pointed toward a pillar of light that appeared on the horizon. The tremendous height of it merged into the prismatic sky. *It's bigger than Dr. Ostherhaut's pillar.*

Rosemary checked Stephanie's flight until they barely drifted with the mist. *Fancy that. You're right. I've never seen a larger pillar. That's an incredibly old soul.*

They began moving again at a moderate pace. Fog rolled past under their feet for some time before they reached the outskirts of the great one. Pillars of every size were massed about it, forcing them to reduce their speed to avoid colliding with the citizen pillars. Massive stationary pillars were thicker than skyscrapers in a city. Smaller pillars meandered between them as if strolling cosmopolitan boulevards.

As Stephanie led them between the residents, the crowd concealed the giant pillar's lower reaches from their view. The upper portion could be seen towering above.

I hope Stephanie's pillar is somewhere near, and she's not just taking us on a sightseeing tour, Rosemary said.

Why are all these pillars here? Callan dropped behind to avoid a wall of pillars blocking her path. *Could its owner be famous and have influence over so many souls?*

Souls are drawn from all over by such a spiritual power. The earthly being, whose pillar this is, doesn't necessarily know the others on the earthly plane. They come for the safety and peace that an old guardian generates. The pillars soak it up and transfer it to the earthly body. It would give the individual an inner harmony, an extra advantage when tackling their life problems. Luck, I suppose you could call it. Can't you feel the unique atmosphere of the place?

Callan could. The air was drenched, not with an insipid calm, but with a harmony and tranquility so positive that reality seemed sharper-edged. Replete with life, the place was without distracting emotional conflict or sensory confusion. The movement, color, patterns, shapes and sizes didn't overwhelm her senses as sometimes happened in an earthly city. Passing by, she could perceive and appreciate the details of each individual pillar's colors and patterns with serenity.

After dodging and waving through the pillars for what seemed like miles, they came to stand before the guardian pillar. The attendant pillars didn't crowd in upon the lordly obelisk, respectfully leaving a large plaza around it.

The guardian pillar's circumference was that of an unimaginably lofty skyscraper, and it was an eye-blinding luminescent white. When Callan squinted, she discovered that it had a moiré pattern, shimmering like mother-of-pearl and tinted with alabaster, ivory, oyster and snow. Faint silver-violet tracery accented the whites like exquisite embroidery on a bridal gown.

From the other side of Stephanie, Callan heard Rosemary's awed whisper. *This must be an almost perfect soul. The last life for it, or very near. No flaws left to purge, no more questions to be answered. Nearly complete purity and enlightenment. Divine eternity for this soul is only a lifetime or two away.*

Is it Stephanie's?

Could be, I suppose. She came directly here.

Callan was skeptical. Stephanie certainly didn't seem to be a saintly person. She was kind and honest and loyal, but also scandalously outspoken and earthy. How had Bianca managed to terrify her enough to send her into a catatonic state? Someone with a soul reflected by this pillar would be hard to intimidate.

Katie lifted her head from her mother's shoulder and looked up at the pillar of light. With a chirp of delight, the infant rose and flew across the open space to cling to the pillar. In her yellow sleeper, she looked like an exotic butterfly perched on an ethereal white flower. Callan and Rosemary stood beside Stephanie, too surprised to move.

Ka-tee, Ka-tee, the baby crooned, as she patted the majestic pillar with her tiny hands.

Rosemary roused from stunned silence and went forward. Callan took Stephanie's arm and followed. The three of them stopped a few feet away and gazed up at Katie, who still embraced the pillar a few feet over their heads. Stephanie made not a sound, but for the first time since their astral trip began, her face was animated with wonder.

Katie turned, looked down on them, and favored them with an angelic smile. The same sweet expression had first appeared when Katie was only a few weeks old. Under the influence of the pillar, an underlying, timeless wisdom and compassion shone through. Katie's gaze was a blessing unlike any Callan had felt before. The mysterious beauty of Katie's face left her feeling both humbled and exalted.

My clairvoyance saved Katie's life last spring, Callan whispered. *I guess if that is all that I ever accomplish, it makes my life worthwhile.*

Saving her life was significant. But life, with its twists and turns, is seldom so uncomplicated. One single action, however heroic and selfless, can't completely define it. I believe we live to master our own souls, not as a cipher in service to another's.

Katie's glowing smile was directed at Rosemary, and Callan knew she agreed. Katie turned again to the pillar and patted it once more, then drifted downward gently as an autumn leaf. Stephanie held out her arms to receive her daughter and folded her securely against her breast. Katie replaced her thumb in her mouth and rested her head against the familiar shoulder.

They regarded Katie with reverence for a moment. Rosemary sighed and asked, *Stephanie, can you find your pillar now?*

Stephanie turned toward the left, skirted Katie's pillar, and reentered the community surrounding it. They spent another lengthy time weaving among the citizen pillars until the crowd thinned out to a few scattered obelisks. Near an isolated life mound far from the community around Katie's pillar, Stephanie stopped before a creamy pillar comparable in size to Callan's own. This pillar, like Callan's, was overlaid with a liberal amount of pink, coral and red, but arranged in a helix pattern. The tints of love, emotion, courage and strength perfectly illustrated Stephanie's maternity and, considering the large amount of red, her healthy sexuality, too.

Katie's got a great mom, Callan said. *I wonder why her pillar is way out here away from the others?*

Impossible to tell. The ways of the pillars are a mystery. Her pillar seems unmarked. Bianca just used telepathy to play her games earlier. However, she's too exposed out here. I think we should move it in closer so Bianca won't be tempted to take another crack at her.

Stephanie efficiently moved her pillar with a few directions. They moved the pillar as far into the crowd around Katie's pillar as they could and still find a place to park it.

That should do it, Rosemary said, as Stephanie unwound her silver cord from her pillar. *Before we go home, let's go find a mound and I'll show you how to draw extra power.*

On the way back to the gateway, a series of life mounds rose up out of the mist and Rosemary stopped beside them.

As I told you the first night we came here, she said, *these hills are concentrated life energy, rather like storage batteries. I warned you not to try to go through them. But, if you're cautious, you can siphon off a considerable amount. Just put your hand in, like this.*

Rosemary eased a hand into the mound. Its surface parted as if it were whipped cream. Her aura flashed with rainbow fire. In a second she withdrew her hand.

Come try, she said.

Stay here, Stephanie, Callan instructed before letting go of her arm. *Don't go drifting off. I'll be right back.* Stephanie's blank expression didn't change, but Katie gave her a sweet smile, a bye-bye wave, and shifted in Stephanie's arms to watch the proceedings.

Callan reached out to touch the life mound. She jerked back when Rosemary exclaimed, *Watch it! Don't get too big a charge or your body won't be able to handle it. It'll make Bianca's termination of your first nightwalk look like a pat on the head.*

As Rosemary monitored, she eased her right hand into the life mound. The mist that defined it tickled her face with tentacles of life force. She jumped in surprise when the energy hit her. On one level, the sensation wasn't much different than getting a mild electrical shock, but the additional energy blooming within her astral mind and body left her more invigorated and alive than an extensive workout and a good night's sleep would her physical body.

Enough! Stop! Rosemary ordered.

That felt wonderful! Will my earthly body get any benefit from this?

Some spillover. Mainly, the body has to manage the energy when you're not in astral form. That's purely an unconscious process. Tapping a life mound is a balancing act. Take enough for both the astral and the earthly but no more than the corporeal body can handle. Otherwise, you'll burn out.

During the long descent to Earth, Callan regarded Katie and asked, *Do you think she will grow up to be influential and famous? Say, like the President of the United States?*

It's doubtful that she would become a politician. Most likely, her life will go unnoticed by the rest of the world. At such an advanced stage, anything her soul may need to work out will be subtle and complex, and she'll not be drawn to a public life. Like Albert, for example. That's only my opinion, of course.

On reaching the front yard of the Ellisons' house, Callan said, *You go on home Rosemary and get some rest. I can put these two to bed.*

Thanks, I will. We'll talk tomorrow. Rosemary faded into the night.

It only took a moment to return Stephanie and Katie's spirits to their sleeping bodies. As she closed the protective shield behind her, she heard Rosemary's mind voice, far away and thin. *Callan, return to the astral plane! Hurry! Meet me by Albert's pillar.*

The gravity of Rosemary's voice sent her shooting skyward in alarm. Something was terribly wrong. There was no time for a leisurely trip, reveling in the starry night sky or the grand scenery below. In an instant, she was wrenching open the gateway, plummeting through, flailing headlong, almost out of control, toward the rendezvous point. Rosemary was there, one hand resting on Dr. Ostherhaut's pillar. She tumbled to a halt in front of her.

Rosemary, what is it?

Rosemary's aura flared brightly and her third eye was out and whirling furiously, tinting the landscape a deep indigo.

Listen carefully, my dear. I haven't much time. I'm afraid that Bianca had my ticket punched. I couldn't leave without a last word with you.

What? Callan said, reaching out toward Rosemary. She wouldn't accept the dreadful idea that was forming in her mind. Shudders of panic ran through her, and her aura oscillated with a gray light. Rosemary grasped her hand and pressed it between both of her own.

You already know. The bitch couldn't get me on the psychic level, so she sent an assassin, a hit man with an obscene little gun, to my house. My earthly body is dead. The bastard ran right through me on his way out. Some psychic I am! I didn't even foresee my own death.

No!

In horror, she realized that Rosemary's silver cord no longer arched from her head. Her astral shield was as vibrant as ever, but the astral body within it wavered, as if it was underwater, and lost some of its solidarity moment by moment. Behind them, Rosemary's pillar had begun to quake and a low-pitched humming issued from it, echoing off the other pillars occupying the glade.

Rosemary took her by the shoulders with still-warm hands and gave her a little shake. *You are not to blame yourself for this or be sad for me. I sought you out, remember? Meeting you, helping you release your powers, well, I haven't had so much fun or felt so useful in years. I had hoped to see this thing with Bianca through, but I don't mind going either. I was really rather tired of the lonely bed and the solitary meals, and Colin's waiting for me now.*

But what will I do without you? Callan asked in anguish, only realizing the selfishness of her question as the words spilled from her mind.

Whatever's needed. You'll find the way. Banish all doubt. Dreams are reality. Remember, 'As you imagine, so shall you be.' Now, listen to me. Don't call the police. Call Sam and have him call Albert. He will take care of everything. Do you hear me Callan?

Yes, Rosemary. Despair nearly choked off the reluctant answer.

I also wanted to do something I've been thinking about lately, Rosemary went on matter-of-factly. *You will be my inheritor of this astral plane. I never had anyone to pass it on to.*

Pulling the white silk scarf from around her neck, Rosemary draped it about Callan's. *I knight you, Dame Callan, as Defender of the Pillars of Light, Champion of the Astral Plane. I bequeath you the power and the responsibility, my daughter. Use them well and pass them on.*

Her aqua eyes laughed at her formal declaration and the little ceremony, but she meant her words.

Callan couldn't assimilate the meaning of Rosemary's charge, only record the words in the back of her mind.

I don't understand. What shall I tell Dr. Ostherhaut? How can I tell him what happened to you? I can't give him your goodbye. Her voice cracked under the encircling grief.

No message to him is necessary. No goodbyes are needed between Albert and me. I must go. Colin is waiting. Impatiently, as usual. Rosemary's astral form was translucent now.

With a touch to Callan's cheek and a smile, she turned and ran, arms wide-flung as if running into a lover's embrace, and merged, absorbed in an instant, with her whirling pillar of light.

The pillar rotated faster, throwing out kaleidoscopic brilliance, and rose to hover for a moment above the shifting white ground mist. A great starship of eternity, it lifted ponderously, gradually picking up speed until suddenly it soared, receding in an eye-blink, until only a glowing disc remained visible far above.

When the disc vanished into the shifting colors of the sky, Callan reached blindly for Dr. Ostherhaut's pillar and pressed her cheek to it. Astral bodies didn't sweat, Rosemary had said, but her tears were as caustic and her sobs as harsh-sounding as any produced by an earthly body on the world below.

* * * * *

The early Labor Day hours crawled through the darkness toward dawn. When the sun finally crept over the horizon to etch the black mountain range in shades of smoke, Callan sat slumped on the floor between the couch and the fireplace hearth in her family room. She had retreated there after her return from the astral plane and her almost incoherent call to Sam to tell him that Bianca's assassin had murdered Rosemary.

Upstairs felt too open, too exposed, much like the unsettled feeling during her first weeks in Colorado. Until she had become accustomed to the panorama, the landscape had intimidated her, making her feel insignificant and vulnerable. The blue sky was too immense, the horizons too distant, and the mountains threatening in their majesty, as if they would tumble down and crush her. Now, to that perception had been added terror and grief.

The house above and the Earth beyond the basement walls, even encased in the multiple layers of protective aura as they were, seemed no more adequate than a spiderweb to shield her from an attack by The Gull. At any moment, a psychic bomb could tear through the house and ravage her and Connor. Or, just as easily, a man with a gun could appear out of the night to invade her home. With Rosemary gone, she had no guidance and nowhere to run except down into her basement to hide. She longed to seek safety deeper in the center of the Earth.

During the last hours of the night, she had attempted to subdue her agitation by meditating. Years before, after much practice, she'd finally learned the yoga technique of focusing on a single image and emptying her mind of distressing attitudes. Visualizing and then concentrating on a single rose had helped her survive the declining years of her marriage.

Instead of finding repose within a perfect flower, she could only see Rosemary's face, lined and aging but merry and so alive, as she had been during the days in Sam's conference room. Then her laughing young astral face appeared as she teased Callan about Sam during their first nightwalk together. Had it only been a week ago that they had met? Rosemary had created a different woman within that short time. A woman who now seemed a stranger to herself.

Not only had her mind been stretched to accept bizarre new abilities, but her body felt altered as well. With eyes sunken and gritty with sleeplessness and tears, her limbs and heart exhausted, sucked dry of every ounce of energy, she couldn't even imagine taking a long run in the morning sunlight.

Sometime after the failed meditation, late into the long night, she had crawled onto the couch and dozed, an uneasy sleep haunted by white mist and pillars of light that flew into a multicolored sky. Jerking awake, she had returned to the floor to rest her back against the couch, needing to be closer to the Earth again, and waited for morning.

Sam had said he would contact her as soon as he had news. What more could he tell her that truly mattered except that Rosemary was gone? To her fear and anxiety over The Gull's threat had been added grief, and she didn't know how to face this September morning alone.

She remembered when she was six, on the spring morning her Aunt Noonan died. Sam had found her hiding behind the lilac bush by the back porch, rocking herself in sorrow. He sat with his arm around her and patted her shoulder, letting her cry.

"You won't never go away, will you, Sam?" she pleaded. "You won't never die?"

"No, I won't ever go away, Callie," he promised.

Forever after, the sweet scent of lilacs evoked a sense of loss relieved by the comforting anchor of Sam's touch. He didn't die, but in the end he had gone away.

The predawn air was chilly, and she huddled deeper into the terry cloth robe she wore over a nightshirt. Sam's adult face, as clearly as if he sat beside her, appeared in her mind, and with the vision came the certainty that he was coming to her, was, in fact, turning off the main thoroughfare into her neighborhood.

She ran upstairs into the kitchen and watched for him through the plants in the bay window. In her mind she followed his car's twists and turns through the streets, and when it pulled up at the curb she was opening the front door. He came up the sidewalk and porch steps, his tall form silhouetted against the rising sun, and folded her into his arms.

"Callie, I'm so sorry. She meant a lot to you, I know."

Her cheek rested against his shoulder as his arms tightened around her. She drew a deep, shuddering breath.

"Rosemary told me just before she left, that dreams are reality. She was right. Thank you for coming, Sam. I needed you."

"I'm sorry I took so long. Let's get some coffee." He drew her into the kitchen, his arm still around her shoulders. "It's been a long night." He looked tired and a little scruffy, with a day's growth of beard and sadness in his eyes.

He made the coffee. Side by side they leaned against the counter, arms touching, and waited for it to brew, silently watching the dawn throw leaf shadows onto the kitchen floor. When the coffee was poured and they were seated at the table, only then could she ask, "How is Dr. Ostherhaut taking it, and what about Rosemary?"

"Albert, I know, is devastated, but of course he didn't show it much. Always calm and efficient. They were friends for so long. He made the necessary calls to their former agency. I met him at her house to let the investigative team in. Everything was as Rosemary said."

"Their former agency? I don't understand."

Sam took another sip of his coffee before answering. "Albert explained that since Rosemary was a former employee of that rather sensitive organization, and as the murder was related to her paranormal powers and not just the usual crime, it was best to let them handle the details. The local authorities were notified, but everything will be handled very discretely. That will prevent media attention or cause speculation about her past. There'll be no publicity to upset Rosemary's friends. Everyone will be told it was a heart attack."

"And let Bianca and her assassin get away with it!"

"There'll be an investigation and search for the man responsible, but more than likely he was on his way out of the country an hour after it happened. And there are no clues." Sam got up to refill their cups. "Charging Bianca would be impossible, much less arresting her. How could anything be proved? You can be sure she gave the man orders by telepathy. There's no trail to her. According to the federal people, that's how she usually works."

Elbows on the table, Callan pushed her hands through her hair and held the handful at the back of her neck, head bowed. Her mind whirled in outrage and disbelief. Bianca would get away with murdering Rosemary. She felt haggard with sleeplessness and the nightly trips to the astral plane. The extra energy she had taken earlier on the plane seemed to have dissipated. She felt she couldn't handle much more, but she had to. There was no other option.

She looked up into Sam's sympathetic brown eyes and said in a haunted voice, "Except in Bernie Rabney's case. We forgot about him. She killed him with her own lily-white hand. So it's up to me alone to see that Bianca is stopped. And I will."

"Mom?"

Connor stood in the kitchen doorway, looking from her to Sam. Sam had been in the house when he went to bed the previous night and was still here when he awoke. His mother was in her bathrobe. A deep furrow between his eyebrows said he was troubled by the situation. The only other man he had ever seen with his mother in such circumstances had been his father. Callan couldn't let Connor direct her romantic life, but she didn't have to throw it in his face either.

"Come in, Connor. Sam and I got some bad news late last night. One of our mutual friends passed away suddenly. Someone you haven't met. Sam stopped by early to fill me in."

"Who was it that died?"

"Her name was Rosemary Sabin. I met her recently, but she was a good friend to us. Both Sam and I are upset and sad, and we were up all night."

By the time Callan had finished explaining, Connor's expression changed from a scowl to sympathetic as he sat down at the table.

"That's a bummer," he said. "I never knew anybody who died. You both look tired out."

Callan reached over and touched his hand, remembering how disturbing death could be for the young. "You're going to have to cut us some slack the next few days. We'll probably be off-kilter for a while. How about some breakfast, you two? Will cold cereal and fruit be okay? Some muffins, too." She didn't feel like eating, but fixing breakfast would give her something to do with her hands.

Sam had remained in the background as Callan reassured her son, obviously wanting to continue their private talk, but he greeted Connor with a smile and accepted the offer of breakfast. The meal was subdued but without uncomfortable undercurrents.

When Connor went upstairs to get dressed, Sam cornered her at the kitchen sink, his expression concerned.

"Callie, love, you've got to get some real rest today. You can't go on nightwalking every night without some uninterrupted sleep. Especially sleep with a normal dream cycle. Albert told me what continual trips to the astral plane can do to a person. Plus, you're maintaining god knows how many protective auras."

He'd called her "Callie love," and her dreary depression lifted a few notches. Perhaps he had forgiven her for what she had done to him the night before.

"I'll try for a nap later this afternoon. Maybe Stephanie will watch Connor for a few hours. I don't want to leave him alone even for a minute after what happened last night. Even in the house while I'm asleep," she said. "Boy, I'm going to owe Stephanie some mega babysitting. I don't think I could sleep anyway."

"Oh, yes, you can." Determination tightened his mouth. He pulled a small packet from his jacket pocket, and held it in front of her eyes. "This is a mild sedative. One pill is a kid-sized dose. Just enough to help you let go and sleep. You take one, and we'll bamboozle Connor some more. I'll look after him."

"What about you? You didn't get much sleep last night either."

"I haven't been traipsing around the astral plane. And in case you've forgotten," he added, removing a cereal bowl from her hands and setting it in the sink, "I'm a doctor and used to some sleepless nights."

"Well…" She longed to lie down and sink into oblivion. Staying conscious was getting harder by the moment.

"It'll give Connor and me a chance to get to know one another without Mom hanging around. Tell some dirty jokes and do man stuff. Here, take the pill, tell Connor he has a new babysitter, and go upstairs and sack out."

"Don't let Connor go outside without me. It's probably fairly safe in here during the daylight hours." She didn't add, *I hope.*

"We won't set foot out of the house. I promise."

"Wake me up by noon. Connor won't tolerate being kept inside all day."

"I'll decide when you should get up. Probably when he gets bored whipping me in computer games," he said, pushing the sedative into her hand and kissing the corner of her mouth. "Go."

* * * * *

Shortly after one o'clock, freshly showered and dressed and with the worst of the exhaustion slept away, she came downstairs to find Connor and Sam putting together some lunch. Three delicatessen meats, chicken slices, two cheeses, tomato, a red onion, pickles, three kinds of mustard and a jar of mayonnaise littered the kitchen table. Two monster sandwiches were in the final stages of construction.

"Pass the corned beef, Sam. Hi, Mom. Want me to build you a sandwich?"

"Sure. Thanks. Just chicken with lettuce, tomato and mayo for me. Maybe a dill pickle on the side, too. Hi, Sam. How're you doing?"

Sam looked wearier than he had early that morning, but the sadness had gone from his eyes. He inspected her with his doctor look. "You're your old self again. Come over here and sit by me."

He made sure her chair was pulled close enough to his to press his knee firmly against hers.

"Sam's real good at the games. Beat me four times." The admiration in Connor's voice surprised her. No anger or resentment at defeat marred his face. In fact, he seemed downright sunny about it.

"Good for Sam. I thought you only approved when Zach won?"

"Nah."

What was going on? Connor losing without a trace of the sulkies? Acknowledging an opponent's skill, too? Sportsmanship? And eating corned beef. An incredible change. She slanted a glance at Sam. He was chewing vigorously, but his return glance said that he had been up to something. Sam sorcery, no doubt.

"Connor's a master on that computer. Taught me a lot," he said after swallowing. "He's going to give me some pointers in baseball too."

Sam's comments were sincere. However, his faint smile contained a trace of smugness somewhere underneath, probably self-congratulation. He was certainly entitled to it. She wanted to throw her arms around him and plant a big sloppy kiss on him for what he had done for Connor.

After lunch, Sam left for home, needing a few hours of sleep too. She didn't want him out of her sight and he seemed to feel the same about her and Connor. When she asked, he quickly agreed to return later for dinner. As he went out the door, he cautioned, "Keep your psychic radar up and rotating."

Connor chattered about Sam from the moment the door shut behind him. Finally, when Connor had begun to repeat himself for the third time, Callan phoned Stephanie to see if she and Zach were available for company. Connor's Sam stories would be new to Zach. Besides, she needed to check that everything was well at the Ellisons'.

Stephanie answered the front door, Katie riding her hip. Neither of them appeared the worse for wear after Bianca's visit or their trip to the astral plane. Connor and Zach took a soccer ball into the backyard. Callan suggested that they sit on the patio and keep an eye on the boys, although being outside in the open made her twitchy.

The moment they were seated and the boys were occupied with the ball, Stephanie asked, "What's going on? I had a weird dream last night. You were there, and Rosemary and Katie, too. I have odd feelings about Katie this morning. It wasn't a dream, was it? It's part of your paranormal doings and this thing with The Gull. I have a right to know what's going on."

As reluctant as Callan was to alarm her, Stephanie had to know what happened, especially Rosemary's murder. Bianca had upped the danger for them all.

"I'm so sorry about Rosemary. What an awful, scary thing," Stephanie said when Callan finished. "That big pillar of light with Katie perched on it was the most vivid memory I have. So she's an old soul and sort of a saint?" She looked both worried and a little awed as she regarded Katie playing a few feet away in the sandbox.

"Not a saint, but special. Don't treat her any differently than you did before. Just be her mom. She was born to you because you are the mother she needs for her purpose here. Let it be." Callan didn't know where that piece of knowledge had come from, but somehow it seemed right.

Stephanie considered that for a moment. "Will Bianca come after Katie or anyone else in my family, now that Rosemary is gone?"

"I don't think so. I've got your house and all of you under dense protective auras. So far, Bianca's really dangerous actions have been on the pragmatic side. Rosemary was killed because she helped me and actively opposed The Gull. Most likely, her attack on you last night was her showing off and trying to intimidate me. You are no threat to her plans. Just be on guard when you're outside out from under the protective shield. Most of all, I'm worried about Connor. Bianca knows my weak point. He must be guarded all the time."

"What can I do to help?"

"I'll continue to take the boys to school every morning and see them inside. Bianca is unlikely to try for them while they're at school. Too public. Her methods are sneaky and clandestine. Can you pick them up from school? They shouldn't go off alone to the park or even play in the yard by themselves. They aren't going to like being watched like that. I know this is a burden on you, Steph, but I don't think it will go on much longer."

Stephanie picked up Katie and smoothed her curls, and then turned to watch the boys, still kicking around the soccer ball with their usual inexhaustible energy and grace, before saying, "Nowadays, violence can come out of nowhere. At any time. Why should we expect to be immune? I'll watch the kids and be careful. Count on it. You can't fight Bianca alone. Isn't opposing evil everyone's responsibility, after all?"

* * * * *

The remainder of the afternoon they watched over their sons, mulling over the events of the past week. Later, she and Connor went home in time for her to start dinner. At six o'clock Sam arrived, somewhat rested, bearing a video and microwave popcorn.

"Low-fat popcorn," he pointed out to Connor. "Won't clog your mom's arteries."

The evening had a dream-like quality. Grief and regret for Rosemary still held her, but Sam's nearness kept her from sinking into depression. The two of them lounged on the couch in the family room, his arm around her shoulders, Connor on the floor in front of them. For a while they munched popcorn and hooted the movie villains, but when it was over, Connor had to wake them. They'd succumbed to their sleepless night and dozed off, Callan with her head on Sam's shoulder, his cheek resting against her hair.

As Callan walked Sam to the door, he told her that Dr. Ostherhaut, as Rosemary's executor, had scheduled her funeral for Thursday at noon. She had no family to complete the arrangements.

"I'll be there. Oh Sam, I'd give anything if this hadn't happened. For Rosemary to be killed because of The Gull and me. It's unbearable!"

"I know it's hard for you, love," he said, wrapping her in a hard embrace. "It's not your fault. What can I do to help?"

"Can you come to dinner again tomorrow? I don't like being alone. It's an imposition…you're busy…"

"Being with you isn't an imposition," he said, cupping her face in his hand. "I'll be here. I don't want to be anywhere else."

His goodnight kiss was tender and comforting, and as usual, left her wanting more. With Connor in bed and the house silent, the depression and fear menaced her again. Tomorrow was a workday, the vacation was over, but she still faced another trip to the astral plane.

Rosemary wasn't outside her window to greet and tease her when she slipped through the bedroom wall and into the faint light of a quarter moon. With some hesitation, she entered the Ellisons' bedroom. Grimly, she recreated jeans and a T-shirt on Matt while he still lay under the covers beside Stephanie. Like Stephanie, he was easily coaxed out of his body. She simply told him that she needed his help, and with a sound like the strum of a guitar, his spirit stood before her. When summoned, Zach promptly followed his dad.

She felt vulnerable and exposed without Rosemary. Bianca could ambush her at any time. But luck held. It was a milk run, with no delays in finding their pillars. The pillars were already under Katie's protection. No black-feathered astral enemy prowled the misty world. In minutes, Matt and Zach were safely back in their bodies, and she was back in her own, sleeping deeply, too exhausted to indulge in worry or fear or grief.

* * * * *

Returning to the routine of work jolted her from the trance-like grief and fear that had descended on her at Rosemary's death. As she fought morning rush hour traffic, for the first time in her life, a craving for full-bodied revenge surfaced in her heart. It was bittersweet with a jittery afterglow, much like the effect of an overindulgence in chocolate and coffee. No amount of rational self-talk could restrain the desire to mutilate The Gull. The creature had devastated vast areas of her life and killed Rosemary.

She relished imagined scenes of retribution. Her favorites involved wringing its black neck or the meticulous plucking of each of The Gull's feathers until it was, indeed, as bald as a Thanksgiving turkey. She wanted to see pebbled, wrinkled bird skin, pitted with holes where feathers had once been lodged. Then she would start on any leftover pinfeathers. The creature should feel pain, the knifing jabs and the slow dull aches, both mental and physical, that she had endured over a lifetime.

The desire and the anger it reflected, she realized now, had been hidden within her always, but during the past week it had crept out and detonated. Rosemary's murder had liberated it full-force. The savagery of the fury shocked her. She had always believed herself to be a mild-mannered, civilized person.

On another level, retribution seemed only right and just, as though inflicting mayhem on The Gull would let sunlight into a dark room. That viewpoint felt somehow pure, although a truly satisfying vengeance would likely rebound and defile her pillar of light with the browns and ash-gray of spiritual degradation. Payback time might be spiritually incorrect, but it certainly would appease her rage.

Arriving at work, she abandoned the fantasy for the time being, as such a retribution wasn't a viable answer. The Gull existed only on the psychic plane. The likelihood of plucking the bird in any physical manner was ludicrous.

To her perplexity, other radical alterations had been made in her outlook during the past eight days. Work had piled up while she was gone, but woolgathering and the urge to doodle broke her concentration. Before the morning was half over, she found that the procedures and details of the law were now tedious and irrelevant to her. By afternoon, it was as though she were looking through the back window of a speeding car, seeing her colleagues and her career dwindling in the distance.

The house was empty and silent when she arrived home from work. Connor was at soccer practice with Zach and Stephanie. Sam had late-afternoon patients to see and wouldn't be over for dinner until after seven. After putting a casserole in the oven, she decided to inspect her garden and cut some flowers for the dinner table. Although she had vowed not to cower in her house, she had been doing exactly that.

With a basket of small gardening tools, she stood on the deck and surveyed the backyard under the slanting afternoon sunlight. Her clairvoyant sense didn't detect a sinister ghost hiding in the long tree shadows that barred the lawn. The area seemed peaceful and non-threatening. She went down the steps and headed for the flowerbeds lining the fence.

The sprinkler system kept the lawn and her flowers well-watered and flourishing, along with the weeds. Digging the latest crop would be good therapy. The small patch of herbs in the far corner of the yard was surrounded. She knelt beside the bed, selected a sharp-edged pointed digging trowel, and began probing for weed roots, turning over the soil as she went. The herbs released an intoxicating cloud as she brushed against the plants. She sat back on her heels, picked a sprig of lemon basil, crushed it in her fingers and inhaled the fragrance. The afternoon sunlight caressed her face and bare arms, and she felt a visceral pleasure in being alive.

Out of the corner of her eye, she caught an undulating movement. Her body went rigid with instinctive revulsion. The basil dropped from her fingers. She turned, moving only her head. A cobra, its hood fully flared, sat coiled less than two feet from her left arm, its head level with her face. The serpent swayed as if entranced by snake charmer's music, eyes fastened on hers, its wide-opened mouth exposing its glistening fangs.

No cobra like this one had ever existed in nature. The beady eyes were sapphire, brilliant and flashing with an eerie light. The reptilian body, instead of a natural dusty-brown color, gleamed like a gold lamé evening gown.

Callan slowly released a held breath. This bizarre phantasm answered the question of whether Bianca had seen her telekinetically move the rattlesnake and overhear her comment about hating snakes. This illusion was specifically designed to terrify her.

Little sister, would you like to play with Us? Would you like to stroke Our beautiful skin? Callan heard the childish voice in her mind. The cobra's body retracted then stretched upward, lengthening itself in display.

With the words came the same revulsion that she felt when mind-lifting the rattlesnake. Bianca was feeding the writhing, coiling, pliant essence of snake directly into her brain. She clenched her teeth against nausea and rejected the mind invasion. Her right hand tightened over the weeding trowel next to her knee.

We're bored, sweet sister. We want you to play. You were no fun at all the other night at the house next door. Please, please play with Us. Don't be scared. We won't bite. We promise.

Bianca's mind voice was sticky sweet and as false as her gold reptilian skin. Keeping a careful guard on her thoughts, Callan let her protective aura flow over the trowel.

You're overdressed, Bianca, she sent, as she swung the trowel in a flat arc.

There was no resistance as the trowel passed through the neck of the astral cobra, but the head separated from the body nonetheless. The severed head did a complete revolution and landed, quivering on its stubby neck, in a pile of soft dirt. The sapphire eyes widened in astonishment. Bianca's outcry began as a low mental growl then ascended into a shriek. Callan toughened her shield before the mind assault could pierce her to her soul.

The snake body, which had remained upright, dissolved and the cobra head followed. The eyes were the last to go, spinning in rage, until they too disappeared.

"I shouldn't have done that," Callan muttered as she stood up. "There'll be hell to pay. But it sure felt good."

Chapter Twelve

ဢ

"Don't mind me. Just passing through," Connor said, waving a dismissing hand as he strolled into the kitchen and made for the refrigerator.

Sam leaned against the kitchen table with Callan between his spread legs. Connor had interrupted a bone-melting kiss and an embrace that had Callan plastered against Sam like a leaf against a wet windowpane. Red-faced, she tried to move nonchalantly away from him. Sam didn't cooperate, simply letting her turn enough in his arms to face Connor, while keeping her backside firmly pressed against him. When she looked over her shoulder at him, he had a preoccupied smile on his face and appeared unfazed by the situation. He grinned at her and rubbed a lock of her hair between his fingers.

Sam wasn't as cool as he would like to appear. Her bottom was pressed against his crotch, and she knew better. His running shorts didn't conceal much, and he was using her for a shield.

"Did you finish your homework, Connor?" she asked. She wanted him out of the kitchen before her embarrassment became intolerable.

"Almost. Carry on," Connor said with a grin, saluting them with his grape soda as he sauntered out of the kitchen.

"Sure, no problem," Sam answered absently after Connor had already disappeared through the door.

"Smart aleck," she said, not knowing whether she meant Connor or Sam.

"I don't believe it," she said over her shoulder. "He caught us necking like a couple of teenagers and acted like he saw it everyday. What are you doing to my kid, Sam?"

"Oh, he's just on my side. You didn't answer me about the benefit dinner and concert Saturday." He turned her around to face him again. "Had you in mind when I bought the tickets last week. Can't let 'em go to waste. We'll get all dressed up in our party duds. Are we going?"

She wrapped her arms around his neck and said, "Have you forgotten the complications I live under right now? Especially after what I did to Bianca this afternoon. She's going to be on the warpath. And what about Connor?"

As she spoke, he began kissing her neck, with delicate bites interspersed, working his way down to the curve of her shoulder.

"Is this an attempt to bend me to your will?" she asked lightly. It was probably going to work.

"No, love. If things haven't calmed down by Saturday, we won't go. But I didn't tell you who will be playing at the concert."

Talking didn't seem to interfere at all with Sam's progress across her throat and up the other side of her neck. "There's this classical guitarist and his band...plays New Age stuff with a flamenco sound."

"I've heard him! Love it! I could dance all night to that rhythm. Is he really playing?"

"Uh huh. So is it a date?"

"Well, maybe."

"It's just a few hours. Connor will be safe with the Ellisons. Can't let a woman who thinks she's a bird run your life. You said that yourself."

His hands moved further down her hips and began a relentless, tantalizing kneading. Molten threads made of lightning wove their way up her spine and back down to pool at the junction of her legs.

"You sure know how to win an argument," she whispered against his mouth.

Her T-shirt got bunched under her arms before they prudently abandoned the kitchen. The rest of the evening they took turns trying to beat Connor in a new computer game that Sam had brought over.

Underneath, the sexual tension between the adults crackled. Their chairs were clustered around the computer, and when not playing, Sam kept his arm slung across the back of hers, finding myriad ways to torment and distract her with touches to her hair, neck and arms. She repaid him when it was his turn on the computer by massaging and squeezing his thigh during every climactic turn of the game.

Callan reflected that they seemed like a family, but superstitiously pushed the notion away, as if it somehow had the power to jinx the future. Then she remembered Rosemary saying, "Dreams are reality," and let the image of love, family and a future with Sam find an anchor in her mind.

Their goodnight at the front door was intense but brief. It was getting more difficult each night to leave each other. Fortunately, Sam hadn't turned skittish or standoffish after the miscalculation with the Earth magic. If Connor hadn't been in the house, she suspected she would have happily found herself stretched out on the kitchen table earlier. Now that was an arresting concept, she acknowledged, turning off the foyer light and heading up the stairs.

Her mom and dad were scheduled for their trip to the astral plane that night. Callan hadn't counted on her father being unwilling to engage in any astral shenanigans, even while asleep. He withstood her coaxing for twenty minutes, ignoring pleas for help, commands that he get up and come along, even disregarding her assertion that burglars were invading the house.

Finally, when she told him he was late for court, his astral spirit snapped out. Her mom was cooperative and released on the first try with the simple inducement of a visit with her daughter. She gave Callan a vague, tender smile and held on to her hand as they traveled from Apple Springs to the transition point. Callan kept a tight grip on her father's astral arm with the other hand.

On locating his pillar of light, he resisted securing it with his silver cord. More coaxing and instruction were needed. He frowned at the cord when she finally got him to hold it, as if asking, "Is this legal?" By the time she got them set up near Dr. Ostherhaut's pillar, returned them to their beds and herself to her own, she got barely four hours of natural sleep before the alarm rang.

On Wednesday, work was even more tedious than the day before. She caught herself nodding off while doing research on the computer. In the middle of the afternoon, she absentmindedly sketched the potted plant that sat atop her bookcase instead of writing a summary for one of the attorneys. Drawing the plant had felt wonderful, filling her with contentment and appeasing the longing to immerse herself in art.

Driving home, she pondered her career as a paralegal. If the previous two days were an example of her enthusiasm for her job, her interest had degenerated beyond recovery. It began dying the moment she healed Bianca's defacement of her pillar of light. Now her eyes craved a wider vista than a windowless, gray cubicle in a high-rise.

Perhaps she could look for a job in the art world. It didn't matter what she did as long as it kept her centered on her calling. Art classes were essential. And should she concentrate on commercial or the fine arts? The questions and possibilities excited her. Finding the answers would be an adventure. That is, if she managed to defeat Bianca and had the freedom of choice. She didn't want to think about what life would be like if The Gull prevailed.

* * * * *

"We've got to make a run to the store," Callan told Connor at 6:30 that evening. "I forgot buns for the hamburgers, and Sam will be along in a half hour. Let's hustle."

"Why do I have to go? I wanna stay here. Sam might come early."

Callan searched for a reason why he had to come with her.

"Evelyn's low on gas, so I need you to help fill her up and wash her windows while I get the stuff. They're buggy from the picnic Sunday. Let's go."

He groused about having to minister to Evelyn, but washed her windows. Connor was right about the Chevy guzzling gas. It took a while to fill her up.

Inside the convenience store, as Callan waited to pay, Connor eyed the candy display.

"Can I have a chocolate bar, Mom?"

"What? You eating candy? You never eat candy. When was the last time you ate candy?" Callan was half amused, half amazed at the small marvel happening before her eyes. Connor the health-food freak wanted sweets like a sugar-crazed kid.

"Last Easter," he answered. "But I've got a real yen for some."

"Okay." She hoped he wouldn't abandon a healthy diet entirely, but one candy bar wouldn't hurt him, and she didn't want to discourage his new, relaxed attitude.

"I'll get one for Sam, too," he said, as he picked up another bar. "You know, Mom, you're getting kind of skinny. If you don't watch it, you're going to lose all your girlie muscles," he said, running the back of his thumbnail down her upper arm as he selected another candy bar.

"Girlie muscles? Girlie muscles! I've raised a raving male chauvinist!"

Explaining how the term "girlie" might be misinterpreted, along with its more suggestive implications, took up the drive home.

"Now an intelligent, competent woman," she was saying as she punched the garage door opener and began the turn into the driveway, "might not like—"

The Gull, huge and black, suddenly appeared on the roof, directly over the garage door. Startled, Callan slammed on the brakes, jerking them against their seat belts. The car halted a few feet from the open garage. Before Evelyn stopped rocking, a splash of white hit her hood and splattered onto the windshield. A rank odor flowed in the open windows. Callan sat, stunned.

Bianca's triumphant shriek sounded, and the grating mental noise reverberating through her head released her from the shock. The crazy bitch had befouled Evelyn—literally.

In the rearview mirror, she saw the black bird landing in the driveway behind them. Connor was yelling something but she couldn't understand him. With a rage-filled screech of her own, she slammed the car into reverse.

Flooring the gas pedal, they shot down the driveway. There was no thump as Evelyn rolled over the spot where The Gull had been, but Callan was positive she had managed to whack her. The Gull's contemptuous screeching had cut off with a squawk. As Callan well remembered, coming in unexpected contact with the physical world while in astral form was unsettling.

Callan turned off the ignition, got out of the car and backed away from it, leaving the door open. The stench from the mess on the hood, windshield and roof was overpowering. Grayish-white, flecked with black and brown, the bird droppings slid down Evelyn's chrome grill and dripped from her shiny mauve fenders. Bianca must have delivered several gallons of it.

Sam suddenly appeared beside her. "What in hell happened?"

"That—that—Bianca," Callan stammered through clenched teeth. Shaking with wrath, she jabbed a finger toward the mess on the Chevy. "Evelyn—she--she—"

"Phew, Colorado sure has some big birds," Connor said, as he backed around the rear of the car, gaping up at the sky.

Trembling with the effort, Callan clamped down on her rage. Through this attack on Evelyn, Bianca insulted the memory of Callan's Aunt Noonan. There was no way she could explain this to Connor. Furthermore, the mess would dry in minutes to the consistency of concrete in the hot, dry Colorado climate. Evelyn must once again be pristine, as fast as possible.

"Connor, go get the car washing stuff!" she yelled.

Sam stared at her, then at Evelyn with a grimace, and shook his head.

Connor reached into the grocery sack he'd brought from the car. "Wanna chocolate bar, Sam? Dinner's going to be real late."

Sam looked stunned, whether by the fouled Chevy or Connor's offer, she didn't know which. "Hurry up, Connor," she snapped and ran up the driveway. "I'll get the hoses."

Stephanie showed up just after they began the cleanup. She surveyed the mess on the car and driveway and wrinkled her nose at the stink.

"What happened?" she asked, standing well away from the activity around Evelyn.

"A seven-forty-seven-sized bird laid one on Mom's old car," Connor informed her. He seemed inordinately pleased by the incident. Over the hood, Callan glared him down and went back to spraying Evelyn. She mumbled, "Hi, Steph." Sam echoed her greeting as he directed a stream of water onto the Chevy's side.

Callan's hair stuck in sweaty strands to her face, and her shirt and shorts were already streaked with filth and water. Sam's jeans and shirt weren't in much better shape. Not only was she physically miserable and nauseous, a cauldron of emotions, from rage to fear, still boiled in her.

Giving the car a wide berth, Stephanie crossed the driveway and came up behind Callan. "Is this what I think it is? A reprisal from The Gull?" she asked in an undertone.

Callan answered with a grim nod. Keeping her fury under control was taking a lot of concentration. She didn't know what kind of psychic phenomena would erupt if it got loose.

"Old Bianca's really gotten into the spirit of the conflict. That stuff's certainly fresh. Do you think she's toying with you?"

She retreated a step under Callan's scowl.

Steph watched Sam working for a moment than leaned closer to Callan and whispered, "Well, anyway, look on the bright side. Any guy who's willing to clean that much bird shit off a woman's car has got it real bad for her."

* * * * *

They ended up at a burger place for a late supper. Only after Evelyn had been scrubbed and polished to Callan's satisfaction and returned to the haven of the garage had Sam and Connor dared mention food. Getting the car and the driveway immaculate had left them unfit for a public appearance. By the time they were cleaned up and at the restaurant, it was 8:30.

Still consumed with a gut-wrenching rage, Callan was edgy, and only nibbled at her burger. Sam spent the meal trying to explain to Connor how such a bizarre phenomenon could happen.

"Colorado has plenty of odd weather patterns," Sam told Connor. "In fact, somewhere back east, toads fell like rain on a little town. A tornado lifted the toads from their habitat and transported them a long way before dumping them."

"That's really weird. When did that happen and where?" Connor asked. He was skeptical. "And it landed only on Mom's old car. Plus there was so much of that crap, and it was really fresh. Where did it come from?"

"I don't know how it could happen, exactly. We can go online and do some research on the toads. I suspect that the incident with Evelyn was a comparable event." Sam oozed sincerity and Connor seemed convinced.

Callan had never known Sam to employ such outrageous evasion, but he was doing it to get her off the hook. She was grateful that he could persuade Connor that it was only a bizarre natural phenomenon. They couldn't tell him the truth. It was even more inexplicable than Sam's tall tale. In gratitude for Sam's creative cover-up, Callan managed a smile for him. A slight lowering of his left eyelid acknowledged her appreciation.

That night after Sam had left and Connor had gone to bed, Callan stood looking out the bay window in the kitchen. She had prepared for bed but came down for a glass of milk, hoping it would help her relax enough to sleep. The room was dark except for the light over the stove, and silent but for the hum of the refrigerator and the sighing of a night wind through the trees. The cul-de-sac was deserted. Only two windows showed faint light. Bernie Rabney's house seemed sinister in its darkness. Would anyone ever want to live there after his murder? She sipped the milk.

The protective aura over her house and the Ellisons' had been reinforced moments ago, but she knew she wasn't sufficiently relaxed to descend deeper into the theta state. She needed time to think.

Tonight's group to the astral plane would include her older brother Steve and his wife and child. Tomorrow night, her brother Mark and his wife would go. She hoped her strength wouldn't give out before Bianca targeted them. By Thursday night all her closest relatives would be sheltered by guardian pillars and protected from radical personality changes. Except for Sam. He had continued to insist that she take her relatives first. On Friday night, he would be secure too.

She considered why Bianca hadn't tried to obstruct her solo escort trips. Each night, she expected The Gull to come swooping across the astral plane in vengeful attack. If Bianca put her mind to it, she could have wreaked havoc in so many ways during the past days. She had the advantage with superior psychic skills and no conscience about how she used them. What was she waiting for? Did she get her kicks out of their little psychic skirmishes — the cobra and this afternoon's debacle with Evelyn?

She went to the kitchen entrance to the garage and unlocked the door. Evelyn sat undimmed, her paint and chrome restored to their former brilliance. Callan ran a hand along a smooth cool fender. The small flexible American flag on the radio antenna had gotten bent and crumpled during the cleanup. She straightened and smoothed it so that it stood out stiff and proud again.

Opening the car door, she slid inside and looked out the windshield at the gray garage wall. Folding her arms on the steering wheel, she lowered her head to rest there and murmured, "I miss you Aunt Noonan. I need you Rosemary. What should I do? Tell me what to do?"

* * * * *

Just before twelve o'clock the next day, Sam was waiting for her on the steps of the small church where Rosemary's funeral was to be held. She'd arrived at the last minute. Each day her job became more difficult to perform effectively. The summary left over from the day before had to be finished in a frantic rush that morning. Procrastination wasn't usually a problem with her. The nervousness caused by dawdling added another layer to her anxiety.

"Callie, I'm glad you made it," Sam said, drawing her arm through his and leading the way inside. "Albert and his wife are holding seats for us."

The church was full. Rosemary had many friends at her retirement community, others from across the city and from out of state. Dr. Ostherhaut greeted her somberly but still warmly. He looked grayer than he had a week ago. His mustache actually seemed to droop, and when he smiled briefly at her, the dimple didn't appear. His sadness hit Callan like a blanket thrown over her head. He had loved Rosemary as much as he would allow himself, and her death had hit him hard.

He introduced Callan to his wife Marty, who sat on his other side. A stout, well-dressed lady, she seemed pleasant, with a cordial smile and a brisk manner.

Callan spent the service trying to reconcile the idea of the wax-like figure in the casket with Rosemary. She couldn't do it. Rosemary, in both her guises, young and old, astral and earthly, whirled merrily through her mind. She missed her droll teasing and grieved over her needless death, but felt confident that the two of them were destined to encounter one another again. On the day they met, little more than a week and a half ago, a life as mother and daughter had been revealed to them. Perhaps, she hoped, they would pass that way once more.

After the service, cars followed the hearse to Fairmount Cemetery at the eastern edge of Denver, where Rosemary was to be buried beside her husband Colin. The cemetery was decades old, and mature evergreen trees stood sentinel over the graves.

Standing beside Sam at the graveside, Callan looked out across the cemetery and through the trees, catching a glimpse of mountaintops in the distance. They no longer intimidated her with their massive grandeur. Not after the glory of the astral plane.

The minister began a final prayer, and Callan returned her attention to the service. An angular shadow passed over the flower-covered coffin and a moment later reappeared. It was a perfect summer afternoon and no clouds were approaching from the west. Callan looked up, thinking an airplane must be passing over, then froze in indignation.

The Gull cruised only a few hundred feet away over the treetops in the north. The black bird banked, obviously intending to cast an astral shadow over the grave again.

Get away, Bianca, she sent, barely able to form the telepathic warning, so deep was her fury. *You don't belong here! Get out!*

Ah, little sister, so the old witch is dead. So, so sad. Now you will accept The Gull as your teacher. We will have much fun. Did you like my present? Bianca's mind voice was so syrupy and so obviously treacherous it made Callan's teeth ache.

Did you like losing your head? she shot back. *I want nothing to do with you. Now get away from here!*

The Gull's astral reflection again overshadowed Rosemary's grave, the mad sapphire eyes contemptuously boring down.

Who are you to tell The Gull to leave? came its sneering voice as it passed. Vitriol poured from the sky.

Callan remembered Rosemary's decree on the astral plane the night she died. *I am Dame Callan,* she answered proudly, putting as much confidence, vitality and threat into her mind voice as she could muster. *I am Rosemary's inheritor. Defender of the Pillars of Light, Champion of the Astral Plane. And I do not like you. You're nothing more than a psychic blight. You couldn't defeat Rosemary fairly using psychic power, so you sent a man with a gun to do your disgusting work. Get away now before I boot you straight back to Brazil!*

She still didn't understand the full implication of the titles Rosemary had bequeathed her. They somehow included power along with obligation.

Bah. Silly, meaningless words, The Gull said, as it turned in the south to make another pass. *For your insolence, you will suffer. The Gull is the greatest, most powerful mind that has ever lived, and We have our ways, sweet, sweet sister. Our patience is not infinite. You will weep and beg for Our friendship.*

The Gull's shadow glided over the gravesite once more, but then disappeared over the northern trees and did not return. The service had ended and people were leaving. Callan expelled a long breath.

"Callie, who were you talking to?" Sam asked. He was gripping her arm painfully and rubbing his right temple. "I heard… I felt that strange humming again."

"Bianca came to pay her respects. I sent her on her way." That might not be entirely the truth, but she had stood her ground, and Bianca had flown away. Callan's recent rebellion and assertiveness probably surprised Bianca, it was so different from her usual passivity.

Sam's face was twisted in a grimace. "What's wrong?" she asked.

"I almost could make out words in the hum. God, this headache is incredible."

Was Sam's sensitivity to telepathy increasing? Or had Bianca deliberately caused the pain? It was possible that he had simply been caught in the backwash of her telepathic chat with Bianca. He had been standing by her side, their shoulders and fingers touching.

His eyes were squinted against the sunlight, brows drawn together. Callan led him across the grass and into a grove of aspen trees, out of sight of the departing crowd. By the time they were away from the crowd, his eyes had closed to slits, face creased in agony. His face was pallid and sweat beaded his hairline. As she held his arms, she felt his shaking. She urged him to lean against a tree.

She cupped his face in her hands, wanting to feel what he did. The pain made her flinch. It was as though fire ants stung their way from the back of his eyes into his temples and on to the back of his skull. The headache was reminiscent of the ones that Bianca had given her all her life, but increased twofold. Her only comparable headache was the one Bianca hit her with on the night of the attack on Stephanie. No one could take much of this. She couldn't let him suffer further. Letting her fingertips rest on his temples, she began a delicate massage.

The grove was alive with Earth energy. The trees, the grass, the warm afternoon sun slanting through the leaves, all surged with the fresh, simple bounty of life. Not letting the energy overwhelm her this time, she carefully gathered its power and imagined Sam feeling well, the headache dissolving. She concentrated the Earth energy into her fingertips, letting it flow into his temples. Under her breath, she hummed, raising and lowering the tone, tuneless and comforting as a lullaby. "As you imagine, so shall you be," Rosemary had instructed. Sam must be healed and returned to his natural state.

Weaving a symphony of well-being, drawing Sam with her into the euphoria, time seemed to stand still under the tree. His face before her, the lines of compassion that she had come to love, the texture of his skin and the contour of the bones under her fingers were all that existed. Sam's kiss against the palm of her hand brought her back.

"The pain's gone," he said, hugging her. "You're a wonder. Thanks."

"Have you ever had a headache like that before?"

"No. But we'll obviously have to explore this telepathy thing. I think it's catching."

"It's contagious all right. Bianca did it to you. She knows you're important to me. For your safety, I need to take you to the astral plane tonight." The knowledge of what Bianca could do to Sam terrified her. She could feel panic welling from the pit of her stomach, leaving her nauseous with dread.

"No, don't do that!" he said sharply as he held her by the shoulders, giving her a shake. "You've got to get your family safe. If anything happened to them, you'd be devastated. Promise me you'll wait. I insist." Sam was abnormally agitated, and the emotions pouring from him included alarm and not a little confusion. Seldom so directly adamant about anything, his usual approach to a disagreement was conciliation or an appeal to reason. He obviously wasn't considering how injury to him would affect her. Was he afraid of a trip to the astral plane or her? Why would he be so?

"Okay, Sam. But it's against my better judgment," she said with a sigh. She didn't like letting him have his way in this matter, but it would be difficult to force him to the astral plane if he resisted. She would get to the bottom of those underground emotions soon. Bianca had him as a target and it was too dangerous to let the situation go on.

Dr. Ostherhaut and Marty were the last of the crowd by the gravesite. As they said goodbye, she considered asking the doctor if he knew what Rosemary meant by Defender of the

Pillars of Light and Champion of the Astral Plane, and enlisting him in her efforts to get Sam to agree to a trip to the astral plane right away. But the Doctor looked exhausted, and the questions would have to wait until she could speak with him alone.

Callan and Sam were silent as he walked with her to her car. He held her hand through the window and kissed her fingertips.

"I won't be able to stop by tonight, Callie. I've had to push back several appointments to be here this afternoon. Plus there's a stack of paperwork on my desk that must be dealt with. I probably won't get finished until after 10:00. Will you be okay? If you need me, call, and I'll phone you at work tomorrow. I hope to get free at a reasonable hour tomorrow night. Have you decided whether we are going to the concert on Saturday?"

That Sam wouldn't be spending the evening with her and Connor was an unexpected disappointment. His presence in her home seemed as natural as seeing her son there. She had been unfairly monopolizing his time.

"I understand. I know how much time you've devoted to us lately and I appreciate it. Please don't worry. The house is secure. And yes, let's go to the concert."

"That's my girl," he said, the warmth from his copper eyes increasing her temperature beyond the natural warmth of the afternoon. "Have you got a fancy dress for the shindig?"

"Not a new one."

"Why not shop for something this afternoon. Get your mind off things for awhile."

He probably believed she needed cheering up, and she did, but she sensed he had an ulterior motive for suggesting a shopping trip. Over two hours remained before Connor was due home. Sam didn't want her alone for any length of time. They were still making the assumption, perhaps erroneously, that Bianca preferred to play her games away from the public eye. Shopping would keep Callan in public places and on the move with less likelihood of being attacked by Bianca.

"Are you suggesting, Doctor, that women use shopping to relieve their melancholy?" She pursed her lips and arched an eyebrow at him in phony disapproval. While looking into his eyes, she added another layer of protective aura about him. The sun blazing through it ignited an incandescent halo about him. *My own mortal warrior angel.*

"Oh, no, not at all," he answered, smothering a grin and raising both eyebrows back at her. "But I'm sure a little unorthodox therapy would be beneficial, just this once."

"Tactful man. Take care."

She didn't really feel like returning to the silent house. That little boutique where she'd found the teal dress might have something spectacular. She drove out the cemetery gate and turned the car toward Cherry Creek Mall. Rosemary would approve the purchase of a new dress. She could almost hear her say, "Don't be a prude. Get a knock-'em-dead eye-popper!"

Chapter Thirteen

ॐ

Sam's absence that evening gave Connor a bad case of the sulks, and in self-defense Callan invited Stephanie and Zach over after dinner. Connor and Zach were in the family room giving the computer another workout.

"You sure know how to pick 'em," Stephanie said, as she let the white chiffon skirt of Callan's new evening gown slither through her fingers. "You've got a devilish flare for sexy clothes. Have you got special plans for Sam after he sees you in this dress? You're definitely flying high these days."

"You're darned right," Callan answered wryly, not intending to reveal what she had in mind for Saturday night. She took the dress from Steph and hung it in the closet.

Stephanie grimaced and waved a finger at her. "You can pick sexy clothes, but your profanity is strictly from 1910. Come on now, get with it. Say 'damned right.' You can do it."

"Not on your life. Saying that would ruin my self-image of old-fashioned rectitude. If that happened, I'd truly be urologically aggrieved." Let Steph chew on that for a while. It would sidetrack her before she could start speculating about Callan's intentions toward Sam on Saturday night.

"Let's go downstairs," she added, heading for the door. "I want to try an experiment and you can act as my lookout."

A mute Stephanie followed her to the kitchen. Callan went into the garage, returned with a trash-filled, white plastic bag, and led the way to the deck. She set the trash bag at the end of the deck and rejoined Steph, who stood by the sliding glass doors under the light.

"Yesterday, when Bianca dumped that stuff on Evelyn—" Callan started to explain.

"Yeah, the bird shit," Stephanie supplied for her. "And you were truly urologically aggrieved. Go on, say it—birrrd shhhhit."

Callan frowned at her and continued with the explanation. There'd be no time for the experiment if Stephanie got on a roll. "Bianca didn't levitate it all the way here from wherever she got it. And she certainly wasn't carrying a bucket. She must have teleported it en masse somehow."

"What?"

Stephanie was a little dense tonight.

"You know, instantaneous movement of an object through space. Like on *Star Trek*, but using the mind instead of a machine," Callan said impatiently.

"Okay, I'll buy that." She crossed her arms and leaned against the doors. "I think."

"So, I have to learn how to do it too. Besides, I might be able to get rid of my trash by sending it into orbit, but levitating it would be impractical," Callan said. Surely Steph could understand how important such a skill would be in getting the upper hand with Bianca. "The cops would get a zillion UFO reports. You keep an eye out for the boys while I give teleporting a try."

"Trash bags in space. That'll sure start an alien invasion scare. Go on," Stephanie ordered, waving her hand in dismissal. "I want to see if you can pull this one off."

"You're such a cynic," she answered shortly. Steph didn't believe she could do it. Her lack of confidence hurt. She'd show her.

Callan marched down the deck until she was four feet from the trash bag. Breathing deeply and dropping into the theta state, she drew both astral and Earth power and released the third eye. With her chin tucked down, she stared at the bag, memorizing every ripple and crease in the plastic, how the deck light reflected off its satiny surface, and exactly how the blue twist tie stood out from the bag neck. When they had etched themselves in her mind, she concentrated on dissolving the trash bag and its contents. She imagined it reforming far, far away, on a long orbit toward the sun. Distance shouldn't matter. The vision ripened until it was too swollen to hold in her mind. The trash bag disappeared with a pop. Rarely had a psychic endeavor gone so well.

She sauntered back toward Stephanie. The grin on her face felt fabulous. A successful psychic experiment, at last. Stephanie's expression combined astonishment and admiration. Showing off the power to an appreciative audience was gratifying.

"Mission accomplished. Would you like a glass of wine and some crackers?"

"Wow, guess I have to eat my words," Stephanie admitted as she turned to slide open the deck door. "Can you get rid of my trash like that too and maybe the weeds in my backyard? Matt's been complaining about them lately."

Something hit Stephanie on the shoulder, and with a yelp she swung around, bumping into Callan. With rustles and pings and plops, more objects rained down around them. Callan flinched as something landed on her head. She shoved up against the door beside Stephanie.

Callan bit her lip and looked around. Was The Gull behind this? She didn't sense her anywhere near. What had happened?

When the patter of falling objects stopped, she reached up and plucked the thing from her hair. The unorthodox hair ornament, which at one time must have been a greasy chicken leg bone with some gristle and meat still attached, had been stretched to pencil thinness and the whole bent into a circle.

Stephanie's wide eyes and dropped jaw said that she could erupt in hysterical giggles or a banshee shriek any second. Either would be noisy. Callan started to raise a hand to clap over her mouth, but Stephanie was unflappable. Her face smoothed into its usual composure. She picked up the plastic gallon milk jug that had hit her and held it up to the deck light. The handle of the jug stuck grotesquely out of the bottom. They surveyed the littered deck.

Next to a planter, two corncobs were braided together in a tight corkscrew with the corn silk and husks neatly compacted and tied like a belt around the middle. On the potted geraniums lining the deck railings, masses of fluffy, shredded newspapers lay draped like Christmas tree tinsel. The white trash bag lay by the deck stairs, stiff with tightly-spaced knots down its length.

Stephanie picked up a soda can by her feet. The top of the can was missing, and the sides were folded back and flattened like the cuff on a pant leg. By a deck chair she picked up another soda can. It had been stretched like the chicken bone to a foot in length, and then coiled like a spring.

"This is truly amazing," Steph said, waving the cans at Callan. Her smirk was rapidly growing into a cheeky grin.

"I don't understand what went wrong," Callan stammered. This was a disaster she never could have imagined. She felt cold with terror that Bianca might be behind it and flushed with humiliation that possibly it was only her own psychic ineptitude.

Stephanie shook her head and considered the grotesque garbage again, then said, "I think this is a sign that you should stick to conventional recycling."

* * * * *

After escorting her younger brother Mark and his wife to the astral plane that night, Callan lay awake trying to figure out how she had miscalculated during the teleport. The fiasco of the grotesque trash, especially in front of Stephanie, was embarrassing, particularly after successfully showing off her other paranormal powers.

The blanket was too hot and she shoved it down and rolled to her other side. Hadn't she pushed the trash bag hard enough?

Or maybe she released the power too soon? Where had it gone to anyway?

Maybe Bianca interfered without her knowing it. The room was a little chilly. She turned on her back and pulled the blanket back up. Maybe her subconscious mind, starved for a creative outlet, had sabotaged the effort by using the trash as a weird art medium. There weren't any sure answers. She finally fell asleep vowing to postpone further teleportation practice until she had some idea how to go about it. At least she would try with something less messy than a bag of trash. It had taken a while to get all the incriminating litter off the deck.

Friday at work was hectic and seemed a month long. She was tired again and several people commented on it, adding that she looked like she had lost weight. Connor was right. She was getting skinny. Her waistband was loose, and her muscle tone would atrophy too if she didn't start working out again soon. A discouraging day, and only the knowledge that Sam and the benefit dinner and concert awaited her over the weekend kept her going. Not seeing or speaking to Sam for nearly twenty-four hours left her lonely and jittery. When he was with her, his sensual allure and companionship did much to blot out the worry about Bianca and what she would do next. Illogically, she also felt safer when he was around.

When he hadn't phoned by 3:00, she called his office and left a message. If he could join them for dinner, she wanted to know. At 5:30, when she picked up Connor at Stephanie's, his first question was whether Sam would be over that night. Sam hadn't called back, which was puzzling. Perhaps he'd had a medical emergency, she suggested to Connor. That could easily happen.

The phone rang at quarter after six as she was preparing vegetables for a stir-fry. Sam! Delight melted through her bones. Dinner wasn't on the stove yet, and they could wait for him. Connor would be tickled.

"Callan? This is Dr. Ostherhaut."

"Yes, Doctor, how are you?"

"Good, but Sam isn't."

His bluntness sent her fumbling at the kitchen counter for support.

"This is a most peculiar situation," he went on. "Sam came to my office a short while ago. He was almost inarticulate. Had trouble telling me what was troubling him. It had something to do with you, but he barely can speak your name. He goes into a panic attack when he tries. Starts shaking and sweating. Even an oblique reference to you causes him inordinate distress. Overnight, he's developed an inexplicable phobia--involving you."

Callan's stomach plummeted toward her knees.

"Phobia? About me? How can that be?"

"In my opinion, this is not natural, in the sense that the condition is unlikely to have developed spontaneously from his own psychological makeup. He was able to tell me that this happened once before, just as abruptly, some months after he moved to Chicago as a teenager. Do you see what I'm saying?"

Callan trembled and sweat ran down her neck. But she was cold, so cold. Sam had believed, both of them had believed, that The Gull considered him insignificant to Callan and wouldn't use him as a hostage. They'd given in to wishful thinking and now Sam had paid for it. Yesterday, at Rosemary's funeral, Bianca had extracted from Sam all she needed to know about their current relationship and then acted upon it. Obviously, she had always known what they meant to each other. They'd been naive to believe otherwise.

"Bianca," she growled into the phone. "That's it, isn't it? She's done something to him. Now and years ago."

"Seems possible. Have you any suggestions on how to handle this, since it's undoubtedly a psychic-induced problem?"

"Is Sam still at the office?"

"Yes. I don't know how he made it through the day. He's pulled toward you, then has to fight the panic caused by his own thoughts. He can't even think about it logically. I haven't mentioned my suspicions to him."

"Don't upset him by trying to talk about it. It won't do any good. In fact, don't mention me at all. Just get him home. He should sleep and not worry. Reassure him that everything will be fine. Do whatever you can to ease his anxiety, but don't drug him heavily. I'll take care of this later tonight. Anything Bianca can do, I can undo."

In an effort to separate them once again, that psychic snake in the grass had interfered with his pillar of light. Bianca probably knew its location from years ago. The only way to counteract the damage was to take him to the astral plane and heal his pillar—if she could.

* * * * *

Moonlight shone through the windows on the landing, flowed down the stairs and into Sam's foyer, turning the parquet floor into a satiny pond. The milky light blended with her astral aura, adding depth with its subtle glow.

She had waited impatiently through a long evening until Sam would likely be asleep. Her clairvoyance now sensed the disjointed mental activity of his dream state.

Ignoring the curved staircase, with a swoop she gained the landing in front of the three long windows and glided toward the right. Sam's bedroom, the first room off the landing, was behind tall double doors. She went through. The moon's glow gilded a path across a pale carpet to the foot of the bed. Gliding to the side of the king-sized bed, she looked down at him.

Sam's protective aura burned with a vigorous rainbow light. He slept on his back, covered to the waist by a sheet, one arm curled above his head. His bare chest rose and fell with his deep, regular breathing. He looked so peaceful that she wished she could curl up beside him, lay her head on his shoulder, and forget all the troubles of the past days. Reaching out, she caressed his cheek. Whiskers prickled under her fingertips.

Sam, she called to him, *come with me.*

He stirred restlessly, moving his arm to his side and turning his face away from her.

Sam, love, she said again, *come nightwalking with me. I'll show you the mountains from above the world.*

He mumbled and flung out an arm, then turned on his side away from her. She stepped back, puzzled at his resistance. He'd responded to her telepathic urging, so Dr. Ostherhaut hadn't drugged him.

Sam!

"No!" he muttered, rolling onto his back again, an arm slashing out.

The arm passed through her astral body, and she jerked back. For a moment it seemed he might awaken. From his dream came an image of her face, distorted with malignancy. That Sam could even dream of her in such a manner stunned her. She backed away toward the double doors. The phobia that held him was so potent that even her astral presence gave him nightmares. Bianca had thoroughly fenced him away from her.

"Go 'way," she heard him mumble.

At his words, she turned and fled onto the landing and out a tall window. Floating down, she landed on a terrace. Across a strip of grass a swimming pool glowed with soft underwater lights.

At his sleeping rejection, the heartache caused by their parting long ago had been explosively resurrected. The night before he left for Chicago, they stood in her front yard holding each other. An early October snow veiled the lights from the house, chilling their cheeks and lips as they clung to one another and made promises that were not kept.

When Sam broke off communication, her clairvoyance had disclosed his jumbled emotions — ambivalence, homesickness and yearning — along with a strange panic and fear. Nothing else came through. He wasn't sick or in trouble exactly, but an impenetrable door had closed between them.

She called him, but his mother said he wasn't home. He was home, but refusing to talk to her. She wrote, frantic, until a despairing pride silenced her pen.

She went to Sam's best friend in Apple Springs, Jerry Quinn, and asked him to contact Sam and find out what was wrong. The reply through Jerry was simple and devastating.

"He says he can't talk to you."

At her insistence on clarification, Jerry would only repeat, "He can't. He says to forget about him."

Sam's cryptic answer left her forsaken. She couldn't hate him for such callousness. He was Sam, after all. Her parents' interpretation was a new girlfriend and simple guilt over it. For a time she considered hopping a bus for Chicago and confronting him, forcing him to tell her straight-out why he was abandoning a lifetime of loving friendship. The word "why" repeated itself over and over in her mind. "He's found someone else," her parents kept insisting. Such a thing was common when young people were apart for long periods, they said. Callan must accept Sam's decision. Perhaps they were right, and Sam had simply grown away from her and Apple Springs. Their childhood affection couldn't offset the allure of an exotic city girl. So she hadn't gone to Chicago. The finality of such a meeting would have been torture anyway.

Disillusionment and sorrow formed around the unanswered question "why" and lingered for years until she met her future husband, Luke Nevins, in her junior year of college. Only then did she begin to set aside Sam's persistent memory as a remnant of childhood. The memory brought back tears of bitterness and hopeless anger.

Tonight she had come face-to-face with the final rejection she had avoided then. It burned through her like a lighting strike. Long ago, Bianca had lured a young Sam to the astral plane, had him lead her to his pillar of light, and defaced it, shutting Callan out with a forged phobia. Bianca had only to revisit his pillar and mark it once more. It wasn't Sam's free choice to reject her then or now. Bianca's scheme was at the root of it.

Ultimately, she had lost Sam because of fear of his rebuff. Her cowardliness was to blame. Somehow, she could have made a difference, changed the outcome and kept them together. He was lost to her again if the psychic barrier that Bianca erected was permitted to remain.

No, not this time. The Gull wouldn't separate them again. The two of them had been cheated, but standing here indulging in sniveling and self-pity wouldn't save Sam. How could she get him to the astral plane? There was no one else to do the job, and Sam reacted to her like a creature from a horror movie. This called for some clever misdirection.

The pool's underwater lights gave the water an aqua tint much like Rosemary's eyes. Rosemary. What would she do? Sam wouldn't be afraid of Rosemary in her astral form. "As you imagine, so shall you be." The words echoed in her mind. She could become Rosemary, be her for the trip to the astral plane. It was the only way it could work.

Closing her eyes, she concentrated on Rosemary, how her young astral form had looked. She remembered the long blonde hair that parted on the left and fell to Rosemary's shoulders. She fixed each ringlet in her mind's eye. The merry aqua eyes and the sultry pout after getting caught ogling Matt Ellison or when she teased Callan about sex and Sam. The slim, straight figure and the fluid way she moved in the astral state filled her mind.

The white silk-fringed scarf, of course, which Callan now wore around her neck with the teal gown, was a part of Rosemary's nightwalking costume. The brown leather bomber jacket with the trim tan pants and knee-high brown boots came next. When Rosemary clearly filled her mind, her physical appearance along with her personality, Callan let the vision overshadow her.

Looking down at herself, she saw Rosemary's flying outfit. The hair resting on the shoulders of the bomber jacket was blond and curling. A touch of her fingers confirmed that her face had transformed too. With luck, Sam would see and sense only Rosemary. Satisfied with the disguise, she flew up and through the bedroom window.

He slept deeply, his fragmentary dreams no longer plagued by nightmares of a hideous Callan. A few steps away from the bed, she stopped and called to him.

Hi, Sam, she said in Rosemary's melodic voice that reached high then swung low when she was intrigued or excited about something.

Want to go outside with me? It's a beautiful starry night. We'll get some moonbeams and fresh air and whatever else you'd like.

She put seductiveness into the voice, much as she imagined Rosemary would have if she were coming on to a handsome man. A dreaming Sam wouldn't be immune to a pretty blonde. She moved closer. He stirred and smiled. Callan wasn't sure she liked this enthusiastic reaction, compared to the one she had gotten in her true form, but what else could she expect? Sam's instincts were all male. But his astral spirit hadn't detached. She hoped he wouldn't be as stubborn as her dad.

How about it, Sam? I have a problem I need to talk over with you. He never could resist an appeal for help. It was his strength and his weakness.

With a soft rushing sound like wind through fir trees, Sam's astral spirit rose, his silver cord arching high from the top of his head, and he was completely, splendidly naked. She'd forgotten to dress him first.

Sam was strong, she knew that, but before her stood the bare evidence. Wide shoulders with planes of muscle extending into well-defined corded arms. His deep chest tapered to a slim waist. As she had surmised from her fleeting explorations, he had a stomach that would shame a washboard. His slim hips and long sinewy runner's legs were impressive too.

She didn't mean to look, but she couldn't help it. He was definitely aroused and getting more so every second. He began gliding toward her. Guiltily, she jerked her eyes up. Her face must be flaming brighter than her aura.

He smiled, knowingly and sensually. The blankness of the non-lucid nightwalker had vanished. He wasn't really awake, but had obviously picked up on her furtive, fascinated inspection of his body. He was all sexual instinct.

His straightforward erotic response unnerved her. As he reached her, she retreated and put a hand up to halt him. If he embraced her, he might see through the masquerade. His resulting panic would wake him, and there'd be no further chance of coaxing his spirit to the astral plane tonight. No way was he making love to her while she wore Rosemary's astral form. He stopped, expression puzzled and disappointed.

Quickly, she clothed him in the first items that came to mind, the chambray shirt and jeans that he had worn at the picnic the previous Saturday. In the second it took to dress him, the lucidity vanished from his face, leaving him indifferent to her and his surroundings.

The insipid look on his face irritated her. She'd buttoned the shirt up all the way to his neck. Impulsively, she unbuttoned him nearly to the waist until his brawny chest was bared. That was better--the he-man look suited him, even if the dull look in his eyes didn't.

She cautiously approached him, touched his arm and said, *Let's go, Sam*, and they rose through the roof, out into the moonlight. Hovering above the roof, she threw a thick protective aura about his house. As he nightwalked with her, the six feet of the silver cord attached to his physical body would be exposed, leaving his astral spirit vulnerable to an attack from Bianca. He'd refused to have a shield before, insisting it was unnecessary, that Callan had too many others to support, and it would just be a beacon to Bianca. Stubborn man.

Their auras touched and flared as they ascended toward the transition point. Watching him as they soared, she was disappointed that he seemed oblivious to the splendor of the world below. *Make up your mind. Do you want him asleep and manageable or awake and randy?*

The trip through the gateway went fast, and soon they stood at the spot where Rosemary had first brought her. The pearly mist bloomed around them as she stopped to get her bearings.

The place was restless and life-intensive as ever, with ghostly vegetation protruding from the ground mist, many animal life forms moving below, pillars in the distance wondering on their own mysterious errands. The sky rotated through its never-ending color wheel of light.

A parting of the mist revealed Dr. Ostherhaut's pillar behind the life mounds on the horizon. Connor, her parents, her brothers and their spouses and children were grouped under his ethereal protection. A visit to his grove of pillars was like a family reunion. Touching a particular pillar released the quintessence of the personality, flooding her with the affection she held for that person. She extended her clairvoyance to search for any sign of Bianca as she had every night since Rosemary's death. When not in the territory of a wise old pillar, she was susceptible to attack.

Once Sam's pillar was secure, maybe there would be some time for a little rest. Each night before returning to the earthly plane, she renewed her psychic strength at a life energy mound, but it wasn't quite enough to fully revitalize the earthly body along with fueling the protective auras she was maintaining.

She looked into Sam's eyes and took care to project her mind voice distinctly. *Sam, listen to me. Find your pillar of light. It's very impressive.*

His wooden expression lifted, and he seemed to truly see her. Slowly, he scanned the astral plane. The laugh lines around his eyes creased, and he smiled at the psychedelic sky, the shimmering mist and the majestic pillars of light on the horizon.

After looking his fill, he nodded, grinned at her and glided forward, heading to the left of Dr. Ostherhaut's grove, in the same direction Callan had taken the night she located her own pillar. Keeping pace beside him, she kept a firm grip on his arm.

They passed what she now considered the home mound, then the hollow where her own pillar had originally been, and continued on, heading for a range of life mounds grouped on the horizon. After gliding through a narrow pass, a single pillar of light appeared in a valley between five mounds. Sam was heading directly for it. How strange that his pillar, like hers, sat solitary, without even one companion pillar to share the isolation. Rosemary had said that the pillars often moved about the astral plane on their own enigmatic errands. Perhaps theirs had been searching for each other, across the astral plane and down through the years.

As they approached, the pillar appeared several lifetimes taller than her column. Its top was barely visible in the billowy clouds. Automatically, as they drew closer, she began to interpret the pillar's colors.

Its current life history possessed a platinum background overlaid with color in a chevron motif. She wasn't surprised to see that the basic color at the bottom was aquamarine, the shade of the psychically empowered. Not as wide and dominant as that on her pillar but definitely an influence, forming the foundation for the other personality traits.

Chevrons of violet, denoting compassion and protectiveness, alternated with the gold of empathy and intelligence. Tentacles of orange for courage, confidence and strength, along with the deep pink of those who love, twined between and over the violet and gold chevrons. And on its right flank a lavish patch of crimson overlay the motif. His sexuality blazoned forth for all to could see. She couldn't have painted a better portrait illustrating Sam's character.

Sam studied his pillar, head tipped to the side, eyes squinted, as though confirming the colors' meanings. With splayed fingers, he pressed his hand upon it, just as she and Connor and Katie had done when first encountering their pillars of light. After a moment, he nodded, as if the confirm, *Yes, this is who I am.*

Evidence of Bianca's tampering wasn't immediately apparent, and Callan didn't want to take the time to examine the pillar thoroughly. The Gull could come streaking across the mist in an effort to stop the rescue mission, just as she had with Connor. They were too far away for Dr. Ostherhaut's intervention. She wanted Sam and his pillar safe before restoration began.

After helping Sam expose a long length of his silver cord, they bound the pillar for transfer. With a tug the obelisk floated above the curling mist, and they began the trek back to the home territory. Callan kept checking the horizon by common sight, not entirely trusting her clairvoyance to warn her of The Gull's stealthy approach.

Sam stopped when they circled the last mound and come upon the wise old one and its colony of pillars. For a moment he just looked, and then spoke for the first time on the journey. *Dr. Ostherhaut?* His mind voice was lucid and tinged with awe and curiosity.

Yes. We'll put your pillar by his.

In answer he moved forward easily again, guiding his cargo skillfully between the other pillars.

Right here, Sam.

She indicated a space beside her column. There was plenty of room now that Rosemary's had gone. He maneuvered the pillar until it came to rest barely three feet from Callan's. With her help, he unwound his cord and stood waiting, watching her inquisitively, a smile in his eyes.

Slowly she walked around the pillar, searching for signs of Bianca's meddling. She found the marks just above eye level on a patch of deep rose that swelled outward from the crimson into the violet. The area was a nearly perfect half circle, the size of a dinner plate cut in half, the flat side facing toward the right. A deep furrow had been gouged around the edge of the half circle and a crisscross slashed over the center. Shadowy gray marks of a previous defacement, Bianca's earlier vandalism, underlay the fresh ones. The shape and color of the half circle looked familiar, but she couldn't quite place it.

She called him to her side and pointed at the disfigurement.

Your pillar must be healed, Sam, she said, trying to keep fury from her voice. What had been done to him was intolerable. *Touch it. Make it right.*

On seeing the defacement, his eyes sparked gold and his mouth twisted in silent anger. *Touch it, think about making it whole again,* she commanded.

He pressed his palm against the scarred area and stroked it as though smoothing the wrinkles from a tablecloth. After each pass of his hand, a section of rose emerged, radiant and unblemished. Only when the marring was erased did Sam's feral expression return to normal.

The familiarity of the half circle haunted her more acutely now that it was restored. Her own pillar was so close that they had brushed against it during the healing. She walked around it, scanning it, Sam following and watching over her shoulder. On the far side, a half circle extended from the crimson patch on her pillar. It was on the same level, the same size and shape as the one on Sam's, but reversed, the flat edge toward the left.

Two parts meant to be together, she said as she traced the rose half circle with her fingertips.

Make it right, Callie, love, he said, as he slipped a hand under her hair to stroke the back of her neck.

He had penetrated the disguise and was no longer terrified, so she dropped Rosemary's form, and let her own astral body emerge. He smiled as her face appeared. She kept Rosemary's nightwalking outfit, in honor of her and all the women before who had borne the mantle of the psychic.

With her silver cord looped about her pillar, she slowly swiveled it until the two half circles faced each other, aligned to form a full circle. With an inner snap, she felt them engage like a bolt snapping home. An elixir of poetry saturated her soul. Sam's eyes called her and they moved simultaneously, auras blending, astral bodies merging until only an oval of rainbow light remained between the pillars.

Combined, they understood where they had sprung from, and how that supported the heart and soul of one another, beginning with his need to heal, her compulsion to create. No words or avowals of love were exchanged. Only emotion and spirit flowing from one to the other. Until there was no other. Just the one.

Gradually, they become separate souls, although still linked on some level and depth that Callan couldn't plumb. *Time to go home, Sam,* she said, wanting to remain like this always, standing within the shelter of their blended auras, but that wasn't possible. Their bodies required a spirit to continue living, and it wasn't yet time for them to take ship from the astral plane. Arms about each other, they soared toward the gateway and the earthly world awaiting them. Moments later, they stood beside his bed, where his body rested.

I don't want to go back in there, he said, looking with distaste at the uninhabited flesh on the bed. *It's coarse, so physical, and yet somehow powerless too. I like the astral body better.*

I know. But the body is where we live and learn. Where we can be together. And the nightwalking is there, when we wish to see clouds beneath our feet.

His astral spirit settled into the body. *Sleep well, love. I'll see you tomorrow.*

She reluctantly turned away and flew toward her house and the body that awaited her there.

Chapter Fourteen

ଚଠ

Callie? Sam's joyful mind voice opened her eyes at seven the next morning. He was on his way to her. She had just enough time to wash her face, brush her teeth and run a brush through her hair. She opened the front door just as he came up the porch steps.

His hair was wet from a shower, and he hadn't bothered to shave. He wore tight running shorts, a tank top and carelessly tied jogging shoes. He looked incandescent, happiness stripping away the years, making him look like a boy of seventeen again.

Laughing, they threw their arms around each other, and whirled about in a dance of celebration, knowing that no one could emotionally separate them again. The laughter subsided and they stood in the foyer, looking into each other's eyes, absorbing the joy each found in the other.

"Do you remember last night and understand what happened to you yesterday, Sam?"

"Most of it, it think. You came to me as Rosemary," he answered, his vision turned inward. "We went to the astral plane and moved my pillar of light. What a fantastic place! We corrected Bianca's sabotage. And fulfilled the bond we began as children. You are going to marry me, aren't you, Callie love?"

"Didn't we do that last night?" She wanted to cry and laugh at the same time. Her eyes tingled with tears while she swallowed a chuckle that crawled at the back of her throat.

"So we did. But the relatives will expect a ceremony and shindig. How long will it take to get it together?"

"Not long. We'll keep it simple."

"Good. We've waited too many years already."

"Let's go downstairs before we wake Connor. We've got so much to talk about."

They stretched out on the family room couch, faces inches apart, legs intertwined. His hands found their way inside her robe. He slid the soft knit of the old orange nightshirt over her body, molding it against her back and waist and down her backside to her thighs.

"This is a great shirt," he murmured into her neck.

"I like you without one," she answered, as she pushed up his tank top and with abandon relished the warm, solid feel of his flesh under her hands. She sank into a sensuous, dreamy state, enjoying the warmth of his body. She felt him follow her into the same hypnotic state that much resembled their joining on the astral plane the night before. They drifted on a warm sea of contentment and sensual awareness.

Callan couldn't hold the dreamy state. She wished they could stay exactly as they were forever, but unanswered questions bubbled up through the pleasure like gases in a lava pool.

Finally, she said into his chest, "It was bad for you, wasn't it? These past two weeks, I kept picking up this buried emotion from you. Doubt and distrust and caution, even fear. Leftovers from what Bianca did to you long ago, I suspect. Tell me about that time."

Sam pushed himself further up on the couch cushions and smoothed her hair back from her face. Looking into her eyes, his were bleak with remembrance.

"That spring after we moved to Chicago was the most horrible time I've ever lived through," he answered. "One morning I woke up convinced that you had found another guy, that you no longer wanted me. The pain was devastating, but I accepted it as a fact immediately. I believed you had used your uncanny ability to foretell or inspire destiny, I suppose, and knew we weren't meant to be together. I told myself that you had communicated your rejection in a dream by using your paranormal powers somehow."

He paused and looked away as if it was difficult for him to continue. She sensed that talking brought up his long ago feelings as though they had just happened. She could understand. Last night above his pool, she had relived that terrible time herself.

"Go on, tell me the rest."

"After that, any more than a fleeting thought of you, and I'd get a panic reaction, sick to my stomach, sweating and trembling. Total irrational terror. I didn't even dare think your name.

"Because you were completely integrated into my childhood," he went on, "the phobia made much of my past in Apple Springs off-limits. I had to be very careful whenever I needed to think about the past. It became a habit, avoiding any memory of you, although at times I believed I was simply going crazy.

"Plus, for years I had a hard time even talking to girls, since friendship with a girl triggered memories of you. It wasn't until I met Julie that I managed to form a relationship with a woman. She was a generous person, straightforward and honest, and she laughed a lot. Living was always an adventure for her, and she infused some fun into my life after years of grind in college and medical school. I guess enough time had gone by and the damage Bianca had done gradually mended, or maybe I healed because I desperately needed to love someone. After we married, I was able to recall more of my childhood and you without it causing unbearable anxiety. I'll always be thankful for the years with her.

"That's the real reason I surprised you at the gym that first day. To be certain that actually seeing you wouldn't send me into an uncontrollable panic attack. It was close at first, but I was able to manage the turmoil I felt. It got easier as time went on."

"I'm sorry that Bianca hurt you so much, Sam." Guilt for what he had undergone clogged her throat with the salty taste of swallowed tears. All these years she'd assumed he'd been guilty of heartlessness, but in reality, he had been tormented and paid a higher price than she.

Callan hugged him closer and murmured into his chest, "Thank god for Julie. I've got so much to thank her for."

There was nothing else to say and no way to make it up to him. Sometime in the last minute, her unacknowledged jealously of Julie had drained away. Feeling envious over Julie's place in Sam's life was exceptionally stupid. Now, there could only be gratitude toward the dark-haired girl who had loved Sam and liberated him from Bianca' terrorism.

"How was that time for you, Callie love?"

She told him what happened and how much she now regretted not seeking him out in Chicago. "I feel so bad, so guilty. I should have known better, that you would never do something like that."

"Wouldn't have done any good. I'd have run from you in terror. It wasn't your fault. Only Bianca's."

"Hi, Sam. You're too late for dinner." Callan had been so absorbed in Sam that she hadn't even sensed Connor approaching. He stood in the doorway in his disreputable cutoff sweatpants and baggy T-shirt.

"But I'm glad you came for breakfast," he added through a yawn. "Are you guys kissing again?" Callan fathomed that his half smile and half grimace implied that kissing was permissible if he got Sam's goodwill as a consequence.

"Oh, I just stopped by to ask your mom to marry me. That okay with you?"

Connor sleepy haze evaporated. "Sure," he said, as a wide grin cracked his face and his deep blue eyes sparkled. "If you let me tell old Eddie Chudy he's out of the running."

* * * * *

"Sam's here!" Connor's yell echoed up the stairs, followed by the murmur of Sam's deep voice.

As she stood before the mirror for a final inspection of the long, white and silver chiffon gown, Callan felt primed for the night. The lace bodice, re-embroidered with delicate silver thread, shimmered, and the multilayered skirt floated like mist. The dress certainly met her criteria for a seduction outfit. It felt sensuous from the inside. A halter top, leaving the back bare to two inches below the waist. No bra, of course. Sheer, white thigh-high stockings with lace edging. Itsy-bitsy white lace bikini panties. High-heeled, white satin sandals. No way could Rosemary or Steph ever accuse her of being a prude in this dress. The gown was simple and classic, just as she liked it. She hoped Sam would like it too. They didn't have much time.

All day an unnatural black density permeated the house, as though a massive storm front rushed from over the mountains. Bianca was planning something, Callan sensed, but her clairvoyance couldn't unravel how or when. It was maddening that with her psychic senses, she would always fall short where Bianca was concerned. Soon though, tomorrow maybe, Bianca would strike. The uncanny tension hovered, waiting to close her in a trap.

While attending to the routine of a busy Saturday, she considered the options in a battle with Bianca and had come to a decision.

She was Dame Callan, Rosemary's inheritor, the psychic power carried in every cell of her body. To her surprise, she could accept that now without reservation. She was also an artist, with the creativity tied into the psychic. And Connor's mother, tied to him in a bond of bone and blood and love. And Sam's beloved. The different roles fused in her soul. That was finally thoroughly understood.

Life as Bianca's slave would be intolerable. None of her loves would survive and she'd be truly empty. No matter how thoroughly Bianca suppressed the genuine Callan, even as a slave she would know what she had lost and what she had become. When the battle commenced, Callan would give no quarter and use every ounce of her psychic, emotional and physical strength to win. The fight would rage until she triumphed or Bianca destroyed her utterly. The acceptance of who she was and the payment required for preserving that true self left her feeling curiously peaceful, almost buoyant with joy in each successive moment.

Before facing The Gull, she hoped for one loving night with Sam. Their soul bonding had been consummated on the astral plane, but her body craved the final earthly joining. After the next hours, they might never have another chance in this life. Who could predict whether they would meet and love again during another lifetime? She couldn't foresee it. Perhaps, if they came together before the last deadly psychic battle, their two souls would be drawn to each other in a future time and place if she lost to Bianca.

Sam could be a problem. He was an unusually principled man, and if he insisted on a marriage license and wedding, she wouldn't have the power to change his mind. In the past his stringent self-control was unshakable. She hoped he would be pliable tonight. It was time for them. Years past time.

After giving a final check in the mirror, she draped a long black taffeta evening coat over her arm and picked up a beaded evening bag. Connor arrived outside the bedroom door just as she opened it.

"He's here!" Connor said. "I've put him in the living room like you said. Hey, you two match. Black and white. He's wearing a monkey suit. He's got suspenders, but he doesn't wear those funny garters to hold up his socks like Grandpa Nevins does. He showed me. Sam's way cool."

"It's great that you like Sam. No garters makes him cool," she said, her mood soaring. Sam, music, good food, and dancing and a possible sexy ending to the evening. What could be better? She felt seventeen again. She turned and started toward the stairs.

"What happened to the back?"

Something wet slid from below her hair to her waist. With a squeak of surprise, she whirled around. Connor stood almost on her heels.

"What was that?"

"Just my baseball," he said hesitantly, holding it up.

"Ick! It's wet! What's that disgusting stuff on it?"

"I dropped it in the aquarium and had to fish it off the bottom."

"You rolled goldfish doo-doo on my back?" Incredulous, she gingerly reached around to investigate. Her hand came away damp and slightly sticky.

"What's gotten into you? Why'd you do that?" she snapped.

"Well—I dunno, I just did." His eyes were downcast under her outrage.

Callan grabbed a handful of his T-shirt and hauled him back into the bedroom. After dumping the purse and coat on the bed, she headed for the bathroom, pulling Connor behind.

"If you've ruined this dress, I'm going to commit more child abuse than feeding you a hamburger!" she said, as she craned her neck to view her back in the bathroom mirror.

"It's only a little bit of stuff."

She only grunted at that, tied a bath towel around her waist and hips, soaped a washcloth and wrung out the excess moisture.

"You're in luck," she said through her teeth. "You didn't get the dress. I haven't time to bathe and change again. Get over here and wash this yuck off me. I can't reach."

Connor obeyed sheepishly, rubbing the washcloth over her back.

"Be careful, don't get the dress wet!" she snapped, as he neared the waistline.

She took back the washcloth, rinsed it, and handed it back to Connor. "Rinse the soap off."

When he was done, she dabbed at her back with a towel. She checked her hair, grimaced at the flushed face in the mirror, smoothed and settled the dress at the waistline, and tried to calm herself. With a sigh, she crossed her arms and considered her son with a perplexed frown. Connor had loosened up all right, reverting to an impulsive, heedless kid. Why couldn't he at least do the expected with a baseball, like break a window? Instead, he had to use his mother for a cleaning rag.

"I can't believe you did that. Is this in retaliation for not taking you along tonight?"

"Nope. I don't know why. I'm sorry, Mom," he said, eyes still downcast.

"Okay, we'll talk about this tomorrow."

She left the bathroom, snatched up the purse and coat from the bed, swept out the door and down the stairs, Connor trailing behind.

Sam was waiting in the foyer with a raised eyebrow and a quizzical half smile. In his tuxedo, he was eye-catching, the white of his shirt emphasizing his tanned face and drawing chestnut highlights from his hair. The suit stressed the broadness of his shoulders and the trimness of his waist. The sight of him sent a shiver down her back, along the same track the slimy baseball had followed, but causing a delightfully sensual reaction.

"I'm in deep shit, Sam," Connor said.

"Watch your mouth, young man!"

"Is there a problem?" Sam asked politely, a trace of concern showing.

"Well, it was really only a little goldfish shi—"

"Connor! Hush up! Stephanie is expecting you. Where's your overnight bag?" Callan demanded, unable to contain her irritation. Connor picked up a bag from the last stair step and waggled it at her.

"Did you shake hands with him, Sam?" Psychiatrist or not, Sam was still an innocent where kids were concerned.

"No, he said his hands were dirty."

"Eesh! You got lucky. I'm neck deep in the stuff!"

She pivoted on a high heel and marched to the front door, giving Sam his first look at her bare back.

When Stephanie answered the front door, her eyes crinkled and a grin blossomed. She checked out Sam first and then Callan's outfit and expression. "You two look absolutely royal," she said.

"Steph, make sure he gets washed up," Callan said with a jerk of her thumb at Connor.

To Connor, she ordered, "All the way up your arms. Change your shirt. Wash that, too." She pointed at the baseball he still held.

"We'll take good care of him. You two have a great time."

"Thanks, Steph," Callan said with a grateful smile. "I'll pay back all the babysitting you've done for me lately." *If I'm still around*, she amended silently.

"Matt and I have plans for a week alone in the Bahamas next winter," she answered, anticipation lighting up her face. "You can pay us back then."

"Gladly."

Between that word and the next breath, she drew on the life energy she now carried like an extra heart and added another layer to the protective aura around the Ellisons' house.

Stephanie winked at Sam and said, "Don't worry about a thing. Have a sensational time."

Sam nodded his thanks to her and said, "See ya, Connor." He added a man-to-man slap on the shoulder and led Callan down the porch steps.

In the car, when Callan told him what Connor had done, he guffawed so hard he nearly missed the exit for the freeway.

"The whole thing's your fault, Sam. You turned him into a typical preadolescent," she accused, and then joined in his laughter, her annoyance dissipating. "Between him and Bianca, I've had a hard time staying clean lately."

"Connor just needed to square his view of the world and get his thinking about himself straight. But do you notice a subtle similarity to your current problem with Bianca?" he asked in a sober voice.

Callan looked down at her hands and considered for a moment.

"Bianca's strategies and actions aren't well thought out or logical. That phony, outlandish cobra, for instance. The bird guano on Evelyn. Even terrorizing Stephanie. They seem impulsive, almost whimsical in a way. None of them effective in conquering me. More like a kid's game of one-upmanship. She's had infinite opportunities to take me over. She's arrogant and reckless, in that she doesn't believe that I could effectively fight back."

"You're right on the money," he said and squeezed her hand. "Deadly, of course, when she wants to be. Don't forget Bernie Rabney and Rosemary. Senseless deaths. Neither of them really endangered her. Many others, apparently, over the years. A gull is an appropriate image for a vicious, amoral child."

"A psychic loony bird, you mean. She's a waste of human skin."

Sam grinned. "Not expressed in textbook medical terms, but an apt colloquial description of the woman."

"I don't want to think about her tonight," she said, anxiety creeping in to surround her again. "This is our night."

"As you say, Callie love, our night. And have I told you how exquisite you look?"

The Gull banished, they gave themselves over to the pleasure of the evening. The dinner and concert were held at a downtown Denver hotel ballroom. The well-dressed crowd's jewels and colorful eveningwear glittered in the chandelier-lit room.

During the cocktail hour before dinner, Sam circulated, introducing her to friends and medical colleagues. With his warm hand resting at her bare waist, she felt his pride and happiness as he pronounced her his fiancée. Envy flowed from many of the women and whispered around her like the mournful sighing of wind through pine trees. The depth of their jealousy shocked her for a moment until she acknowledged that Sam's looks and charm had captured these women. They only saw the surface of him and wouldn't they be even more envious if they knew the wonderful inner man. She felt smug until she reminded herself that destiny might change for her at any moment.

What truly amazed her was the men's deep subliminal reaction to her. She knew she was pleasing to look at in the white and silver gown, but her allure was more than physical attractiveness, more than the sparkle created from happiness, more than that she was a mysterious stranger who had appeared as Sam's fiancée.

Under the scrutiny of a tall, steely-eyed surgeon, she caught the thought, *An enigma.*

I'm mysterious to them, she realized, *because I'm no longer a mystery to myself. It's rare to meet someone who knows exactly who and what they are and what they are meant to be. That must generate a unique aura. Although few people have the privilege of examining their pillar of light, as well.*

As evening progressed through the multicourse dinner, more people stopped to greet Sam. *No wonder he is obviously liked and admired. His charisma is even more potent than during the years at Apple Springs.*

After the dinner, when the concert began, flamenco, jazz and pop came together to create an exotic, sultry Latin night. They held hands under the tablecloth, let their emotions merge, and as one they flowed into the rhythms of the elegant guitar music.

In the sonorous throb of the guitar came the call to fiesta, and an image of a brightly-colored gypsy skirt flaring in an unending spin. A high-stepping stallion pranced under a full moon, and in the shadows of a mysterious courtyard two lovers kissed as palm leaves pattered like night rain. The moan of background horn became the mournful crying for a love that failed to step out of a sunrise.

When the music ended, Callan emerged from a gratifying emotional and sensory high. Each molecule in her body seemed to be frolicking in delight. Anything and everything seemed possible.

"My feet won't stop tapping for days," she sighed in pleasure.

"Mine either. I caught those images you sent me. You put on quite a show."

"You added a few of your own. That gypsy dancer was quite alluring," she teased.

"Didn't you notice the white and silver dress, *senorita*?" he whispered in her ear. "By the way, I especially liked the horse. Very symbolic."

"Wasn't mine. Must have been yours."

"Maybe," he grinned. "Our fantasies seemed to have gotten blended. Anyway, if you feel like dancing, we can join some of this crowd. They're sure to be heading to a club."

"I'd love to dance with you again, but I wish it could be to the music we just heard."

"In that case, I know just the place."

"Where?"

"My house."

* * * * *

Sam unlocked his front door and ushered her into his foyer. "I don't know why I bought such a big place," he said, sounding a little tense, "except that my accountant said I needed a tax deduction. But I just use the kitchen, family room and one bedroom. Otherwise, I just rattle around in here. It's not even furnished. We can decide later whether to live here, or your house, or somewhere else entirely."

He adjusted the chandelier's light level until the expanse of satiny parquet floor softly glowed as though illuminated by candlelight.

"This is stunning, Sam, and a wonderful ballroom." She slipped off her evening coat.

"Not as stunning as you are tonight." He took her coat and handbag and brushed his fingertips along her cheek. She shivered in anticipation of the night to come. "Wait, and you'll have your music and dance."

Sam disappeared into the room far down on the right, where she had found him on her first nightwalk. She hadn't told him what she'd done that night, sneaking in to sit in his lap while he slept. She smiled at the memory and walked to the foot of the stairs to look at the dark landing windows above. A faint blue glow from the reflected pool shone through. Perhaps, she wouldn't tell him. Not right away, at any rate. Some secrets weren't meant to be told, just treasured. Haunting guitar music suddenly filled the foyer with the memory of love, long ago times and nostalgia.

Sam reappeared out of the shadows and extended his hand. She slipped into his arms, and the rhythmic guitar took them and joined their movements. Her skirt flared out from her ankles and the soft glow of the chandelier highlighted the silver threads in the white lace. In Sam's arms, she felt as light and as free as when floating through clouds during a nightwalk. At times, she was sure their feet left the floor.

Sam knew how to make a woman feel beautiful. He turned the dance into distilled flight, fluid but controlled, giving Callan gentle momentum in her movements. The Latin beat tempted them, swayed them, stretched them, turned them, pushed them apart, pulled them together to lock thighs and spin, and finally pause at the foot of the stairs. They hesitated, her back arched over his arm, her hand held against the beat of his heart. Her other hand caressed the back of his neck. They swayed gently to the music.

The sensual light in his half-closed eyes teased her, but he remained silent, an elusive smile slipping across his face.

He wanted her. She didn't need empathic ability to know that. She expected he would turn and lead her up the stairs to the room behind the big double doors. Ripples of desire coursed through his body and her own. But he didn't move, just held her close and gently swayed in place. Looking into his eyes, she perceived that the initiative was to be hers, then, this first time.

Perhaps Sam's failure to act was his form of revenge for the provocative dress she wore. No, he wasn't so petty or given to retaliation in any form. Or, maybe, because he had always called a halt to their lovemaking during their teenage years, he was offering her the chance to finally decree that now was their time.

The erotic attraction building between them for the past two weeks had reached a pinnacle tonight. His Sam-perfume muddled her head. She was enraptured and breathless, and not a little flustered by the enticing, enigmatic look in his eyes. Embarrassed all of a sudden, she wished she had more moxie, like Stephanie or Rosemary. She was no good at this seduction business. *Do the simple thing*, instinct told her. So she straightened in his arms and kissed him.

The fever heightened between them, but when it gradually ended, he continued with feather-light kisses across her cheek and down her bare shoulder. He still didn't move up the stairs. When he lifted his head and looked down into her eyes, she knew he was going to tease her, make her say what she wanted. She didn't know how to say what she wanted. Not with any grace or class, anyway. This night must be beautiful, as it might set a standard for the rest of their lives. Standing there silently, not knowing what to do, was a torment. A memory floated up through the turmoil.

"Do you remember that old chicken coop on your folks' property when we were little?" she finally blurted out.

"Sure do. You and I had a disagreement down there. I gave up a yellow truck I was fond of to make up with you."

"Do you remember what the argument was about?" she pressed on, her stomach fluttering with embarrassment.

"I was upset because you didn't look like me. As I recall, you compared me to a warty frog — with its tongue hanging out, I believe." He was holding back a smirk, she could tell. His laugh lines had grown deeper, although the grin hadn't broken through and his voice remained solemn.

"Well, I was wondering, am I going to make the warty frog's acquaintance again any time soon, or is he going to hold out on me in revenge?" The raw clumsiness and raunchiness of the question appalled her. Her cheeks were sizzling.

A grin broke through, as brief as the flicker of a candle flame. "Since he's all grown up now, I think that can be arranged."

He was whooping with laughter inside, she could tell. Waves of amusement flowed from him, robust as a strong red wine and as effervescent as champagne.

"That's one of the things I love about you," he whispered as he nuzzled her neck, "you're always original."

"So love me."

With his warm hand caressing her back, he turned and led her up the stairs.

* * * * *

Behind the big double doors, music played. They drifted into the bedroom as if the dance continued. Sam flicked a switch and a bedside lamp came on. In the muted light, the room's colors were pale grays accented with burgundy. Sam paused as they reached the center of the room. He pulled her against his chest and slipped his hand under her fall of hair, tipping her face up to his.

"I'm sorry, Callie." His voice was gruff and his eyes remorseful. "I was unkind to force you to take the lead. But it's strange. At the last moment I couldn't quite make the move up the stairs," he said, irony in his voice. "I think I'm a little scared."

Her hand rested on the stiff tucks of his tuxedo shirt. Under it she could feel his racing heart and turbulent emotions.

"Why would you be scared?" She was puzzled and a little worried by his confession. Looking into his eyes, she knew he loved and desired her, now more deeply than he had as a boy. That was true of her feelings as well. Their emotions had evolved, become more complex, intensified by the years they had been apart and the maturing each had done. The night before on the astral plane, they had touched each other's souls in a way few had experienced. There should be no hesitation now.

He sighed and lifted her hand from his shirtfront to place a kiss on the palm of her hand.

"It's irrational, I know, but for some reason I feel that fate will find a way to punish me for my rigid, priggish standards when we were kids. Because I left you and denied the gift of love then. It's crazy, but I feel as if something will keep us apart at the last moment. Here I am, trained in the workings of the mind, but I've been carrying this unsettling superstition around all day. I can't seem to shake it." His voice was husky with unease.

She bowed her head and let her forehead rest against his shoulder. Weariness and rage swept through her, one after another, like flashes of cold and then heat. Even in this moment that should have been dedicated to them alone, Bianca intruded. Sam had picked up on her clairvoyant awareness that The Gull would soon provoke the last battle for her mind and soul.

With an inner start of dread, she thought she heard the thrum of wings beating. For a moment, the sound obliterated the crickets' whirring. She stared past Sam's shoulder to the windows flanking the bed. Unreality washed over her, as if this moment were only a mirage, an illusion created out of passion.

No voyeur with malevolent sapphire eyes glared back at her. Only stars glowed there. The chirp of a sleepy bird dropped delicately into the room. The note blended with the music, and the reassuring sound broke her paralysis. The foreboding was only imagination. Her inner eye saw that the protective aura still radiated softly about the house. The night beyond the window remained empty of a great bird. Her psychic sense told her so. And Sam's apprehension must be relieved.

"We are alone and safe here. Don't worry. And no regrets about the past. You did what you thought best and what you were forced to do. Nothing will keep us apart tonight. I promise."

His fingers found the hooks that secured the halter of her dress. The whisper of chiffon settling upon the carpet merged with the notes of the music. A scrap of white lace and sheer stockings drifted down upon the dress. A black jacket fell beside them. Soft light gilded the turn of breast and hip, highlighted a muscular shoulder and thigh as shirt and pants were discarded. Sam was even more splendid in the flesh than the night before in astral nakedness.

With an arm about her waist, he guided her to the bed. The rustle of bedclothes reverberated with temptation and the freedom at last to do as they needed. What they desired now was to know the feel of earthly flesh, one against the other. To merge on the physical plane as they had on the astral plane.

Hands warm and strong on her skin, with one long stroke he traced her body from shoulder to breasts, to the curve of the waist, across her stomach and downward to her thigh. The caress left her quaking. She stretched, a long supple movement. Again, he ran his hand over her, much slower this time, pausing to cup a breast, trailing the backs of his fingers over her stomach and down to the juncture of her thighs.

In reply, her hands trailed over the sculptured muscles of his back and down to cup his taut buttocks. She urged him closer and sought his mouth. She was hungry for his taste, so hungry, starved during the passing years. Each touch of his mouth on her skin was as nourishing as raindrops on sun-baked earth.

She reveled in the sensation of the hair on his chest rubbing against her breasts, the stroking of his tongue across her lips and the inside of her mouth. His leg was thrown over hers, and his arousal pressed against her hip.

His lips followed the line of her cheek, down her neck, to settle at the crest of her breast, around the side and under, lavishing delicate wet kisses upon her.

"Here?" he asked.

"Yes."

"And here?"

She could no longer answer him except with shivery sighs and urging hands. He stroked and kissed her taut waist and came to hover above her navel. She knew his sensitive lips would detect the two-inch scar just above it. The memory of the origin of the scar intruded and brought her down from the sensual bliss. Slight as it was, his lips would register the telltale mark. But it no longer mattered now, that badge of failure and inadequacy. She let it go in a long moan.

As she had done once before, she reached outward for the sexual Earth energy woven into the protective astral aura surrounding the house. Monitoring its potency, she siphoned it into her mind then let it enfold them gently. Her passion increased tenfold, flaming unbearably. On and on the astral energy flowed through them, heightening their senses. Their movements together were as fluid as wind rippling over grass, supple body upon supple body. Until the grass caught fire, blazed up and fused their bodies as their spirits had on the astral plane.

Completion filling them, they favored each other with caresses, sultry kisses and contented murmurs.

"I feel like a pebble washed down a mountain in a flash flood," Callan said much later, stretching in satisfaction.

"I've got a remedy for little sore pebbles," Sam replied, tickling the offended area.

"Sam!"

His rowdy laugh echoed through the bedroom. "Come on," he said and rolled out of bed. "I've got just what you need."

Leading her by the hand, he headed across the big bedroom. The flexing of his backside as he strode in front of her was fabulously provocative.

"Oh, my," she whispered under her breath. His rear was so taut she could hardly gather enough skin for a good pinch.

He jumped and whirled around, an astounded look on his face. He caught her up in a bear hug. "You little devil!"

She looked at him through her lashes and said in a prim voice, "You don't swing a butt like yours in front of a woman and not expect a reaction."

"I'll be damned. Callie, love, you've turned brazen on me."

In revenge he got behind her, fondled her all the way across the bedroom, and waltzed her into a sumptuous bathroom. The white and green tiled room overflowed with plants. They hung from brackets in the ceiling, sprouted from planters in every corner, and edged the rim of the tub. The greenery nearly concealed the fact that the bath was big enough for two.

"This will get you back in shape in no time. It's a whirlpool." His hand drifted down, slowly appreciating each delicate curve and sensitive area. His touch arrested her laughter, smothered by the electric sensation flickering through her body. By the time he stopped the teasing and turned on the water, Callan's knees were quivering.

"Hop in," he said, and handed her into the rising warm water.

As she settled back into the water, he pulled on a navy robe while his eyes roved appreciatively over her. "I'll go get us a snack and a drink fitting for my decadent spa."

"Dr. Cavendar, I've always though you were uptight and straight-laced. But you're a fake. You're really a closet sensualist."

"Fooled you. Psychics don't know everything. I'll be right back. Keep the water moving."

With a contented sigh, Callan lay back in the waist-deep water and studied the bathroom. Unlike most of the house, this room had been completely decorated. Above the whirlpool, the white tile was inlaid with green tiles, each individual tile etched with a different cluster of leaves and flowers. A white, fluffy round rug covered most of the floor. Brass holders and racks held thick white and green striped towels. The wide, high-set windows were covered with green louvered shutters. Ferns and variegated vines in brass pots hung in front of the windows and out over the whirlpool, creating a verdant bower.

She poured a small amount of herbal body shampoo from an ornately shaped green bottle into the rippling water. Foam and a rich, mossy fragrance rose around her. Relaxing deeper in deliciously scented water, she propped a leg on the tub's tiled rim, and closed her eyes with a satisfied sigh. Soothing jets of water massaged her body, enhancing her dreamy, lazy serenity.

I feel young and new. Sam's magic is certainly potent. Oh, yes, definitely potent.

She giggled softly and pushed wet hair up and away from her neck, then rested her elbow on the tub's edge. Something slid under her armpit and across the instep of her elevated foot. Her toes curled. Sam had crept back into the bathroom. He liked to tickle. She wasn't unusually sensitive, except in a specific private area, so he was out of luck. With a grin she said, "That was quick," turning her head and opening her eyes.

A slender, grass-green snake with a long, tapered nose was trapped under her upper arm. The head wove in a lazy arc inches from her eyes. The vertical black pupils, surrounded by speckled yellow, looked directly into hers.

Her mind froze and she simply stared into the dead-black pupils. Feather-like, the snake's forked tongue grazed the tip of her nose. Recoiling, her arm slid from the side of the whirlpool, taking the snake with it. As it fell, the snake struck her breast. The green body disappeared under the water.

The thing squirmed against her stomach. The feel of it made shivers dance down her spine and rush out across her skin. In revulsion, she flailed at the creature, slapping at the water. The writhing body eluded her. A long gasp blocked her throat, a scream caught behind it. Only a feeble wail escaped her.

Her left ankle was hooked on the tub edge. A pencil-thin, dark green garter snake draped her big toe. She flinched in horror and jerked her leg into the tub. Riding her foot down, the snake disappeared into the swirling water.

Moaning, she struggled to stand. As she lurched to a half-crouch, coiled serpents rained from the potted plants above the whirlpool. They struck out as they fell. Flickering tongues tickled her naked skin. Coils and tails of serpentine bodies churned the frothy water.

Their mass and her panic overbalanced her and toppled her back into the water. A bulky, speckled, reddish-brown snake encircled her thigh and began to squeeze. Panting in terror, she grasped the snake and tried to wrest it from her leg. Another, turquoise and ringed with coral, poked its head up between her spread lags and crawled over her pubic mound. Its diamond-shaped head poked at her navel. She let go of the boa circling her thigh and slapped it away from her stomach.

A daffodil-yellow boa dropped from above, curled around her neck and began to tighten. The golden eyes glittered as the snout nuzzled her cheek in a serpentine kiss. More brightly colored bodies slithered over the tub's edge. The water boiled with lithe, squirming flesh. She clumsily struggled to stand again, uncoordinated in hysteria, hands slapping and brushing frantically at the reptiles.

Under the swish of pulsing water, the thrashing and hissing of snakes and her own agonized moaning, she heard giggles. The smell of rotting onions obliterated the herbal scent.

Tee, hee, tee, hee, came the shrill titter. The mind voice immobilized her. *Got ya, got you good this time. Do you like Our little friends?*

A huge black and tan diamond-backed rattler slithered onto the tub edge and coiled there. Its castanet rattling echoed off the tiled walls and harmonized with the giggles. Whitish mouth gaping wide, fangs forward, the snake lunged. The fangs fastened into the nipple of her right breast. Callan descended into mindless darkness and slipped under the water.

Chapter Fifteen

ಐ

The snakes — the snakes — the snakes.

From the blackness inside, the words unrolled with a hopeless horror that wouldn't end. They held her prisoner with their strength, constricting her arms, pinning her legs. Biting, over and over. Oh god, the excruciating tickle of their tongues brushing her skin. She fought, but there were so many lashing, whip-like bodies. They held her helpless. She couldn't breathe. She couldn't get away.

"Noooooo," she keened, and struggled harder.

Callie, Callie, Callie. A whisper at first in the basement of her mind, without meaning, then evolving into sounds that came from without. "Callie, it's okay." Over and over the voice repeated the word. Callie. Her name, she understood after what seemed a million years.

"It's Sam. Callie, I'm here…I'm here…"

Sam? There was something special about that word. A safe word. Hang onto the word Sam. Follow the word Sam.

Sam. The word conjured a face. A good face. And the voice, which had always resonated in her mind and carried with it safety and rapture, spoke from somewhere close. Yes, Sam was nearby. Find Sam.

"Callie, open your eyes and look at me," the voice of Sam demanded. "You're okay, you're safe. I have you safe."

It was possible to obey that voice. She opened her eyes and Sam was there. He looked down at her, his eyes squinted in alarm, sweat running into them, with a long bloody scratch below the left one.

They were in the dimly lit bedroom, lying crosswise on the bed, Sam's leg hooked around hers weighing her down, his arms pinning hers. The world rushed into focus, their evening together, and the minutes in the whirlpool. Her body convulsed in terror at the memory. He tightened his hold.

"Easy, easy," he reassured her. "Relax. Take a deep breath. Don't fight me. Do you know where you are?"

She took a long breath, slowly let it out, and said hoarsely, "In your bedroom. Oh, Sam, she…Bianca…she made snakes in the whirlpool. They fell on me. Touched me with their awful tongues. Bit me." She began to sob, long hiccupping groans.

His hold loosened, but he pulled her closer to cuddle her against his body. As he held her, he stroked her back.

"I saw no snakes, love," he said. "I'd just reached the kitchen when I knew something was wrong up here. I don't know how I knew. When I rushed into the bathroom, you were under the water. No snakes, Callie. It was only a hallucination. When I pulled you out, you fought me."

"They felt real enough. So real I can still feel them crawling over me." She shuddered deeply, skin crawling as though long-legged spiders walked over her. Exhaustion and shock tinged her voice with despair. Sam pulled up the comforter, cocooning their damp bodies in its warmth.

"I lost myself, Sam. And I hurt you too," she said, touching his cheek below the scratch. "Bianca's playing her games again. But she made no attempt to take my mind when I was fighting the snakes. I was defenseless. She could have overpowered me easily."

"How did she get in?" he asked. A psychic horror had penetrated his home to torment them. "Didn't you have a shield around the house?"

"I don't know." She closed her eyes and cautiously extended a tentacle of psychic sense to investigate the shield. Only a thin, amorphous shell remained of the once thick aura. During their lovemaking, she must have drained enough power from the shield to leave them vulnerable to Bianca's mania. Or, perhaps, sex somehow disrupted the psychic channel that funneled astral life energy to the shield. Her intuitive perception said that both explanations were likely, unless Bianca wielded power beyond imagining. Another psychic principle she hadn't known about.

"It did have a shield," she said, new panic flooding her. "But most of the shield is gone now. Oh, god, I wonder if it's disappeared from around the Ellisons' house too. Connor! I've got to get home."

They frantically pulled on clothes, Callan in her rumpled gown with the black taffeta evening coat thrown over it. Sam hastily donned jeans and a T-shirt.

The lights in the Ellisons' house were blazing as they pulled into the cul-de-sac. As soon as the car stopped, Callan jumped out and ran for the house, Sam at her heels. Stephanie flung open the front door as they ran up the porch steps.

"Connor's gone!" Stephanie burst out as they rushed into the foyer. "I got up to check on Katie and stopped by the boys' room. He wasn't there. The screen was pulled off and the window lock snapped. There was a ladder against the wall. Zach said he didn't hear anything."

Matt stood with Katie in his arms at the foot of the stairs, a dazed look on his face. A white-faced Zach stood on the stairs behind him.

Grief and remorse flowed from Stephanie in a torrent. "Callan, I'm so sorry. We didn't protect him like we promised."

Callan stood frozen for a moment. It was all real. Bianca had her son. She could no longer hope otherwise. The Gull had distracted her with the snakes so she wouldn't sense his danger. Sam put his arm around her waist, and she leaned against him.

"It's not your fault, Steph. It's mine, for not facing up to Bianca before this. For giving her the chance to take him."

"Who is this woman you're talking about?" Matt interrupted, outrage hardening his usual mellow voice. "We should call the police right now!"

"No, don't!" Callan's sharp command startled Matt into silence. "They can't help."

Callan tilted her head back against Sam's shoulder and let her senses flow upstairs to Zach's corner bedroom. The essence of her son, like a lingering fragrance, led from the empty twin bed on the left to the window and out into the predawn chill. A vehicle had parked in the field behind the cul-de-sac. She could mind smell its gassy, metallic scent as if she stood beside it. It had returned overland, across a field where a colony of prairie dogs lived, to a track at the edge of the golf course. The trace led into the club parking lot and then out into the street. Faint, but definite, the psychic trail led west then angled north. Bianca was taking Connor into the mountains.

On the dawn breeze came the familiar accented voice and the challenge, distant, but solid in its resolution. *If you want your precious boy, come to me, find me if you can, my sister.*

So, the final battle began with a game of hide and seek, with Connor as the prize. Childish, yet so dangerous in its potential outcome. She had expected to face The Gull alone with only herself to worry about. All her efforts to protect her loved ones had been useless and naïve. No attack on the astral plane would come as she had anticipated. Bianca had simply come in the night to kidnap Connor physically. *You've been gullible,* she condemned herself, *always assuming Bianca would do the expected.*

With an inner sigh, she returned her attention to Stephanie and her family, who were staring at her, waiting for directions.

"I'll find Connor myself. No police. Promise me, Steph. You know it's the only way. Explain it to Matt."

"Callie," Sam said. "What are you planning?"

She didn't look at him or answer, simply waited for Stephanie's nod of agreement, then whirled from his embrace. Hurrying through the door onto the porch, she ran down the steps and across the lawn toward her house. The hem of the taffeta coat swished across the grass, the muted sound pursuing her as surely as destiny.

At the driveway, Sam caught her arm and spun her to face him. "You can't go after Connor alone. I'm going with you."

"No. You can't. If you do, Bianca will acquire another hostage. She'll use you against me in some horrible way. I don't have the power to defend both Connor and you. Don't put me in a position where I have to choose between you." Callan's voice was flat, devoid of entreaty. Her blunt evaluation of the situation left Sam without a comeback. What she said was indisputable. They stood facing each other, letting her statement taint the fresh, chilled air.

"There must be some way I can help," Sam said, voice rough with dismay.

"Stay here. Be my lifeline. Think of me, and in your thoughts send all the psychic hope and power you can muster. Just knowing that you are here, safe, will be the bedrock I can fight from. That's all you can do. I'm sorry." Callan stepped around him. Sam came after, his silence like a feral creature stalking her.

She unlocked the front door, flipped on the foyer lights and those in the kitchen. Crossing the room, she stopped by the connecting door to the garage, and took from a hook the keys that belonged to Evelyn. Only when she held them in her palm did she realize her intent.

"I have to take Evelyn," she said, puzzled at first at the knowledge. Her hand closed into a fist over the keys, and she looked up at Sam. "I don't know why or how I know. I just do. Rosemary told me to always trust my instincts in psychic matters."

His jaw clenched, Sam looked bleak and ashen under the fluorescent kitchen light. She caught his masculine instinct to imprison her within the safety of his arms to prevent her from driving off alone. Looking into his eyes, she shared the moment when he successfully repressed the urge. He had no other choice. To let Bianca keep Connor without a fight would destroy Callan as surely as any psychic battle. And going with her would only increase her danger. It was a hard-won acceptance for Sam.

How ironic, said one corner of her mind. Throughout history, warriors had gone off to war, leaving behind their women, fearful and grieving, to await the outcome. Only a man of uncommon bravery would step back at such a moment, without further protest to delay her, and let his woman go off alone into battle.

It was hard to leave. She had wished for a night of physical love, just one night, vowing that was all she would ever want and that she would be satisfied. They had had their time together, but it didn't seem enough. The heart and body were greedy entities, apparently never satiated. But the call toward Connor was inexorable, pulling like barbed wire twisted around her psychic center.

A brush of her lips across his in salute and in hope, and she turned to open the door.

"Be careful, love," he said.

A punch of a button sent the garage door rumbling up, revealing a thin flamingo pink lip of sunrise. She mourned that Sam had to know the gut-wrenching feeling of the one left behind, but it would be a comfort to know that he was safe, waiting for her to come home. If she came home. But she mustn't think about the ending, only the necessary steps, taken one by one, to retrieve Connor from The Gull.

A turn of the ignition key and Evelyn's engine roared, then settled down to a steady murmur. After a last look at Sam standing in the kitchen doorway, she backed out of the garage, down the driveway and into the street. A glance in the rearview mirror as she turned out of the cul-de-sac showed Sam standing on the lawn, watching her drive away.

Chapter Sixteen

so

The C-470 tollway that encircled the Denver metro area was a mile from Callan's house. Evelyn took the northbound on-ramp with a gratifying roar. After a pause to pay the toll, the Chevy settled onto the multilane expanse of concrete as though it was propelled on a cushion of air. The sun had ascended further, illuminating the mountains on the left in golden light. The evergreen trees on the foothills radiated in emerald glory. The link, a reassuring guide to Connor, pulled steadily at Callan.

This early on Sunday morning, the traffic was light with stretches of vacant highway. As she transferred to the far left lane, Callan speculated on how fast Evelyn would run. She'd never pushed the old car to its limits, even during honor challenges at traffic lights. She hoped that no patrol cars were about, because she intended to find Evelyn's limit and would not stop for anything. Connor's life was in Bianca's capricious, evil hands. In seconds the speedometer read eighty miles per hour. A little more pressure on the accelerator, and with a throaty growl, Evelyn reached for a hundred and captured it.

Slowing her brainwave pattern, Callan hovered between the alpha state of relaxed hyper-awareness and the theta state of psychic perception. Through her hands on the steering wheel, her heartbeat seemed to merge with the steady, satisfying drone of Evelyn's engine. Her senses spread outward upon the shrieking wind as the Chevy cut through it. Her mental radar scanned and interpreted the flow of the sparse traffic ahead and behind. With a gentle cerebral nudge, drivers of slower vehicles were persuaded to graciously move from her path. The speedometer read one hundred and ten and continued climbing.

A feathery tickle grazed the edge of her awareness, so faintly that at first she couldn't be sure she had really felt a mental touch. Again the illusive stroke brushed her mind, more firmly this time. For a moment her theta state wavered. Had Bianca changed her mind and decided to begin the fight for Connor immediately? Or was she simply checking to see if Callan was complying with her summons? But the phantom touch had a different feel to it than the usual savage contact with Bianca. The connection from Connor was passive. But this new probe was dynamic and aware.

She corrected her momentary lapse in attention, sank deeper into the theta state, and cautiously let her inner awareness expand farther. Sam. Since their merge on the astral plane, his mental emanations were becoming nearly as familiar to her as her own. He was miles behind, but coming on steadily. He hadn't been able to defeat his innate need to protect after all. And he'd absorbed enough psychic lore in the past few days to use their bond to track her. It gave her a grim pleasure to know that he was back there. It didn't matter though. She had to stay well ahead of him. He mustn't get involved.

Without shutting down all psychic impressions, including the trace to Connor, the link with Sam couldn't be severed. To keep Sam safe, the battle must be engaged, and won, before he attracted Bianca's attention. Increased pressure on the accelerator, and Evelyn's engine snarled in response. The wind howled and shrieked like blood-hungry demons outside the closed windows. Callan withdrew her awareness of Sam and concentrated once more on the connection to Connor and the traffic.

The subtle lead to her son now pulled toward the northwest and into the foothills. She had to slow at the freeway exchange where C-470 fed into the highway for Boulder. The reduced speed caused her such anxiety that the smooth flow of the psychic pull to Connor was interrupted. For minutes she couldn't sense him. The link had fragmented, leaving her uncertain and unfocused. Should she continue on toward Boulder?

With deliberation, she breathed slowly and deeply, relaxing and coaxing the theta state to return to her mind. The link to Connor flowed back, filling her once more with the essence of his psyche. The pull definitely led toward Boulder and beyond. She roared on into the morning. At over eighty miles per hour, Boulder's outskirts appeared in less than fifteen minutes.

Threading the morning traffic through the city in the foothills slowed her again, but this time the delay didn't interrupt her concentration. Evelyn seemed to pick her own way through the traffic without her guidance, until they finally burst free north of the city. Here, housing developments and small hamlets were interspersed with new-mown hayfields lying golden on gently rolling hills. As the road angled more acutely westward, the terrain changed to densely forested foothills, and then to the canyon that led to the town of Estes Park.

Traffic to Estes Park proceeded in slow, sedate swoops around the wide curves that followed the course of the Big Thompson River. As the road ascended into the mountain pass, small groups of houses, a gas station, a restaurant and an antique store appeared beside the highway. Scattered between the tourist shops, cabins catering to fishermen and tourists nestled beside the river. Across the stream, deluxe resorts were tucked into wider areas along the river and in side canyons. Morning sunlight glinted off foaming rapids and glimmered on the smoother stretches of water.

Groves of aspen and vast tracts of pines dotted the riverbank and the ridge tops across the narrow valley. At these higher elevations, some aspens had already begun the autumn turn and their vivid leaves, ranging from green to golden yellow to a pinkish-orange, flamed against the deeper green of the pines and the vast cobalt sky. In the wind funneling down the pass, the mint-green aspens shimmied in the wind, tossing up their leaves to display silvery undersides.

Further on, the road mounted to hug gray cliffs, edged by a steep fall-off to the river below, and became a two-lane with only brief passing lanes. Evelyn leaned into the long curves, regally sweeping up the inclines, then swooping down the long slopes below with a purring engine. Passing slower cars where she could, Callan kept their speed up, the curves rushing toward her, some wide and leisurely, some tight and fast. Traffic seemed to scatter before her, as the speedometer alternated between fifty and sixty-five. On some curves the speed limit was a modest forty. Too slow, much too slow. Bianca could become impatient at the wait for Callan and take her pique out on Connor.

Get out of my way – get over, Callan aimed the thought, grim and anxious, as she tried to edge around an unyielding pickup truck. Coming out of a tight curve and into a clear straightaway, the truck obligingly crept onto the narrow shoulder of the road.

The pull to Connor grew stronger with every mile that passed, along with a deepening panic. The link with Sam had gone underground, and she didn't bother to search for it. Better that he lose her now among these cliffs.

The canyon became a long tunnel, rugged, sheer rocks on one side and the long drop to the river below. Her outward senses narrowed to her hands and eyes, limited by the necessity of holding Evelyn on the road and making the next fast curve without spinning out into the river or into oncoming traffic. Her forearms and hands ached from twisting the steering wheel mile after mile. She wanted to stop driving for a moment and rests her eyes from the glare of the morning sunlight off Evelyn's hood. Time seemed to be compressed and measured only by the endless whistling of the wind past the car's windows.

The pass spiraled downward and gradually opened to a high meadow with snow-dappled peaks beyond. Ringed by regal mountains, Estes Park lay in the valley just ahead.

She slowed as she entered the town and cast about for a more definite sense of Connor. Bianca must have gone to ground, as the leading trace seemed to have stabilized, no longer shifting and twitching through the ether as it had earlier. The area around the town proper was a maze of roads leading off into side canyons, twining around or over ridges and low hills, leading to homes concealed between their folds and on ridge tops. The general pull toward Connor still led west and north. She rejected the urge to peel off and explore side roads leading in that direction, since her instinct said Connor was still some distance off and not within the town.

The town catered to tourists, and early morning people strolled the sidewalks and spilled out into the street. Holding to the speed limit and watching for jaywalkers, she maneuvered Evelyn through the hamlet. A mountainside abruptly blocked the main street. In necessity, the road twisted south and then north in a steep hairpin curve. A sign indicated that it led to the Rocky Mountain National Forest.

Snow-dusted peaks well exceeding ten thousand feet loomed over her. As they had done when she first arrived in Colorado, these behemoths of creation intimidated her, as if at any moment they would come tumbling down to crush the world.

This road had been carved into the stone wall of an even higher canyon. She deepened the theta state, sharpening the link to Connor, narrowing her perception until the majestic surroundings disappeared, evicted from her awareness. Nothing existed except her hands on Evelyn's steering wheel, the immediate road before the car's hood, and the knowledge that her son was somewhere close ahead. Time narrowed along with the canyon as she turned off to follow a rough, unpaved track. The grade increased and the turns tightened as they climbed the gulch through the mountain. With each twist of the path, the sense of Connor grew more intense.

The trail turned right and just ahead was a cabin. It sat on what appeared to be a large pile of crushed rock heaped in front of a cliff. No vegetation crowded around it. The small log shack had only a sagging door and one broken window in its face. Gray and splintered with weathering, it canted slightly, as if it could topple from its rocky perch and slide down the mountain into the trees below. Golden morning light touched the still mound of ancient wood gently, but the building seemed to repel it. To its left, a dark hole in the cliff indicated that long ago this had been a mine of some kind. Now only blackened debris topped by the lopsided shanty and the ominous opening in the mountain remained.

Connor was there in that aged ruin. She drove Evelyn as close to the edge of the rubble as she dared and shut off the engine. The final contest loomed ahead. Callan sat staring at the shack and realized that she had formed no plan of action to free Connor. A method or even an idea on how to overpower The Gull still eluded her. She was as clueless as the first time The Gull had intruded into her life all those years ago. She'd wasted the time on the trip up by not forming at least an idea of how to proceed.

The theta state seeped away and terror filled the car. The air was too thin. She couldn't breathe. She cranked down the window a few inches and gulped in the chilly mountain air. Terror bubbled like lava in the primitive part of her mind, ready to erupt into the glacial pit of her stomach. Terror was sometimes hot, sometimes cold. This time it seemed both, the sensations each fighting for supremacy over her body. In a moment, they cancelled each other out, leaving only numbness. Perhaps a French aristocrat felt like this on the way to the guillotine.

Welcome, sister, came a whisper on the cool breeze.

She knows I'm here. The excruciating headache that usually accompanied any interaction with The Gull didn't appear. Just the chill voice in her mind. With no time left, she could only hope that a plan occurred to her when she actually faced The Gull. *As you imagine, so shall you be.* She could only trust that her imagination was up to the trial of a lifetime.

So open the car door and meet the beast.

Chapter Seventeen

ಬಂ

Pebbles and dust filled her white satin sandals as she made her way up the slope to the cabin. Although the sun shone golden on the cliffs and mountains, the chilly mountain air seeped through the black taffeta coat. Except for the twitter of birds and the soft sigh of the wind through the pines below, an eerie silence held the morning. No emanations radiated from Connor. No challenge issued from The Gull. The shack simply waited.

A jolt of panic stopped her breath for a moment. She ruthlessly forced it down. Cold-bloodedness was strategically best. The Gull would have less emotional ammunition to use against her. Uncertain whether a physical or a psychic defense would be needed, she kept her consciousness hovering between the alpha state and the theta state, not wanting to commit to either.

A flat slab of rock served as the cabin's doorstep. The cabin's door hung from one hinge and gaped partly open. She stepped up and pushed it open.

Light spilled through the cracked glass of a window in the back of the cabin. Spotlighted by sunlight, Connor lay sprawled on a narrow splintered bench set in the center of the room. One hand and bare foot trailed down onto the dusty littered floor. She sensed he was unhurt but deeply asleep, and the relief nearly sent her to her knees. But the presence in the room wouldn't allow that maternal luxury.

A charming sprite stood at the end of the bench where Connor lay. Bianca looked much as she had in Dr. Ostherhaut's photo. She was startlingly tiny, fragile, standing barely higher than Callan's elbow. She wore a tan leather vest over a red checked shirt, a short, matching fringed-leather skirt, and cowboy boots. A red felt cowboy hat hung from a cord around her neck. Her blue-black hair swirled in a cloud of curls around her shoulders. And she smiled a sweet, cherubic smile as though a much-anticipated guest had arrived. Impossible for such a creature to harbor such evil. She looked like a ten-year-old kid ready for a trip to Disneyland.

You have arrived quickly, dear sister. We are pleased at your promptness, the cherub said.

I didn't have much choice. You took my son. The telepathic words snapped out so forcefully that it seemed their sharp edges cut her mind as they flew outward. The theta state was fully operational. The light of the hot third eye blazing indigo from her forehead washed the room in a flickering blue luminescence.

Oh, well, yes. What can you expect? You would not receive Us. You refused Our friendship. Bianca's words were sweet and reasonable. *But now you are here and We can finally get acquainted after all these years. Do you like Our outfit? We do so love American Western style.*

The woman was demented. Did she think that Callan had come to discuss her wardrobe?

A shadow in the corner shifted. Someone stood by the window. Callan hadn't sensed another presence. She stepped into the light and Callan saw a South American Indian woman. Well over six feet, with at least two hundred pounds of massive muscle attached to her large bones, she possessed the look of someone who had spent a hard life on a mountainside. The dark skin, channeled by deep furrows resembling those on the mountain outside the window, stretched over sharply angled cheekbones and a large hooked nose. The woman pulled back her lips and showed broken, black teeth. Although the grimace must have been intended as a smile, the result was more like a suddenly animated Halloween pumpkin. Callan wanted to grab Connor and make a run for Evelyn. Only the knowledge that Bianca would stop her mentally or this strange bodyguard would bring her down physically stopped her from bolting.

So, Bianca had increased the odds in her favor. Callan could not hope to fight both Bianca and this mammoth person. *The bodyguard has to go.* With that idea came instant reaction. Callan released the brake on the theta state and let go of as much focused telekinetic energy as she could muster. The Indian woman shattered the remaining fragments of glass as she sailed through the window. A screech echoed off the cliffs, along with the rattle of debris and the snapping of branches as she rolled down the mountain. Then silence.

Appalled at what she'd done, Callan watched for a violent reaction from Bianca.

Oh, that was so amusing. Maria bounced like a basketball all the way down! she giggled instead. *We like your style, sister. We will make a great team.*

No, we won't ever be a team. You are loony tunes. Callan let all her venom and distaste taint the statements. *I want you out of my mind and out of my life. What normal person would associate with a woman who thinks she's a bird? I'm sane, you're not.* Getting The Gull worked up was unwise, she suddenly realized. *Too late.*

Bianca's mouth puckered as if she had swallowed vinegar. *And haven't you learned yet that We always have what We want? It can be no other way.*

There was nothing to do but keep on sparring. *Oh, yeah? Psychic or not, you're a freak on all levels. I won't follow you into darkness. My soul is my own. I'll fight for it.* The possible repercussions from the curt statements aroused no alarm in Callan this time. The numbness had come back. *How peculiar. I wonder where it went before.*

So be it, sister.

Bianca reached back for the cowboy hat. The motion distracted Callan. With a mind dislocation that pulled a groan from her, she was suddenly outside in Evelyn.

No, not in the car. I am the car!

Somehow she had melded into the body of steel and rubber. The Gull had driven her mind out of her body once before when she killed Bernie Rabney. Then she had taken Callan's consciousness into her own. This was even more ghastly. No flesh encased her. Massive hardness and a chill rigidity enclosed her mind and spirit. Without blood and body, there was no human correlation for the senses she now had. The perceptions were alien, both physically and mentally. The early sunlight warmed the metal chassis. Her sight extended above, below and alongside her. The deep blue of the sky spread like an airy blanket from mountain to mountain as, at the same time, she received a detailed view of the rubble under the carriage of the car. The ticking of the cooling engine sounded like the working of a great clock heart. Gravel imprinted itself on the tires rather like a bare foot on a nubby carpet. The perspective was rather nauseating although there seemed to be no particular physical location where that sensation was centered.

Evelyn's engine revved and caught, and the new flesh of metal rolled across the rocky yard. The car slid around the cabin and nosed up a narrow trail that edged a cliff behind it. When the car wavered toward the edge of the trail, Callan realized that she had to guide the car. No one was in the driver's seat and Bianca apparently didn't intend to drive. She fought to relax within the strange steel body, sinking deeper into the theta state, and fought for control of Evelyn. Gravel pinged against Evelyn's undercarriage as they lurched up the winding cliff path.

The car picked up speed — too fast for the narrow track that was barely wide enough to accommodate Evelyn's width. A rear wheel slipped on the crumbling cliff edge as they whipped around another tight curve. As fast they were going, there was no time to figure out how to slow down, only to concentrate on keeping to the rutted, rocky trail. Her all-encompassing vision gave her a sickening panoramic view of the deep gorge below on her right. A lapse in concentration and a misjudgment and they'd go over the edge. Callan knew that she would experience the fall as though she were a crashing automobile. She'd die as surely as if her physical body were thrown from the cliff.

The trees and brush below in the chasm glowed with incandescence and with a whoosh exploded into flame. The eerie fire seemed to consume the rock walls as it swiftly climbed the cliff toward the trail. The canyon was an inferno. The whole thing was just an illusion produced from Bianca's fertile imagination, Callan knew, but she could still feel the heat against Evelyn's body, so fierce the car's glossy paint would surely blister within seconds.

Above the inferno, The Gull appeared. Connor's astral spirit, limp in unconsciousness, was held by one ankle in its claw.

He'll be awake when We let go. The fear will destroy his spirit. Obey Us now!

Oh, god, someone help, Callan prayed. Terror shredded her focus. The car waived toward the edge. Alarmed, Callan clamped down on her concentration.

Forced to retain Evelyn's form by Bianca's mental constraint, she couldn't go after Connor. Before she could fight free of Bianca's power, she'd have lost control and plunged into the flames.

Need a good chauffeur, honey? said a cheerful voice from the driver's seat. *Your driving is a menace.*

Rosemary! Where did you come from? You're dead! Seated nonchalantly behind the steering wheel, Rosemary didn't look ghostly at all. In her fly girl outfit, blonde hair and white scarf blowing in the astral wind, she looked the picture of old-fashioned romance and adventure.

I've been around keeping an eye on unfinished business. Don't worry about the car. I'll drive. Go get your boy.

Callan relinquished command and concentrated on returning to her own astral form. With a mental wrench, the metal around her dissolved and she was unfettered. Get Connor, and then deal with Bianca.

A long silver thread shot out from The Gull. Like a striking snake, it reached her and wrapped about her waist. With a jerk, the canyon, the car and Bianca and Connor were gone. She was in front of the cabin, lying on her back. Bianca's astral lasso turned into a rough, thick rope that coiled around her from shoulders to ankles. She could barely lift her head to look down her body, the rope cocoon was so tight. Metal pressed against her back and thighs. Bianca had tied her to some rusty railroad tracks.

From higher on the slope behind came the long wail of a whistle. By rolling to the side and tilting her head back, she could see an old-fashioned train with a stack that belched smoke. The thrum of the rails under her testified to Bianca's plan. It would pass over her in seconds. She heard shouts from her other side. Around the cabin ran six men, each dressed in a black uniform with round gold buttons and bucket helmets on their heads. Handlebar mustaches quivering, they waved axes over their heads, and yelled just what they intended to do when they reached her. She made out the words "cut" and "smash" and "head" clearly. The Gull was trying to scare her into submission.

Oh, damn! Bianca has been watching silent movies. Now I'm supposed to play the lead role in the Perils of Pauline *to amuse her.* Well, at least Bianca hadn't been watching the more modern gory stuff that featured mad slashers with chainsaws or alien beasts. What luck!

She had to get out of this astral straightjacket. She concentrated on long and thin and supple and with a mental jerk, turned into a snake. Shiny black with silvery white spots. She didn't know what particular brand of snake she'd turned herself into, but at least she wasn't as gaudy as Bianca's gold cobra. Quickly, she slithered out of the ropes and onto the rocks.

Enough of letting Bianca play musical chairs with her form! She concentrated on her own shape and it formed around her. She stood up, turned, and with a wave of her hand dispelled the illusion of the Keystone Cops and the runaway train.

The Gull still hovered over the flaming chasm, swinging Connor by an ankle.

You — you, ridiculous turkey butt! Callan yelled. It was the worst insult she could think of at the moment, but seeing Connor in danger filled her with mind-numbing fury.

She shot out over the canyon. The black taffeta coat flapped in the hot updraft from the flames. As an illusion, this version of hell was extraordinary. She smelled the acrid hot rocks burning. The brightness of the flames and fumes made her eyes water. The heat prickled her skin. The edge of her skirt and coat hem began to smoke. She jerked her feet up and her high-heeled sandals fell into the void.

The Gull swung Connor back and forth like a pendulum as if she intended to fling him as far as possible into the inferno. The flames dyed his hair and silver cord a garish crimson. He wailed and began to thrash.

You call Me turkey butt! How would you like your sweet little boy dumpling, my sister? Singed, medium rare or well done?

Don't you dare! Don't you dare!

Giggling, The Gull swung Connor faster and higher. Callan was almost there, only a few more yards.

Teleport, Callan, she heard Rosemary call. She shifted her mind to obey.

The Gull let go of Connor.

He fell, it seemed, in slow motion.

Suddenly, she was beside him, reaching out to catch him in her arms. She clutched him around his calves, the tops of his feet resting on her shoulders.

Connor, now in a lucid state, screamed and struggled. *Go to sleep, Connor, I have you,* she said, and teleported to the cabin.

She lay his astral spirit on his limp body and it merged into his flesh. Best to keep his physical body and astral spirit together. She couldn't stay to watch over him. He was quiet now, in a non-lucid state again, so she created a protective aura around him. It writhed about him like thick impenetrable ice glittering with fireflies, the most formidable aura she had ever wrought.

He was as safe as she could make him. Hopefully, Bianca would concentrate on her. She turned away and saw her physical body. It lay crumpled on the dusty floor, the hair spread in a fan about the ashen face. The silver cord seemed almost drained of its ethereal luminescence. The hems of the coat and dress were charred. The sandals lay a few feet away, almost unrecognizable black lumps. Apparently, Bianca had let the astral energy of the flaming canyon flow into the corporeal world. She wasn't playing. She intended to acquire Callan or see both Connor and herself dead.

The screeching of a scavenger bird and the flapping of wings could only be Bianca arriving for the kill. She had to get out of here and gain more power. Both her physical and astral bodies, nearly depleted of life force, felt as though she had been mugged by evil extraterrestrials. Bianca wouldn't allow her time for the usual scenic trip through the gateway to the astral plane. She shot through the cabin roof, dropped deeper into the theta state, and directed her concentration on the energy hills not far from Dr. Ostherhaut's pillar.

Life force billowed about her in great white clouds. Astral power threw her to her knees. She'd arrived on the astral plane all right, without going through the gateway, and materialized in the middle of a life mound. The force was too much to handle. She felt bloated, as if she were an over-filled tire that might explode any second. And oh, it hurt so. Every cell in her body shrieked with it.

She flailed about for what seemed like hours, picking up more energy, until the mound spat her out like a cherry pit. Too swollen with energy to move, like she'd indulged in a hundred Thanksgiving dinners, she lay there staring up at the shifting multicolored sky. Apparently, The Gull hadn't been able to track her when she teleported to the astral plane. Just as well. If she moved to fight now, she'd explode.

She drifted with the ground mist for a while to let the astral energy stabilize and considered the situation. Bianca had the upper hand as she always had, just because she was more ruthless than Callan and more experienced in the astral arts. Somehow, she had to get the upper hand, because Connor might soon be in danger again. And Sam was getting close to the cabin. He was there, drawing nearer, like a small sun in the back of her mind. She mustn't think of him. If Bianca discovered that, she would turn her vindictive tricks on him.

She had to concentrate. What weapon would intimidate or destroy The Gull?

A vague picture of a peculiar airplane formed in her mind. The fighter plane was obsidian, blacker than The Gull, infinitely bigger and certainly dangerous in the real world. Zach had a model of it prominently displayed in his bedroom. It would be a formidable weapon when fueled by the astral energy she'd absorbed.

Carefully, she reconstructed the details of the plane in her imagination. The image wasn't clear, as she hadn't paid that close attention to the model plane at the time. Angles. Yes, it had been composed of sharp edges, like the facets of a diamond. The wings swept back, longer than the fuselage, she remembered. The nose was as sharp as creased paper with angular protuberances on each side like sinister eyes. Two short tail fins stuck up in a V shape. Notches and subtle indentations in the body and wings hinted at armaments. Perfect! The warplane would scare the you-know-what out of Bianca. And Callan felt no hesitation in using the plane's weapons.

The astral energy seemed to have settled into a compact force in her body. Spreading arms and legs, she let herself rise to a standing position. The fighter plane's image locked firmly in mind, her body flowed like heavy water to shape the fighter. The form was heady. Unlike her sojourn as Evelyn, she felt omniscient, light and invincible. This must be how pilots felt going into combat. She laughed and her voice emerged as the scream of a powerful engine. Astral mist surged like whitecaps about the black avenger.

It would take a minute to learn the plane's capacity. Then she realized only her imagination could limit its potential. She wanted Bianca's terror, she wanted to see blood, she wanted vengeance. In this astral machine, there were energy bolts to spare. The Gull's tail feathers hadn't long to flutter. Time to find The Gull and enforce some humility. With that thought, the fighter slid forward.

A moment of visualization and the plane shot out over the burning canyon. She yelled in jubilation and rolled the fighter over and over through the hellish flames. Frying The Gull's feathers would be one of the most satisfying moments of her life.

Where's that turkey butt? she yelled.

Pull up, Callan, pull up, she heard Rosemary shout.

In her euphoria, she hadn't seen the canyon wall looming before her. With an inner flinch, she flung the plane skyward, barely avoiding a merge with a mountain crag. Shaken at her carelessness, she turned the plane and headed back.

As you imagine, so shall you be. Pay attention, before you turn yourself into a boulder, Rosemary warned.

Right. Thanks.

Ahead, flying above where Rosemary guided Evelyn along an endless track going nowhere, The Gull cruised along the canyon edge, sweeping its wings in languid strokes. Even at this distance, Callan could hear her contemptuous cackling. The bird bitch was laughing at her. Anger roiled in her guts like boiling water. Even if she died for it, destroying this fiend would purge her rage and save her family. Callan turned her angled nose toward The Gull and glided toward her prey. The critter would regret the day she messed with Callan Nevins' life.

As she promised Stephanie, her friend would also be avenged. The loony bird would be roasted a juicy golden brown. But first, Callan was going to enjoy sending her tail feathers up in flames. Satisfaction at last for all the stolen, distorted years of her life was imminent. The realization left her exhilarated and giddy with anticipation.

The fighter growled like a prowling jungle cat. In an instant, the air above the canyon became thick, as though this astral dimension had developed a pollution problem. The fires below were obscured, their flickering barely visible through the murk.

The ambiance around here certainly mirrors Bianca's character, Callan thought. *I have to hurry and get in the first shot.* The Gull, as a phantom flitting around the crags in the astral smog, could hide in a moment and then stage an ambush. Releasing her fury, the fighter leapt forward.

Hold, hold. Don't let go too soon.

She couldn't wait a moment more. Black and silver life energy shot from the plane's nose and streaked toward the gliding bird. The bolt struck a glancing blow just under The Gull's tail feathers. With a squawk, it erupted skyward, smoke trailing behind. It thrashed about, tearing at the burning feathers with its hooked beak, then dropped onto a ridge.

How about that, Rosemary? Callan yelled in triumph.

Nice shooting!

Callan moved closer. The shot hadn't been fatal. While The Gull was distracted, she could deliver the ultimate blow. The silly bird didn't even have the sense to transform into her human shape to escape the smoldering feathers. Before she could release another energy strike, the plane came to a total, abrupt standstill. She hadn't willed the halt. Without a jolt, the plane had simply ceased its forward motion. A few yards ahead, between Callan and The Gull, a slender figure floated in midair.

The woman was tall and young with dark shoulder-length hair that blew in the astral wind. Dressed in jeans, sweater and athletic shoes, she looked as if she came off some college campus. Her smile was gentle and radiated a mysterious wisdom, and her aura glowed a pure silver white. She seemed familiar to Callan.

Auntie Callan, what are you doing?

Callan suddenly recognized the dark brown eyes. They had looked down at her from a gigantic pillar of light not long ago.

The power, gentleness and understanding of her expression were unmistakable.

Katie?

Yes, it's me.

But you're just a baby!

In this life, yes, but I've borrowed a former appearance. What are your intentions here?

Giving The Gull some of her own medicine.

Murder, you mean?

Well, no, not exactly. That was certainly a dishonest answer. Lying to this angelic creature was inadvisable—if not impossible. She felt like a naughty little girl caught in some delinquent act by her mom. *Well, yes. I want to punish her for all that she's done to me and mine. Most of all, make her stop tormenting me,* she admitted.

You know if you kill Bianca in her true form, you'll blacken your pillar of light and cast your soul back dozens of incarnations. Please find some other way to address your grievances. Katie's astral spirit faded away into the murky astral haze.

Stunned and ashamed, Callan let the jet fade from her consciousness and returned to her natural astral form. Slowly she drifted down toward where Rosemary waited in the Chevy, now parked on the trail below. Apparently, the shot to The Gull's tail feathers had at least interrupted her control of the car. The Gull was still flopping around on the ledge, trying to extinguish the fire on her behind.

Callan settled into the passenger seat of the Chevy, turned to Rosemary and asked, *Did you see Katie? What am I going to do now?*

Yeah, I did. And you've still got a problem here, Rosemary answered, her eyes squinted in concern. *I don't have any suggestions off-hand.*

Callie, came a murmur in Callan's mind. She strained to catch the ghostly voice.

Callie? She recognized the whisper. Sam was close by, on the trail to the shack in fact, and he'd somehow acquired enough psychic power to communicate with her and was certainly near enough to draw Bianca's attention. Callan looked for her on the ledge, but the bird form had vanished. Terror swallowed her like a tidal wave.

She forced her fear down to the bottom of her mind. Emotional control and using her head was the only way she and Sam could survive.

Sam, get out of here! she whispered fiercely, keeping her telepathic answer at low power and in a narrow directional beam. Their conversation mustn't leak out to The Gull. She remained in control, as the canyon illusion hadn't disappeared while she fought her flaming tail feathers.

No, Callie, listen. You've got to use a different approach with The Gull. Sam's mind voice grew stronger and more urgent with every word. *You can't beat her one-on-one with psychic powers alone. She's ruthless and more experienced than you. Get into her mind. Try to discover the root of The Gull form. Why did she choose it? It must have something to do with the way she is.*

That's chancy. And what do I do if I find out?

Let me stay with you and I'll watch and advise. I'm a damn good psychiatrist you know! With a bleak heart she agreed. There was nothing else to do. They were backed into a corner.

Callan, why are you just sitting there? Rosemary interrupted, jerking her back to the Chevy and the blazing canyon. *The Gull is coming back. I can feel her malevolence growing.*

Just thinking, Rosemary, she said. At that moment The Gull sailed over the rim across the canyon, powerful wings stirring the rising heat and fumes, and came majestically toward them.

Take care, Rosemary, and thank you. I've got to handle this now, whatever may come of it. She reached over and brushed a lock of hair from Rosemary's cheek. She suspected that she wouldn't see her again in this world. Maybe somewhere else or some other time, she didn't know. Then again, maybe today her own pillar of light would rise from the astral plane and Rosemary would be waiting for her.

Rosemary's aura brightened to a deep pink, she smiled and said, *Luck, my dear,* then faded into the astral fog.

Taking a deep breath, Callan launched herself upward to meet Bianca. From now on, she would only think of the creature as Bianca. The Gull alias gave her too much mystique and with it the power to intimidate, so she would only recognize the child-like being as real. She didn't know how she knew that mindset was vital. Perhaps Sam was feeding her information subconsciously, which would be the most efficient method of communication, because there certainly wouldn't be time for a telepathic conference call once the encounter began.

Stay with me Sam, she sent as she rose to meet Bianca. A fuzzy emotional answer came back filled with love and encouragement. She hovered a few feet above Evelyn, reluctant to stray far from the beloved and familiar.

You are a nasty, nasty person to hurt Us so! Bianca spiraled down toward her and her mind voice resembled the shriek of a bird of prey diving on its kill. *We will punish you without end for the burning!*

Cut the Queen Victoria, omniscient goddess crap, Bianca, Callan interrupted, before the creature could get into one of her long revenge spiels. *I'm tired of it.* She projected nonchalance like a cloud of expensive perfume. Bianca mustn't know how scared she was. The matter-of-factness of Callan's comment caused The Gull's plummet to falter.

Ask her about herself, where she's from, Callie. Be friendly, Sam whispered.

I give up anyway. So if I'm going to be one of your lieutenants, I'd really like to know more about you. It'll help me to know what would please you. Mistress, Callan added. *Might as well get into the spirit of the part,* she thought to herself.

The bird halted and hovered less then twenty feet away, whether in surprise or wariness at the submission, Callan couldn't tell. She had to give the woman credit for her control. The flames and lava from the canyon still glowed and the astral smog still billowed, thick as storm clouds. The hugeness of the creature at close range panicked her. For a moment she doubted that Bianca could be distracted or defeated, but she felt the pressure of Sam's mind deep in her own and affirmed again that she had no choice but to proceed.

What do you mean? Bianca asked. She was definitely suspicious.

She remembered Rosemary's theory that Bianca wanted a psychic sister to share her world. *Well, aren't we going to be friends, too? You know all about me, from when I was a little kid, but I don't know anything about you except you're from South America. Isn't that right?*

Brazil, yes. You want to be Our friend? The offer of friendship seemed to astonish the woman.

It seems reasonable, don't you think? Much more pleasant all around. Callan projected all the sincerity she could muster. Then she feared she might be overdoing the deceit business. She'd never had much practice. So much for being a Miss Goody-Two-Shoes. *I need to get to know you so I can understand what you want, what you believe is important in your business, what you will expect of me. Then I'll be more helpful to you.*

You want to know about Our business? Bianca asked. She radiated less vitriol than before. Her mind voice indicated that her temper tantrum had moderated into mild irritation.

Maybe later, Callan said, *but right now, what about you? Do you have a family and a home?* Bianca's response at being treated like an ordinary person meeting someone at a cocktail party was encouraging.

A home, yes, a beautiful house on a cliff by the sea, where We've always lived. Perhaps one day We will allow you to visit us. If you please Us. You burnt Our tail! she screeched as her anger flared again, churning the astral mist into a gray froth.

I'm so sorry about that, Callan hurried to appease. *You scared me so, and I didn't know what to do. Of course you always look beautiful. I particularly liked the western outfit you were wearing earlier. You have marvelous taste in clothes. You should appear that way more often.*

Can this woman possibly believe this con job? Talk about social naïveté! Callan thought. *A four-year-old in preschool wouldn't fall for this. The woman obviously never had a friend in her life.* For a moment Callan felt like a rat for deceiving her, but pushed the feeling aside. Compassion right now could get her killed.

Bianca fluffed her feathers and made a noise, partly a shriek and partly an indignant huff. *You are trying to delay Us,* she said. *And We always look beautiful.*

Of course. You were going to tell me about your family, Callan hastened to add. *Do they live with you in the house by the sea?*

No, all dead. The poppa, the momma, and the ugly brothers. Long ago. They weren't much use to Us. The sapphire eyes whirled and pinned Callan like a laser beam.

Dr. Ostherhaut had said that Bianca had more than likely murdered her family, Callan remembered then.

Better get off that subject, Sam's voice urged. *She killed them, all right. Try to get her to tell you about when she became The Gull. She refers to herself in the plural. That's a clue to follow.*

Well, yes, I understand. Relatives certainly can be tiresome, Callan continued to Bianca. *I'd be delighted if you would show me, mentally anyway, what your home looks like. And tell me about when you were little. Were you a happy little kid? When did you become The Gull?*

Callan was guessing, but more than likely Bianca had adopted the gull image at a young age and that it had happened in the house by the sea. Sam must be feeding her these ideas subliminally, she realized. Anxiety still smothered in her and made it hard to form strategy.

The sapphire eyes dimmed and Callan felt less like she was being chopped into digestible pieces.

Very well, We will take you for a visit to Our house. Be aware that any impertinence will be punished! Open to Us!

The concept of allowing Bianca into her mind staggered Callan. Swallowing headfirst one of those snakes from the whirlpool last night would be easier. But if she didn't retain strict control, Bianca would read her plot and discover Sam hidden just above her subconscious level.

Do it, Callie. I'll drop a little deeper, but I'll stay with you, Sam said. She felt him slip deeper into her mind, like a lion vanishing into a jungle. His essence remained, his Sam-perfume, wrapping her in its warmth. No other choice remained but to comply.

I can do that, Callan said, answering both Sam and Bianca, and let her personal shield slip a little.

Instantly, Bianca's feelings surged into her mind. The familiar headache blossomed and she gulped back a scream of agony. Raw, vicious emotions emanated from the women and scalded her mind like boiling water. The rotting onion odor gagged her. Violent colors swirled through her mind, shattering her control and nearly dissipating her inner astral image. She felt herself dissolving on the astral wind.

You do not open to Us! Bianca accused.

Sorry. Give me a minute. This is difficult for me. I've been closed up for a long time and don't know how to open. You need to be gentle with me.

Callan struggled to reform her astral body and mind before she snapped back into her body. If she was unconscious, Bianca might loose patience and simply take her over, regardless of the consequences to Callan. She groped for something to steady her psyche, and an inspiration, hardly more than instinct, urged her to say, *Do you suppose we can go in my Chevy? It will relax me and I'd like to show her off to you,* she said on impulse. Was that Sam's suggestion? No matter. Evelyn reminded her of the normal world and was something to cling to.

Such silliness, but you may bring it.

Callan floated into the driver's seat, but The Gull hovered leisurely and made no move to enter the car.

I'd be pleased to have you join me, but I don't think The Gull will fit into the car. Maybe you could ride as Bianca? Callan suggested.

The Gull considered the request for a moment, then abruptly Bianca appeared in the passenger seat, sporting her cowboy hat, boots and fringed-leather outfit. She gave a bounce as if testing the comfort of the seat, grinned like a cherub, and said, *Let Us go! We will drive.* Callan felt pressure against her mind, but the force produced only a moderate throb in her temples. She could live with it. She had to let go—swallow the snake—for all their lives. She opened her mind tentatively to Bianca and a cold murkiness engulfed her mind. The flaming canyon fell away.

* * * * *

The world dissolved into a tunnel of white nothingness, much like the entrance to the astral plane that Rosemary had shown her what seemed ages ago. She felt movement, as if the Chevy hit ninety miles an hour, then blackness for a moment, and suddenly the Chevy burst into an overcast morning above a green sea. Humidity-laden air slapped her face and she breathed in the scent of the tropics.

With a jerk Callan pulled away from Bianca's control, her cloak of individuality closed around her and her dizziness passed. *I might have known she'd drive like a maniac.*

Ahead, cliffs rose from a turbulent surf. As they drew closer, Bianca pointed and shouted above the wind, *There! That's Our home!* She sounded exuberant, like a kid on an amusement park ride. A stone mansion topped the cliff and looked almost organic as it flowed over the precipice, following the sharp contours of the rock. The dwelling, smothered in moss and vegetation, looked as though the jungle was devouring it.

We will go down now. You drive, Bianca instructed with an amused, malevolent glance at Callan.

She suspects something, Callan thought, and sent a weak questing call for Sam. He drifted there, fairy-fine, hidden deep within her soul.

Callan sent Evelyn spiraling down toward the cliff mansion. As they approached the cliff, Bianca directed her to a wide terrace overlooking the ocean, and Callan edged in to park just above and next to the stone balustrade. Across the terrace, wide French doors stood open. Within, Callan glimpsed elegant antique furniture, including a four-poster canopied bed draped with crimson silk.

This suite, these rooms, are Our place, Our home, Bianca said with a proud wave of her hand. *Always have we been here, born here as child and gull, and dreamed Our dreams of the world here. We've rarely left it. Until we went to the United States to obtain you, stubborn one, We had never been so far away from here in body.*

Callan supposed she should be flattered, but she certainly could have done without the honor. However, the information sparked Sam's interest. Callan could feel him edging upward in her mind. *Careful, Sam.*

She said she was born here as a gull, Sam said. *That's a vital clue. Get her to talk about it.*

Callan sent a big question mark to him and waited for further instructions, but nothing more was forthcoming. Sam must have run into that shiftless clairvoyant imp that resided down there in her mind and gotten distracted, she decided, or to give him the benefit of the doubt, maybe he was just cautious.

I've always wondered why you appeared as a gull, Bianca. It's certainly an impressive form. But how did you choose? Callan finally asked. The blunt questions contained none of the subtle interview techniques that Sam might have used with a patient. She hoped Bianca wouldn't get suspicious of her motives. But Bianca was confident of her power and eager to talk. She now had a friend and an almost-equal, with an unfettered mind, wanting to chat.

Let Us show you, sister, how it was, Bianca said. *Open to Us now and We will become one heart and mind.*

With the command, Bianca's mind flowed over hers and she felt them fall into a smothering, bodiless blankness, as she had when Bianca had first taken her over when she murdered Bernie Rabney. Panic welled up, but she firmly shoved it down, and submitted to the inevitable.

They lay enclosed within low walls on a smooth, soft surface. Morning sunlight flickered through leaves to one side. Birds flew above, across their field of vision, but they didn't know the name of the creatures that soared above. They only knew that their movements created pleasure within their being, and brought relief from the loneliness that stretched forever behind and extended forward into eternity. They watched and slept until pain in their middle made them cry out. Hunger, but they hadn't acquired that concept yet. Their wails rose up to mingle with the shrieks of the gulls above. After a time, a rustling noise sounded beside them and huge hands reached down to roughly remove the dampness that also accompanied the hunger. It put something in their mouth, and when they finished suckling, it was quickly removed.

Your mother? Callan managed to surface into individuality to ask the question.

The nanny, Bianca answered with a caustic scorn. *A useless human, as they all are. Our mother could never be bothered to tend Us personally. We spent Our days here watching the gulls. The family didn't care what happened to Us. They left Us to the whims of that incompetent nanny creature. But the gulls were always there. They watched over Us.*

The nanny disappeared. They dozed and woke again to late afternoon sunlight. The birds, gulls, still flew above, constant guardians of the desolate terrace. They watched the birds and at twilight a gull landed on the balustrade next to their bassinette. The thing seemed huge as it fluttered its wings and pecked at a lizard scuttling across the stone. They could clearly hear its beak as it struck the rock barrier. It gobbled the reptile, then cocked its head and stared at them with interested beady black eyes.

Their infant, unformed psychic mind reached out and brushed against the bird's. Cold and detached and avaricious, without intellect, the mind held only self-interest. It would never allow itself to be a victim of another's needs. Totally self-contained, it responded only to its own desires. To the infant, that seemed an advantageous condition. That is the way we must be, they knew. They reached with their newfound power and ripped away the essence of the gull's instinct. Greed mixed with the familiar rotten onion smell swamped Callan's senses. Smothered by the stench and instantly panicked, she fought Bianca for release from the nightmare and won through. Callan suddenly found herself slumped in the driver's seat of the Chevy. *That was like drowning, and then reaching the surface for a gasp of life-giving air*, she thought.

You attempt to deceive Us! You will die for it! You are not Our friend! Bianca screeched. Somehow she'd caught on to the deception when Callan panicked and exposed her revulsion.

The Gull crouched on Evelyn's hood with wings spread ready to attack. The sapphire eyes swirled furiously and seemed to merge into one gigantic Cyclops eye. It flapped its wings and a whirlwind of onion stink gusted into Callan's face. *We will think of a disagreeable way for you to die. And that boy dumpling of yours, too. And some others We know about. We will send your souls to hell.*

Sam? Callan sent a question within. *She's getting really worked up. I could use your advice here. What now?*

Sam's mind voice and presence filled her mind with sweet perfume. *Her psychic mind imprinted on a gull rather than a human*, he answered. *The original gull image is still on the terrace. Destroy it!*

What? How?

The original gull is only in Bianca's memory. With the gull imprint eliminated from Bianca's mind, she will have no template for the gull delusion, Sam answered. *You only need to destroy that memory, nothing else.*

How to destroy an illusion? She had to hurry. The Gull looked as though she had made up her mind about Callan's fate. Hopefully, the primary gull's extermination wouldn't kill Bianca, too. If she died, Callan's pillar of light would certainly acquire some long-standing nasty stains. She explored inward for a solution, but nothing came to mind and Sam didn't respond with an idea.

Evelyn's radio antenna sparked in the last of the sunset, sending out gold and silver rays, its United States flag standing out straight and proud, as though it called to her clairvoyantly. *Why not?*

The Gull advanced a step on the hood, hooked beak slashing from side to side. Reaching out, Callan grasped the antenna with her mind and transformed it into a slender, golden-tipped lance of light. It coiled and vibrated in her hand as if it were alive. With a powerful mental heave, she hurled it toward the gull roosting on the balustrade, piercing the bird through the breast. The gull vanished in a burst of rainbow light. A wail of grief and rage and hopelessness echoed though the astral world.

The tropical night dissolved, and Callan fell though light and dark, dark and light, through infinite ages of cold and heat. Then silence and peace received her.

Epilogue

ဆ

Callan awoke in the shack on the mountain. At first she didn't know where she was, and exhaustion kept her glued to the dirty floor until she smelled smoke. Bianca! Had she survived the lance and ignited the cabin to carry out her revenge? She rolled to her side and pushed to her knees. Connor still lay on the bench in the middle of the room. Bianca's body lay facedown behind him. She couldn't tell if she was breathing.

Snaking lines of fire traced the cabin's back wall. It had taken the impact of the psychic energy generated in the fight. They had to get out now. The place was as dry as well-seasoned firewood. She struggled to her feet and went to Connor. He was breathing well enough, but still asleep. She pulled him into a sitting position and paused for a second to get her strength back. She was incredibly weak. Getting him to his feet used up most of her energy.

"Connor, wake up," she said. He didn't respond, so she clasped him around the waist, hefted him under her arm, much like she had done on the astral plane when they'd been threatened by the alligator creature, and dragged him toward the door. She'd almost reached it, and then Sam was there.

"Let's get you out of here," he said, as he took Connor from her and ducked out the door.

Smoked filled the room and she could barely see Bianca slumped on the floor. She wanted to follow Sam in the worst way, but she couldn't leave Bianca to die in the burning cabin. She reminded herself that Bianca might already be dead. But since she didn't know, her pillar of light and her soul would take a beating if the woman wasn't dead and she left her behind.

The smoke had thickened and she began to cough, but she trudged over, grabbed the back of Bianca's shirt and vest, and started to drag her across the floor. She probably didn't weigh more than a six-year-old, but that was almost more than Callan could handle. It seemed like the shack door moved farther away with each step and heave she took.

Then Sam was there, taking the burden away and leading her into the crystalline morning air. The morning sun surprised her. It was barely mid-morning. She felt as though she had been gone from the earthly world for days. She tilted back her head and drew in the cool air. It was good to be alive. But was Bianca still with them, and what condition was she in? Was she still a threat? And Connor? Had he suffered harm in the ordeal? None of it would come into focus to be analyzed, and she didn't want to think about any of it anyway. Falling to the ground and curling up for a long sleep seemed her best option. *Get moving or you'll fall down*, she instructed herself.

Sam had Connor and Bianca stretched out beside Evelyn. He leaned over Connor and examined him. "He's fine, Callie. Just drugged and asleep," he said. "He'll wake up soon."

He then went to Bianca and looked her over. Callan waited patiently for his verdict.

"Bianca's in a coma. Totally unresponsive. She needs a hospital."

So it was finished. Callan wanted to say, "Just roll her down the mountain. That's all she deserves." But she didn't have the energy to even say that.

In just a few minutes the cabin was almost completely consumed. Sam used his car fire extinguisher to put out the last smoldering embers, and then loaded Connor into Evelyn and Bianca into the backseat of his car. After restoring Callan with a bottle of warm orange juice and a granola bar and a little rest, she was able to drive Evelyn down the mountain. In Estes Park, Dr. Ostherhaut and an ambulance met them, and he took Bianca off their hands. The ambulance driving away was the most heartening sight she'd seen in a long time. When she asked Sam how the doctor knew he was needed, Sam just waved his cell phone at her.

Connor roused from his drugged state halfway home. He was groggy, headachy and sick to his stomach, and his misery left him indifferent to how he happened to be far way from home without a memory of leaving his bed at Stephanie's house. But not for long.

By that evening, after hours of his incessant questions, she and Sam gave in and told him about his mother's psychic powers and the battle with The Gull. He had trouble associating his ordinary mom with their exorbitant claims. He required a demonstration. Callan served him grape juice without ever leaving her place at the kitchen table. He was wide-eyed and momentarily speechless. They attempted to swear him to silence forever while he was still awed. After mulling over their revelations and demands for secrecy, his response was a cheeky, "Okay, but only if you fix it so I beat Zach every time we play computer games."

Three weeks later, Bianca still resided in an exclusive mountain sanitarium under Dr. Ostherhaut's care. According to the doctor, she was a sweet child and making excellent progress in learning to talk, but showed no signs at all of paranormal powers.

Within a week of the battle, Callan resigned from her job at the law firm. As Sam stated, she would need all her time to pursue her art career. In his opinion, she was going to be famous. Her first project was a portrait in pastel chalk of Stephanie and Katie, wearing their denim outfits. Katie's eyes in the portrait were strangely wise and more intense than would normally be expected in one so young. But Stephanie, on seeing the painting, said with approval, "Yes, that's my Katie."

Their wedding in the third week of October came off without a hitch. Stephanie, as her matron of honor, presented Callan with a special gift of a chicken coop, rendered in porcelain. "For inspiration," she said. The artwork depicted an avian palace, with a red-tiled roof and an enclosure of gilded chicken wire. A daffy white hen perched on its peaked roof, eyes rolled heavenward. Below, a rooster patrolled the coop yard while eyeing the hen.

Except for a loud, bullheaded argument between Connor and his Grandfather Noonan over who would give the bride away, the wedding was sedate. They compromised. Both escorted her down the curving staircase of Sam's home.

As a wedding gift, Dr. Ostherhaut offered his mountain cabin for their honeymoon. Filled with every luxury, including a large whirlpool bath, it should have been called a mountain villa.

On the fourth morning of their honeymoon, Callan awoke to find Sam's head propped on his hand, maple-sugar eyes observing her lovingly.

Yum, breakfast, she thought, as she curled an arm around his neck to pull him down for a kiss.

"You're mighty perky this morning," he said against her mouth when she eased her hold.

"Tanked up at a life mound before I came home last night."

"Did you get Connor's dad straightened out?"

"Bianca really did a job on him," Callan answered. "But Luke's pillar has been mended and moved over by Katie's now. She'll be a good influence. After a while, when Luke reverts to his more normal self, Connor might be able to visit Apple Springs. Get to know his father again."

Seeing Luke in a different light, as a victim rather than as a villain, had been a revelation. Soon he would again be much like the young man she married, but she couldn't go back. What was, was, and the past that had been distorted by The Gull couldn't be changed.

Responsibilities fulfilled, her hands explored the muscles in Sam's back. Kissing her way down his chest got the hoped for response.

"Do you always wake up this horny?" Sam asked. "Is it a condition particular to psychics?"

"With you, I do." With devilish glee she rubbed his nipple with her thumb just to see him twitch. "And if you're going to go all medical on me, why does the hair on the right side of your chest grow counter-clockwise, and the hair on the left, clockwise?"

"Screwy hair genes, I guess."

"A likely story. You going to bring out Mr. Warty Frog this morning?"

Sam slumped back on the pillow and pulled the blanket primly up under his chin. "I think he's out of hop. Been in a lot of long races this week," he said, a rascally grin hiding in the corner of his mouth.

Her eyes went to his feet where his toes pushed up the tautly drawn blanket. Slowly, she traced his long form, pausing midway where the cover was suspiciously tented, and then on up to meet his warm gaze.

"Oh, yeah?" she said, pinning him with her eyes and a siren smile. "You can't fool me — I'm psychic."

Now Available

From

Heaven and Lace
By Linda Bleser

Best-selling romance novelist Lace Kincaid is the darling of the romance industry. There's only one problem—Lace Kincaid doesn't really exist. Identical twins Ashley and Alexis are the team behind the pseudonym. Quiet and demure Ashley writes the best-selling books. Lexi handles marketing and promotion, and outrageously plays the diva role of "Lace Kincaid" at public events.

On the eve of winning the prestigious Crystal Quill Award, Ashley's and Lexi's charade could come crashing down if they can't hide the truth from handsome journalist Rick Orlando, who is unwittingly courting them both—a complicated and comical deception that might just put their careers and love lives in jeopardy.

Heaven and Lace was previously released elsewhere under the title A Little Bit of Heaven.

Enjoy An Excerpt From:
HEAVEN AND LACE

Copyright © LINDA BLESER, 2006

The Copper Café was only ten minutes away and Ashley was early. Since the reporter thought they'd already met, it would look suspicious if she didn't recognize him, so she chose a secluded table across from the entrance where he'd be sure to spot her. Even though Lexi had described him, she couldn't trust her sister's powers of description where men were concerned. Lexi found them all incredibly handsome and sexy.

Her precautions were unnecessary. The moment he strode through the door she knew this was the man she was waiting for. He said something to the hostess then scanned the room. When his gaze swept over her he smiled, and she felt as if someone had flipped a switch and turned the lights a little brighter.

She caught her breath and smiled back, wondering why Lexi had let this one get away. He turned and thanked the hostess before making his way to the table, his movements confident and purposeful. Although he looked all business, she detected a boyish playfulness behind those sparkling amber eyes. One look in those eyes and she forgot all about Steve, her stopped-up toilet and her writer's block. Nothing else existed. Nothing but the copper glints in his eyes and the play of dimples when he smiled.

"I see you already ordered coffee," he said, setting his notebook on the table. "Do you mind if we order something to eat? I forgot to have dinner."

She laughed. "I thought I was the only one who forgot to eat when I was working."

He looked at her with what seemed like surprise, tilting his head and studying her in the candlelight. Ashley wondered if she'd given herself away already. What would Lexi have said? Probably something suggestive.

She blushed thinking of the possibilities and studied the menu, not trusting herself to get lost in those eyes again. "I'll have a salad," she said to fill the silence.

"That sounds good," he said, grinning. "Except I'll have mine with a burger on the side."

Ashley laughed again, her heart doing flip-flops when his grin broadened into a smile. She had to remind herself that this was an interview, not a date.

When the waitress refilled their coffee, they both reached for the sugar at the same time and their fingers brushed. She laughed nervously and pulled back, and Rick found himself enchanted by the delicate blush that sprang to her cheeks.

Was this the same Lace Kincaid he couldn't wait to escape from only hours ago? She seemed sweeter, more innocent somehow.

His notebook sat forgotten on the table while they ate. Although he'd been guarded at first, before long they were laughing and sharing more than coffee. Like the fact that they both adored "I Love Lucy" reruns and strawberry licorice, would rather own a dog than a cat, and preferred fishing to the opera.

"Speaking of fishing," he said. "I've got a little camp up on Saratoga Lake. It's just a two-bedroom, lakeside cabin that once belonged to my grandfather, but it comes complete with an array of reels and rods and a nice little fishing boat. Nothing fancy," he finished, feeling suddenly shy. What was he doing inviting Lace Kincaid fishing? He would have laughed at the idea this afternoon, but tonight it felt right. Perfect, in fact.

"I'd love that," she said, her face lighting up. "I'll bring the bait."

That smile was all the bait he needed. Her lips were full and sensuous. It was all he could do not to reach out and trace the gentle curve, imagining how they'd feel brushing against his. She looked away and he realized he'd been staring at her lips far too long.

The intimate little corner of the Copper Café began to feel like their own private haven as Ashley relaxed, surprised to realize how much she enjoyed his company. It was almost midnight before he turned the conversation around to her writing, and his insightful questions impressed her.

"You've read one of my books?" she asked.

Rick frowned slightly. "Well, to be honest, not until now. And only because I wanted to be prepared for this article."

Ashley waited, trying to read the expression on his face, but he didn't offer any further explanation. She wanted to ask which book he'd read and whether he liked it, but stopped herself. What if he hadn't? His opinion suddenly mattered to her. Did she want to know if he hated it? Especially now, when she was struggling with her own writing demons?

When he reached for the check, his fingers brushed against her wrist and Ashley felt a delicious tingle run through her. Her breath quickened and she held his gaze for what seemed an eternity.

He broke the connection first and cleared his throat. "Where shall I meet you tomorrow?"

Her heart fluttered. Tomorrow? She smiled and started to answer, then realized he wasn't meeting *her*. He was meeting Lace Kincaid, and Lexi would be playing that role for the rest of the week. Lexi would be sitting across from him, getting lost in his eyes, running her perfect fingernails across his hands. How long would it take her sister to seduce and win him? How long before Lexi had Rick Orlando wrapped around her little finger?

"I'll call and let you know," Ashley said. Something inside her wanted to fight for him, to win his heart before Lexi had a chance to charm him away.

Her shoulders slumped. That was silly. When had she ever been able to compete with her sister?

Never, she realized, reaching for her purse. And men like Rick Orlando didn't fall in love with plain, vanilla yogurt women in the real world.

Why an electronic book?

We live in the Information Age — an exciting time in the history of human civilization, in which technology rules supreme and continues to progress in leaps and bounds every minute of every day. For a multitude of reasons, more and more avid literary fans are opting to purchase e-books instead of paper books. The question from those not yet initiated into the world of electronic reading is simply: *Why?*

1. ***Price.*** An electronic title at Ellora's Cave Publishing and Cerridwen Press runs anywhere from 40% to 75% less than the cover price of the exact same title in paperback format. Why? Basic mathematics and cost. It is less expensive to publish an e-book (no paper and printing, no warehousing and shipping) than it is to publish a paperback, so the savings are passed along to the consumer.

2. ***Space.*** Running out of room in your house for your books? That is one worry you will never have with electronic books. For a low one-time cost, you can purchase a handheld device specifically designed for e-reading. Many e-readers have large, convenient screens for viewing. Better yet, hundreds of titles can be stored within your new library — on a single microchip. There are a variety of e-readers from different manufacturers. You can also read e-books on your PC or laptop computer. (Please note that Ellora's

Cave does not endorse any specific brands. You can check our websites at www.ellorascave.com or www.cerridwenpress.com for information we make available to new consumers.)

3. *Mobility.* Because your new e-library consists of only a microchip within a small, easily transportable e-reader, your entire cache of books can be taken with you wherever you go.

4. ***Personal Viewing Preferences.*** Are the words you are currently reading too small? Too large? Too... ANNOYING? Paperback books cannot be modified according to personal preferences, but e-books can.

5. ***Instant Gratification.*** Is it the middle of the night and all the bookstores near you are closed? Are you tired of waiting days, sometimes weeks, for bookstores to ship the novels you bought? Ellora's Cave Publishing sells instantaneous downloads twenty-four hours a day, seven days a week, every day of the year. Our webstore is never closed. Our e-book delivery system is 100% automated, meaning your order is filled as soon as you pay for it.

Those are a few of the top reasons why electronic books are replacing paperbacks for many avid readers.

As always, Ellora's Cave and Cerridwen Press welcome your questions and comments. We invite you to email us at Comments@ellorascave.com or write to us directly at Ellora's Cave Publishing Inc., 1056 Home Avenue, Akron, OH 44310-3502.

COMING TO A
BOOKSTORE
NEAR YOU!

ELLORA'S
CAVE

Bestselling Authors Tour

UPDATES AVAILABLE AT
WWW.ELLORASCAVE.COM

Cerridwen Press

Cerridwen, the Celtic goddess of wisdom, was the muse who brought inspiration to storytellers and those in the creative arts.

Cerridwen Press encompasses the best and most innovative stories in all genres of today's fiction.

Visit our website and discover the newest titles by talented authors who still get inspired—much like the ancient storytellers did

once upon a time...

www.cerridwenpress.com